**e about this job you'd like
do for you.'**

owe her for her signature on their divorce
if by doing this he could end things
em on a more pleasant note then
d find the closure he so desperately

yes, you have my word that I will never
eal to another soul what you're about to tell me
nless you give me leave to.'

he stared at him as if trying to sum him up. With
tart he realised she was trying to decide whether
rust him or not.

don't trust my word of honour?'

ou were after any kind of revenge on me, what
n about to tell you would provide you with both
e means and the method.'

e didn't want revenge. He'd never wanted
revenge. He just wanted to move on with his life.

d to kiss her.

A DEAL TO MEND THEIR MARRIAGE

BY
MICHELLE DOUGLAS

First Published in Great Britain 2016
By Mills & Boon, an imprint of HarperCollins*Publishers*
1 London Bridge Street, London, SE1 9GF

© 2016 Michelle Douglas

ISBN: 978-0-263-91959-2

23-0216

Our policy is to use papers that are natural, renewable and recyclable products and made from wood grown in sustainable forests.The logging and manufacturing processes conform to the legal environmental regulations of the country of origin.

Printed and bound in Spain
by CPI, Barcelona

Michelle Douglas has been writing for Mills & Boon since 2007 and believes she has the best job in the world. She lives in a leafy suburb of Newcastle, on Australia's east coast, with her own romantic hero, a house full of dust and books and an eclectic collection of '60s and '70s vinyl. She loves to hear from readers and can be contacted via her website www.michelle-douglas.com.

For Greg, who brings me glasses of red wine whenever I need them and supplies hugs on demand— the benchmarks of a romantic hero. :)

CHAPTER ONE

THE FIRST PRICKLE of unease wormed through Caro when the lawyer's gaze slid from her to Barbara and then down to the papers in front of him—her father's will, presumably. The lawyer picked up a pen, turned it over several times before setting it back to the table. He adjusted his tie, cleared his throat.

Even Barbara noticed his unwillingness to start proceedings. Turning ever so slightly, her stepmother reached out to pat Caro's hand. 'Caro, darling, if your father has disinherited you—'

Caro forced a laugh. 'There'll be no *if* about that, Barbara.'

It was a given, and they both knew it. Caro just wanted all the unpleasantness over so she could put it behind her. Her father was about to utter the last words he ever would to her—albeit on paper. She had no expectation that they'd be any kinder in death than they had been in life.

'Mr Jenkins?' She prodded the lawyer with the most pleasant smile she could muster. 'If you'd be so kind as to start we'd both appreciate it. Unless—' she pursed her lips '—we're waiting for someone else?'

'No, no one else.'

Mr Jenkins shook his head and Caro had to bite back a smile when the elderly lawyer's gaze snagged on the long, lean length of Barbara's legs, on display beneath her short black skirt. At thirty-seven—only seven years older than

Caro—Barbara had better legs than Caro could ever hope to have. Even if she spent every waking hour at the gym and resisted every bit of sugar, butter and cream that came her way—which, of course, she had no intention of doing.

The lawyer shook himself. 'Yes, of course, Ms Fielding. We're not waiting for anyone else.'

'Come now,' she chided. 'You've known me my entire life. If you can't bring yourself to call me Caro, then surely you can call me Caroline?'

He sent her an agonised glance.

She made her smile gentle. 'I *am* prepared, you know. I fully expect that my father has disinherited me.'

She didn't add that the money didn't matter. Neither Mr Jenkins nor Barbara would believe her. The fact remained, though, that it had never been money she'd craved but her father's approval, his acceptance.

Her temples started to throb. With a superhuman effort she kept the smile on her face. 'I promise not to shoot the messenger.'

The lawyer slumped in what had been until recently her father's chair. He pulled off his spectacles and rubbed the bridge of his nose. 'You have it all wrong, Caro.'

Barbara clasped her hands together and beamed. 'I *knew* he wouldn't disinherit you!'

The relief—and, yes, the delight—on Barbara's face contrasted wildly with the weariness in Mr Jenkins's eyes. Cold fingers crept up Caro's spine. A premonition of what, exactly…?

Mr Jenkins pushed his spectacles back to his nose and folded his hands in front of him. 'There are no individual letters I need to deliver. There are no messages I need to pass on nor any individual bequests to run through. I don't even need to read out the will word for word.'

'Then maybe—' Barbara glanced at Caro '—you'd be kind enough to just give us the general gist.'

He slumped back and heaved out a sigh. 'Mr Roland James Philip Fielding has left all of his worldly goods—all of his wealth and possessions—to…'

Caro braced herself.

'Ms Caroline Elizabeth Fielding.'

It took a moment for the import of the lawyer's words to hit her. When they did, Caro had to grip the arms of her chair to counter the roaring in her ears and the sudden tilting of the room. Her father had left everything…*to her*? Maybe…maybe he'd loved her after all.

She shook her head. 'There must be a mistake.'

'No mistake,' the lawyer intoned.

'But surely there's a caveat that I can only inherit if I agree to administer my mother's trust?'

Her father had spent the last twenty years telling her it was her duty, her responsibility…her *obligation* to manage the charity he'd created in homage to her mother. Caro had spent those same twenty years refusing the commission.

Her father might have thought it was the sole reason Caro had been put on this earth, but she'd continued to dispute that sentiment right up until his death. She had no facility for figures and spreadsheets, no talent nor desire to attend endless board meetings and discuss the pros and cons of where the trust money should be best spent. She did not have a business brain and had no desire whatsoever to develop one. Simply put, she had no intention of being sacrificed on some altar of duty. End of story.

'No caveat.'

The lawyer could barely meet her eye. Her mind spun…

She shot to her feet, a hard ball lodging in her chest. 'What about Barbara?'

He passed a hand across his eyes. 'I'm afraid no provision has been made for Mrs Barbara Fielding in the will.'

But that made no sense!

She spun to her stepmother. Barbara rose to her feet, her

face pinched and white. Her eyes swam but not a single tear fell, and that was somehow worse than if she'd burst into noisy weeping and wailing.

'He doesn't make even a single mention of me?'

The lawyer winced and shook his head.

'But…but I did everything I could think of to make him happy. Did he never love me?' She turned to Caro. 'Was it all a lie?'

'We'll work something out,' Caro promised, reaching out to take Barbara's hand.

But the other woman wheeled away. 'We'll do nothing of the sort! We'll do exactly as your father wished!'

Barbara turned and fled from the room. Caro made to follow her—how could her father have treated his young wife so abominably?—but the lawyer called her back.

'I'm afraid we're not done.'

She stilled and then spun back, swallowing a sense of misgiving. 'We're not?'

'Your father instructed that I give you this.' He held out an envelope.

'But you said…'

'I was instructed to give this to you only after the reading of the will. And only in privacy.'

She glanced back at the door. Praying that Barbara wouldn't do anything foolish, she strode across and took the envelope. She tore it open and read the mercifully brief missive inside. She could feel her lips thinning to a hard line. She moistened them. 'Do you know what this says?'

After a short hesitation, he nodded. 'Your father believed Mrs Fielding was stealing from him. Valuables have apparently gone missing and…'

And her father had jumped to conclusions.

Caro folded the letter and shoved it into her purse. 'Items may well have gone missing, but I don't believe for one moment that Barbara is responsible.'

Mr Jenkins glanced away, but not before she caught the expression in his eyes.

'I know what people think about my father and his wife, Mr Jenkins. They consider Barbara a trophy wife. They think she only married my father for his money.'

He'd had *so much* money. Why cut Barbara out of his will when he'd had so much? Even if she *had* taken the odd piece of jewellery why begrudge it to her?

Damn him to hellfire and fury for being such a control freak!

'She *was* significantly younger than your father…'

By thirty-one years.

'That doesn't make her a thief, Mr Jenkins. My father was a difficult man and he was lucky to have Barbara. She did everything in her not insignificant powers to humour him and make him happy. What's more, I believe she was faithful to him for the twelve years they were married and I don't believe she stole from him.'

'Of course you know her better than I do—but, Miss Caroline, you do have a tendency to see the best in people.'

She'd been hard-pressed to see the best in her father. She pushed that thought aside to meet the lawyer's eyes. 'If Barbara did marry my father for his money believe me: she's earned every penny of it several times over.'

Mr Jenkins obviously thought it prudent to remain silent on the subject.

'If my father's estate has passed completely to me, then I can dispose of it in any way that I see fit, yes?'

'That's correct.'

Fine. She'd sell everything and give Barbara half. Even half was more than either one of them would ever need.

Half an hour later, after she'd signed all the relevant paperwork, Caro strode into the kitchen. Dennis Paul, her father's butler, immediately shot to his feet.

'Let me make you a pot of tea, Miss Caroline.'

She kissed his cheek and pushed him back into his seat. 'I'll make the tea, Paul.' He insisted she call him Paul rather than Dennis. 'Please just tell me there's cake.'

'There's an orange syrup cake at the back of the pantry.'

They sipped tea and ate cake in silence for a while. Paul had been in her father's employ for as long as Caro could remember. He was more like an honorary uncle than a member of staff, and she found herself taking comfort in his quiet presence.

'Are you all right, Miss Caroline?'

'You *can* call me Caro you know.' It was an old argument.

'You'll always be Miss Caroline to me.' He grinned. 'Even though you're all grown up—married, no less, and holding a director's position at that auction house of yours.'

In the next instance his expression turned stricken. 'I'm sorry. I didn't mean to mention that bit about you being married. It was foolish of me.'

She shrugged and tried to pretend that the word *married* didn't burn through her with a pain that could still cripple her at unsuspecting moments. As she and Jack had been separated for the last five years, 'married' hardly seemed the right word to describe them. Even if, technically, it was true.

She forced herself to focus on something else instead. 'It's not *my* auction house, Paul. I just work there.'

She pulled in a breath and left off swirling her fork though the crumbs remaining on her plate.

'My father has left me everything, Paul. *Everything.*'

Paul's jaw dropped. He stared at her and then sagged back in his chair. 'Well, I'll be…'

His astonishment gratified her. At least she wasn't the only one shocked to the core at this turnaround. To describe her relationship with her father as 'strained' would be putting it mildly. And kindly.

He straightened. 'Oh, that *is* good news Miss Caroline. In more than one way.' He beamed at her, patting his chest just above his heart, as if urging it to slow its pace. 'I'm afraid I've a bit of confession to make. I've been squirrelling away odd bits and pieces here and there. Things of value, but nothing your father would miss, you understand. I just thought… Well, I thought you might need them down the track.'

Good grief! Paul was her father's thief?

Dear Lord, if he knew her father had written Barbara out of his will, thinking her the guilty party… *Oh!* And if Barbara knew what Paul had done…

Caro closed her eyes and tried to contain a shudder.

'Paul, you could've gone to jail if my father had ever found out what you were doing!'

'But there's no harm done now, is there? I mean, now that you've inherited the estate I don't need to find a way to…to get those things to you. They're legally yours.' His smile faded. 'Are you upset with me?'

How could she be? Nobody had ever gone out on a limb like that for her before. 'No, just…frightened at what might've happened,' she lied.

'You don't have to worry about those sorts of what-ifs any more.'

Maybe not, but she still had to find a way to make this right. 'It's only fair that I split the estate with Barbara.'

A breath shuddered out of him. He glanced around the kitchen pensively. 'Does that mean selling the old place?'

What on earth did she need with a mansion in Mayfair? She didn't say that out loud. This had been Paul's home for over thirty years. It hit her then that her father had made no provision in his will for Paul either. She'd remedy that as soon as she could.

'I don't know, Paul, but we'll work something out. I'm not going to leave you high and dry, I promise. Trust me. You, Barbara and I—we're family.'

He snorted. 'Funny kind of family.'

She opened her mouth and then closed it, nodding. Never had truer words been spoken.

'Will you be staying the night, Miss Caro?'

Heavens, where Paul was concerned, *Miss Caro* was positively gushing—a sign of high sentiment and emotion.

From somewhere she found a smile. 'Yes, I think I'd better.' She had her own room in the Mayfair mansion, even though she rented a tiny one-bedroom flat in Southwark. 'Hopefully Barbara will… Well, hopefully I'll get a chance to talk to her.'

Hopefully she'd get a chance to put the other woman's mind at rest—at least about her financial future.

'Mrs Fielding refuses to join you for breakfast,' Paul intoned ominously the next morning as Caro helped herself to coffee.

Caro heaved back a sigh. Barbara had refused to speak to her at all last night. She'd tried calling out assurances to her stepmother through her closed bedroom door, but had given up when Barbara had started blasting show tunes— her father's favourites—from her music system.

'You will, however, be pleased to know that she did get up at some stage during the night to make herself something to eat.'

That was something at least.

'Oh, Miss Caroline! *You* need to eat something before you head off to work,' he said when she pushed to her feet.

'I'm fine, Paul, I promise.' Her appetite would eventually return. Although if he'd offered her cake for breakfast…

Stop thinking about cake.

'I'm giving Freddie Soames a viewing of a rather special snuffbox this morning.' She'd placed it in her father's safe—*her* safe—prior to the reading of the will yesterday. 'After that I'll take the rest of the day off and see if I can't get Barbara to talk to me then.'

As a director of Vertu, the silver and decorative arts division at Richardson's, one of London's leading auction houses, she had some flexibility in the hours she worked.

She glanced over her shoulder at Paul, who followed on her heels as she entered her father's study—*her* study. 'You *will* keep an eye on Barbara this morning, won't you?'

'If you wish it.'

She bit back a grin, punching in the combination to the safe. Ever since Paul had caught Barbara tossing the first Mrs Fielding's portrait into a closet, he'd labelled her as trouble. 'I *do* wish it.'

The door to the safe swung open and—Caro blinked, squinted and then swiped her hand through the empty space.

Her heart started to pound. 'Paul, please tell me I'm hallucinating.' Her voice rose. 'Please tell me the safe isn't empty.'

He moved past her to peer inside. 'Dear God in heaven!' He gripped the safe's door. 'Do you think we've been burgled?'

Something glittered on the floor at her feet. She picked it up. The diamond earing dangled from her fingers and comprehension shot through her at the same moment it spread across Paul's face.

'Barbara,' she said.

And at the same time he said, 'Mrs Fielding.'

She patted her racing heart. 'That's okay, then.'

'She'll have been after those jewels.'

'She's welcome to those jewels, Paul. They're hers. Father gave me Mother's jewels when I turned twenty-one.'

He harrumphed.

'But I really, *really* need that snuffbox back—this instant.'

She sped up to Barbara's first-floor bedroom, Paul still hot on her heels. She tapped on the door. 'Barbara?'

'Not now, Caro. Please, just leave me in peace.'

'I won't take up more than a moment of your time.' Caro swallowed. 'It's just that something has gone missing from the safe.'

'That jewellery is *mine*!'

'Yes, I know. I'm not referring to the jewellery.'

The door cracked open, and even the way Barbara's eyes flashed couldn't hide how red they were from crying. Caro's heart went out to the other woman.

'Are you accusing me of stealing something? Are you calling me a *thief*?'

'Of course not.' Caro tried to tamp down on the panic threatening to rise through her. 'Barbara, that jewellery belongs to you—I'm not concerned about the jewellery. Yesterday I placed a small item in the safe—a silver and enamel snuffbox about so big.' She held her hands about three inches apart to indicate the size. 'I have to show it to a potential buyer in an hour.'

Barbara tossed her hair. 'I didn't see any such thing and I certainly didn't take it.'

'I'm not suggesting for a moment that you did—not on purpose—but it's possible it was accidentally mixed in with the jewellery.' Behind her back she crossed her fingers. 'I'm *really* hoping it was. Would you mind checking for me?'

Barbara swept the door open and made a melodramatic gesture towards the bed. 'Take a look for yourself. *That's* what I took from the safe.'

The bed didn't look as if it had been slept in. Caro moved tentatively into the room to survey the items spread out on the bed. There was a diamond choker, a string of pearls, a sapphire pendant and assorted earrings and pins, but no snuffbox. Her heart hammered up into her throat.

'It's not here,' Paul said, leaning over to scan the items.

Caro concentrated on not hyperventilating. 'If…if I don't find that snuffbox I'll… I'll lose my job.'

Not just her job but her livelihood. She'd never get another job in the industry for as long as she lived. In all likelihood legal action would be taken. She'd—

Breathe! Don't forget to breathe.

Barbara dumped the contents of her handbag onto the bed and then slammed her hands on her hips. 'Once and for all—I haven't taken your rotten snuffbox! Would you like to search the entire room?'

Yes! Though of course she wouldn't.

Her gaze landed on a tiny framed photograph of her father that had spilled from Barbara's bag. An ache opened up in her chest. How could he have treated Barbara so badly? She understood Barbara's anger and disappointment, her hurt and disillusionment, but she would never do anything to intentionally hurt *her*—of that Caro was certain. She just needed to give the other woman a chance to calm down, cool off…think rationally.

'Did you not sleep at all last night, Barbara?'

Barbara's bottom lip wobbled, but she waved to the chaise lounge. 'I didn't want to sleep in the bed that I shared with…'

Caro seized her hands. 'He loved you, you know.'

'I don't believe you. Not after yesterday.'

'I mean to split the estate with you—fifty-fifty.'

'It's not what *he* wanted.'

'He was an idiot.'

'You shouldn't speak about him that way.' Barbara retrieved her hands. 'If you're finished here…?'

'Will you promise to have dinner with me tonight?'

'If I say yes, will you leave me in peace until then?'

'Absolutely.'

'Yes.'

Caro and Paul returned to the study to search the room, in case the snuffbox had fallen during Barbara's midnight raid on the safe, but they didn't find anything—not even the partner to that diamond earring.

'You didn't take it by any chance, did you, Paul?'

'No, Miss Caroline.'

'I'm sorry. I thought I'd just check, seeing as…'

'No offence taken, Miss Caroline.' He pursed his lips. '*She* has it, you know. I'm not convinced that the second Mrs Fielding is a nice lady. I once saw her throw your mother's portrait into a closet, you know.'

Caro huffed out a sigh. 'Well… I, for one, like her.'

'What are you going to do?'

She needed time. Pulling her phone from her purse, she rang her assistant.

'Melanie, a family emergency has just come up. Could you please ring Mr Soames and reschedule his viewing for later in the week?'

The later the better! She didn't add that out loud, though. She didn't want to alert anyone to the fact that something was wrong—that she'd managed to lose a treasure.

Her assistant rang back a few minutes later. 'Mr Soames is flying out to Japan tomorrow. He'll be back Thursday next week. He had asked if you'd be so good as to meet with him the following Friday morning at ten o'clock.'

'No problem at all. Pop it in my diary.'

Friday was ten days away. She had ten days to put this mess to rights.

She seized her purse and made for the door. Paul still trailed after her. 'What do you mean to do, Miss Caroline?'

She wanted to beg him not to be so formal. 'I need to duck back to my flat and collect a few things, drop in at work to pick up my work diary and apply for a few days' leave. Then I'll be back. I'll be staying for a few days.'

'Very good, Miss Caroline.'

She turned in the entrance hall to face him, but before she'd swung all the way around her gaze snagged on a photograph on one of the hall tables. *A photograph of her and Jack.*

For a moment the breath jammed in her throat. She pointed. 'Why?' she croaked.

Paul clasped his hands behind his back. 'This house belongs to you now, Miss Caroline. It seemed only right that you should have your things around you.'

Her heart cramped so tightly she had to fight for breath. 'Yes, perhaps… But…not that photo, Paul.'

'I always liked Mr Jack.'

'So did I.'

But Jack had wanted to own her—just as her father had wanted to own her. And, just like her father, Jack had turned cold and distant when she'd refused to submit to his will. And then he'd left.

Five years later a small voice inside her still taunted her with the sure knowledge that she'd have been happier with Jack on *his* terms than she was now on her own terms, as her own woman. She waved a hand in front of her face. That was a ridiculous fairytale—a fantasy with no basis in reality. She and Jack were always going to end in tears. She could see that now.

Very gently, Paul reached out and placed the photograph facedown on the table. 'I'm sure there must be a nice photograph of you and your mother somewhere.'

She snapped back to the present, trying to push the past firmly behind her. 'See if you can find a photo of me and Barbara.'

Paul rolled his eyes in a most un-butler-like fashion and Caro laughed and patted his arm.

'The things I ask of you…'

He smiled down at her. 'Nothing's too much trouble where you're concerned, Miss Caro.'

She glanced up the grand staircase towards the first-floor rooms.

'I'll keep an eye on Mrs Fielding,' he added. 'I'll try to dissuade her if she wants to go out. If she insists, I'll send one of the maids with her.' He glanced at the grand-father clock. 'They're due to come in and start cleaning any time now.'

'Thank you.' She didn't want Barbara doing anything foolish—like trying to sell that snuffbox if she *did* have it. 'I'll be as quick as I can.'

Despite the loss of the snuffbox and all the morning's ker-fuffle, it was Jack's face that rose in her mind and mem-ories of the past that invaded Caro, chasing her other concerns aside, as she trudged across Westminster Bridge.

The sight of that photograph had pulled her up short. They'd been so happy.

For a while.

A very brief while.

So when she first saw his face in the midst of the crowd moving towards her on the bridge, Caro dismissed it as a flight of fancy, a figment of her imagination. Until she realised that blinking hadn't made the image fade. It had only made the features of that face clearer—a face that was burned onto her soul.

She stopped dead. Jack was in London?

The crowd surged around her, but she couldn't move. All she could do was stare.

Jack! Jack! Jack!

His name pounded at her as waves of first cold and then heat washed over her. The ache to run to him nearly undid her. And then his gaze landed on her and he stopped dead too.

She couldn't see the extraordinary cobalt blue of his eyes at this distance, but she recognised the way they narrowed, noted the way his nostrils flared. She'd always wondered what would happen if they should accidentally meet on the street. Walking past each other without so much as an acknowledgment obviously wasn't an option, and she was fiercely glad about that.

Hauling in a breath, she tilted her head to the left a fraction and started towards the railing of the bridge. She leaned against it, staring down at the brown water swirling in swift currents below. He came to stand beside her, but she kept her gaze on the water.

'Hello, Jack.'

'Caro.'

She couldn't look at him. Not yet. She stared at the Houses of Parliament and then at the facade of the aquarium on the other side of the river. 'Have you been in London long?'

'No.'

Finally she turned to meet his gaze, and her heart tried to grow bigger and smaller in the same moment. She read intent in his eyes and slowly straightened. 'You're here to see me?'

His demeanour confirmed it, but he nodded anyway. 'Yes.'

'I see.' She turned to stare back down at the river. 'Actually…' She frowned and sent him a sidelong glance. 'I don't see.'

He folded his tall frame and leaned on the railing, too. She dragged her gaze from his strong, hawk-like profile, afraid that if she didn't she might reach across and kiss him.

'I heard about your father.'

She pursed her lips, her stomach churning like the currents below. 'You didn't send a card.'

He didn't say anything for a moment. 'You send me a Christmas card every year...'

He never sent her one.

'Do you send *all* your ex-lovers Christmas cards?'

She straightened. 'Only the ones I marry.'

They both flinched at her words.

In the next moment she swung to him. 'Oh, please, let's not do this.'

'Do what?'

'Be mean to each other.'

He relaxed a fraction. 'Suits me.'

She finally looked at him properly and a breath eased out of her. She reached out to clasp his upper arm. She'd always found it incredibly difficult not to touch him. Through the fine wool of his suit jacket, she recognised his strength and the firm, solid feel of him.

'You look good, Jack—really good. I'm glad.'

'Are you?'

'Of course.' She squeezed his arm more firmly. 'I only ever wanted your happiness.'

'That's not exactly true, though—is it, Caro?'

Her hand fell away, back to her side.

'My happiness wasn't more important to you than your career.'

She pursed her lips and gave a nod. 'So you still blame me, then?'

'Completely,' he said without hesitation. 'And bitterly.'

She made herself laugh. 'Honesty was never our problem, was it?' But the unfairness of his blame burned through her. 'Why have you come to see me?'

He hauled in a breath, and an ache started up in the centre of her. 'Hearing about your father's death...' He glanced at her. 'Should I give you my condolences?'

She gave a quick shake of her head, ignoring the burn of tears at the backs of her eyes. Pretending her relationship with her father had been anything other than cold and combative would be ridiculous—especially with Jack.

'You don't miss him?'

His curiosity surprised her. 'I miss the *idea* of him.' She hadn't admitted that to another living soul. 'Now that he's gone there's no chance that our relationship can be fixed, no possibility of our differences being settled.' She lifted her chin. 'I didn't know I still harboured such hopes until after he died.'

Those blue eyes softened for a moment, and it felt as if the sun shone with a mad midday warmth rather than afternoon mildness.

'I am sorry for that,' he said.

She glanced away and the chill returned to the air. 'Thank you.'

The one thing the men in her life had in common was their inability to compromise. She couldn't forget that.

'So, hearing about my father's death...?' she prompted.

He enunciated his next words very carefully and she could almost see him weighing them.

'It started me thinking about endings.'

Caro flinched, throwing up her arm as if to ward off a blow. She couldn't help it.

'For pity's sake, Caro!' He planted his legs. 'This *can't* come as a surprise to you.'

He was talking about divorce, and it shouldn't come as a shock, but a howling started up inside her as something buried in a deep, secret place cracked, breaking with a pain she found hard to breathe through.

'Are you going to faint?'

Anger laced his words and it put steel back in her spine. 'Of course not.'

She lifted her chin, still struggling for breath as the knowledge filtered through her that just as she'd harboured secret hopes of reconciling with her father, so she had harboured similar hopes where Jack was concerned.

Really? How could you be so...optimistic?

She waved a hand in front of her face. The sooner those hopes were routed and dashed, the better. She would *never* trust this man with her heart again.

She lifted her chin another notch against the anger in his eyes. 'You'll have to forgive me. It's been something of a morning. We had the reading of my father's will yesterday. Things have been a little...fraught since.'

He rubbed a fist across his mouth, his eyes hooded. 'I'm sorry. If I'd known, I'd have given you another few weeks before approaching you with this.' His anger had faded but a hardness remained. His lips tightened as he glanced around. 'And I should've found a better place to discuss the issue than in the middle of Westminster Bridge.'

She had a feeling her reaction would have been the same, regardless of the where or when. 'You've just been to my flat?' she asked.

He nodded. 'I was going to catch the tube up to Bond Street.' It was the closest underground station to where she worked. 'But...'

'But the Jubilee Line is closed due to a suspicious package at Green Park Station,' she finished for him. It was why she was walking. That and the need for fresh air. 'I'm on my way to the flat now. We can walk. Or would you prefer to take a cab?'

Jack didn't like Caro's pallor. Rather than answer verbally, he hailed a passing cab and bundled her into it before the motorists on the bridge could start tooting their horns. The sooner this was over, the better.

Caro gave the driver her address and then settled in her seat and stared out of the side window. He did the same on his side of the cab, but he didn't notice the scenery. What rose up in his mind's eye was the image of Caro when he'd first laid eyes on her—and the punching need to kiss her that had almost overwhelmed him. A need that lingered with an off-putting urgency.

He gritted his teeth against it and risked a glance at her. She'd changed.

It's been five years, pal, what did you expect?

He hadn't expected to want her with the same ferocity now as he had back then.

He swallowed. She'd developed more gloss…more presence. She'd put on a bit of weight and it suited her. Five years ago he'd thought her physically perfect, but she looked even better now and every hormone in his body hollered that message out, loud and clear.

After five years his lust should have died a natural death, surely? If not that then it should at least have abated.

Hysterical laughter sounded in the back of his mind.

Caro suddenly swung to him and he prayed to God that he hadn't made some noise that had betrayed him.

'I hear you're running your own private investigation agency these days?'

'You hear correctly.'

Gold gleamed in the deep brown depths of her eyes. 'I hear it's very successful?'

'It's doing okay.'

A hint of a smile touched her lips. She folded her arms and settled back in her seat.

'Calculating the divorce settlement already, Caro?'

Very slowly her smile widened, and his traitorous heart thumped in response.

'Something like that,' she purred. 'Driver?' She leaned

forward. 'Could you let us out at the bakery just up here on the right? I need to buy cake.'

Cake? The Caro he knew didn't eat *cake*.

The Caro you knew was a figment of your imagination!

CHAPTER TWO

'JACK, I FIND myself in a bit of a pickle.'

Caro set a piece of cake on the coffee table in front of him, next to a steaming mug of coffee. She'd chosen a honey roll filled with a fat spiral of cream and dusted with glittering crystals of sugar.

Jack stared at it and frowned. 'Money?'

'No, not money.'

He picked up his coffee and glanced around. Her flat surprised him. It was so *small*. Still, it was comfortable. Her clothes weren't cheap knock-offs either. No, Caro looked as quietly opulent as ever.

She perched on the tub chair opposite him. 'You seem a little hung up on the money issue.'

Maybe because when they'd first met he hadn't had any. At least not compared to Caro's father.

Don't forget she was disinherited the moment she married you.

She hadn't so much as blinked an eye at the time. She'd said it didn't matter. She'd said that given her and her father's adversarial relationship it was inevitable. And he'd believed her.

He bit back a sigh. Who knew? Maybe she'd even believed the lie back then.

'Perhaps we should clear that issue up first,' she continued.

'You didn't have to buy cake on my account, you know.'

He wished she hadn't. Her small acts of courtesy had always taken him off guard and left him all at sea. They'd oozed class and made it plain that she'd had an education in grace and decorum—one that he'd utterly lacked. It had highlighted all the differences between them. He'd lived in fear of unknowingly breaking one of those unknown rules of hers and hurting her.

You hurt her anyway.

And she'd hurt him.

He pushed those thoughts away.

Caro gazed at him and just for a fraction of a second her lips twitched. 'I didn't buy cake on *your* account.'

She forked a mouthful of honey roll to her lips and while she didn't actually close her eyes in relish, he had a feeling that deep inside herself she did.

'This cake is very good. Jean-Pierre is a wizard.'

That must be the baker's name. She'd always taken pains to find out and then use people's names. He'd found that charming. Once. Now he saw it for what it was—a front.

'But if you don't want it please don't eat it.'

He leaned towards her, his frown deepening. 'You never used to eat cake.'

'I know! I can't believe what I was missing.' Her eyes twinkled for a moment and her lips lifted, but then she sobered and her face became void of emotion. 'But people change. Five years ago you wouldn't have been at all concerned with the threat of me taking you for half of all you owned.'

He'd worked hard during the last five years to make a success of his security and private investigation firm. Such a success, in fact, that if he were still alive even Caro's father would sit up and take notice. He sat back. It seemed he'd been making money while Caro had been eating cake. It summed them up perfectly.

'Five years ago I didn't have anything worth taking, Caro.'

She looked as if she might disagree with him, but after a moment she simply shook her head. 'Let me waste no further time in putting your mind at rest. I don't want your money, Jack. I never did. You should know that yesterday I was named as my father's sole beneficiary.'

Whoa! He straightened. Okay...

'As we're still married I expect you could make a successful claim on the estate. Do you wish to?'

His hands clenched to fists. 'Absolutely not!'

She shrugged and ate more cake. '*You* haven't changed that much, then. Earlier today I'd have staked the entire estate on you not wanting a penny.'

Damn straight! But her odd belief in him coupled with her utter lack of concern that he could have taken her for a financial ride pricked him. 'So, this *pickle* you're in?'

She set her plate down, clasping her hands to her knees. 'Jack, I'd like to hire you for a rather...delicate job.'

He tried to hide his shock.

'But before we continue I'd like an assurance of your discretion and confidentiality.'

'You wouldn't have asked me that once.' She'd have taken it for granted.

'True, but when you walked away from our marriage you proved my trust in you was misplaced. So I'm asking for an assurance now.'

He glanced down to find his knuckles had turned white. He unclenched his hands and took a deep breath. 'I should warn you that if this "delicate" matter of yours involves murder or threats of violence then I'm honour-bound to—'

'Don't be ridiculous! Of course it doesn't. Don't take me for a fool. I'm a lot of things, but I'm not a fool.'

He bit back something very rude. Bending down, he

pulled the divorce papers he'd had drawn up from his satchel and slapped them onto the coffee table.

'I don't want to do a job for you, Caroline. I simply want you to sign the divorce papers and then never to clap eyes on you again.'

Her head rocked back, hurt gleamed in her eyes, and that soft, composed mouth of hers looked so suddenly vulnerable he hated himself for his outburst.

She rose, pressing her hands to her waist. 'That was unnecessarily rude.'

It had been.

She glanced at her watch. 'As interesting as this trip down memory lane has been, I'm afraid I'm going to have to ask you to leave. I have to be somewhere shortly.' She picked up the papers. 'I'll have my lawyer read over these and then we can get divorce proceedings underway.'

'And you'll draw the process out for as long as you can to punish me for refusing this job?' he drawled, rising too.

Her chin came up. 'I'll do nothing of the sort. You can have your divorce, Jack. The sooner the better as far as I'm concerned.'

A weight pressed down on him, trying to crush his chest. It made no sense. She was promising him exactly what he wanted.

With an oath, he sat again.

Caro's eyes widened. 'What are you doing?'

'Finishing my coffee and cake. Sit, Caro.'

'Really, Jack! I—'

'It's hard, seeing you again.'

Her tirade halted before it could begin. She swallowed, her eyes throbbing with the same old confusion and hurt that burned through him.

The intensity of emotion this woman could still arouse disturbed him. It was as if all the hard work he'd put in over the last five years to forget her and get his life back on track could be shattered with nothing more than a word or a look. He couldn't let that happen. He straightened. He *wouldn't* let that happen.

'No woman has ever made me as happy as you did.' He sipped his coffee. 'Or as miserable. I wasn't expecting the lid to be lifted on all those old memories. It's made me… testy—and that's why I said what I said. It was a mean-spirited thing to say. I'm sorry.'

Finally she sat. 'It doesn't make it any less true, though.'

'It's not true. Not really.' He didn't look at her as he said it. 'I expect things will be more comfortable once we put this initial meeting behind us.'

'I expect you're right.'

She frowned suddenly and glanced a little to his left. With a swift movement she reached down and picked up…

His cufflinks!

Jack bit back a curse. They must have fallen from his case when he'd pulled out the divorce papers. He could tell from the way her nostrils suddenly flared that she recognised the box. They'd been her wedding present to him when he'd said he'd prefer not to wear a ring—rose gold with a tiny sapphire in each that she'd claimed were nearly as blue as his eyes. He'd treasured them.

His glance went to her left hand and his gut clenched when he saw that she no longer wore her wedding ring.

Without a word she handed the box back to him. 'You really ought to be more careful when you're pulling things from your bag.'

He shoved the box back into the depths of the satchel. 'Tell me about this job you'd like me to do for you.'

He didn't owe her for her signature on their divorce papers, but if by doing this he could end things between them on a more pleasant note, then perhaps he'd find the closure he so desperately needed.

'And, yes, you have my word that I will never reveal

to another soul what you're about to tell me—unless you give me leave to.'

She stared at him, as if trying to sum him up. With a start he realised she was trying to decide whether to trust him or not.

'You don't trust my word of honour?'

'If you're after any kind of revenge on me, what I'm about to tell you will provide you with both the means and the method.'

He didn't want revenge. He'd never wanted revenge. He just wanted to move on with his life.

And to kiss her.

He stiffened. *Ridiculous!* He pushed that thought—and the associated images—firmly from his mind.

'I have no desire to hurt you, Caro. I hope your life is long and happy. Would it ease your mind if I didn't ask you to sign the divorce papers until after I've completed this job of yours?'

She leaned back, folding her arms. 'Why is this divorce so important to you now?'

'I want to remarry.'

She went deathly still. 'I see.'

She didn't. It wasn't as though he had a particular woman in mind, waiting in the wings, but he didn't correct the assumption she'd obviously made. It was beyond time that he severed this last tie with Caro. He should have done it before now, but he'd been busy establishing his company. Now it was thriving, he was a self-made success, and it was time to put the past to rest.

If Caro thought he'd fallen in love again, then all well and good. It would provide another layer of distance between them. And while he shouldn't need it—not after five years—he found himself clinging to every scrap of defence he could find.

'Well...' She crossed her legs. 'I wish you well, Jack.'

She even sounded as if she meant it. That shouldn't chafe at him.

'Tell me about this job you want to hire me for.'

He bit into the cake in an effort to ignore the turmoil rolling through him and looked across at her when she didn't speak. She glanced at the cake and then at him. It made him slow down and savour the taste of the sweet sponge, the smooth cream and the tiny crunch of sugar.

He frowned. 'This is really good.'

Finally she smiled. 'I know.'

He'd have laughed at her smugness, but his gut had clenched up too tightly at her smile.

She leaned forward, suddenly all business. 'I'm now a director at Vertu, the silver and decorative arts division at Richardson's.'

'Right.' He didn't let on that he knew that. When they'd married she'd been only a junior administrator at the auction house.

'Yesterday I placed into my father's safe a very beautiful and rather valuable snuffbox to show to a client this morning.'

'Is that usual?'

She raised one elegant shoulder. 'When selected customers request a private viewing, Richardson's is always happy to oblige.'

'Right.'

'When I went to retrieve the snuffbox this morning it wasn't there.'

He set down his now clean plate, his every sense sharpening. 'You have my attention.'

'I put it in the safe myself, prior to the reading of my father's will.'

'Which took place where?'

'In my father's study—the same room as the safe.'

He remembered that study. He nodded. 'Go on.'

Her expression was composed, but she was twisting the thin gold bangle on her arm round and round—a sure sign of agitation.

'The fact that I am sole beneficiary came as a very great shock to both Barbara and I.'

He raised an eyebrow. 'Your father and Barbara have remained married all this time?'

'Yes. I believe she loved him.'

Jack wasn't so charitable, but he kept his mouth shut.

'When Barbara retired to her room, the lawyer gave me this letter from my father.' She rose, removed a letter from her purse and handed it to him. 'More cake?'

He shook his head and read the letter. Then he folded it up again, tapping it against his knee. 'He thought she was stealing from him.'

Knowing Roland Fielding, he'd have kept a very tight rein on the purse strings. What kind of debts could his lovely young wife have accrued that would have her risking being caught red-handed with stolen goods?

'He was wrong. It wasn't Barbara who was pilfering those bits and pieces. It was Paul.'

'Paul is still working…?' He blew out a breath. 'Shouldn't he have retired by now?'

She pressed her hands together. 'My father wasn't a man who liked change.'

That was the understatement of the year.

'And, to be fair, I don't think Paul is either. I suspect the thought of retirement horrifies him.'

The bangle was pushed up her arm and twisted with such force he thought she'd hurt herself.

'He and Barbara have never warmed to each other.'

'And you're telling me this because…?'

'Because Paul was putting all those things he'd taken—'

'Stolen,' he corrected.

'He was putting them away for *me*.'

Jack pressed his fingers to his eyes.

'He was as convinced as I that I'd be totally written out of the will. He thought that I might need them.'

He pulled his hand away. 'Caro, I—'

She held up a hand and he found himself pulling to a halt.

'If Barbara finds out why my father wrote her out of the will and that Paul is responsible, she'll want him charged. I can't let that happen—surely you can see that, Jack? Paul was doing it for *me*.'

'You didn't ask him to!'

'That's beside the point. I know Barbara has been wronged, and I mean to make it up to her. I intend to split the estate with her fifty-fifty.'

He let the air whistle between his teeth. 'That's very generous. You could probably buy her silence for a couple of million.'

'It's not generous and I don't want to "buy her silence"! I want her to have half of everything. Half is certainly far more than I ever expected to get, and I'm fairly certain she won't begrudge me it.'

Was she?

'Where does the snuffbox come in?'

She hauled in a deep breath. 'During the middle of the night Barbara removed the jewellery from the safe. As it's all hers she had every right to remove it.'

He straightened. 'Except the snuffbox went missing at the same time?'

She nodded. 'When I asked her about it she claimed to not have seen it.'

'But you don't believe her?'

Her fingers started to twist that bangle again. 'She was upset yesterday—understandably. She wasn't thinking clearly. I know she wouldn't do anything to deliberately hurt me, but my father has treated her so very shabbily and

I suspect she panicked. I fear she's painted herself into a corner and now doesn't know how to return the snuffbox while still maintaining face.'

'And you want me to recover said snuffbox without her being aware of it?'

'Yes, please.'

It should be a piece of cake. 'What happens if the snuffbox isn't restored to Richardson's?'

'I'll lose my job.' She let out a long, slow breath. 'I'll never work in the industry again.'

He suddenly saw what she meant by revenge. Her job had been more important to her than starting a family with him. Now he had the potential to help destroy all the credibility she'd worked so hard to gain in one fell swoop. The irony!

'Worse than that, though…'

He lifted a disbelieving eyebrow. 'Worse than you losing your job?'

Her gaze didn't waver. 'Richardson's prides itself on its honesty and transparency. If I don't return that snuffbox there will be a police investigation.'

'The scandal would be shocking,' he agreed.

'For heaven's sake, Jack—who cares about the scandal?' She shot to her feet, hands on hips. 'Barbara does *not* deserve to go to jail for this. And Paul doesn't deserve to get into trouble either.'

They were both thieves!

'This mess is of my father's making. He forces people into impossible situations and makes them desperate. I won't let that happen this time around. I won't!' She pulled in a breath and met his gaze squarely. 'I mean to make this right, Jack. Will you help me?'

He stared at her. This woman had dashed all his most tightly held dreams. Five years ago she'd ground them underfoot as if they hadn't mattered one iota. The remembered pain could still make him wake up in a lather of sweat in the middle of the night.

He opened his mouth.

His shoulders slumped.

'Yes.'

Since when had he ever been able to say no to this woman?

Caro tiptoed past the disused pantry, and the butler's and housekeeper's offices—both of which had been vacant for as long as she could remember. The kitchen stretched all along the other side of these old rooms, with the small sitting room Paul used as his office on the other side of the kitchen. She'd chosen this route so as to not disturb him, but she tiptoed just the same. The man had bat-like hearing.

Lifting the latch on the back door, she stepped out into the darkness of the garden, just as she'd promised Jack she would. She glanced around, wondering in what corner he lurked and watched her from. Feigning indifference, she lifted her head and gazed up at the night sky, but if there were any stars to be seen they were currently obscured by low cloud.

She knew from past experience, though, that one rarely saw stars here—the city lights kept the stars at bay and, as her father had always told her, star-gazing never got anybody anywhere in life.

'Tell that to astronomers and astronauts,' she murmured under her breath.

'Miss Caroline?'

Paul appeared in the kitchen doorway. Caro wiped suddenly damp palms down her skirt. No one was supposed to see her out here.

'Dinner will be ready in ten minutes.'

She turned towards him. 'Are you sure there isn't anything I can help you with?'

'Certainly not.'

In his youth, Paul had trained as a chef. With the help of an army of maids, who came in twice a week, Paul had kept this house running single-handed for nearly thirty years. Although, as her father had rarely entertained, the position hadn't been a demanding one.

When she was a child she'd spent most of the year away at boarding school. So for nearly fifteen years—before her father had married Barbara—it had just been her father and Paul rattling around together in this big old house.

Some sixth sense—a hyper-awareness that flashed an odd tingling warmth across her skin—informed her that Jack stood in the shadows of a large rhododendron bush to her left. It took all her strength not to turn towards it. She'd wanted to let Paul in on their plan—his help would have been invaluable, and for a start she wouldn't be tiptoeing through the house in the dark, unlatching doors—but Jack had sworn her to secrecy.

And as he happened to be the surveillance expert…

She reached Paul's side and drew him to the right, away from Jack, pointing up at the steepled roofline. 'Did you know that one night, when I was ten, I walked all the way along that roofline?'

Paul glanced up and pressed a hand to his chest. 'Good grief!'

'I'd read a book about a cat burglar who'd made his way across London by jumping from roof to roof.'

'Tell me you didn't?' Paul groaned.

She laughed. From the corner of her eye she saw a shadow slip through the door. 'Mrs Thomas-Fraser's Alsatian dog started up such a racket that I hightailed it back to my room before the alarm could be raised.'

'You could've fallen! If I'd know about that back then it would have taken ten years off my life.'

Caro shook her head. 'I can hardly believe now that I

ever dared such a thing. Seriously, Paul, who'd have children?'

He chuckled and patted her shoulder. 'You were a delight.'

To Paul, perhaps, but never to her father.

'Come along.' He drew her into the house. 'You'll catch a chill if you're not careful.'

She wanted to laugh. A *chill*? It was summer! He was such a fusspot.

'I don't suppose I could talk you into joining Barbara and I for dinner?'

'You suppose right. It wouldn't be seemly.'

Seriously—he belonged in an England of a bygone age. 'Oh, I should go and lock the other door.'

'I'll take care of it.'

To insist would raise his suspicions. 'Paul, do we have any headache tablets?'

He pointed to a cupboard.

When he'd gone, she popped two tablets and unlatched the kitchen door—just in case. This sneaking around business was not for the faint-hearted.

Barbara sliced into her fillet of sole. 'Caroline, do I need to remind you that if your father had *wanted* me to inherit any portion of his estate, he'd have named me in his will?'

Caro swallowed. 'You only call me Caroline when you're cross with me.'

Barbara's gaze lifted.

'I didn't know he was going to do this, Barbara. I swear. I wish he'd left it all to you.'

Her stepmother's gaze lowered. She fiddled with the napkin in her lap.

'And if he *had* left it all to you,' Caro continued, 'I know you'd have made sure that I received a portion of it.'

'Of course—but that's different.'

'How?'

'This money has been in your family for generations. It's your birthright.'

Twaddle. 'I mean to give Paul a generous legacy too. He'll need a pension to see him through retirement.'

'That man's a rogue. I wouldn't be surprised if he hasn't weaselled enough bonuses out of your father over the years to see him through *two* retirements.'

'Even if he has, he'll have earned every penny.'

The other woman's gaze narrowed. 'You and your father—you never could find any common ground. You didn't understand each other. You never brought out the best in him. And—you'll have to forgive me for saying this, Caro, darling—you were never at your best when you were around him either.'

Caro opened her mouth to dispute that, then shot her stepmother a half smile. How could Barbara still defend him after he'd treated her so shabbily? 'Okay, I'll concede that point.'

Where was Jack at this very moment? Was he in Barbara's room, scanning its every hiding place? Had he found the snuffbox yet?

The thought of Jack prowling about upstairs filled her with the oddest adrenaline rush—similar to the one she'd had as a ten-year-old, when she'd inched across the mansion's roof. It made her realise how boring her life had become.

Not boring! Predictable.

She stuck out her chin. She *liked* predictable.

'Caro?'

She snapped her attention back to Barbara.

'You had the oddest look on your face.'

Jack had *always* had that effect on her. 'Just trying to work out the morass that was my father's mind. *And* yours.'

'Mine?' Barbara set her fork down. 'Whatever do you mean?'

'If our situations were reversed you'd be happy to share my father's money with me. Why aren't you happy for me to share it with you?'

Barbara picked up her clutch purse and rose. 'I find my appetite has quite fled. I really don't wish to discuss this any further.'

Caro nearly choked on her sole. *Jack!* If Barbara should happen to find him in her room...

'Please don't go! I—' She took a hasty sip of water. 'I'm tired of feeling lonely in this house.'

Barbara's face softened. She lowered herself back to her chair. 'Very well—but no more talk about your father and his money.'

'Deal.' Caro did her best to eat her new potatoes and green beans when all the while her stomach churned.

Please be careful, Jack.

She glanced over at her stepmother. 'Paul tells me you've barely been out of the house lately? Don't you think you should get out more? Being cooped up like this can't be good for you.'

Barbara sent her a tiny smile. 'On that subject we happen to be in complete agreement, darling. Lady Sedgewick has invited me down to their place in Kent this very weekend. She's having a house party. I thought I might accept her invitation.'

'Oh, yes, you should! The Sedgewicks are a lovely family. I was at school with Olivia. Do go. You'll have a lovely time.'

It was beyond time that Barbara started enjoying herself again.

Caro tiptoed into her room ninety minutes later. 'Jack?' she whispered into the darkness, before clicking on the light.

Her room was empty. She tried to crush the kernel of disappointment that lodged in her chest. He hadn't said that he'd wait for her in her room. She'd just assumed he would. She checked her phone for a text.

Nothing.

Maybe he'd sent her an email?

She was about to retrieve her laptop when a shadow on the far side of the wardrobe fluttered and Jack detached himself from the darkness. Her mouth went dry and her heart pounded. She tried to tell herself it was because he'd startled her, but she had a feeling her reaction was even more primal than fear.

Dressed in close-fitting jeans and a black turtleneck sweater, Jack looked dark, dangerous and disreputable.

Delicious, some part of her mind pronounced.

She wanted to tell herself to stop being ridiculous, but 'delicious' described him perfectly. What *was* ridiculous was the fact that every atom of her being should swell towards him now, with a hunger that robbed her of breath.

But why was it ridiculous—even after five years? It had always been this way between them.

Yes, but five years ago he'd broken her heart. *That* should make a difference.

She lifted her chin. It did. It made a huge difference. Obviously just not to her body's reaction, that was all.

She pulled in a breath. 'Well…?'

She held that breath as she waited for him to produce the snuffbox. She'd get her snuffbox and he'd get his divorce, and then he could marry this new woman of his and they'd all be happy.

He lifted a finger to his lips and cocked his head, as if listening to something.

Actually, she had serious doubts on the happiness aspect. She had serious doubts that Jack was in love.

Not your business.

Jack moved in close, leaned towards her, and for a moment she thought he meant to kiss her. Her heart surged to the left and then to the right, but he merely whispered in her ear.

'Go and check the corridor.'

His warm breath caressed her ear, making her recall the way he'd used to graze it gently with his teeth…and how it had driven her wild. The breath jammed in her chest. She turned her head a fraction, until their lips were so close their breaths mingled. She ached for him to kiss her. She ached to feel his arms about her, curving her body to his. She ached to move with him in a union that had always brought her bliss.

His lips twisted and a sardonic light burned in the backs of his eyes. 'Caro, I didn't come up here to play.'

His warm breath trailing across her lips made her nipples peak before the import of his words hit her. From somewhere she found the strength to step back, humiliation burning her cheeks.

'You should be so lucky,' she murmured, going to the door and checking the corridor outside, doing all she could to hide how rubbery her legs had become. 'All clear,' she said in a low voice, turning back and closing the door behind her. 'What did you hear?'

He merely shrugged. 'It's better to be safe than sorry.'

She did her best not to notice the breadth of his shoulders in that body-hugging turtleneck or the depth of his chest. 'Do you also have a balaclava?'

He pulled one from the waistband of his jeans.

She rolled her eyes and shook her head, as if having him here in her bedroom didn't faze her in the least.

'Did you get it?' She kept her voice low, even though Barbara's room was at the other end of the house and Paul's was another floor up, and he used the back stairs to get to it anyway. Nobody would be passing her door unless they'd come deliberately looking for her.

'No.'

'*No?*' She moved in closer to whisper, 'What do you mean, no?' She had to move away again fast—his familiar scent was threatening to overwhelm her.

'If it'd been in that room I would've found it.'

She didn't doubt him—not when he used that tone of voice. Damn! Damn! *Damn!*

She strode to the window, hands clenched. 'Where can it be?'

'Did she have a handbag or a purse with her at dinner?'

Caro swung around. 'A little clutch purse.' In hindsight, that *had* been odd. She hadn't had any plans to go out this evening, so why bring a purse to dinner in her own house?

'It's in there, then.'

'So…what now? You can't creep into her room with her in it.'

'It wouldn't be ideal,' he agreed, moving to the window and raising it. In one lithe movement he slid outside.

'So?'

'So now I go home and ponder for a while.'

She should have known it wouldn't be that easy. She planted her hands on her hips. 'Jack, you *can* use the front door. Everyone else is in bed. No one will see you.'

'But you've made me eager to try out your cat burglar method.'

So he'd heard her conversation with Paul about that…

She leaned out to peer at him. 'Be careful.'

He moved so quickly that she wouldn't have been able to retreat even if the gleam in his eyes *hadn't* held her captive. His lips brushed her hair, his breath tickling her ear again. She froze, heart pounding, as she waited for him to murmur some final instruction to her.

Instead his teeth grazed her ear, making her gasp and sparking her every nerve ending to life.

CHAPTER THREE

'I *KNEW THAT* was what you were remembering earlier. And your remembering made *me* remember.'

Jack's voice was so full of heat and desire it made Caro sway. 'So…' Her voice hitched. 'That's my fault too, is it?'

Jack, it seemed, considered everything to be her fault.

He ignored that to lean in closer again and inhale deeply. 'You smell as good as you ever did, Caro.'

She loathed herself for not being able to step away.

He glanced down at her and laughed—but it wasn't a pretty sound, full of anger and scorn as it was. She sensed, though, that the anger and scorn were directed as much at himself as they were at her.

He trailed a lazy finger along the vee of her blouse. Her skin goosepimpled and puckered, burning at his touch with a ferocity that made her knees wobble.

'If I had a mind to,' he murmured, 'I think I could convince you to invite me to stay.'

And the moment she did would he laugh at her and leave?

The old Jack would never have enjoyed humiliating her. And yet that finger continued trailing a tantalising path in the small vee of bare flesh at her throat. Heat gathered under her skin to burn fiercely at the centre of her.

She made herself swallow. 'If I had my heart set on you staying, Jack, you'd stay.'

That finger stopped. He gripped her chin, forcing her gaze to meet the cold light in his. 'Are you sure of that?'

She stared into those eyes and spoke with an honesty that frightened her. 'Utterly convinced.'

Air whistled between his teeth.

'You want me as much as you ever did,' she said. And, God help her, the knowledge made her stomach swoop and twirl.

'And you want me.' The words ground out of him from behind a tight jaw.

'But that wasn't enough the last time around,' she forced herself to say. 'And I see no evidence to the contrary that it'd be any different for us now either.'

She found herself abruptly released.

Jack straightened. 'Right—Barbara. Now I've had time to think.'

He'd *what*? All this time his mind had been working? It was all *she'd* been able to do to remain upright!

'If she's keeping that trinket so close then she obviously has plans for it.'

'Or is she looking for the first available opportunity to throw it into the Thames and get rid of incriminating evidence?'

He shook his head. 'Barbara is a woman with an eye on the main chance.'

She found herself itching to slap him. 'You don't even *know* her. You're wrong. She's—'

'I've come across women like her before.'

Did he class Caro as one of those women?

'And I'm the expert here. You've hired me to do a job and we'll do it my way—understand?'

She lifted her hands in surrender. 'Right. Fine.'

'Can you get us an invitation to this country party of Lady Sedgewick's?'

She blinked. 'You *heard* that?'

'I thoroughly searched Barbara's room and your father's study, as well as checking the safe.'

She stared at him. 'You opened the safe?'

He nodded.

'But you don't know the combination.'

He waved that away as if it were of no consequence. 'And on my way to the study I eavesdropped on what might prove to be a key piece of information. By the way, it's a nice touch to keep letting Barbara think you mean to give her half of the estate. Hopefully it'll prevent her from feeling too desperate and doing something stupid—like trying to sell something that doesn't belong to her.'

Caro's fingers dug into the window frame. 'It's *not* a ploy! I fully intend to give her half.'

'Lady Sedgewick?'

She blew out a breath and tried to rein in her temper. 'I can certainly ensure that *I* get an invitation.'

'And me?'

'On what pretext?' She folded her arms. *'Oh, and by the way, Lady S, my soon-to-be ex-husband is in town—may I bring him along?* That won't fly.'

He pursed his lips, his eyes suddenly unreadable. 'What if you told her we were attempting a reconciliation?'

A great lump of resistance rose through her.

'Think about it, Caro. Your snuffbox goes missing and then the very next weekend Barbara—who's apparently hardly left the house in months—makes plans to attend a country house party. Ten to one she has a prospective buyer lined up and is planning to do the deal this weekend.'

Hell, blast and damnation!

'This is becoming so much more complicated than it was supposed to.'

'If you don't like that plan there are two other strategies we can fall back on.'

* * *

'Was it difficult to swing the invitation?'

'Not at all.'

It was early Saturday morning and she was sitting beside Jack in his hired luxury saloon car. It all felt so right and normal she had to keep reminding herself that it was neither of those things. Far from it. She still didn't know how they were going to negotiate sharing a bedroom. She kept pushing the thought from her mind—there was no point endlessly worrying about it—but it kept popping back again.

'Tell me how you managed it.'

So she told him how on Thursday she'd 'just happened' to bump into her old schoolfriend Olivia Sedgewick at a place she knew Olivia favoured for lunch, and they'd ended up dining together.

The house party in Kent had come up in their idle chit-chat, and Caro had confided her concerns that this would be Barbara's first social engagement since Roland had died. A bit later she'd mentioned meeting up with Jack again after all these years, and how the spark was still there but they were wanting to keep a low profile in London in case things didn't work out.

Of course things weren't going to work out.

'And…?' Jack prompted.

'Well, from there she came up with the brilliant plan of inviting us down for the weekend. We'll get a chance for some out-of-London couple time, with the added bonus that I can keep an eye on Barbara too.'

He laughed. 'You mean you deviously planted the idea in her mind and she ran with it!'

She shrugged. 'She's a lovely person. It wasn't hard.'

'It was masterfully done. I should hire you for my firm.'

He didn't mean it, but his praise washed over her with a warmth that made her settle back a little more snugly in her seat. 'I fear I'm not cut out for a life of subterfuge and undercover intrigue. I don't know how you manage it without getting an ulcer.'

His chuckle warmed her even more than his praise had.

'Barbara has no idea that we're coming?' he asked.

'None whatsoever. I told Olivia I didn't want Barbara thinking she was being a burden to me. I asked her if we could say that we'd met up only last night and she invited us down to her parents' for the weekend on the spur of the moment.'

'Excellent. I've had her tailed over the last few days, but there's nothing suspicious to report. It appears you've not had any suspicious visitors for the last couple of days either.'

'Oh, well…that's good.'

And at that point they ran out of conversation.

'I've…um…taken most of next week off as leave from work.' Just in case they had to do more sleuthing.

'Right.'

She itched to ask him about the woman he had back home in Australia—the one he planned to marry. How had they met? What was she like? Was she very beautiful? Did they set each other alight the way she and he once had? Or…?

She folded her arms. Or was this other woman simply a brood mare? A means to an end?

She couldn't ask any of that, of course. What Jack did with his life was no longer any concern of hers. It was none of her business.

She lifted her chin. 'We're having a glorious summer so far.' She gestured at the blue sky and the sunshine pouring in the windows.

At the same time he said, 'I take it you're not seeing anyone at the moment?'

She stiffened. None of *his* business. 'What does that have to do with anything?'

He sent her a sidelong glance, his lips twisting. 'Let's just say it could be awkward for all concerned if we happened to run into your current squeeze in Kent.'

She laughed. It was either that or cry. 'That would be terribly bad form indeed. We're safe, Jack. I have no current paramour.'

Unlike him.

For heaven's sake, let it go!

She shifted on her seat. 'You'd better fill me in on the plan.' She bit her lip. 'You *do* have a plan, don't you?'

'My plan is to watch and listen. I'm good at my job, Caro. And I'm very good at reading people.'

He'd been terrible at reading *her*.

'I can nose out a fishy situation at fifty paces.'

'Fine, but… What am *I* supposed to do?'

'Be your usual charming self.'

From anyone else that would have sounded like a compliment.

'Don't forget our cover story. We're supposed to be attempting a reconciliation.'

She had no hope of forgetting *that*.

'So the odd lingering look and a bit of hand-holding won't go astray.'

She swallowed, her mouth suddenly dry and her pulse suddenly wild. 'Absolutely.'

'And just be generally attentive.'

To him? Or to what was going on around them?

'Take your cues from me.'

Suddenly all she wanted to do was return to her tiny flat, crawl into bed and pull the covers over her head.

He sent her another sidelong glance and then reached out to squeeze her hand. 'Whenever you feel your resolve slipping think about the consequences of not getting that snuffbox back.'

Worst-case scenario? She'd lose her job with no hope

of another and she'd be visiting Barbara in jail. She shuddered. No, no, *no*. She couldn't let that happen.

She squeezed his hand back. 'Excellent advice.'

'With the two of you, that brings our numbers up to a merry dozen,' said Cynthia—Lady Sedgewick—leading Caro and Jack into the drawing room, where she introduced them to several of the other guests. 'Olivia should be here any moment. Oh, and *look*, Barbie dear…' Cynthia cooed as Barbara walked in from the terrace. 'Did you know that Caro and Jack were joining us this weekend?'

Barbara pulled up short, her mouth dropping open.

'It was all very last-minute,' Caro said, going across to kiss her stepmother's cheek. 'I never had a chance to tell you.'

Jack moved across to shake Barbara's hand. 'Lovely to see you again, Barbara.'

For an awful moment, Caro had the oddest feeling that Barbara meant to snub Jack completely, but at the last moment she clasped his hand briefly before slipping her arm through Caro's and drawing her away.

'Why don't I help you to unpack? You can fill me in—' she glared over her shoulder at Jack '—on all the gossip.'

'I've put them in the room next to yours, Barbie.'

'I'll see that Caro's safely settled.' With that, Barbara led Caro out of the drawing room and up a rather grand staircase.

'Doesn't it set your teeth on edge, the way she calls you Barbie?' Caro asked in a low voice.

'It's just her way. More pressing at the moment is the question of what you're doing here with Jack?'

'Ah…'

'No, no.' Barbara held up her free hand. 'Wait till we've gained the privacy of your room.'

So arm in arm they climbed the stairs in silence and

walked along the grand gallery with all its family portraits until they reached the wing housing their bedrooms.

'Are you completely out of your mind?' Barbara demanded, the moment she'd closed the bedroom door behind them. 'That man broke your heart into a thousand little pieces and stamped all over it without so much as a by-your-leave. Have you taken leave of your senses?'

Caro opened her mouth. Closing it again, she slumped down to the blanket box sitting at the end of the bed—which, thankfully, wasn't some huge big four-poster monstrosity.

'How long?' Barbara asked.

She and Jack should have discussed their cover story in a little more detail. She decided to go with the truth. 'Only a few days. I… I didn't know how to tell you.'

'A few *days*! And already you're spending the weekend with him?'

Caro grimaced at how that sounded. 'Well, technically we *are* still married. And I thought coming down here this weekend would…would…' She trailed off, wishing this all felt as make-believe as it actually was.

Barbara sat beside her and reached out to halt the constant twisting of her bangle. 'Caro, darling, I know your father's death came as a very great shock to you, but do you *really* think this is the best way to deal with it?'

'You think I'm making a mistake?'

'Don't you?'

Her shoulders sagged. 'You're probably right. Why are we so attracted to the things that are bad for us?'

Barbara opened her mouth and then closed it, her shoulders sagging too. 'It's a very strange thing,' she agreed.

'Seriously, though,' Caro said, strangely close to tears, 'what hope does a woman like me have of holding the attention of a man like Jack?'

Barbara stiffened. 'Don't you *dare* sell yourself short! Any man would be lucky to have you.'

Her stepmother's concern warmed her to her very bones. Surely Barbara wouldn't steal from her? She'd just got herself into a fix and she didn't know how to extricate herself. That was all.

She met Barbara's gaze. 'You really do care about me, don't you?'

'Of course I do. What on earth would have you thinking otherwise?'

'Father.'

'Look, darling, the will—'

'Not the will. I meant before that. All Father's disapproval and disappointment where I was concerned.' She lifted a shoulder and then let it drop. 'You must've resented all the…disharmony I caused.'

Barbara patted Caro's hand. 'I was married to your father, and I loved him, but it doesn't follow that we agreed on every point.'

She stared at the other woman, wondering what on earth that meant.

'And now Jack's back in your life…'

Not for long.

'And you think the spark is still there?'

She huffed out a breath. 'No doubt about that…'

Barbara went to Caro's suitcase and flung it open, rummaged through its contents. 'Here.' She pulled out a pair of tight white Capri pants and a fitted blouse in vivid blue. 'Slip into these. They'll be perfect for croquet on the lawn later.'

Caro grimaced. 'There's nowhere to hide in that outfit.' She normally wore a long tunic top with those Capris. 'And there's no denying I've put on a little weight in the last few months.'

'Despite what torture we women put ourselves through

in the name of beauty, men appreciate a few curves on a woman. Jack won't be able to take his eyes off you.'

Barbara smiled at her and Caro found herself smiling back. Dressing to attract Jack suddenly seemed like the best idea in the world.

And fun.

Besides, *he* was the one who had insisted on their ridiculous cover story. She was only doing what he'd insisted was necessary. No harm in enjoying herself in the process…

Jack watched Caro ready herself to take her next shot and had to run a finger around the collar of his shirt when she gave that cute little tush of hers an extra wiggle. He wasn't the only man admiring her…uh…feminine attributes. His hand tightened about his croquet mallet. It was all he could do not to frogmarch her up to the house and order her to put on something less revealing.

Except what she was wearing was perfectly respectable! The only bare flesh on display was from mid-calf to ankle, where her Capris ended and her sand shoes started. Those sand shoes made her look seriously cute. The only problem was they kept drawing his attention to the tantalising curves of her calves.

Who was he trying to kid? Her entire ensemble made her look cute. Not to mention desirable.

Barbara trailed over to him, a glass of fruit punch dangling elegantly from her fingers. 'Caro is looking well, isn't she?'

He couldn't lie. 'She's looking sensational.' But then he'd *always* thought she looked sensational.

Some things never change.

Barbara smiled up at him pleasantly. 'May I give you a word of warning, darling?'

'Of course.'

'If you break her heart again, I will cut *your* heart out with a knife.'

Whoa!

With a bright smile, she patted his arm. 'Enjoy your game.'

He stared after her as she ambled off again.

'You're up, Jack.'

He spun around to see Caro pointing to the hoop that was his next target. Croquet? He scowled. What a stupid game!

'Cooper!' Caro called to one of the other players. 'Have you added any new pieces to your collection recently?'

Good girl.

'Dear me, yes. I picked up a rather splendid medieval knife at the quaintest little antique place.'

Don't tell Barbara that. It might give her ideas.

'I must show it to you next time you're over.'

How well did Caro know these people?

He took his shot and tried to focus as the conversation turned to collectibles and antiques. He entirely lost the thread of it, though, when Caro took her next shot. Did she *practise* that maddening little shimmy?

He glanced around, gritting his teeth at the appreciative smiles on the other men's faces. He couldn't frogmarch her up to their bedroom and demand she change her clothes! If he marched her up to their bedroom he'd divest her of those clothes as quickly as possible and make love to her with a slow, serious intent that would leave her in no doubt how much he, for one, appreciated her physical attributes.

Every cell in his body screamed at him to do it.

He ground his teeth together. He was here to do a job. He was here to put the past behind him. It had taken too long to get this woman out of his system. He wasn't letting her back into his life again. Regardless of how cute her tush happened to be.

Find the snuffbox.

Get the divorce papers signed.

Get on with your life.

He kept that checklist firmly in the forefront of his mind as he turned his attention back to the conversation.

Croquet was followed by lunch. After lunch it was tennis and volleyball. A few of the guests went riding, but as Barbara was lounging in a chair on the lawn, alternately chatting with their hostess and flicking through a glossy magazine, he and Caro stuck close to the house too. Besides, Jack didn't ride.

It suddenly struck him that he had no idea whether Caro rode or not. Just another of the many things that hadn't come up during their short marriage.

Caro smiled a lot, chatted pleasantly and seemed utterly at ease, but it slowly and irrevocably dawned on him that while she'd always been somewhat reserved and self-contained that was even more the case now. She seemed to hold herself aloof in a way she never had before. She'd become more remote, serious…almost staid.

Dinner was followed by billiards for some, cards for others and lazy conversation over drinks for the rest. The other guests were a pleasant lot, and despite his low expectations he'd found it an oddly pleasant day.

Except for the lingering glances Caro sent him. And the secret smiles that made him want to smile back…and then ravish her. He'd lost count of the number of touches she'd bestowed on him—her hand resting lightly on his arm, her fingers brushing the back of his hand, her arm slipping through his…

Goddamn endless touches!

He raised his hand to knock on their shared bedroom door, but then pulled it back to his side. He had to get a grip. Caro was only following his instructions. Even if she *was* in danger of overdoing it.

Overdoing it? Really?

He ground his teeth together. No. She'd struck the perfect balance. He just hadn't realised that her flirting with him would stretch the limits of his control so thoroughly.

Be cool. Keep a lid on it.

Hauling in a breath, he knocked. He'd given her a good thirty minutes to get ready for bed. He hoped it was enough. It would be great if she were asleep.

The door opened a crack and Caro's face appeared. *No such luck.* She moistened her lips and opened the door wider to let him enter. She wore a pair of yoga pants and an oversized T-shirt…and her nerves were plain to see in the way she was pushing her bangle up and down her arm. It sent an answering jolt through him and a quickening of his pulse. If she'd had access to some of his earlier thoughts she'd have every right to her nerves.

He resisted the urge to run his finger around his collar again. He had to get his mind off the fact that they were in a bedroom. Alone.

He draped his jacket across the back of a chair. 'I've been meaning to ask—has Barbara ever exhibited any signs of violence?'

Caro settled on the end of the bed, her feet tucked up beneath her. 'Heavens no. Why would you ask such a thing?'

He raked both hands back through his hair, trying not to look at her fully. 'During croquet she threatened to cut my heart out with a knife if I broke *your* heart.'

'Ah.' She bit her lip and ducked her head. 'So that's what put you off your game.'

He could have sworn her shoulders shook. He settled himself in the chair—the only chair in the room. It was large and, as he'd be spending the night in it, thankfully comfortable.

'Are you laughing at me?'

'Not *at* you.' Her eyes danced. 'But she's such a tiny little thing, and you have to admit the thought of her doing you any damage is rather amusing.' A smile spilled from her. 'And it's kind of sweet for her to fluff up all mother-hen-like on my account.'

That smile. He had a forbidden image of her sprawled across that bed, naked…wearing nothing but that smile.

A scowl moved through him.

She shrugged. 'It's nice.'

Nice? He stared at her, and for the first time it occurred to him that extracting Barbara from this mess—one of her own making, he might add—might, in fact, be more important to Caro than her job. Which was crazy. He'd had firsthand experience of all Caro would sacrifice in the interests of her career.

'That's why she whisked me away the moment we arrived. She wanted to warn me of you—to tell me to be careful.'

He stared at her. 'Careful of what?'

'Of *you*, of course. Of getting my heart broken again.'

'*Your* heart?' He found himself suddenly on his feet, roaring at her. 'What about *my* heart?'

Her jaw dropped. '*Your* heart? *You* were the one who walked away without so much as a backward glance!' She shot to her feet too, hands on hips. 'You mean to tell me you *have* a heart?'

More than she'd ever know.

He fell back into the chair.

She folded her arms and glared. 'Besides, *your* heart can't be in any danger. You're in love with another woman, right?'

He moistened his lips and refused to answer that question. 'Are you saying *your* heart is in danger?'

She stilled before hitching her chin up higher. 'When you left five years ago I thought I would die.'

He wanted to call her a liar. Her heart was as cold as ice. It was why he'd left. He hadn't been able to make so much as a dent in that hard heart of hers. But truth shone from her eyes now in silent accusation, and something in his chest lurched.

'I am *never* giving you the chance to do that to me again.'

For a moment it felt as if the ground beneath his feet were slipping. He shook himself back to reality.

'Sending me on a guilt trip is a nice little ploy, Caro, but it won't work. I *know* you, remember?'

'Oh, whatever…' She waved an arm through the air, as if none of it mattered any more, and for some reason the action enraged him.

He shot to his feet again. She'd started to lower herself back to the bed, but now she straightened and held her ground.

'You!' He thrust a finger at her nose. 'You made it more than clear that while I might be suitable rebellion material, to put Daddy's nose out of joint, I was nowhere near good enough to father your children!'

That knowledge, and the fact that she'd taken him in so easily, should have humiliated him. He wished to God that it had. He wished to God that he'd been able to feel anything beyond the black morass of devastation that had crushed him beneath its weight.

All he'd ever wanted was to build a family with this woman. A family that he could love, protect and cherish.

Before Caro, he hadn't known it was possible to love another person so utterly and completely. When he'd found out that she didn't love him back, he hadn't known which way to turn.

One thing had been clear, though. He'd had no intention

of leaving her. He'd blamed her father, with all his guilt-tripping emotional blackmail, for stunting Caro's emotional development. He'd figured that half or even a quarter of Caro was worth more than the whole of any other woman.

That was how far he'd fallen.

She'd stamped all over him—and he'd spread himself at her feet and let her do it.

When he'd asked her if they could start a family, though, she'd laughed. *Laughed.*

He dragged a hand down his face. He would never forget the expression on her face. He hadn't been able to hide from the truth any longer—Caro would never consent to have a family with him.

So he'd left before he could lose himself completely.

He'd fled while there was still something of him left.

'*Your* heart?' he spat. 'What use did *you* ever have for a heart? Stop playing the injured party. You haven't earned the right.'

CHAPTER FOUR

'I HAVEN'T EARNED the right…?'

Caro's hands clenched and she started to shake with the force of her anger. He watched with a kind of detached fascination. Back when they'd been married—*they were still married*—Caro had rarely lost her temper.

In fact, now that he thought about it, she might have got cross every now and again, but he couldn't recall her *ever* losing her temper. To see her literally shaking with anger now was a novel experience…and bizarrely compulsive.

Her eyes flashed and a red flush washed through her cheeks. She looked splendid, alive—and tempting beyond measure. There was nothing staid or remote about her now.

He loathed himself for the impulse to goad her further.

He loathed himself more for the stronger impulse to pull her into his arms and soothe her.

He watched her try to swallow her anger.

'In your eyes, my not wanting children made me unnatural. Having children was more important to you than it ever was for me. It's a very great shame we didn't discuss our views on whether or not we wanted children *before* we married.'

He stabbed a finger at her. 'What's a *very great shame* is that your job—your stupid, precious job—was more important to you than me, our relationship and the potential family we could've had.'

The old frustration rose up through him with all its associated pain.

'What's so important about your job? What is it, after all, other than vacuous and frivolous? It can hardly be called vital and important!'

Her eyes spat fire. 'What—unlike *yours*, you mean?'

He swung away and raked a hand through his hair, trying to lasso his anger before swinging back to face her. 'When you get right down to it, what do you *do*? You sell trinkets to rich people who have more time and money than they do sense.'

Her hands clenched so hard her knuckles turned white. 'While *you* find things rich people have lost? Oh, that's *right* up there with saving lives and spreading peace and harmony throughout all the land.'

He blinked as that barb found its mark. 'My job's saving your butt!'

'Not yet it isn't!'

They stared at each other, both breathing hard.

'If people like me didn't care about our jobs, Mr High and Mighty, *you'd* be out of work.'

Touché.

'Sometimes jobs aren't about performing an important function in society. Sometimes they're about what they represent to the people doing them.' She thumped a hand to her chest, her voice low and controlled. '*My* job is the only thing I've ever achieved on my own merit. Against my father's wishes, strictures and censure *I* chose the subjects *I* wanted to study at university.'

She'd chosen Art History rather than the Trust Law and Business Management degree her father had demanded she take. He'd wanted her groomed in preparation for taking over that damn trust he'd set up in her mother's name. Caro had always sworn she wouldn't administer that trust, but her father had refused to believe her, unable to countenance the possibility of such rebellion and defiance.

'*My* job,' Caro continued, 'has provided me with the means to pay the rent on my own flat and to live my own life. How dare you belittle that? My job has given me independence and freedom and the means—'

'I understand you needing independence from your father.' Fury rose through him. 'But you didn't need it from *me*! I'm nothing like your father.'

'You're *exactly* like my father!'

She'd shouted at him, with such force he found himself falling back a step. His mouth went dry. She was wrong. He was nothing like her father.

'You wanted to control me the same way he did. What *I* wanted didn't matter one jot. It was always what *you* wanted that mattered!' Her voice rose even higher and louder. 'You didn't want a wife! You wanted a…a *brood mare*!'

The accusation shot out of her like grapeshot and he stared at her, utterly speechless. He couldn't have been more surprised if she'd held a forty-five calibre submachine gun complete with magazine, pistol grip and detachable buttstock to his head and said, *Stick 'em up.*

He found himself breathing hard. She was kidding— just trying to send him on a guilt trip. That couldn't be how she'd felt all those years ago.

The bedroom door flew open and they both swung round to find Barbara standing in the doorway, her face pinched and her eyes wide. 'I will *not* let you shout at Caro like that!'

Him? Caro had been the one doing most of the shouting.

'Come along, darling, you can bunk in with me tonight.'

She moved past Jack to take Caro's arm and tug her towards the door. She shot a venomous glare at him over her shoulder.

Caro didn't look at him at all. Not once. His heart started to throb. He opened his mouth to beg her to stay.

To what end? It was madness even to consider it. He snapped his mouth shut, clenching his hands into fists.

'Oh, *really*, Caro…' He heard Barbara sigh before the door closed behind them. '*This* is what you wear to bed to attract a man? It won't do.'

He wanted to yell after them that there was absolutely nothing wrong with what Caro was wearing, that she looked as delectable as ever. But, again, to what end?

He collapsed back into the chair, his temples throbbing and his chest burning.

'You wanted a brood mare!'

Behind her calm, composed facade, was that what she'd really been thinking? He rested his head in his hands. Was that truly how she'd felt? Was it how *he'd* made her feel?

'Are you okay, darling?'

Caro managed a shaky smile. 'This will probably sound stupid, but that's the very first time I've ever yelled at Jack.'

Barbara lowered herself to the bed. 'Coming from anyone else I would be surprised—shocked, even—but not from you. You've always been a funny little thing.'

'Funny?'

'Very controlled and self-contained. You have a tendency to avoid confrontation. It can be very difficult to get a handle on how you truly feel.'

Caro blinked and sat too. 'I'm sorry. I didn't realise.'

'Oh, I know you don't do it on purpose. Besides, you're getting better.'

She rubbed a hand across her forehead. 'Fighting like that doesn't feel *better*.'

'So things with you and Jack aren't going so well?'

She recalled, despite their fight, that she and Jack had

a cover story to maintain. She forced a shrug. 'That fight has been brewing for five years.'

'Well, then, maybe it's cleared the air,' Barbara said briskly. 'In the meantime, it won't hurt him to stew for a night. Now, come along—jump into bed. Things will look brighter in the morning, after a good night's sleep.'

'Are you sure you don't mind me sharing with you?'

'Not in the slightest.'

Caro climbed under the covers. Just before the light clicked out she noticed Barbara's clutch purse, sitting on the dressing table on the other side of the room like an unclaimed jackpot.

She blinked, her mind growing suddenly sharp. With a heart that pounded she lay still, staring into the dark, willing Barbara to fall asleep. The sooner she retrieved the snuffbox, the sooner Jack would be out of her life.

It seemed an age before Barbara's slow, steady breaths informed Caro that she was asleep. As quietly and smoothly as she could, she slid out from beneath the covers and stood by the side of the bed for a couple of moments, holding her breath to see if Barbara would stir.

When she didn't, she made her way carefully around the bed to the dressing table. Reaching out a hand to its edge, she nearly knocked over the can of hairspray sitting just behind the purse. With a dry mouth she righted it and waited. When nothing happened, she edged her fingers forward until they skimmed across the purse.

With her heart pounding so loudly she was sure Barbara must hear it, she opened the purse and pushed her hand inside. At the same moment the bedside light was flicked on.

'Caro, what are you doing?'

Caro stared into the clutch purse, afraid that if she turned around her expression would betray her. *No snuffbox.* 'I was… I was looking for some painkillers.' She turned and blinked in what she hoped was a bleary fashion.

'Here you go.' Barbara handed her a pill from a bottle on the bedside table beside her, along with a glass of water.

There was nothing for it but to take the headache tablet, even though she didn't have a headache. Granted, Jack was a major headache, but she'd need something stronger than an aspirin to get rid of *him*.

'Thank you, and I'm sorry I disturbed you.'

She climbed back into bed, her stomach feeling suddenly odd. Seriously, she wasn't cut out for all this sneaking around.

She wondered if Jack was sleeping soundly next door. She wondered what would have happened if she'd stayed there. Would they have made wild, abandoned love?

She tingled all over at the thought.

Just as well she was on this side of the wall!

The fuzziness of sleep settled over her, but when Barbara slipped from the bed Caro tried to push it away. What was Barbara doing? This could be a *clue*!

The other woman padded over to the window. Caro tried to rouse herself from the darkness trying to claim her.

As if from a long way away, she thought she heard Barbara say, 'Oh, Roland, why did you have to make things so hard?'

Caro wouldn't mind an answer to that question herself. She tried to lift herself up onto her elbows, but her body refused to comply with the demand.

'Why are you making me do this?'

Do what?

Caro opened her mouth to ask, but the words wouldn't come. Her last coherent thought before a thick, suffocating blanket descended over her was that Barbara hadn't given her an aspirin. She'd given her a sleeping tablet.

* * *

Caro found it nearly impossible to shrug the fog of sleep from her brain, but she did manage to push herself upright into a sitting position.

What time was it?

Sunlight flooded in at the window, but finding the energy to locate a clock in this unfamiliar room seemed beyond her at that moment. She turned her head a fraction to check the bed. No Barbara. At least not in the bed.

'Barbara?'

She barely recognised that voice as her own.

She cleared her throat and tried again. 'Barbara?'

The result wasn't much better. Eventually she forced herself to sit on the edge of bed, and then to stand and turn around. It only confirmed what she already knew—Barbara wasn't in the room.

She hoped Jack knew where Barbara was.

She pulled in a breath. *Right.* She needed to go next door and dress and then join everyone else for the day's activities.

She made swaying progress across to the door. She had to rest for a moment before opening it, forcing herself through it and then closing it behind her. She'd almost reached the door to the room she and Jack shared when his voice sounded behind her.

'Caro?'

She rested back against the wall—needing its support—before turning her head in his direction. *Heavens.* A sigh rose up through her. With his height and his breadth, Jack cut a fine figure. A pair of designer denim jeans outlined his long lean legs and strong thighs to perfection. She'd bet the view looked even better from behind.

It suddenly occurred to her that if he'd come in a few minutes later he'd have almost certainly caught her in a state of undress. For some reason she found that almost unutterably funny, and a giggle burst from her.

'Morning, Jack.'

His eyes narrowed as he drew nearer. 'Have you been drinking?'

'Most certainly not.' She tried to straighten, but only lasted a couple of seconds before she found herself slumping again. She pointed a finger at him. 'Barbara gave me a pill last night.'

His face darkened. 'You accepted a pill from Barbara? Are you *insane*?'

She didn't like his opinion of Barbara, and she *hated* his opinion of her. 'I thought it was an aspirin. And I had to take it to maintain my reason for why she'd caught me with my hand in her purse.' She frowned. 'I think it was a sleeping tablet... I'm still feeling kind of fuzzy.'

His nostrils flared, and he made a move as if to pick her up, but she held up both hands to ward him off.

'Ooh, please don't do that. My stomach is feeling...um... queasy. A bathroom would be a very good idea about now.'

He took her arm with a gentleness that had the backs of her eyes prickling. 'Come on—it's just a couple of doors this way.'

She tried not to focus on his strength, his warmth, or how much she was enjoying the feel of him beside her. It was this physical craving for him that had been her undoing before. It was something that went beyond sex. It had brought her peace and a sense of belonging that she'd felt right down in her very bones.

And it had obviously been a lie. So she needed to ignore it now.

'Where's Barbara?'

'She and a couple of the other women have gone into the village. Apparently there's a little boutique Cynthia has been gushing about.'

'Then why are you here?'

'I have an operative tailing them.'

She stopped and blinked up at him. 'You have *operatives*?'

His lips twitched. 'I have several, and this one is female. Believe me, she'll blend in much better than I ever could on a shopping trip.' He gestured to the door where they'd stopped. 'Do you need a hand?'

'Certainly not.'

'Then you have to promise me to not lock the door.'

'Will *you* promise not to come in?'

He crossed his heart. 'Unless you call me.'

'Deal.'

She wasn't sick, although it felt like a close run thing for a minute or two. Splashing cold water on her face had helped. So did the glass of water Jack pressed on her once they reached their room again.

He fluffed up the pillows and then helped her onto the bed to sit up against them. It made her feel oddly cared for.

'I'm sorry to be such a bother,' she mumbled. 'I've never had a sleeping tablet before.' She wouldn't have had one last night either if she'd known what it was.

'They don't agree with everyone.' He touched the backs of his fingers to her forehead. 'But your colour is returning and you don't feel hot.'

Don't focus on his touch! 'That's good, right?'

One side of his mouth hooked up. 'That's good.'

Don't focus on his smile! 'The snuffbox wasn't in Barbara's purse.'

He eased away from her, all businesslike and professional again, and she tried to tell herself that she was pleased about that.

'I'm going to go and check her room.'

'What? *Now?*'

'No time like the present.'

She swallowed and called out, 'Be careful.'

But as he was practically out of the room by the time she'd uttered the caution, he probably didn't hear it.

Sitting there, with her pulse racing too hard and her ears primed for Barbara's return, was even more nerve-racking than the night he'd searched the house in Mayfair.

She wondered why he was doing this when he didn't have to. She'd made it clear that she'd sign the divorce papers whether he helped her or not.

Because he wanted closure?

She rested her head back against the pillows. Things had grown so complicated between them five years ago. It occurred to her now that she hadn't moved on from then—last night's argument had proved that. She'd only pretended to. And this morning proved that she needed to stop craving that sense of belonging she'd only ever felt with him. She had to put that behind her too.

It was time to stop feeling like half a person. It was time to get on with her life.

And there was only one way to achieve that.

The door opened and Jack moved back inside. She raised an eyebrow.

He shook his head. 'Nothing.'

'I'm starting to think she's telling the truth—that she didn't take it.' She frowned. 'Except…'

He sat in the chair on the other side of the room. 'Except…?'

'Before I fell asleep last night, I heard her talking to my father.'

He raised an eyebrow.

'Not a hallucination—give me some credit, Jack. She was staring out of the window, talking to the dead like we all probably do from time to time.'

'Speak for yourself.' He shuffled forward an inch. 'What did she say?'

'She asked my father why he'd made things so hard, and...' She frowned trying to remember more clearly. 'And something about why was he making her do this...or something along those lines.'

'Your father left you *everything*?'

'Everything.'

'Without a single condition?'

'Condition-free.'

He shook his head and settled back in the chair. 'I could've sworn he'd make the management of your mother's trust a condition of the will.'

'I told him not to bother—that I refused to be dictated to that way.'

'And he believed you?'

She almost laughed. 'He ought to have done. I told him often enough. Why?'

'Just trying to get a handle on why he did what he did.'

She'd given up on that. It was an impossible task.

She and Jack both fell quiet. Her heart started to pound. She recalled Barbara's words from last night—about the way Caro was controlled and self-contained, and how she avoided confrontation. Five years ago she'd thought Jack had *known* how much she loved him. Maybe he hadn't. Maybe she hadn't been demonstrative enough.

'I'm going to talk about the elephant in the room,' she announced, her mouth going dry.

'What elephant?'

'The termination I had five years ago.'

Every muscle in his body bunched, as if she'd just hit him and he was waiting to see if the blow would fell him. Her heart burned so hard it made it difficult to continue. Except she had to continue. If Jack knew the truth maybe he wouldn't hate her so badly—maybe he wouldn't carry such a great weight of bitterness around with him. And...

and maybe he'd find happiness with this new woman he had in his life.

The thought reduced her heart to ashes.

She moistened her lips, ignoring the blackness welling inside her. 'I spent hours and hours in those first weeks after you'd gone trying to work out why you'd left the way you had.'

She'd returned from work one evening to find every trace of him removed from their shared flat and a note informing her that he'd realised they wanted different things and he was returning to Australia. He'd left her no contact number, no way for her to get in touch with him. It had taken her months before she'd finally believed that he was never going to ring.

'And did you come to any conclusions?'

Oh, his bitterness! How could it still score her heart so deeply?

'Of course I did. I do have a fully functioning brain in my head.' Her voice came out too tart, but she couldn't help it. 'I decided that you must've somehow found out about the termination I was planning to have.'

He gave one terse nod. 'The clinic rang to confirm your appointment.'

'They *told* you?' That shocked her. They'd assured her of confidentiality.

'No, Caro, they didn't. But I'm a detective, remember? It didn't take much for me to put two and two together.'

'And yet you still only came up with three and three-quarters of the answer.'

He didn't yell, he didn't storm around the room flinging out his arms and accusing her of killing their child, but the way he stared at her with throbbing eyes didn't feel much better.

He tilted up his chin. 'I understand your right to make your own decisions when it comes to your body. I don't dis-

pute that. But to get rid of a child I so desperately wanted...'
He turned grey. 'That was when I realised you'd *never* have
children with me.'

The children that had always been more important to
him than she'd ever been.

'That was when I realised you'd meant it when you said
you didn't want children.'

'I said I wasn't *ready* for children.'

There was a difference. Why had he never been able to
understand that? She'd asked him to give her three years.
Not that she'd been able to promise him for certain that
they'd have children after that time either, but she'd needed
time to consider the issue, to make sure in her own mind
that she was up to the task of being a mother.

The thought of becoming a parent in the image of her father had filled her with horror. Jack's idea of family hadn't
helped much either—it had seemed more like a fantasy
she'd never be able to bring off. The whole issue of creating a family had left her all at sea, and it had been too big
a decision to get wrong.

'Caro—'

'Jack, my pregnancy was ectopic.'

He froze. If silence could boom, it boomed now.

'Do you know what that means?' she ventured.

'Yes.'

She barely recognised the voice that croaked from his
throat. She wanted to cover her eyes at the expression of
self-disgust that spread across his features, millimetre by
slow millimetre.

'It means the fertilised egg implanted itself in your tubes
rather than in your uterus.'

She nodded and swallowed. 'In an ectopic pregnancy
the foetus has no chance of surviving.'

'And if the foetus isn't removed it will kill the mother.'
Her surprise at his knowledge must have shown, because

he added, 'I had a foster mother who had an ectopic pregnancy.' He lifted his head. 'You had no choice but to have a termination.'

'No,' she agreed.

He shot to his feet, his body shaking and his eyes blazing. 'Why the *hell* didn't you tell me?'

'I was trying to find a way, but you left before I could! Why didn't you confront me about it as soon as you took that call from the clinic?'

He paced the room, a hand pressed to his forehead.

Caro pushed her bangle high up onto her arm, where the thin metal cut into her. She loosened it and tried to get her breathing back under control. 'I was trying to find the courage to face your disappointment,' she said.

He swung back to stare at her.

'To tell you I was pregnant in one breath and then to take it away in the next…' She shook her head. It had seemed unnecessarily cruel. 'It brought my most frightening fears to the surface. I couldn't help wondering if, down the track, it ever came to a question of my life or a baby's—which would you choose?'

He fell down into the chair.

'When you walked away I had my answer.'

Jack stared at Caro, his heart feeling as if it had been put through a grater and then the pieces collected up and shoved back into his chest willy-nilly. Had he ever really known her?

He'd walked away from his marriage believing Caro had betrayed him and his dreams…and in the end it was he who'd betrayed *her*.

'You should've told me.' He didn't yell the words this time, but they shook with the force of emotion ripping through him.

'And *still* you blame me.'

Her remote smile troubled him. 'No!' His hands clenched. 'I'm just as much to blame. I can't believe I walked away over such a stupid misunderstanding.'

'That misunderstanding wasn't *stupid*, Jack. And with the benefit of hindsight it wasn't unforeseen either. Maybe you *should* blame me—because God knows I was glad the decision had been taken out of my hands. I was glad I wasn't faced with the choice of working out what to do with an unexpected pregnancy.'

It didn't change the fact that he'd walked away from her at a time when she'd needed his support.

'I'm sorry you had to go through that alone.'

She blinked, and her surprise at his apology hurt.

She moistened her lips. 'Thank you.'

He rubbed the back of his neck, silently calling himself every dark name he could think of.

'Was the procedure…gruelling?'

She shook her head. 'It was very simple keyhole surgery. The procedure was performed in the morning and I was home again in the afternoon.'

But he hadn't been there to cosset her afterwards.

She lifted a hand to push her hair off her face. Her hand shook and his heart clutched.

'I had a couple of stitches in my belly button and—' She swallowed. 'It didn't seem like much to show for… for all that was lost.'

Her words ran him through like a knife. He had to brace his hands on his knees to fight the nausea rising through him.

'I'm sorry I wasn't there for you. I'm sorry I left like I did.'

She glanced away, but not before he'd seen the tears swimming in her eyes.

In two strides he was in front of her and pulling her into

his arms. She pressed her face into his shoulder and sobbed silently for a few seconds.

'When I first found out I was pregnant, there was a part of me that was excited.' One small hand beat against his chest. 'For a few moments I thought I could make everything work.'

His eyes and throat burned. She wrenched herself out of his arms and he felt more bereft than ever.

She seized a handkerchief from the nightstand and dabbed her eyes. 'You want to know something funny? If I ever *do* decide I want children I now have less chance of conceiving.'

His head rocked back. 'That's not funny! It's—'

'You leaving like you did…' She swung around. 'Maybe it was for the best after all.'

Did she really believe that?

She lifted her chin. 'What you said in your letter was true. We did want different things. We probably still want different things. You still obviously want children.'

His heart thumped.

She lifted a hand and let it drop. 'Me…? Even after all this time I'm still not certain I do. That would never have worked for you in the long run, Jack.'

In five years his desire for a family had never waned. If anything, it had grown. And in his pursuit of that he'd hurt this woman badly.

'I know it's a moot point now, but I wonder if you'd have married me if you'd known I couldn't have children.'

He stared at her and shook his head. 'I can't answer that. I haven't a clue.'

And now they'd never know.

He pulled in a breath. One thing was clear—this time he wasn't leaving until the job was done and he and Caro had said everything they needed to say.

Five years ago he'd misjudged her and her actions. He'd

make that up to her, and then maybe he'd be able to draw a line under this part of his life and move on. Without bitterness and without blame.

CHAPTER FIVE

'WHAT DO YOU MEAN, you believe Barbara drugged me on purpose? You really are set against her, aren't you?'

Jack kept his eyes on the road, but his every sense was attuned to the woman sitting next to him in the car. She smelt like caramel, and with every agitated movement she sent another burst of sweetness floating across to him.

It would take less than seventy-five minutes to reach Mayfair from the Sedgewick country estate, but he had no faith in his ability to last the distance with that scent tormenting him.

'She wanted nothing more than to comfort me after the fight you and I had, and to make sure I got a decent night's sleep.'

'She wanted to make sure you didn't find the snuffbox.'

His hands clenched about the steering wheel. He'd put Caro in danger. He'd underestimated Barbara's desperation and the lengths she'd go to in an effort to not get caught. His jaw tightened. What if Caro had reacted adversely to the sleeping pill? What if—?

'Barbara *cares* about me.'

His knuckles turned white. 'Barbara is determined to save her own skin! Why can't you see this issue in black and white for once, instead of a hundred shades of grey?'

The words burst from him more loudly than he'd intended and they reverberated through the car with a force that made her flinch. He cursed himself silently.

Except… 'You need to be on your guard around her, Caro. You need to tread carefully where she's concerned.'

He glanced across and her deep brown eyes momentarily met his. The confusion in them made his chest ache. Her gaze lowered to his hands and his white-knuckled grip on the steering wheel. He tried to relax his fingers. He wanted her on her guard—not frightened witless.

'Regardless of what you think, this issue is *not* black and white.'

He had to bite his tongue. This had always been a bugbear between them. She'd always claimed he was too quick to make snap judgments. He'd retaliate by saying she lacked judgment.

'I think she has a lover,' he bit out.

Barbara had buried her husband three months ago—a husband she claimed to have loved. If she had taken up with another man so soon after Roland's death it wouldn't add credibility to her claims of devotion.

Caro straightened and swung towards him. It was all he could do to keep his eyes on the road and his hands on the wheel.

'What makes you think that?' she asked.

'She bought lingerie on her shopping trip to the village this morning.'

To his chagrin, she started to laugh. 'Heaven forbid that a woman should buy pretty undergarments for her own pleasure.'

'In my experience—'

'*Your* experience?' She folded her arms. 'Exactly how many lovers have you had in the last five years, Jack?'

His head rocked back, the question barrelling into him and knocking him off balance. No doubt as it had been intended to.

His heart thudded. 'You first.' The savagery that ripped

through him made his stomach churn. 'If you really want to know the answer to that, then you answer first.'

Spots appeared at the edges of his vision while he held his breath and waited for her to answer. That was what the thought of Caro with another man did to him. Even after five years.

'It's none of my business,' she said after a long pause. 'I'm sorry.'

At her apology, it was as if a hand reached out and squeezed his chest in a grip that stole his breath. One moment he wanted to rip her apart and the next he wanted to draw her into his arms and never let her go. It made no sense whatsoever.

'It doesn't feel that way, though, does it?' he growled. 'Our *business* still feels intertwined.'

'I know.' Her chest rose and fell in a sigh. 'Which is ludicrous after all this time.'

He swallowed the ball of hardness doing its best to lodge in his throat. 'It could be because our relationship had no formal ending.' He'd just…*left*. 'There were no last words, no proper goodbyes.'

'Perhaps,' she agreed, her voice full of dejection and… and secrets?

'One,' he snapped out.

'I beg your pardon?'

He didn't need to turn his head to imagine in technicolour detail the slow blink of her eyes and the cute wrinkle of confusion that would appear between her eyebrows.

'In the last five years—since I left you—I've had one lover, Caro.'

One. He didn't turn his head. He didn't want to see the surprise that would be plastered across her face.

She coughed. 'One? *You—one?*'

He almost smiled then, because he knew that in about five seconds she'd be internally beating herself up for re-

vealing her surprise, her shock. She'd deem it rude and
insensitive.

'One,' he repeated.

'But…' Her hands made agitated movements in the air.
'But you like sex so *much*!'

He'd loved it with Caro.

'So do you.'

He couldn't continue this conversation and keep driving at the same time.

On impulse he turned in at a small pub. 'Hungry?' At a
stretch they could make this an early dinner.

'Not in the slightest.' She unbuckled her seatbelt and
opened her door. 'But a glass of burgundy would go down
a treat.'

They sat at a table by the far wall, nursing their drinks.

'And I can hardly call her a lover,' Jack said.

Caro shot back in her seat, one hand pressed to her chest
just above her heart, drawing his attention to the pale perfection of her throat.

'Please, Jack, you don't have to explain. You don't owe
me anything.'

Yes, he did.

'It was a one-night stand,' he continued, 'and it was a
disaster.'

The entire time the only person he'd been able to think
about had been Caro. It had been Caro's touch he'd craved,
and he'd used another woman in an attempt to drive Caro
from his mind. Not only hadn't it worked, it had been unfair. The encounter had left him feeling soiled, dirty and
ashamed. He hadn't been eager to repeat the experience.

Caro brought her wine to her lips and sipped. Her hand
shook as she placed the glass back to the table. 'It's only
been the once for me too. I wanted to get on with my life.
I wanted to feel normal again.'

He could tell it hadn't worked.

'It was terrible. It left me thinking I should join a convent.'

He grimaced.

She stilled. He glanced across at her. She twisted her bangle round and round with sudden vigour.

'What?' he demanded.

'You don't have a woman waiting back home for you in Australia, do you?'

He glanced away.

'You want to remarry, and you still want children...' She let out a breath. 'But you don't have anyone specific in mind yet.'

Something inside him hardened. 'Why are you so relieved about that?'

'Because I *knew* you weren't in love. I thought you were about to make another mistake.'

He stared at her, at a loss for something to say.

'You want to feel normal again too. That's what all this is about.'

He thrust out his jaw. 'It's time to draw a line under us.'

She stared down into her red wine, twirling the glass around and around instead of her bangle. 'So...we're working towards—what? An amicable divorce?'

Acid burned in his stomach. He took a sip of his beer in an attempt to ease it. 'And getting your snuffbox back.' He owed her that much.

She suddenly straightened, and although she leaned towards him he couldn't help feeling she'd erected some emotional barrier between them.

'Barbara doesn't have a lover, Jack. She bought that lingerie for *me*. I'm afraid she doesn't subscribe to the view that yoga pants and a T-shirt are suitable attire for the bedroom. She thinks I should be making more of an effort to attract you.'

A groan rose up through him.

'So, in case you need to know this in support of our cover story, it's a long gold negligee with shoestring straps and some pretty beading just here.'

Her hands fluttered about her chest and it took an effort of will for him not to close his eyes. 'Right…'

Her eyes grew sharp. 'And yet you still think she could hurt me?'

He straightened too. 'Why don't you just throw her to the wolves?' The woman was a thief, for God's sake!

'I care about her. She…she and Paul…are like family to me.'

She said the word *family* carefully, as if afraid it might hurt him.

He gulped back a generous slug of beer. 'Some family!'

She sipped her red wine, but her jaw was tight. 'You *do* know your idea of family is too romantic, don't you?'

That was what happened when you grew up without one of your own.

Her eyes narrowed, as if she'd read that thought in his face.

'I hope you find what you're looking for, Jack. I really do. I hope it makes you as happy as you seem to think it will.'

He sensed her sincerity. And her doubt. 'Not all families are as screwed up as yours, Caro.'

'That's very true. But Barbara…' She shrugged. 'I feel a certain affinity with her. My father turned her into a trophy wife, never correcting the widely held view that people had of her. Probably because he found the depth of his feelings for her too confronting. So he tried to control her…and she let him. Unlike me, she did everything he asked of her— everything she could to please him. And if you think that was easy then you're crazy.'

He could feel his mouth gape. He snapped it shut. 'You're *nothing* like Barbara.'

'That's where you're wrong. All I'd have had to do was agree to have children with you, Jack, and I'd have been exactly like her.'

'That was totally different!'

'How?'

'I *never* tried to turn you into a trophy wife.'

'No—just into the mother of your children.'

He ground his teeth together. 'Asking you if we could start a family was not an unreasonable demand.'

'My father didn't see ordering me to take over the administration of my mother's trust as an unreasonable demand either. He thought it a worthy goal. And he was right—it is. But it's not a role I want in life.'

In the same way, she obviously didn't want the role of mother.

'For God's sake, Caro, I *loved* you!'

'But not unconditionally! It was clear you'd only continue to love me if I bore your children.'

His hand clenched about his glass. 'What you're saying is that what you wanted was more important than what *I* wanted.'

She lifted her glass, but she didn't drink from it. 'I don't recall you ever offering to be the primary caregiver. I don't recall you ever making any attempt at compromise.'

Each word was like a bullet from a Colt 45.

'I was the one who was expected to make all the sacrifices.'

Bull's eye. For a moment Jack could barely breathe.

'But that's all old ground.' She waved a hand in the air and sipped her wine. 'Do you seriously think Barbara could present a physical danger to me?'

It took an effort of will to find his voice…his balance… his wits. 'I'm not ruling it out.'

'Then let's call the search off.'

She drained the last of her wine and he found it impossible to read anything beyond the assumed serenity of her countenance.

'For God's sake, why?'

'I don't want to force her into actions she'd otherwise avoid. If she's as desperate as you're implying, then she's welcome to the snuffbox.'

'But your job…?'

'I'll have to explain that I've lost the snuffbox, make financial reparation to the seller, and then tender my resignation.'

She'd sacrifice her *job*? She *loved* her job.

'I could go back to university.'

'To study what?'

'Something different from my undergraduate degree, obviously. Or I could enrol in a doctorate programme. It's not like money will be an issue.'

But there'd be a cloud hanging over her head, professionally, for the rest of her working life. Regardless of their differences and their history, she didn't deserve to take the blame for someone else's wrongdoing. Caro was innocent and he was determined to prove it.

'No!'

She raised an eyebrow and rose casually to her feet, though he sensed the careful control she exerted over her movements.

'I believe we're done here.'

He rose too. 'Give me until the end of the week, Caro. Like we planned. Give me until Friday. It's only five days away.'

She opened her mouth and he could see she was going to refuse him.

'Please?'

His vehemence surprised her, but he couldn't help it.

'I swear I won't put Barbara in any position that will incite her to violence.'

She glanced away and then glanced back. Finally she nodded. 'Okay—but then it's done, Jack. It's finished.'

He knew what she really meant, though. They'd be done. Finished.

The resistance that rose through him made no sense.

He nodded, and then took her arm and led her out to the car. 'Am I taking you back to the house in Mayfair or to your flat?'

'The flat, please.'

Good. He didn't want to run into her when he bugged the Mayfair house tonight…

Caro frowned at the knock on her door. She dumped her notepad on the sofa before seizing the remote and clicking the television off.

Daytime television, Caro? How low do you mean to sink?

Shaking her head, she padded to the door and opened it.

'Hello, Caro.'

Jack!

She moistened suddenly dry lips, wishing she'd bothered to put on something more glamorous than the default yoga pants when she'd dragged herself out of bed this morning.

'Uh, good morning?'

She started and glanced at her watch, huffed out a sigh. 'Yep, it's still morning.'

'Just.'

Right.

'May I come in?'

She blinked, realising she'd been holding the door open and just staring at him. 'Of course. I'm afraid I wasn't expecting to see you today.'

He entered without saying a word. He sported those same designer jeans he'd worn yesterday and the view from the back was indeed spectacular. It wasn't his physique that held her attention, though—as drool-inducing as those shoulders and butt might be—but the odd combination of stiffness and stillness in his posture that hinted at…nervousness? What did Jack have to be nervous about?

Oh, dear Lord! Unless he had news for her. *Bad* news.

She pushed her shoulders back, forced her chin up. She'd already decided the snuffbox was lost forever, hadn't she? She'd accepted the fact that she'd lose her job. She pulled in a breath.

'You've found out something? You have…bad news?'

He shook his head. 'I'm currently collecting information and analysing data.'

No, he wasn't. He was here in her flat. Her *tiny* flat.

Widening his stance, he eyed her up and down. Warmth crept across her skin and a pulse fired to life deep inside her. Soon, if she weren't careful, he'd have her throbbing and pulsing with the need he'd always been able to raise in her.

She crossed her arms, not caring how defensive it made her look. Once upon a time she'd have sashayed over to him, run her hands along his shoulders and reached up on tiptoe to kiss him—long, slow, sensuous kisses that would have had him groaning and hauling her close…

She clenched her hands. But that had been back before he'd left. That had been before he'd broken something inside her that she hadn't been able to put back together. She wasn't kissing Jack again and they most certainly weren't going to make love together. It would set her back five years!

She stared back at him. She didn't know if there was a challenge in her eyes or not, but the hint of a smile had touched his lips.

'I'm afraid Barbara wouldn't approve.'

It took a moment for her to realise he referred to her

yoga pants and T-shirt. 'Barbara never drops around un-announced.'

He took neither the bait nor the hint, just nodded and glanced around her sitting room. For once she wished it were larger, not quite so cosy. His gaze zeroed in on the plate of cake perched on the coffee table. He turned back and raised both eyebrows.

Her cheeks started to burn. Dear Lord! She'd been caught sitting around in her slouchy pyjamas, eating cake and watching daytime television. What a cliché!

She refused to let her humiliation show. 'I'm on leave this week. It's a well-known fact that when one is on holiday, cake for breakfast is mandatory.'

He didn't point out that it was nearer to lunchtime than breakfast.

'Besides, that orange cake is utterly divine—to die for. Would you like a slice?'

He shook his head.

She pulled in a breath, counted to three and then let it out. 'I really wasn't expecting to see you today, Jack. I don't mean to be rude, but what are you doing here?'

His eyes shone bluer than she remembered. They seemed to see right inside her—but that had to be a trick of the light.

'I was hoping to take you to lunch.'

Her heart gave a funny little skip. 'Why?'

'There are some things we should discuss.'

Divorce things? She didn't want to talk about the divorce. Why couldn't they just leave it up to their lawyers? She wanted to say no to lunch. She wanted to say no to spending more time in his company. She wanted to resist the appeal in those eyes of his. Those eyes, though, had always held a siren's fascination for her.

'Is it really such a difficult decision?'

To admit so would be far too revealing, but to go to lunch with him…

'I just don't see the point.'

'Does there need to be a point? It's a beautiful day outside.'

Was it? She glanced towards the window.

'And maybe I'm striving for the *amicable* in our amicable divorce.'

Was she supposed to applaud him for that?

In the next moment she bit her lip. Was he worried that she'd become difficult and spiteful if he didn't recover the snuffbox?

She frowned. Surely not? Surely he knew her better than that…

Her heart started to pound. Very slowly she shook her head, recalling the expression on his face when she'd revealed the true reason behind her medical termination. His shock had swiftly turned to self-disgust and guilt. She didn't want him racked with guilt. She was just as much to blame as him for that particular misapprehension. Besides, that one incident hadn't been responsible for the breakdown of their marriage. It had just been the proverbial last straw.

'Caro?'

She raised her hands in surrender. 'Fine. I'll go and get changed.'

Twenty minutes later they were outside, walking in the sunshine. Jack was right—it was a glorious day.

She lifted her face to the sun and closed her eyes. 'I love this time of year. I wish it could be summer all year long.'

'Which begs the question, why were you cooped up in your flat when you could've been outside, enjoying all of this?'

'Maybe because my leave is for a family matter rather than a true holiday? Maybe because I don't actually feel in a holiday mood?'

'So the cake…?'

'Cake is its own reward,' she averred stoutly, trying to resist the way his chuckle warmed her to her very toes.

They were quiet until they reached the Thames. Caro turned in the direction of several riverside cafes and restaurants. The river was dark, fast-flowing and full of traffic. She loved its vibrancy…the way it remained the same and yet was always changing.

'When did you stop having fun, Caro?'

Her stomach knotted. 'I beg your pardon?' She slammed to a halt, planting her hands on her hips. 'I have fun!'

How dare he try to make her life all black and white with his judgments?

The dark seriousness in his eyes made her heart beat harder. 'I'll have you know that I have plenty of fun! Oodles of it! I catch up with my girlfriends regularly for coffee.' *And cake.* 'I see shows, go to movies, visit art galleries. I live in a city that offers a variety of endless activities. I have plenty of fun, thank you!'

'You've had nothing in your diary for the last three months.'

She clenched her hands to stop from doing something seriously unladylike. 'You went through my diary?'

'It was on the coffee table…open. I figured if it were sacrosanct you'd have put it away.'

'Or maybe I expected better manners from my visitors!' Heat scorched her cheeks. 'That is one of the rudest things I've ever heard. An invasion of privacy and—'

'Not as rude as stealing a snuffbox.'

She folded her arms and with a loud, 'Hmph!' set off again at brisk pace. 'You were looking for clues?'

'Just wondering if you'd made any enemies lately.'

She rolled her eyes, wondering why it was so hard to rein in her temper. 'I'm not the kind of woman to make enemies, Jack.'

Except of her father.

And her husband.

'Is there anyone at Richardson's who's been fired recently? Someone who might hold you responsible? Is there some guy who's been pestering you for a date over the last three months? Have you had a disgruntled client who's cross they've missed out on a particular treasure? Is there—?'

'No!'

'Caro, your diary is full of work commitments, the odd work-related lecture at London University or an art gallery, and one weekend conference in Barcelona. You didn't have a single dinner date, coffee date, movie date, *any kind of date* scheduled into your diary at all.'

'Maybe because it's a *work* diary. I remember my social engagements. I don't need to write them down.'

It struck her now that there were so few invitations these days they were easy to remember. She went cold and then hot. When had that happened? She'd once had a full calendar.

'You always were a good liar.'

He said it as if it were a compliment!

'I'm sorry to say, though, that I don't believe you.'

'And that should matter to me because...?'

He flashed her a grin that set her teeth on edge. 'Getting under your skin, aren't I, kiddo?'

'Don't call me that!' It had been a pet name once. Jack had drawled it in Humphrey Bogart fashion and it had always made her smile.

Not any more.

'You were only ever that rude when you were fibbing or hiding something.'

'And it seems you can still try the patience of a saint.'

God knew she wasn't a saint. But his perception had her

grabbing hold of her temper again, and her composure, and trying to twitch both into place.

'You wrote *everything* down. You were afraid you'd forget otherwise. You were big on making lists too.'

'People change. Believe it or not, in the last five years even *I've* changed.'

'Not that much.' He pulled a folded sheet of paper from his pocket. 'You still make lists.'

She snatched it from him, unfolded it and started to shake. 'This… You…'

'That's a list you're making of options in the eventuality of losing your job.'

'*I know what it is!*' She scrunched the sheet of paper into a ball. 'You had no right.'

'Maybe not, but it brings us back to the original question. When did you stop having fun, Caro?'

Before she could answer, he marched her to a table for two at a nearby riverside restaurant and held a chair out for her. For a moment she was tempted to walk away. But that would reveal just how deeply he'd got under her skin, and she was pig-headed enough—just—not to want to give him that satisfaction.

Besides—she glanced around—the sun, the river and the warmth were all glorious, and something deep inside her yearned towards it. She didn't want to turn her back on the day—not yet. For the first time her flat suddenly seemed too small, too cramped.

Blowing out a breath, she sat. For the briefest of moments Jack clasped her shoulders from behind in a warm caress that made her chest ache and her stomach flutter.

He took the seat opposite. 'Caro—'

'Pot.' She pointed to him. 'Kettle.' She pointed to herself. 'When was the last time *you* had fun?'

The waitress chose that moment to bustle up with menus. *Manners, Caro.*

'They do a really lovely seafood linguine here.' The Jack of five years ago had loved seafood. She figured he probably still did.

'Oh, I'm sorry,' the waitress said, 'but that's no longer on the menu. We've had a change of chef.'

Jack glanced at Caro and then leaned back in his chair. 'When did you change chefs?'

'It'd be four months ago now, sir.'

Caro swallowed, staring at the menu without really seeing it. 'My...how time flies.'

Jack said nothing. He didn't have to. Had it really been over four months since she'd been down here for a meal?

They ordered the prawn and chorizo gnocchi that the waitress recommended, along with bottles of sparkling mineral water. When the waitress moved away, Caro hoped that Jack would drop the subject of fun. She hoped she could simply...

What? Enjoy a pleasant lunch in the sunshine with her soon-to-be ex-husband? That didn't seem likely, did it?

She gestured to the river, about to make a comment about how fascinating it always was down here, watching the river traffic, but she halted at the expression on his face.

'You're not going to let the subject drop, are you?'

'Nope.'

'Why does it matter to you one way or another if I have fun or not?'

'Because I can't help feeling that I'm to blame for the fact you don't have fun any more—that it's my fault.'

He couldn't have shocked her more if he'd slapped her.

She folded her arms on the table and leaned towards him. 'Jack, I get a great deal of enjoyment out of many things—a good book, a good movie, cake, my work—but I think it's fair to say that I'm not exactly a pleasure-seeker or a barrel of laughs. I never have been.'

'You used to make me laugh. Now, though, seems to me you hardly ever laugh.'

'Has it occurred to you that it's the company I'm currently keeping?'

He didn't flinch—not that she'd said it to hurt him—but his gaze drifted out towards the river and she couldn't help feeling she'd hurt him anyway.

Their food arrived, but neither one of them reached for their cutlery. She touched the back of his hand. His warmth made her fingertips tingle.

'I didn't say that to be mean, but neither one of us should pretend things are the same as they used to be between us—that things aren't…difficult.'

She went to move her hand, but in the blink of an eye he'd trapped it within his. 'When was the last time your soul soared, Caro? When was the last time you felt like you were flying?'

Her mouth dried. She wasn't answering that.

The last time had been on a picnic with Jack in Hyde Park. They'd packed a modest meal of sandwiches, raspberries and a bottle of wine, but everything about that day had been perfect—the weather, the world…them. They'd gone home in the evening and made love. They'd eaten chocolate biscuits and ice cream for dinner while playing Scrabble. That day had felt like perfect happiness.

Had that day been worth the pain that followed?

She shook her head. She didn't think so.

He released her hand. 'I see.'

Did he?

'Just as I thought.'

She forced a morsel of food into her mouth. 'The gnocchi is very good.'

'I bought a boat.'

She lowered her cutlery with a frown. *Okaaay.*

'I go boating and fishing. And some days when I'm

standing at the wheel of my boat, when I'm whipping along the water at a great rate of knots and the breeze is in my face, sea spray is flying and the sun is shining, I feel at peace with the world. I feel alive.'

He lived near water? 'What made you get a boat?'

'A couple of friends, tired of my…grumpiness, dragged me out on their boat.'

Her jaw dropped. 'Grumpiness?' Caro felt like an idiot the minute the word left her. She tried to cover up her surprise by adding, 'You obviously enjoyed it enough to buy your own boat.'

'When I left you and returned to Australia I threw myself into work.'

He'd made such a success of his firm that only an idiot could accuse him of wasting his time.

'But I didn't do anything else—just worked. I didn't want to be around people. I just wanted to be left alone.'

She could relate to that.

'Apparently, though, being a bear of a boss isn't the ideal scenario.'

Ah…

'A couple of friends dragged me out on their boat, where I was quite literally a captive audience, and proceeded to tell me a few home truths.'

She winced. 'Ouch.'

'They pointed out that I had no balance in my life.'

'So you bought a boat?'

He shrugged. 'It helped.'

'I'm glad, Jack, I really am. But…' She leaned back, her stomach churning. 'Why are you telling me this?'

'Because I want to help you find *your* boat.'

CHAPTER SIX

HE WANTED TO help her rediscover her passion, but she was suddenly and terribly afraid that they'd simply discover—rediscover—that *he* was her passion. What would they do then?

You could offer to have a family with him.

No! She didn't want to live with a man who placed conditions on his love. She'd had enough of that growing up with her father. Why couldn't *she* be enough?

Oh, stop whining!

Jack stared at her, as if waiting for her to say something, but she was saved from having to answer when a little girl moved close to their table, her face crumpling up as is she were about to cry.

Caro reached out and touched the little girl's shoulder. 'Hello, sweetie, have you lost your mummy?'

The little girl nodded, her eyes swelling with tears.

'Well, I'll admit that's frightfully easy to do,' Caro continued in her usual voice—she hated the way adults put on fake voices where children were concerned, 'but shall I let you into a secret?'

The child nodded.

'Mummies are very good at finding their little girls.'

'You think Mummy will find me?'

'Oh, yes, I know she will.'

Caro was aware of Jack's gaze—the heaviness in it, the heat…his shock.

'The trick, though, is to just stay put and wait.' She glanced at the food on the table. 'Would you like a piece of garlic bread while you wait? My friend here—' she gestured to Jack '—thought I was hungry and ordered a lot of food, but…' She started to laugh. 'I had cake for breakfast, so I'm not really hungry at all.'

The little girl's eyes went wide. 'You ate *cake* for breakfast?'

'Uh-huh.'

'Is it your birthday?'

'Nope—it's just one of the good things about being a grown-up.'

In no time at all the little girl—Amy—was perched on Caro's lap, munching a piece of garlic bread. Caro didn't want to meet Jack's eyes, so she looked to the left of him, and then to his right.

'You might want to keep an eye out for a frantic-looking woman.'

'Right.'

She turned her attention back to the little girl. It was easier to look at her than at the yearning she knew would be stretching through Jack's eyes.

The sight of Caro holding that little girl, her absolute ease with the child, burned through Jack. A dark throb pulsed through him. They could have had this—him and Caro. They could have had a little girl to love and care for. If only Caro hadn't been afraid.

If only I'd been patient.

The thought slid into him, making his heart pound. She'd asked him for time but he'd thought she was putting him off, making excuses. So he hadn't given her time. In hindsight he hadn't given her much of anything.

Unable to deal with his thoughts, he stood and scanned the crowd, doing as Caro had suggested and trying to locate a worried mother in the crowd. It took less than a minute for a likely candidate to appear. He waved to get the woman's attention, and in no time flat—with a multitude of grateful thank-yous—the pair were reunited.

He sat.

Caro reached for her mineral water. 'Stop looking at me like that.'

'Like what?'

'Just because I don't know if I want children of my own it doesn't mean I don't like them.'

'Right…'

She glared at him then, before skewering a prawn on the end of her fork. For some reason, though, *he* was the one who felt skewered.

'Why on earth did you—*do* you,' she amended, 'want children so much?'

He shrugged, but his chest tightened, clenching in a cramp, and for a moment he couldn't speak.

Eventually he leant back. 'I've always wanted children… for as long as I can remember.'

'Well, now, *there's* a strong argument to convince a woman to change her entire life to fit children into it.'

With that sally, she popped the prawn into her mouth and set to picking through what was left of her pasta, obviously in search of more prawns.

A scowl built through him. 'Can't a person just want kids?'

She shrugged. 'Maybe. My next question, though, would be… Do you want children because you believe you can give them a good life and help them to grow up to be useful members of society? Or…?'

'Or…?'

'Or do you want children because you've never had a proper family of your own, have always felt lonely, and feel that children will fill that lack in your life?'

He stared at her, breathing hard. 'That's a mean-spirited thing to do, Caro—to use my background against me.'

Her forehead crinkled. 'I'm not trying to use it against you. I'm truly sorry you had such a difficult childhood. I sincerely wish that hadn't been the case. But at the same time I don't believe children should be used to fill gaps in people's lives. That's not what children are meant for.'

'Why didn't you ask me any of this five years ago?'

She set her fork to the side. 'I doubt I could've verbalised it five years ago. Your craving for children made me uneasy, but I could never pinpoint why.'

Jack wanted to get up and walk away—which, it appeared, was his default position where this woman was concerned.

'And, you see,' she continued, staring down at her plate rather than at him, 'back then it played into all of my insecurities.'

Her what?

'And that made me withdraw into myself. I realise now I should've tried to talk to you about this more, but I felt that in your eyes I wasn't measuring up.'

Her words punched through him. 'Just as you feel you never measured up in your father's eyes?' He let out a breath, seeing it a little more clearly now. 'If I'd had a little more wisdom… But your withdrawal fed into all of *my* insecurities.'

Her forehead crinkled in that adorable way again. *Don't notice.*

'Insecurities? *You*, Jack? Back then I thought you the most confident man I'd ever met.'

When he'd been sure of her love he'd felt like the most invincible man on earth.

'I saw your refusal to have children with me as a sign that I…' He pulled in a breath and then forced the words out. 'That I wasn't good enough for you to have children with.' He dragged a hand back through his hair. 'I thought that as a brash colonial from the wrong side of the tracks I was only good enough to marry so you could thumb your nose at Daddy...'

She straightened. 'I'll have you know that I've never thumbed my nose at anyone in my *life*!'

'I thought I wasn't the right *pedigree* for you.'

Her shoulders slumped. 'Oh, Jack, I was never a snob.'

He nodded. 'I can see that now.'

Her shoulders slumped further. 'I'm sorry you felt that way. If I'd known...'

'If you'd known you'd have set me straight. Just like I'd have set *you* straight if I'd known I was making you feel like *you* weren't measuring up.'

She pulled in a breath and lifted her chin. 'It's pointless wallowing in regrets. We live and learn. We'll know better than to make the same mistakes in the future...with the people who come into our lives.'

He understood what she was telling him. That there was no future for them regardless of whatever acknowledgments and apologies they made for the past now.

Beneath the collar of his shirt his skin prickled. Of *course* the two of them had no future. She didn't need to remind him!

She pushed away from the table a little. 'It's been a lovely lunch, Jack, but—'

'We were talking about boats.'

She rolled her eyes. 'I don't need a boat. I don't *want* a boat.'

'When did you become so risk-averse? *Everyone* needs a boat, Caro—a figurative one—even you. You had passions once.'

Her cheeks flushed a warm pink. His skin tightened. He hadn't been referring to that kind of passion, but he couldn't deny that as lovers they'd had that kind of passion in spades.

The one place where they hadn't had any problems had been in the bedroom. She'd been everything he'd ever dreamed of…and everything he hadn't known to dream of.

He wanted her now with the same fierceness and intensity with which he'd wanted her five years ago. The way her eyes glittered told him she wanted him too. They could go back to her flat and spend the afternoon making wild, passionate love. That would help her rediscover her passion for life.

For how long, though? Until he left and returned to Australia?

A knot tightened in his stomach. They couldn't do it. It would only make matters worse.

Caro glanced away and he knew that regardless of how much he might want it to, she'd never let it happen.

Which was just as well. His hands clenched. This time when he left he wanted to leave her better off than when he'd found her. They might still want different things out of life, but that didn't mean he couldn't help her rediscover her joy again.

He set his shoulders. 'You said you'd give me to the end of the week.'

'To find my snuffbox!'

'We need people to believe we're reuniting…we don't want them suspecting that I'm working for you.'

That was a lowdown dirty trick, but he could see that it had worked.

She folded her arms and glared at him. 'To the end of the week,' she growled.

He had to hook his right ankle around his chair-leg in order to remain seated rather than shoot to his feet, reach across the table and kiss her.

The fingers of her right hand drummed against her left arm. 'What I'd like to know, though, is what *precisely* does this entail?'

'That you be ready when I come to collect you at six o'clock this evening.'

He shot to his feet. He needed to breathe in air that didn't smell of Caro. He needed to clear his head before he did something stupid.

She blinked. 'Where are we going?'

'You'll see.'

'What should I wear?'

He'd started to turn away. Gritting his teeth, he turned back and tried to give her a cursory once-over. But his hormones said *To hell with cursory* and he found himself taking his time. Her heightened colour told him she wasn't as averse to his gaze as she no doubt wished she were.

'What you're wearing now will do nicely.'

With a half-muttered expletive, he bent down and pressed his lips to hers, refusing to resist temptation a moment longer. The kiss lasted no longer than two beats of his heart—a brief press and a slight parting of his lips to shape his mouth to hers, a silent silky slide—and then he stepped away.

Stunned caramel eyes stared back at him.

'Please excuse me if I don't walk you home.'

Walking her home would be asking for trouble.

He turned and left before he could say another word— before he did something dangerous like drag her to her feet and kiss her properly. One touch of his lips to hers hadn't eased the need inside him. It had turned it into a raging, roaring monster. Her scent and her softness had made him hungrier than he'd ever been in his life before. He needed to get himself back under control before their date tonight.

Caro changed from her earlier outfit of jeans and a peasant-style top into a pair of white linen trousers, and then flipped through her selection of blouses.

The blue silk, perhaps?

No, Jack had always loved her in blue. She didn't want him thinking she was dressing to please him.

The red?

Good Lord, no! She swished that along the rack. Red and sex were too closely aligned, and that wasn't the signal she wanted to send.

The black?

Low neckline—not a chance!

What about the grey?

She pulled it out, but shoved it back into the closet almost immediately. It showed too much midriff. She needed something asexual. She didn't want Jack kissing her again.

Liar.

Even if that lunchtime kiss had only been for show…in case anyone had been watching.

Don't be an idiot.

He'd kissed her because he'd wanted to. End of story.

A breath shuddered out of her, her fingers reaching up to trace her lips. Lips that remembered the touch and taste of him as if it had been only yesterday since she'd last kissed him. Lips that throbbed and burned with a violence she'd thought she'd managed to quell. That was bad news. *Very* bad news. She had to make sure he didn't kiss her again.

Or if he tried to she had to take evasive measures—not just sit there like a landed duck, waiting and hoping for it to happen.

Now choose a blouse!

In the end she decided on a soft pink button-down with a Peter Pan collar. As it wasn't fitted, no one could possibly accuse it of being sexy. With a sigh, she tugged it on. And not a moment too soon either, as Jack's knock sounded on the door while she was still buttoning it up.

How do you know it's Jack? It could be anyone.

She shook her head, slipping the strap of her purse over her shoulder. It would be Jack, all right. Nobody else knocked with quite the same authority. Besides, he was bang on time. He'd always had a thing for punctuality.

She took a deep breath and then opened the door, immediately stepping outside and pulling the door closed behind her. She did *not* want Jack in her tiny flat again, with its temptation of a bedroom a mere door away. The less privacy Jack and she had, the better.

'Hello, Jack.' She prevented herself from adding a snippy *again* to her greeting.

'Caro.'

The heat from his body beat at her. He wore an unfamiliar aftershave, but it had the same invigorating effect as dark-roasted coffee beans. She breathed in deeply, her nose wrinkling in appreciation.

He gave her a flattering once-over. 'You changed.'

'Just freshened up.'

'You look nice.'

She went to say thank you, but he reached out to flick one of her buttons—the second button down...*the one right between her breasts*.

'These are kinda cute.'

She glanced down and then groaned. The buttons were bright red plastic cherries! 'If you knew the lengths I went to tonight to choose an appropriate shirt you'd laugh your head off.'

'Appropriate? You'd best share. I enjoy a good laugh.'

She moved them towards the elevator. 'I wanted to choose a shirt that was...demure.' She jabbed the elevator button and the door slid open.

'So I wouldn't kiss you again?' he said, ushering her inside and pushing the button for the ground floor.

She couldn't look at him. She moved her handbag from her right shoulder to her left. 'Something like that.'

'You hated it that much?'

'Can…can we continue this conversation once we're outside, please?'

They travelled the rest of the short distance in thin-lipped silence. At least, *his* lips were thin.

'You hated it that much?' he repeated, once they stood outside on the footpath.

She pulled in a breath of warm evening air. It didn't do much to clear her mind. 'No, Jack, the problem is that I liked it too much.'

He swung to stare at her, his lips going from thin-lipped sternness to erotic sensuality with a speed that had her tripping over her own feet. He reached out to steady her, but she held both hands up to ward him off. Although he didn't actually turn around and stare back the way they'd come, she could practically feel his mind moving back to her fifth-floor flat.

'Not going to happen,' she said, wishing her voice had emerged with a little more resolution.

'We still generate heat, kiddo.'

'What good did heat do us five years ago?'

A slow grin spread across his face, turning him into a rakish pirate and her insides to molten honey. 'If I have to explain that to you then—'

'Hey, mister!' a taxicab driver shouted from the kerb. 'Do you want the cab or not?'

Caro gestured. 'Is that for us?'

Jack nodded.

She set off towards it at a half-trot. 'He wants it,' she called back to the driver, trying not to run. But she wanted to be away from her flat *now*.

Jack followed, a scowl darkening his features. He gave the driver directions, closed the dividing window and settled on the seat beside her.

'We're five years older and wiser, Caro.'

Older, maybe—but wiser? She wasn't so sure about that.

'What good do you think it would do us? We generate heat. So what? It's the kind that burns, and you know it.'

He stared down at his hands for a moment. 'Maybe this time we could make it work.'

Their marriage? She wanted to cover her ears. He *had* to be joking! She gave a hard shake of her head. 'No.'

His eyes flashed. 'You won't even think about it?'

She told herself that thin-lipped and forbidding was better than steamy sex-on-legs pirate. Not that she managed to convince herself about that.

She shook the thought away. 'Do you really believe I've been able to think of anything else since I saw you five days ago?'

She recognised the quickening in his eyes but she shook her head again, awash with a sorrow that had her wanting to curl up into a ball.

'Hell, Caro,' he ground out. 'Don't look at me like that.'

She dragged her gaze back to the front, not wanting to make him feel bad. She'd never wanted him to feel bad.

'Even though you told me you wanted a divorce, I haven't been able to stop wondering—what if we came to understand each other properly this time around? Could we make a go of it? Could this be the second chance I craved and fantasised about in those first few months after you left?'

Her throat closed over. Beside her, waves of tension rolled off Jack in a silent storm of turmoil. She passed a hand across her eyes and swallowed.

'The thing is, Jack, I keep circling back to the same conclusion. I don't believe I have what it takes to make you happy.'

'I—'

She held up a hand to cut him off. She met his gaze. 'And with you I would always be wondering… *Is he only with me because I agreed to have children?*'

He slumped back, pain tearing across his features, and she ached to hold him, to wipe that pain away and tell him that they could work it out—but if she did she feared she'd only hurt him worse later, and that would be unforgivable.

She forced herself to continue. 'I can't see things between us working out any better if *you* were the one to make the big sacrifice either. If we didn't have the children you want so much I'd be riddled with guilt.'

She clenched her purse in a death grip on her lap.

'I don't believe love and marriage should be all about self-sacrifice. It should be about two people making compromises, so they can both be happy.'

She didn't think that was possible in her and Jack's case.

'It's about both people being equally important.'

She tried, unsuccessfully, to unclench her hands from around her purse.

'I can't help feeling that in either scenario the things that drew you to me, the things you loved about me, would fade...and in the end you'd leave me anyway.' She stared at her hands. 'I'm not saying this to be mean. I'm saying it because this time I want to be completely honest with you.'

She finally turned to look at him. His eyes were alternately as soft as a kiss and as hard as adamantine.

His lips finally twisted with self-mockery. 'You really have thought about it, haven't you?'

She wanted to cry. When he'd come searching for closure had he pictured *this*?

He turned to gaze out of the window. 'No amount of mind-blowing sex can compete with that.'

A chasm opened up inside her. 'I wish I could have that great sex without paying the price.'

'But that wouldn't be the case. Not for either one of us.'

It helped a little to hear him admit it too. 'Some people subscribe to the view that the loving is worth the losing, but

I don't believe that. It took me too long to get over you the last time, Jack. And I know now it was just as hard for you.'

'You don't want to risk it again?'

Did he? *He couldn't!* She shook her head. 'The odds are just too high.'

He took her hand, pressed it between both his own before lifting it to his lips and placing a kiss to her palm. Her blood danced and burned.

'I'm so sorry, Caro. For everything.'

The backs of her eyes stung. 'Me too.'

He laid her hand back in her lap with a gentleness that had her biting her lip. How could she still want to throw herself at him with such fierceness after the conversation they'd just had?

'I swear I won't kiss you again.'

She closed her eyes and concentrated on her breathing. 'Thank you.'

'I only want to make things easier for you. Better. It was all I ever wanted.'

She couldn't speak. She could only nod. She knew that too. It was why she'd fallen so hard for him in the first place.

The taxi stopped. Caro glanced at her watch. It felt as if a whole lifetime had passed, but in reality it had been only ten minutes. She slid out from the door Jack held open for her and waited as he paid the cab driver, pulling in deep breaths to try and calm the storm raging through her.

She'd hoped such a frank conversation would ease the storm. That wasn't going to be the case, evidently. She was at a loss as to what else to try.

She glanced around, searching for distraction. She'd paid next to no mind to where they'd been going, but their location looked vaguely familiar.

Jack moved up beside her. 'Do you know where we are?'

The taxi pulled away and drove off into the warm summer evening. She had no right to feel abandoned.

Huffing back a sigh, she pointed to a sign. 'That says this is Red Lion Square. So…we're in Holborn?'

He nodded. 'We're heading for a building on the other side of the park—and then my dastardly plan will be revealed.'

He smiled, but she saw the effort it cost him. Reaching out, she pulled him to a halt. His warmth immediately flooded her, daring her to foolishness, and she reefed her hand back.

'Are…are you sure you still want to do this?' She wouldn't blame him if he wanted a time out. It wasn't his job to help her find happiness again, her relish for life.

'Of course I still want to do this.' He stared at her for a long moment before shoving his hands into his pockets. 'I have no desire, though, to force you into something *you* don't want to do. If you want to leave, Caro, just say the word.'

She didn't even know what *this* was yet, but that wasn't really what he was referring to anyway. He wanted to see her smile and have fun again. She wanted the same for him. And she sensed that by helping her he'd be helping himself.

From somewhere she dug out a smile. 'I'm game if you are.' The force of his smile was her reward. She turned away, blinking. 'Lead on, Macduff.'

He led her into the headquarters of one of London's premier Scrabble clubs. Her jaw dropped as she took in the sight of the boards and players set up around various tables.

A young man brimming over with energy came bustling up. 'You must be Caro Fielding. I'm Garry.' He turned to Jack. 'You're—?'

'A friend,' he supplied, with a wink at Caro. 'I rang yesterday.'

'I remember. You said Caro might be interested in joining our club.'

He had, had he? 'I—'

'She's a brilliant player,' Jack inserted.

Good grief! 'I haven't played in an age. And he exaggerates.' She elbowed Jack in the ribs but he just grinned down at her, utterly unrepentant.

'Well, why don't we set you up with Yvonne? She's pretty new to the club too.'

Before Caro knew it she found herself deep in a fierce game of Scrabble. She'd loved the game once. She and Jack used to play it—though he'd never really been a match for her. He'd only ever played to humour her. But when had *she* stopped playing?

When Jack had left.

Her heart thudded.

At the end of the game she sat back and stared at the neat rows of tiles. 'You just wiped the board with me.' A thread of competitiveness squirmed its way to the surface. 'Again?' She wanted a chance to redeem herself.

They started another game. Caro was vaguely aware of Jack strolling around the room, watching the other games, but she had to block him out to concentrate on the game in front of her.

'You might be rusty,' her opponent said, 'but you're picking it up again at a fast rate of knots.'

Caro lost the second game as well—but not by a margin that made her wince. An old fire she'd forgotten kindled to life in her belly. 'Best of five?'

Yvonne simply grinned and started selecting a new set of tiles.

Caro was amazed to find that three hours had passed when a bell sounded and they were instructed to finish up their games. Where had the time gone?

She glanced about, searching for Jack. When she found

him, leaning back in a chair at a neighbouring table, he grinned at her, making her heart pitter-patter.

'Ready?' he said, standing and ambling over to her.

'Just about. I have to hand in my registration form and pay my club dues.'

He started to laugh. 'You don't want to think about it for a bit, then?'

'Heavens, no.'

For some reason that only made his grin widen.

'Do you know they hold competitions—and there's a Scrabble league? Did you know there are world championships?'

'You have your eye on the main prize?'

'Not this year.' She tossed her head, a little fizz of excitement spiralling through her. 'But next year could be a possibility.'

'C'mon.' Throwing an arm across her shoulders, he led her outside. 'Let me buy you a burger.'

'Ooh, yes, please! I'm starved!'

'And I owe you a meal.' He grimaced down at her in apology. 'I didn't realise until much later that I'd left you holding the bill for lunch today.'

They both remembered the reason why Jack had left so abruptly.

He removed his arm from her shoulders and she edged away from him a fraction. She cleared her throat and tried to grab hold of the camaraderie that had wrapped itself around them so warmly just a few short moments ago.

'It's a small price to pay for this.' She gestured back behind her to indicate the Scrabble club. 'I had a great time tonight. I'd forgotten how much I enjoyed Scrabble. It was an inspired idea, Jack. Thank you.'

The burgers were delicious, but while they both did their best to make small talk the easy camaraderie had fled.

'Where are you staying?' she asked him afterwards.

He named a hotel in Covent Garden. 'Oh, Jack, you could walk there from here. Please—you don't need to see me home.'

'But—'

'Truly! I'd prefer it if you didn't.' She wanted to avoid any fraught goodnight moments on her doorstep. 'But I'd appreciate it if you'd flag me down a cab.'

'You insist?' he asked quietly.

She gave a quick nod. He looked far from happy, but he didn't argue. He hailed a cab and insisted on paying for it.

As he helped her inside he said, 'Tomorrow. Six p.m.'

A ripple of anticipation squirrelled through her. 'Again?'

'Wear a dress and heels. Small heels—not stilettos.'

She did everything she could to prevent her breath from hitching. 'Will we be cabbing it again?'

'Yes.'

'Then I'll wait downstairs for you. Goodnight, Jack.'

With that she sat back, before she did something daft... like kiss him.

CHAPTER SEVEN

'SALSA CLASSES?'

Caro's mouth dropped open, but Jack kept his concentration trained on the expressions flitting across her face rather than the temptation of her lips, shining with a rose-pink lipstick.

Lips he ached to kiss fully and very, *very* thoroughly. Lips he wanted to tease, tempt and taste. The longer he stared at those lips, the greater the need that built inside him.

Who was he trying to kid? What he wanted was Caro, warm and wild in his arms, wanting him just as much as he wanted her.

Except he wasn't supposed to be thinking about that!

He dragged his attention back to her expression, trying to decide whether she was excited or appalled. Maybe a bit of both.

'What do you think?' he found himself asking.

They'd attended dance classes once—back before they were married. At the time he hadn't been all that keen—except on the thought of holding Caro in his arms. He hadn't let on, though. He'd been too intent on wooing her. To his utter surprise, the dance classes had been a blast.

She frowned up at him. 'I'm really not sure this is such a good idea.'

She was afraid of the physicality of the dance, afraid of where it would lead…and maybe a little afraid of herself and her own body's yearnings. He needed to put her mind at rest and reassure her that they could survive one dance class together.

The results of the few enquiries he'd made into Caro's life since returning to London—showing the extent of her withdrawal into herself—had shocked him. That was the price she'd paid for the breakdown of their marriage. It was a price she should never have paid and it was time for it to stop.

He touched a finger to her temple—gently and very briefly. 'The Scrabble is for your mind and the dance classes are for your body. A healthy mind and a—'

She blew out a breath that made her fringe flutter. 'And a healthy body,' she finished for him. 'If you say one word about me eating too much cake…'

'Wouldn't dream of it. Cake is necessary too. I don't see why you should feel guilty about eating cake.'

She rolled her shoulders. 'I don't.'

'Then stop being so defensive.'

He moved them to one side as a couple bounded up the steps to push through the door.

The young woman turned just before entering. 'Are you thinking of joining the class? You should. It's great fun—and a really good workout.'

'My friend here is,' Jack said, before Caro could pooh-pooh the whole idea. 'The problem is that I can only attend tonight.'

'That's not a problem. There are two guys in the class who are currently looking for partners—Marcus and Timothy.' She leaned in closer. 'I'd go with Tim. He's a bit shy, but really lovely. See you inside.'

With a smile, she and her partner disappeared through the door.

Jack turned back to Caro and spread his hands, saying

nothing, just letting the situation speak for itself. She bit her lip, glancing once again at the flyer on the door.

Her uncertainty pricked him. 'You loved dancing once.'

'Yes.'

He wanted to ask her what she was afraid of. He didn't. He decided to try and lighten the mood instead. 'It's either this or rock wall climbing.'

She spun back to him, her eyes widening. 'I beg your pardon?'

'There's a gym not too far from your flat that has a climbing wall. I bet it'd be great fun. A great workout for the arms too.'

A laugh shot out of her. 'You can't be serious?'

'Why not?' He grinned back at her. 'Except as we're here, and not there, I did come to the conclusion that you'd prefer this to that. If I'm wrong, just say the word.'

When had she become so risk-averse?

With another laugh, she took his arm and hauled him into the hall.

She wore an amber-coloured dress with a fitted bodice and a skirt that flared gently to mid-calf. It looked deceptively plain until she moved, and then the material—shot through with sparkling threads of gold and bronze—shimmered. Beneath the lights she sparkled, until he had to blink to clear his vision. He led her to a spot on the dance floor before moving away to speak to the dance instructor for a few moments.

He drew in a fortifying breath before returning to Caro and waiting for the class to begin.

He was insanely careful to keep a respectable distance between their bodies when the music started and the instructor began barking out instructions, but her warmth and her scent swirled up around him, playing sweet havoc with his senses. The touch of her hand in his, the feel of her through the thin material of her dress where his hand rested at her waist, sent a surge of hot possessiveness coursing through him.

He had no right to that possessiveness.

He gritted his teeth. He only had to get through one night of salsa. Just a single hour. He gritted his teeth harder. He could do it.

'I can't believe how quickly it's all coming back,' Caro murmured, swinging away and then swinging back.

Her throaty whisper told him that their proximity bothered her too. *That* didn't help. He pulled in a deep breath, but it only made him draw in more of her scent. That *really* didn't help. *Don't think about it.*

'I was worried your feet might be black and blue after an hour of dancing with me.'

'Liar! If you were worried about anybody's feet it was your own. You were always better at this than me.'

'Not true. I mastered the moves quicker, but once you had them down pat you were a hundred times better.'

Their gazes snagged and locked. They moved across the dance floor with an effortlessness that had Jack feeling as if they were flying. Staring into her dark caramel eyes, he could almost feel himself falling...

Stop! a voice screamed through his mind.

With a heart that beat too hard, he dragged his gaze away. He had to swallow a couple of times before he trusted his voice to work. 'I checked with the teacher and found out that's Tim over there.' He nodded across the room to a slim, well-groomed man with light hair and a pleasant smile.

Caro mistimed her step and trod on Jack's foot. 'Oops.' She grimaced up at him in apology. 'It's a challenge to count steps, talk and look round all at the same time.'

Fibber. But he didn't call her on it.

'Why don't we introduce ourselves at the end of the lesson?'

One of her shoulders lifted. 'Seems to me he's found a partner.'

'She's an instructor here. She's filling in to make up the numbers.' He glanced across at the other man again. 'He seems pleasant enough. He's not tramping all over her feet either, so that's a plus.'

'For heaven's sake, Jack! Do you want to give him my phone number and set me up on a date with him too?'

He snapped back at her biting tone. 'Don't be ridiculous.' He glanced across at the other man again. This Tim wasn't her type…was he? 'Your private life is your own to do with as you will.'

It suddenly occurred to him that encouraging Caro to get out more would throw her into the company of men. Men who would ask her out. Men she might find attractive.

He had a sudden vision of Caro in the other man's arms and—

'Ouch!'

He pulled to an abrupt halt. 'Hell! Sorry!'

He bent down to rub her foot, but she pushed him away, glaring at him. 'What are you doing?'

'I was…um…going to rub it better.'

'Not necessary!'

Those amazing eyes of hers flashed cinnamon and gold fire and all he could think of was kissing her foot better, and then working his way up her leg and—'

'Come! Come!'

The dance instructor, who had a tendency to repeat everything twice, marched up to them now, clapping his hands, making Jack blink.

'You must concentrate! *Concentrate*, Jack. Take your partner in your arms.'

He adjusted their positions, moving them a fraction closer to each other, pressing a hand into the small of Caro's back to force her to straighten. The action thrust her chest towards Jack. Jack stared at those delectable curves, mere centimetres from his chest, and swallowed convulsively.

Good God! Torture. Utter torture.

'You must maintain eye contact,' the teacher barked at them.

With a superhuman effort Jack raised his eyes to Caro's.

'This is the salsa!' The man made an exaggerated gesture with his hands. 'This is the dance of flirtation!'

Caro's eyes widened. It was all Jack could do to swallow back a groan.

'So…you must flirt.' He performed another flourish. *'Flirt!'*

Caro's eyes started to dance, and Jack could feel answering laughter building inside him. The instructor moved away to harangue another couple.

'You *will* flirt,' Caro ordered in a mock authoritarian tone. 'We have ways of *making* you flirt!'

He gulped back a bark of laughter.

'It's quite a conundrum,' Caro continued, this time in her own voice. 'How exactly *does* one flirt while dancing?'

She made her eyes innocent and wide. Too innocent. He felt suddenly alive.

He grinned and nodded towards their teacher. 'According to him, lots of eye contact.'

She eyeballed Jack, making him laugh. 'Tick,' she said. 'We have that down pat. But we can't accidentally brush fingers when we're already holding hands.'

'And with your hands already engaged you can't do that cute twirling of your hair around one finger thing, while giving me a come-hither look.'

She snorted back a laugh. 'Ah, but I *can* lasciviously lick my lips in a suggestive fashion.'

She proceeded to do so—but she did it in such an over the top fashion he found himself hard pressed not to dissolve into laughter.

'Your turn,' she instructed. 'You *will* flirt!'

He copied her move in an even more exaggerated way, until they were laughing so hard they had to hold onto each other to remain upright.

'Excellent! Excellent!' The instructor beamed at them. 'Now, *dance.*'

The rest of the hour flew by.

'That was fun,' Caro said a little breathlessly when they stood on the footpath outside afterwards.

Jack put her breathlessness down to the unaccustomed exercise.

'Night, Tim,' she called out when the other man bounded down the steps.

'See you next week, Caro,' the other man called back, with a smile that set Jack's teeth on edge.

He refused to put Caro's breathlessness down to the fact she'd made a *new friend*.

'Stop glaring like that,' Caro chided. 'It was your idea.'

Not one of his better ones, though. It felt as if he was handing her over to another man. Without a fight.

He scowled up at the sky. 'Just remember I don't want an invitation to your wedding.'

'I'm not even going to dignify that with an answer.'

He shook himself. He wouldn't blame her for simply walking away. 'Sorry. Uh…hungry?'

She eyed him for a moment before finally nodding. 'Yes.'

Excellent! He refused to dwell on why he wasn't ready for the night to end. 'There's a great little restaurant around the corner that has—'

'No.'

He frowned at her. 'No?'

'A restaurant meal is too much like a date, Jack, and we aren't dating. C'mon—I know a better place.'

The dance school was in Bermondsey, just a couple of

stops on the tube from Caro's nearest station. He'd chosen it for the convenience of its location. He'd wanted to make attending classes there as easy and trouble-free for her as possible. He scowled down at his feet. He hadn't meant for it to be that easy for her to hook up with another man, though.

He tried to shrug the thought off. It shouldn't matter to him. He wanted a divorce, remember?

Ten minutes later he found himself in a large park, with people dotting the green space, making the most of the summer evening.

She pointed. 'There.'

He grimaced. 'A fish and chip van?'

'You can get a burger if you prefer.'

Without further ado she marched up to the van and ordered a single portion of fish and chips. She shook her head when he reached for his wallet. She paid for it herself. She didn't offer to pay for his meal.

He received the message loud and clear.

He ordered the same, and then found them a vacant park bench. He figured her dress wasn't made for sitting on the grass.

'So, if this isn't a date,' he said, unwrapping his fish and chips, 'what is it?'

'The kind of meal friends would share.'

Was this how she and Tim would start out—sharing a friendly meal in the park? Maybe they'd eventually progress to dinner in a pub, and then romantic candlelit dinners for two in posh restaurants?

Stop it! Caro deserves to be happy.

He closed his eyes. She *did* deserve to be happy.

'Are you okay?' she asked quietly.

It was one of the things he'd always appreciated about her—she never made a fuss, never drew attention unnecessarily.

He shook his head, and then nodded, and finally shrugged, feeling oddly at sea. 'I wanted to say that I've thought about what you said the other day.'

'Hmm...?' She popped a chip into her mouth. 'You might need to be a bit more specific than that.'

'About my reasons for wanting children.'

She paused with a chip halfway to her mouth. 'You don't have to explain anything to me, Jack.'

'If not to you, then who?'

She lowered the chip back to the packet. 'To yourself.'

He stared around the park, at the family groups dotted here and there, and his soul yearned towards them. To belong like that, to be loved like that...to *create* that—it was all he'd ever really wanted.

He turned back to Caro. 'It's occurred to me that I'm better prepared for fatherhood now than I was five years ago. You were right. I wanted children too much back then.'

'I'm not sure it's possible to want something like that *too* much,' she said carefully.

'You were spot-on. I wanted them for *me*—to make me feel better and...and whole.'

She stilled, staring down at the food in her lap. 'Even if that was the case, I don't doubt that you'd have been a fabulous father.'

'Maybe—but I'd have had a few rude awakenings along the way.'

She went back to eating. 'That's just life.'

'I wanted you to know that, after looking back, I don't blame you for the misgivings you had.'

She slumped, as if her spine no longer had the strength to support her. She stared at him, her eyes sparking copper and gold. 'That...' She swallowed. 'Thank you. That... It means a lot.'

She deserved to be happy.

He forced himself to continue. 'You've also made me confront my own selfishness.'

Her head rocked back.

'When I said I wanted to have a family, what I really wanted was for you to *give* me a family. I expected you to give up work and be a full-time mother.' He stared down at his hands. 'But if someone had asked *me* to give up everything I was asking you to give up when I was twenty-five, I wouldn't have given it up without a fight either. I'm... I'm sorry I asked that of you.'

She reached out to grip his hand. She didn't speak until he turned to look at her. 'What you wanted wasn't a bad thing, Jack. Stop beating yourself up about it. Apology accepted, okay?'

Her words and her smile made him feel lighter. She released his hand and it took all his strength not to reach for her again.

'Wow...' She shook her head. 'When you say you want closure you really mean it, huh?'

He didn't want closure. He wanted her back.

The knowledge he'd been trying to ignore for two days pounded through him now.

'For my part...' She pushed her shoulders back. 'I'm sorry I withdrew into myself the way I did. I should've tried to talk to you more, explained how I was feeling. You're not a mind reader. It was unfair of me.'

But she'd been scared—scared that he'd reject her. Just as she was too scared to take a chance on them again now.

'I am truly sorry for that, Jack.'

'Likewise—apology accepted.'

Could he change her mind? His heart beat hard. Could he find a way to make her fall in love with him again? What about the issue of children? Could he give that dream up for Caro?

* * *

Caro tried to ignore how hard her heart burned at the care-worn, almost defeated expression on Jack's face.

She tried to dredge up a smile. 'We're a classic example of marry in haste, repent at leisure.'

They should have made more time to get to know each other on an intellectual level, discussed what they wanted out of life. Instead they'd trusted their instincts—had believed so strongly that they were fated for each other. Because that was what it had felt like—and they'd ignored everything else.

Being with Jack had felt so *right*. The world had made sense in a way it never had before. The fact of the matter, though, was that their instincts had led them astray. They'd wanted to believe so badly in the rightness and the *uniqueness* of their love that they'd left logic, clear thinking and reality behind. Arrogant—that was what they'd been…too arrogant.

'You don't believe what's been broken can be fixed, do you?'

He was talking about *them*. Her stomach churned. He wasn't thinking clearly—muddled by a combination of hormones, nostalgia and an aching sentimentality that she could—unfortunately—relate to. The fact that he found himself liking her again had rocked him—shocked him to his marrow. It was no surprise to her that she still liked *him*.

She glanced across and a chasm of yearning opened up inside her. Not liking each other would make things so much easier. If only…

She bit back a sigh. No, she couldn't think like that. One of them had to keep a clear head.

'No.' She made herself speak clearly and confidently. 'I don't believe we can be fixed.'

His shoulders slumped and it took all of Caro's strength

not to lean across and hug him, unsay her words. Jack hated failure. He always had. But in a day or two he'd see that she was right—that she was saving both of them from more heartbreak.

'Eat your chips,' she ordered. 'They'll make you feel better.'

He cocked a disbelieving eyebrow. 'Chips will make me *feel better*?'

'Deep-fried carbohydrate cannot help but boost the soul.'

Five years ago Jack had left angry—in a white-hot fury. And he'd stayed angry for all this time. It was what had fuelled him. Now that the anger was dissipating it was only natural that he should find himself grieving for their lost love. She'd already done her grieving. He was just catching up.

It was odd, then, how she found herself wanting to be there for him as he went through it.

Dangerous.

The word whispered through her and she acknowledged its innate truth. She had to be careful not to get sucked back into the disaster their marriage had become. She couldn't go through that a second time.

She went back to diligently eating her chips. Wallowing wouldn't do either one of them any good. What they needed was a sharp reminder of their differences.

'You know,' she started, with a sidelong glance in his direction, 'I always envied your confidence that you could make a family work.'

His gaze grew keener. 'What do you mean?'

She munched a chip, desperately searching for a carbohydrate high. 'My own experience of family wasn't exactly positive. It didn't provide me with role models of any note.' She gave a short laugh. 'Let's be frank, it was totally dysfunctional. You met my father. For as long as I can remember he was remote and controlling. Paul tells me he was different when my mother was alive, but…'

'You don't believe that?'

She shrugged. 'I don't have any strong memories of my mother before she died.'

'You were only five.'

'In the same vein, I don't have any memories of my father being different before she died.' She couldn't recall *ever* connecting emotionally with him. 'Although I don't doubt her death affected him.'

Her mother had died of breast cancer, and she knew, because Paul had told her, that her mother had been seriously ill for the eight months prior to her death. It must have been hell to witness.

She shook herself and glanced at Jack. The look in his eyes made her mouth suddenly dry and she didn't know why.

'You think he loved her?' he asked.

She tried to get her pulse back under control. 'I guess the fact it took him fourteen years to remarry is probably testament to that.'

He frowned. 'You're saying you think you'd take some of that dysfunction into your relationship with any children you might have?'

'Well…yes. It seems plausible doesn't it? I mean, in my kinder moments I tell myself my father was simply a product of his own upbringing…'

'But doesn't the fact that you're aware of that mean you'll take extra steps to make sure you're *not* like him?'

She shoved a chip into her mouth and chewed doggedly. 'I don't know. It all seems such a…*gamble.*'

What if she couldn't help it? What if she made those hypothetical children's lives a misery? The thought made her sick to the stomach.

She turned to face him more fully. 'Jack, your child-hood was far worse than mine.'

He shook his head. 'I'm not so sure about that.'

'I grew up with wealth. Money makes a big difference. It couldn't buy me a family, granted,' she added, when he went to break in. 'But it was a hundred times better than being in the same situation and struggling financially. A *thousand* times better. I've been lucky in a lot of ways.'

Lucky in ways Jack had never been. She'd done noth-ing to earn those advantages. He'd deserved so much bet-ter from life.

He'd deserved so much better from her.

'You think my confidence is misplaced?'

'No!' She reached out to grip his arm, horrified that he'd interpreted her words in such a way. 'I *always* believed you'd be a wonderful father. I just wished I could believe in my own abilities so wholeheartedly. That's what I meant when I said I envied you. I… I didn't understand where that confidence came from. I still don't.'

He glanced down at her hand. She reefed it back into her lap, heat flushing through her. 'I…uh…sorry.'

'You don't need to apologise for touching me, Caro. I like you touching me.'

His words slid over her like warm silk, and for a mo-ment all she could do was stare at him. Her breathing be-came shallow and laboured. Had he gone mad? She eyed him uncertainly before shuffling away a few centimetres. He couldn't be suggesting that they…?

Don't be daft. He'd promised to not kiss her again. *You didn't promise not to kiss him, though.*

She waved a hand in front of her face.

Jack scrunched up what was left of his dinner and tossed it into a nearby bin. His every movement reminded her of his latent athleticism. He'd always been fit and physical, and he'd been very athletic in bed.

Don't think about that now.

He settled back, stretching his legs out in front of him and his arms along the back of the bench. His fingers toyed with her hair. He tugged on it gently and she tried not to jump.

'There was one particular foster family that I stayed with when I was twelve...'

She stilled. Jack had rarely spoken about his childhood, or about growing up in foster homes. All that she knew was that his mother had been a drug addict who'd died from an overdose when Jack was four. But whenever she'd asked him questions or pressed him for more information, he'd become testy. The most she'd ever extracted from him was that he hadn't suffered any particular cruelties, but he hadn't been able to wait until he was an adult, when he could take charge of his own life.

As for the rest of it... She'd automatically understood his loneliness in the same way he'd understood hers.

'What was this family like?' She held her breath and waited to see if he would answer.

'They were everything I ever dreamed a family could be.' He smiled, his gaze warm, and it made something inside her stir to life. 'Through them I glimpsed what family could be. Living with them gave me hope.'

Hope?

He told her how Darrel and Christine Jameson hadn't been able to have children of their own, so they'd fostered children in need instead. He described picnics and outings and dinner times around the kitchen table when the television would be turned off and they'd talk—telling each other about their day. He laughed as he told her about being grounded when he'd played hooky from school once, and being nagged to clean his room. He sketched portraits of the two foster brothers he'd had there, and how for twelve short months he'd felt part of something bigger than himself—something good and worthwhile.

Something he'd spent the rest of his life trying to recapture, she realised now.

Envy swirled up through her. Envy and longing. 'They sound wonderful. Perfect.'

'They were going to adopt me.'

Her heart dipped and started to throb. This story didn't have a happy ending.

'What…what happened?' She had to force the words out. Jack had deserved to spend the rest of his life enfolded within this family's embrace. Why hadn't that happened?

'Darrel and Christine were tight with a core group of other foster carers.'

That sounded like a *good* thing. They'd have provided each other with support and advice.

'One of their friends' foster sons got into some serious trouble—taking drugs, stealing cars.'

Her heart thumped.

'It was a mess. He became violent with his foster mother.'

She pulled in a jagged breath. 'That's awful.'

'Nobody pretends that taking on a troubled child is going to be easy, but common wisdom has it that the good gained is worth the trouble and the heartache.'

'You don't believe that?'

He pulled in a breath. 'Seems to me that all too often "well-intentioned" and "idealistic" are merely synonyms for "naive" and "unprepared".'

She swallowed, wanting to argue with him but sensing the innate truth of his words.

'The incident really spooked them—especially Christine. And when my older foster brother was caught drinking alcohol, we were all farmed back to Social Services.'

Although he didn't move, the bleakness in his eyes told her how that had devastated him.

She pressed a hand to her mouth for a moment. 'I'm so sorry.'

He shrugged, and she didn't know how he managed to maintain such an easy, open posture. All she wanted to do was fling herself against his chest and sob for the thirteen-year-old boy who'd lost the family of his dreams. She could feel his fingers in her hair, as if touching it brought him some measure of comfort. She held still, willing him to take whatever comfort he could.

'You never found another family like that one?'

He cocked an eyebrow. 'How do I grieve, Caro?'

She stared at him and then nodded. 'You get angry.'

'I stayed angry for the next five years. I acted out. Got a name for myself within the system. I spent my last two years in a group home.'

She swallowed. 'A detention centre?'

'No, it wasn't that bad, but it wasn't really a…a *home*, if you catch my drift.'

She did. And everything inside her ached for him.

'It was a place to mark time until I became an adult and the state could wash its hands of me.'

She tried to control the rush of anger that shook through her. 'Boarding school was a hundred times better than that!'

He twisted a strand of her hair around his fingers. 'I'm glad.'

She bit her lip, the touch of his hand in her hair sending spirals of pleasure gyrating deep in her belly. She shifted in an attempt to relieve the ache. 'Why aren't you bitter about losing that family?'

'I was for a long time, but they taught me that my dream could come true. I'll always be grateful to them for that— for providing me with a yardstick I could cling to.'

She moistened her lips. He zeroed in on the action, his

eyes darkening, and a groan rose up through her. The pulse at the base of his jaw started to pound and her heart surged up into her throat to hammer in time with it. She tried to draw a steadying breath into her lungs, but all she drew in was the scent of him.

'Have you…have you ever considered becoming a foster carer yourself?'

His fingers in her hair stilled. 'No.'

'Maybe you should. You'd know the pitfalls and understand the stumbling blocks. You'd be brilliant.'

He'd be a wonderful father.

'I…'

He faltered and she shrugged. 'It's just something to think about. Obviously not the kind of decision you'd make on the spur of the moment.'

'But worth considering,' he agreed slowly.

She had no intention of wasting such a rare opportunity when he was in such an amenable mood. 'So you didn't feel you belonged anywhere again until you joined the police force?'

When she'd first met Jack he'd been working for the Australian Federal Police. He'd been stationed in London, on secondment to the British Intelligence Service as a surveillance instructor.

Those blue eyes of his sparked and grew even keener if that were at all possible. 'The police force gave me a direction in life. But, Caro, I didn't feel I belonged anywhere again until I met *you.*'

CHAPTER EIGHT

CARO'S MOBILE PHONE RANG, making her jump. Her fountain pen corkscrewed across the page in an example of less than elegant penmanship. She glared at the blot of ink she'd left behind. *Botheration!*

The phone rang again. She pressed it to her ear. 'Hello?'

'Are you home?'

Her hand about the phone tightened. 'Good morning, Jack. How are you? I'm well. Thank you for asking.'

His chuckle curled her toes. 'Caro, as ever, it's a delight.'

She wanted to stretch and purr at the warm amusement in his voice. *So* not good.

'I'm running up your stairs as we speak.'

He didn't sound the slightest bit breathless. If she walked, let alone jogged up the stairs, she'd huff and puff for a good five minutes.

'Really, Jack, is running necessary?'

This time he laughed outright.

Don't bask. Stop basking!

'Your door has just come into view.'

She snapped her phone off and turned to stare at her door. What was he doing here? If they had to meet, why couldn't they have done it somewhere public?

The snuffbox!

Her stomach tightened. With reluctant legs, but a madly beating heart, she moved across to the door and opened it. She tried not to look at him too squarely as she ushered him in. 'To what do I owe the pleasure?'

'Your manners are one of the things I've always admired about you, Caro.'

Was he laughing at her? Or did he sense her resentment at his intrusion? 'Do you have news about the snuffbox? Have there been any developments?'

He glanced down at the table and frowned. 'What are you doing?'

A scowl she didn't understand started to build inside her. She swallowed and sat. 'You're the detective. What do you *think* I'm doing?'

He lifted the sheet of paper she'd been practising on. *"'My darling Barbara. Wishing you many happy returns for the day. May you always be happy. To my darling wife. Love. Much love. All my love. Roland.'"* He turned the paper sideways to follow her scrawls. *"'Your Roland. Roland. Your loving husband, Roland.'"*

She grimaced. Would her father ever have signed himself as Barbara's loving husband? How on earth could she gush it up a little and still sound sincere?

Jack set the sheet of paper down and lifted one of the letters her father had sent to her while she'd been away at university. She'd received one or two missives from him every semester. Cursory things that never actually said much. She didn't even know why she'd kept them.

Dropping the letters back to the table, he reached for the jewellery catalogue and sales receipt sitting nearby. His nostrils flared, but whether at the picture of the diamond necklace or at the amount on the receipt, she wasn't sure.

'That is worth…'

'A significant amount of money,' she agreed.

'It's hideous.'

'Very true. However, it's not its beauty that matters, but

its value.' Besides, it was the kind of piece her father would have admired. If he'd still been alive to admire it, that was.

Jack tossed the catalogue and the receipt back to the table. 'My detective brain informs me that it's Barbara's birthday soon.'

'Today.'

'And that you're faking a gift to her from your father… from beyond the grave.'

She summoned up her brightest smile. 'I *knew* you were more than just a pretty face.'

He didn't smile back. 'When were you going to tell me about this?'

His lips thinned when she blinked. She pushed her bangle up her arm. 'I wasn't. I don't see how it has any bearing on…on other things.'

'You try and guilt Barbara into giving the snuffbox back and you don't think that's relevant?'

No, she wasn't! This—

'How much more is this worth than the snuffbox?'

She could tell from the way he'd started to shake that he was getting a little…um…worked up. 'It's…' She moistened her lips. 'It's probably worth about three times as much, but that's beside the point. I—'

'You really think Barbara is the kind of woman who can be worked on like this? Have you lost your mind completely? She'll take the necklace *and* the snuffbox and run!'

Caro shot to her feet. 'Stop talking about her like that!' She strode around the table and stabbed a finger at his chest. 'You're wrong! I know her far better than you do, and yet you automatically assume your assessment of her is the right one and that mine is wrong!'

'You're too close.' The pulse at the base of his jaw ticked. 'Your emotions are clouding your judgment.'

'No!' she shot back. 'It's your prejudices that are colouring your judgment. You're just like my father.' She whirled away. 'You think because Barbara is young and beautiful she must've married my father for his money.'

'If your father thought that, then why the hell did he marry her?'

She swung back. 'He didn't think that about her. He thought it about *you*!'

A silence suddenly descended around them. All that could be heard was the harsh intake of their breath.

Caro forced herself to continue. 'When you married me, you married a potential heiress. There are some people who would insinuate that your showing up now, like you have, is so you can collect your cut of the spoils. That's how people like my father and his lawyers think.'

His eyes grew so glacial the very air grew chill. 'I thought we'd already covered this.'

'I *don't* think like that. I *don't* believe you ever married me for my money and I *don't* believe money is the reason you're back in London. Why do I think that? Ooh, let's see…' She cocked her head to one side and lifted a finger to her chin. 'Could it be because I'm a good judge of character?'

Jack closed his eyes and dragged a hand down his face.

'Believe me, Jack. If there's one person who clouds my judgment, it's you. Not Barbara. I *know* she didn't marry my father for his money.'

He slammed his hands to his hips. 'But you believe she stole the snuffbox?'

'Not out of malice or for vengeance! It was a stupid spur-of-the-moment thing, done in a fit of pique and hurt, and now… Well, I expect she's bitterly regretting it and trying to find a way to get it back to me.'

He blew out a breath. 'May I sit?'

Good Lord, where were her manners? 'Please.' She gestured to a chair.

He fell into it and then motioned to the paraphernalia on the table. 'And this?'

She lowered herself back to her own chair. 'This has nothing to do with the rest of it.'

'I don't understand.'

She could tell from the low timbre of his voice that he wanted to. She moistened her lips. It meant talking about love. And talking about love to Jack…

She pushed her shoulders back. 'Believe me when I tell you that Barbara loved my father. She believed that he loved her too.'

It took a moment or two, but comprehension eventually dawned across his face. 'And when he cut her out of his will…?'

She nodded. 'I mean, *we* know the reason for his sudden coldness.'

'But she has no idea he thought she was stealing from him?'

'I can't tell her the truth. She and Paul have no warmth for each other. With him, I fear she would retaliate. To be honest, a part of me wouldn't blame her.'

'Damn it, Caro. Part of me wants to say not your monkeys. Not your circus.'

'But it's not true, is it? I know they're not the kind of family you've always dreamed about, but they're all I have.'

Jack lifted the sheet of paper she'd been working on, stared at it with pursed lips. 'You're pretty good, you know.'

'Yes, I developed quite the reputation among my school friends.'

He glanced up, his eyes alive with curiosity. 'You'll have to tell me about it one day.'

When? At the end of the week he'd be gone and she'd never see him again. There wouldn't be any cosy nights in, laughing over reminiscences. Not for them.

'You're hoping this necklace will reinforce the fact that your father did love her?'

'Yes.'

He stared at the sundry messages she'd written when copying her father's handwriting. 'Men are less verbose than women.'

She leaned towards him. 'What are you trying to say?'

'I think you should just sign the card *Love, Roland* and leave it at that—leave all of this other stuff out.'

'Are you sure?'

'Positive.'

She glanced through the letters her father had sent her and realised Jack was right. Her father had never been demonstrative. At least not in his letters. Pulling the card towards her, she carefully wrote *Love, Roland.*

'Utterly authentic,' Jack said.

'It seems I've developed an unfortunate taste for deception. I've made the jeweller swear on all he holds dear that should Barbara contact him he'll say he was acting on my father's wishes—that all this was organised months before he died.'

'You've covered all bases?'

She hoped so. 'All I have to do now is drop this card in at the jeweller's and the package will be ready for delivery this afternoon.'

He stared at her for a long moment, making the blood pump faster around her body. It took a concerted effort not to fidget.

'What?'

'You're a woman of hidden talents, and at the moment that's to our advantage.'

'What are you talking about?'

'Can you forge Barbara's signature as well as you do your father's?'

'I don't know. I've never tried.' She'd never had to forge

her stepmother's signature on a permission slip. Not that it had ever really been necessary to forge her father's either. It had just been easier than asking him—quicker and cleaner. It had saved her from having to look into his face and be confronted anew with his disappointment.

She pushed the thought away and pursed her lips. 'From memory, though, Barbara's isn't a difficult signature.' Unlike her father's, which was all bold strokes and angry slashes. 'I'd have to see it again before...'

She trailed off when he whipped out a form. Barbara's signature appeared at the bottom.

'Right...' She stared at it. After five attempts she had it down pat. 'How is this going to help us?'

He pulled a key from his pocket and set it on the table. 'Do you know what this is?'

'A key, obviously, but I have no idea what it's supposed to unlock.'

'A safety deposit box.'

She pulled in a quick breath. 'Barbara's?'

He nodded and handed her the appropriate paperwork.

'Good Lord, Jack! Where on earth did you get this?'

He raised an eyebrow and she held both hands up, palm outwards.

'You're right. I don't want to know.' She studied the paperwork. 'This isn't held at the bank my father did business with.' Her father had dealt with a bank in the city. This branch was in Chelsea.

'Do you know anyone who works there?'

She stared at the name of the bank and nodded. 'Lawrence Gardner—in another branch of the same bank. He's the father of an old school friend.' She shook her head. 'I'm sorry, Jack, but I can't ask him to check this safety deposit box. I—'

'What I'm trying to assess is the likelihood of us running into anyone you know if we were to go to that branch with you posing as Barbara.'

'I… What? Oh, God! I think I'm going to hyperventilate.'

He didn't turn a hair. 'We have two days to reclaim the snuffbox.'

Two days before a police inquiry descended on her head.

Caro swallowed. Barbara might have made a mistake, but she didn't deserve a police record and jail. 'You think the snuffbox is in that safety deposit box?'

'I can't think where else it'd be.'

'But…but I don't even *look* like Barbara,' she croaked. Barbara was tall, thin…gorgeous.

'You're both blonde.'

'She's ash-blonde.' Caro was a honey-blonde. 'And her hair is long.' So were her legs…

'I can get you a wig. And if you wore one of those sharp little power skirts she fancies, with a twinset and dark glasses…'

'Those things won't make me tall and thin.'

'No, the disguise won't hold up to close scrutiny,' he agreed. 'Not for someone who knows you or her…like this Lawrence Gardner. Would he recognise you?'

'Oh, that won't be a problem. He works from the bank's main office, which is in Knightsbridge.'

Her heart pounded hard.

She stared at him. 'You believe that if I go in there with this key, the ability to forge Barbara's signature and a blonde wig that I could pass for her?'

'Especially if you have some additional ID.' He handed her a credit card and an ATM card.

She squished her eyes shut. 'I'm not going to ask…'

'I'll have them back to her before she even knows they're missing.'

She hoped he was right.

'But, yes, I believe all of those things combined will gain us access to the box…if you dare.'

The way he said it reminded her of the way he'd challenged her on not having fun any more, on being *risk averse*. She pushed up her chin. She wanted that snuffbox back. She wanted Barbara in the clear. She dragged in a breath. *And* she wanted to keep her job and her professional reputation.

She folded her arms. Mostly to hide how badly her hands were shaking. 'When do we do it?'

'Today.'

Dear Lord!

Nerves jangled in Caro's stomach when Jack switched off the car's engine. She pulled down the sun visor to scrutinise her reflection in the mirror again.

'You look perfect,' he assured her.

He'd parked in an underground car park not too far from the bank. He didn't want to rely on taxis or public transport. He didn't want them to be seen. Which made her nerves jangle harder.

She pushed the visor back into place. 'I've been thinking. I should go in on my own.'

If she didn't pull this off then at least Jack wouldn't get into trouble too. She refused to dwell too deeply on the kind of trouble *she* could get into if this didn't go to plan. If she did that she'd freeze.

'Not a chance, kiddo. I'm in charge of this operation. I'm not sending you in there alone.'

She wanted to weep in relief. *Coward.*

'I'm not letting you have all the fun.'

She turned to gape at him. *'Fun?'*

'You and me—we're partners in crime.'

'Fun?' she repeated. *'Crime?'*

He grinned, exhilaration rippling in the depths of his eyes. 'Besides, we're not doing anything wrong. Not really.'

'Tell that to the judge.'

His grin widened. 'We don't want to steal anything. We don't want to hurt anyone. We just want to right a wrong.'

His words made her feel like a cross between Robin Hood and the Scarlet Pimpernel.

'To achieve that end we have to pit ourselves against the system—a worthy adversary. Are you going to tell me you're not experiencing even the tiniest flicker of anticipation?'

'Adrenaline junkie,' she accused, but there was no denying the fever that seemed to be working its way through her blood. *Keep breathing.* 'Any last instructions?'

'Do your best to channel Barbara.'

'That won't be difficult, darling.'

'Perfect.' He rubbed his hands together. 'Once inside, try and keep your head down. Stare at your hands or feign preoccupation with the contents of your purse. I don't want the CCTV cameras getting a good shot of you.'

Dear Lord!

There were two people ahead of her in the queue, and Caro's nerves steadied as they waited their turn. The fact that no alarms or sirens had sounded when they'd entered through the bank's sliding glass doors helped.

She twirled the wedding band Jack had suggested she wear round and round her finger. *Her* wedding band. She'd taken it off two years after Jack had left. Wearing it again now, she felt as if a missing part of her had been reclaimed. Which was an utterly crazy notion, because the thin circle of gold was nothing more than an empty symbol.

Don't think about it. Stay in character.

She pursed her lips and tapped her foot. She didn't watch a lot of thrillers, preferring dramas and comedies, but she did her best to summon a list of kick-ass heroines to mind. There was that Lara Croft *Tomb Raider* character—she was pretty handy in a tight situation. Oh, and Julia Roberts's character in *Ocean's Eleven*—very suave. They were women who strode out confidently and held their heads high.

She was about to toss her hair and lift her head when she recalled Jack's strictures to keep her head down. Hmm, on second thoughts they might not be the best archetypes to use as models in this particular situation. Still, she made a resolution to watch more movies with capable, efficient, devil-may-care, thrill-seeking female protagonists. And now that she thought about it, amateur dramatics might be a spot of fun. Maybe she should look into—

'We're up.'

She started at Jack's words, but her preoccupation helped her not only to keep her legs steady, but her voice steady too. 'Good afternoon,' she greeted the teller. 'I'd like to access my security deposit box, please.'

She handed over the paperwork Jack had procured. Heaven only knew when or how he'd done it, but she had visions of him dressed in black, prowling silently through the house in Mayfair.

Mind you, the vision wasn't without merit…

'If you'd like to follow me, Mrs Fielding?'

A thrill shot through her. This was working! They were going to get away with it.

'Certainly,' she said, following the teller along the length of the counter to a door. This was almost too easy. It occurred to her then that she could become a bit of an adrenaline junkie too.

The teller had started to punch in the door's code when it opened from the other side and a man strode out. Caro's heart leapt into her throat. She ducked her head, using Jack's body as a shield.

Please, please, please...

'Caro!'

Her heart thundered so hard she thought her whole body must pulse with the force. What on earth was Lawrence doing *here*?

The teller frowned and glanced down at the paperwork. 'Caro…?'

Think fast!

'Lawrence, darling, it's *Barbara*.' She made herself beam. 'You do that every single time—mix me up with Caro. We're not even related. It must be the blonde hair.' She reached up to kiss his cheek. 'Please don't give me away…' she whispered. Throwing herself on her sword was the only option.

He stared at her for a long moment, before taking her hand and bringing it to his lips. 'That was clumsy of me. How have you been coping since the funeral?'

To Caro's utter horror she could feel tears start to prick the backs of her eyes. She gave an awkward shrug. 'Oh… you know.'

'What are you here for?'

Caro let the teller explain, while she tried to gain control over the pounding of her heart. What on earth was Lawrence doing in Chelsea rather than Knightsbridge?

'I'll take care of Ms Fielding,' Lawrence told his underling.

Caro swallowed a wince at Lawrence's use of Ms rather than Mrs.

Taking Caro's arm, he led her and Jack back the way he'd come, not releasing her until they reached an office. He closed the door before swinging back. 'Caroline Elizabeth Fielding, what on *earth* do you think you're playing at?'

She swallowed. 'Hello, Uncle Lawrence.'

* * *

Uncle Lawrence! Jack closed his eyes. What on earth had he got Caro into?

He cleared his throat and stepped forward. 'Sir—'

'Uncle Lawrence, this is my husband, Jack. I don't believe the two of you ever met.'

As she spoke she led Jack to a chair and pressed him down into it. She squeezed his shoulder briefly—a not so-subtle signal to keep his mouth shut. Jack fully intended on taking the complete blame for whatever trouble was about to rain down on their heads, but he'd let her have her way for the moment. He was curious to see what she'd do.

'Jack, this is my Uncle Lawrence. It's an honorary title, of course.' In the same fashion as she'd led Jack to a chair she now led her 'honorary uncle' to the chair on the other side of the desk. 'He's my best friend's father. I spent most of my summers at their house in the Lake District.'

Her best friend? He thought for a moment. 'Suzie?'

Her eyebrows shot up as she took the seat beside him. 'You remember her?'

'Sure I do—the super-smart brunette addicted to *Twilight* movies and Hobnob biscuits.'

She'd been at their wedding. He frowned, trying hard to remember something else—anything else. If they could soften the father through the daughter…

'Wasn't she relocating to Switzerland, to run a department of some trading bank?'

Both Caro and Lawrence laughed. 'She's practically running the entire operation now,' her father said with pride, and Jack gave thanks for the tack Caro had taken.

'Good for her. I'm glad she's doing so well.'

'Well, she is now,' Caro said. 'Things were a bit bumpy there for a while, after her second little girl was born. Suzie had postnatal depression, but she's doing great again now.' She shot Lawrence a smile. 'We had a long, slightly wine-fuelled chat the week before last. She's doing wonderfully. You must be so proud of her.'

'I am.' He paused, his eyes keen. 'You know I'll always be grateful to you, Caro, for taking leave like you did, to be with her for those first few weeks after she was released from hospital. It made all the difference.'

It struck Jack how much pressure career-minded women who wanted children were put under. Men rarely suffered the same pressures. He eyed Caro now, his lips pursed.

'It's what friends do…and godmothers.'

Caro was a *godmother*?

'I'd do anything for Suzie and her family. Just as she'd do anything for me and mine.'

That was a masterstroke of emotional manipulation. Jack wanted to shoot to his feet and give her a standing ovation.

'Caro—'

'Uncle Lawrence, I find myself in something of a pickle…'

Without further ado Caro told Lawrence the entire story. By the time she finished the older man had taken off his glasses and was rubbing his eyes.

Caro leaned towards him. 'You *have* to see that I can't let Barbara go to jail.'

He pushed his glasses back to the bridge of his nose. 'Caro, if I take you through to that safety deposit box I will be breaking so many codes of conduct, not to mention laws, that I wouldn't be able to hold my head up in public and—'

'*I* don't actually want to look inside her safety deposit box.'

Jack swung to her. *What on earth…?*

From her bag she pulled out a photograph. 'This is a picture of the missing snuffbox. I don't want to know what else Barbara is storing in the deposit box—that's none of my business. But maybe *you* could check the box to see if that's there.' She pressed the photo into his hand. 'I'm not asking you to remove it—just to see if it's there.'

She stared at her Uncle Lawrence with pleading eyes and Jack held his breath right alongside her.

Lawrence stared at them both for several long moments. 'Do *not* move from those seats.'

Caro crossed her heart. Without another word, Lawrence rose and left.

Caro turned to Jack, sagging in her seat, her hand pressed to her heart. 'I'm so sorry. I can't believe he turned up here today of all days.'

Jack shook his head. 'Not your fault. And this may, in fact, work out better.'

Her shoulders drooped. 'Except now I've involved someone else in my life of crime.'

He meant to say, *Nonsense.* What came out of his mouth instead was, 'You're a godmother?'

A smile suddenly peeked out and he had to catch his breath at the way her face lit up. 'Twice over. To both of Suzie's little girls. Would you like to see a picture?'

'Love to.'

His heart thumped madly when he glanced down at the picture of Caro sitting on a picnic blanket with a toddler in her lap and a baby in her arms. She looked…so happy. His chest twisted. Had he ever made her that happy?

He *wanted* to make her that happy. He wanted—

He blinked when Lawrence came back into the office. Caro reached across and took the photo from his fingers, flashing it towards Lawrence with an abashed grin before slotting it back into her purse.

They all stared at each other and then Caro shuffled forward to the edge of her chair. If he didn't know better he'd think she'd started to enjoy all this subterfuge and intrigue.

'Well?'

Lawrence slumped down in his chair. 'I didn't find the snuffbox.'

Damn! Jack's hands fisted. Had Barbara managed to dispose of it in that half-day before he'd come on the case? He'd had her tailed ever since. He'd had all the guests at the country house party thoroughly investigated, and had come to the conclusion that Barbara hadn't even taken the snuffbox with her that weekend. Instinct told him she'd gone there to make initial contact with someone. He kept waiting for her to visit one of those guests…or for one of them to turn up at the house in Mayfair. So far, though, there'd been nothing.

'I did, however, find this.'

Jack snapped back to attention when Lawrence placed a locket on the desk in front of Caro.

She stilled, before reaching out to trace it with one finger. 'Mother's locket…'

'That belongs to you.'

Exactly! What on earth was Barbara doing with it? It must be worth a fortune.

'Although I have no real memory of her, all my life I've felt overshadowed by my mother.' She stared at the locket with pursed lips. 'My father set that charity up in her name and then expected me to devote my life to running it. He turned my mother into a kind of saint, and there's not a living, breathing woman who can compete with that. It wouldn't surprise me in the least to find that Barbara has felt overshadowed by the first Mrs Fielding too.' She scooped up the locket with its heavy ornate gold chain and put it in Lawrence's hand. 'Put it back. I have so much. I don't need this.'

Lawrence stared down at the locket, his face grim. 'There are some rather interesting items in that deposit box…'

Caro shook her head. 'Barbara is entitled to her secrets.

I have no right to them. I have no desire to pry further than I already have.' She moved to where Lawrence sat and pressed a kiss to his brow. 'I can't thank you enough for all you've done. May I come to dinner some time soon?'

'You know you're welcome any time. Your Auntie Kate would love to see you.'

He rose and kissed both Caro's cheeks. As he did so he held his business card out to Jack behind Caro's back. Jack pocketed it before Caro could notice the exchange.

'It was nice to meet you, sir.'

'I'm reserving my judgment,' Lawrence said in reply.

Jack and Caro walked back to the car without exchanging a single word. As soon as they reached it, however, Caro started hopping from one foot to the other. Her eyes glittered and her cheeks flushed pink with what he guessed was an excess of adrenaline.

'That was…' She reached out as if to pluck a word from the air.

'A close call,' he finished for her. 'If Lawrence Gardner didn't hold you in such high esteem we'd be toast by now.'

She grabbed his arm, all but dancing. 'Jack, I can't remember the last time I felt so…*alive*!'

'And you call *me* an adrenaline junkie.'

He kept his voice teasing, but all the while he was aware of her grip on his arm and the warm smile dancing across her lips. An ache as big as the Great Barrier Reef opened up inside him. His every molecule screamed at him to kiss her.

'I could get addicted to that.'

Addiction? He stared down at her luscious mouth. Yes, he understood addiction. He thought he might explode into a thousand tiny pieces if he didn't kiss her.

You can't kiss her. You promised.

'Thank you.'

'What for?' he croaked.

'For believing I could pull that off.'

Tenderness rose up through him, warring with his desire—and they entwined, forming something stronger and brighter. 'You were brilliant.' It was nothing less than the truth. 'You saved the day.'

'I can't remember the last time I had to think quickly on my feet like that. For a split second I didn't know whether to lie or to confide in Lawrence.'

'You followed your instincts and they didn't let you down.'

She reached up on tiptoe and kissed his cheek. He bit back a groan.

'I...'

Her voice trailed off at whatever she saw in his face. Her eyes met his and darkened. Her gaze lowered to his lips and her own lips parted ever so slightly—as if she were parched, or as if she couldn't quite catch her breath. Wind roared in his ears. She wanted him. With the same desperate hunger that ravaged him. He'd promised not to kiss her, but...

He moved in closer, traced a finger down the soft flesh of her cheek. Her breath hitched. Her eyes never left his.

'You...' She hiccupped again as his finger moved down the line of her throat. 'You promised,' she whispered.

'I promised not to kiss you,' he murmured. 'I don't recall promising not to touch you. You can tell me to stop any time you want to and I will.'

Her lips parted, but no words emerged.

A surge of something hot and primal pulsed through him. 'And I don't recall *you* promising not to kiss *me*.'

Her breath hitched again. Maintaining eye contact, he took her hand and raised it to his lips, nibbled on the end of her ring finger and then her middle finger, drawing it ever so slightly into the warmth of his mouth.

'You didn't promise you wouldn't kiss me,' he whispered

again. 'And I want you to kiss me, Caro. I want that more than I've ever wanted anything in my life.'

A shiver shook through her. He went hard in an instant.

'I didn't promise that I wouldn't put my arms around you…'

Very slowly she shook her head. 'No, you didn't promise that.'

Very slowly he backed up until he was leaning against the car. He drew her towards him to stand between his legs—not quite touching, but their heat swirled and merged and another shiver shook through her.

He kissed the tips of each of the fingers of the hand he still held. 'I didn't promise not to place your arm around my neck…'

He put her hand on his shoulder, snaking an arm about her waist and pulling her closer. The feel of her in his arms was familiar and strange both at the same time. Her other hand slid about his neck too.

'Jack…' she whispered.

He moved his face to within millimetres of hers. 'I didn't promise not to ask you to kiss me…'

'Oh…'

The word was nothing more than a breath and it whispered across his lips, drawing everything inside of him tight. Her hands tightened about his neck.

'I'm not asking, Caro,' he groaned. 'I'm begging. Please kiss me. I—'

She leant forward and pressed her lips to his.

CHAPTER NINE

THE MOMENT HER lips touched his Jack had to fight the torrent of need that roared through him. It took all his strength to let her take the lead and not crush her to him. He didn't want to overwhelm her with his intensity. He didn't want to frighten her with his hunger. He wanted her to remain right here, where she belonged—in his arms.

His hunger was all about *him* and he wanted this kiss to be all about *her*—he wanted to give her everything she needed, everything she craved. He wanted their kiss to tempt, to tease and to tantalise her on every level.

He didn't want the kiss ever to stop. He wanted it to whet her appetite—for him, for *them*. He wanted it to challenge her belief that they couldn't be fixed.

She pressed in closer and a groan broke from him. 'You're killing me.'

She laughed, her breath feathering across his lips. 'And here I was thinking I was kissing you.'

He grazed his teeth across the sensitive skin of her neck, just below her ear, and she melted against him. 'Jack...' His name left her on a whisper, filling him with vigour and a lethal patience.

He kissed a slow path down her throat, revelling in the taste of her and the satin glide of her skin. He moulded her to him—one hand in the small of her back, the other between her shoulderblades. Slipping his lower hand beneath the soft material of her shirt, he lightly raked his fingernails across her bare skin as he kissed his way up the other side of her throat.

She gasped and shivered and pressed herself all the more firmly against him. He wanted to give her so much pleasure it would blot everything else from her mind—the pain he'd caused her, the mistakes they'd made five years ago.

He wanted her filled—body and soul—with the promise of their future. A future he had utter faith in.

He moved his lips back to hers, pressing light kisses at the corners of her mouth, wanting to drive her wild with wanting. Her hands slid up through his hair to hold him still, and his heart pounded until he thought it might burst. She slanted her mouth over his—all open-mouthed heat and wild need—and Jack couldn't contain himself any longer. It was like coming home. It was like being welcomed home.

Fireworks of celebration exploded behind the backs of his eyes. He crushed her to him, wanting the line between where she started and he ended to blur until they became one.

Caro wrapped her arms around Jack's neck and held on for dear life as the maelstrom of desire they'd always ignited in each other rocked through her, lifting her off her feet and hurtling her along with a speed that would have stolen her breath if Jack hadn't already done so. It should frighten her, except she knew Jack would keep her safe. He would never let any harm come to her.

To feel him, to taste him again, alternately soothed and electrified her. It was so familiar, and yet so dark and dangerous. An utter contradiction. Kissing Jack was like every risk she'd ever taken rolled into one—and it was like every warm blanket she'd ever pulled about herself. Kissing Jack was like being flung out of her mind and body at the same time. It was heady and wild.

And it was frightening too—what if she never found

herself again? She didn't want to lose herself. Not completely. Not for all time. If she made love with Jack now where would she ever find the strength to be true to herself? How would she be able to resist all that he would ask of her? She would try to become everything he wanted—needed—and in the process she'd become something neither one of them would recognise.

And then she would have nothing.

Half sobbing, she reefed herself out of his arms. Backing up a couple of steps, she leaned against the car to try and catch her breath. Jack closed his eyes and bent at the waist to draw in great lungfuls of air. She forced her gaze away from him, tried to stamp down on the regrets rising through her, tried to ignore her body's insistent demand for release.

An hour of heaven was not worth another five years of hell.

She started when two arms slammed either side of her on the car, trapping her within their circle. 'You are the most divine woman I have ever met.'

And he was the most divine man she'd ever met—but she wasn't going to say that out loud. She hitched up her chin. 'That could be a sign that you need to get out more.'

He stared down at her, and she didn't know what he saw in her face, but it left her feeling naked.

One corner of his mouth hooked up. 'You never were a pushover.'

Could've fooled her.

'We need to talk, Caro.'

'About the fact we're still attracted to each other?' What was the point of that?

'We could start there.'

She shook her head. 'I can't see there's much we can do about it.'

'Really?' he drawled, cocking a suggestive eyebrow.

She found it hard to stamp down on the laugh that rose through her. In the back of her mind the salsa teacher's voice sounded: *You will flirt!*

'Not going to happen, Jack.'

He raised that eyebrow higher.

She shook her head, but it was harder than it should have been. 'An hour of pleasure is not worth a lifetime of regrets.'

He leaned in closer. 'I can make it last longer than an hour.'

God forgive her, but her breath hitched at the promise lacing his words.

'Do you really think we'd have been able to stop if we'd been at your flat or in my hotel room rather than in a car park?'

She didn't know the answer to that, and she had no intention of finding out. 'I never thought I'd say this, but I'm glad this happened in a public place.'

He reached out and brushed his thumb across her over-sensitised lips. It was all she could do not to moan and touch her tongue to him.

'You still want me.'

'With every atom of my body,' she agreed.

His eyes darkened and his breathing grew shallow at her admission.

'But I am not a mindless body controlled by impulse. I possess a brain, and that brain is telling me not to just walk away from this, Jack, but to run.'

'You're frightened.'

'You should be too! You didn't emerge unscathed the last time we did this.'

He made as if to cradle her cheek, but she snapped upright.

'You're crowding me.'

He immediately dropped his arms and moved back. She

paced the length of the car before coming back to stand in front of him.

'We have no future together, and I cannot do some kind of final fling with you. I've worked too hard to get over you to risk undoing all my hard work now.'

He stared at her for a long moment. 'I beg to differ with you on one point, Caro.'

She folded her arms and tapped a foot. 'Really?'

'I believe we *could* have a future together.'

Her arms slackened. Her jaw dropped. 'You *can't* be serious.'

His eyes grew keen and bright. 'I've never been more serious about anything in my life.'

Fear, raw and primal, scrabbled through her, drawing her chest tight.

'What makes you—' he leant down so they were eye to eye '—so certain we *don't* have a future?'

'Our past!' she snapped. He was being ridiculous! Nostalgia was making him sentimental.

'We can learn from the mistakes of our past.'

'Or we could simply repeat them.'

He shook his head. 'I'm smarter now. I know what it is I really want—and that's you.'

No! She wouldn't believe him. She *couldn't*. 'What about children.'

'I don't care if we have children or not.'

How long would that last? 'I don't believe you.' This time she moved in close, invading his personal space. 'I think you want children as much as you ever did.'

His eyes flashed. 'I want you more.'

She stepped back. She wouldn't be able to live with him making that kind of sacrifice.

'Does *nothing* of what I say make any impact on you?' he demanded, his voice ragged.

She swung away and closed her eyes against the pain

cramping her chest. 'Jack, for the last five years you've held me solely responsible for the breakdown of our marriage. In the last eight days you've been confronted with your own culpability. I understand your sense of guilt, I understand your desire to make amends and to try and put things right, but…' She turned, gripping the tops of her arms tightly. 'We cannot be put to rights. There's no longer any *"we"* that can be salvaged.'

Her words seemed to beat at him like blows and each of them left her feeling bruised and shaken.

He seized her by the shoulders, his face pale though his eyes blazed. 'I love you, Caro. Doesn't that mean anything to you?'

Yearning yawned through her. To have…

No!

She hardened her heart and shook her head. 'I don't wish to be cruel, Jack, but no, I'm afraid it doesn't.'

Turning grey, he let her go, his shoulders slumping as if she'd just run him through with a sword. She had to bite her lip to stifle the cry that rose up through her.

Why had he ever come back to London?

Why hadn't he simply sent the divorce papers through the post?

She'd rather he'd continued to blame her—hate her—than put him through this kind of emotional torment.

She had to leave before she did something stupid, like hurl herself into his arms and say sorry, tell him she loved him too. Love wasn't enough. It never had been. It was better they face that now than another twelve months down the track.

She pulled herself up to her full height. 'I'll see myself home.'

He stiffened. 'Get in the car, Caro. I will take you home.'

Her hands clenched. 'I am not a child who can be ordered about or cajoled. I have a free will, which I'm choosing to assert now. I would much prefer to see myself home.' She tried to pull in a steadying breath. 'But thank you for the offer.'

He stared at her, shoved his hands in his pockets. 'Right.'

She moistened her lips. 'I think it'd be for the best if we didn't see each other again.'

His head jerked up. 'The snuffbox—'

'Is lost forever, I expect.'

'I haven't given up hope.'

She had.

'At nine o'clock on Friday morning—' the day after tomorrow '—I'll be informing my boss that I've lost the snuffbox and I will tender my resignation.'

The pulse in his jaw jumped, but he didn't say a word.

'I'd like you to send me a bill for your time and expenses, though I suspect you won't.'

'You suspect right.'

'I'll sign the divorce papers and have them sent to your lawyer.'

She couldn't say any more. Her throat ached too much from saying the word *divorce*—it lodged there like a block of solid wood, its hard edges pressing into her with such ferocity it made her vision blur.

She spun away and made for the exit. 'Goodbye, Jack.'

The letters on the car park exit sign blurred, but she kept her focus trained on their neon glow rather than the throb at her temples or the pain pressing down on her chest. It took all her strength to remain upright and to place one foot in front of the other.

This was for the best. She could never trust Jack again. She could never be certain that the next time she failed to measure up to his expectations he wouldn't just walk away again. And she wouldn't be able to bear that.

She hadn't made him happy five years ago. Oh, they'd had great sex—there was no denying that—but a solid mar-

riage needed stronger glue than great sex. She and Jack...
they didn't have that glue.

The sunshine made her blink when she finally arrived
outside. She scowled at it. How dared the day be so...*summery*?

She caught the tube home. *Please, please, please, don't
be one of those people who cry on the train.* She couldn't
bear the mortification of that.

She might not be able to turn the pain off, but she could
try and corral her thoughts. She recited the alphabet silently
until she reached her stop. On wooden legs, she turned in
at Jean-Pierre's bakery.

He spun with a smile that faded when he took in her expression. *'Ma cherie.'* He shook his head. 'Not a good day?'

'Dreadful, dreadful day,' she agreed tonelessly. 'The
worst.' She gestured to his counter full of cakes. 'I'm looking for something that will make me feel better.'

Sugar wasn't the answer. They both knew that. But
she blessed his tact in remaining silent on the subject. He
packed her up an assortment. She trudged upstairs to her
flat and sat at the table. She stared at the cakes for several
long minutes—a chocolate éclair, a strawberry tart, a vanilla slice and a tiny lemon meringue pie.

She couldn't dredge up the slightest enthusiasm for a
single one of them.

The longer she stared at them the more her eyes stung.
A lump lodged in her throat. Shaking her head, she lifted
the chocolate éclair to her lips and bit into it. She chewed
and with a superhuman effort swallowed. She set the éclair
back down. Its dark brown icing gleamed the exact same
colour as Jack's hair—

Slamming a halt to those thoughts, she picked up the
lemon meringue pie, bit into it, chewed and swallowed.
She did the same with the strawberry tart and then the vanilla slice. With each bite the lump in her throat subsided.

It lodged in her chest instead, where it became a hard, bitter ache.

She stared at the delicacies, each with a dainty bite taken out of them, and pushed the cake box away to rest her head on her hands.

Jack started when he realised darkness had begun creeping across the floor of his hotel room. He barely remembered returning here earlier in the afternoon, but the stiffness in his muscles told him he'd been sitting in this chair for hours.

He glanced across to the window. The grey twilight on the other side of the glass complemented the greyness stretching through him.

He closed his eyes. Every fibre of his being ached to go and find Caro and change her mind—to fight harder for her—but...

He rested his head in his hands. The look on her face when he'd told her he loved her... He'd wanted to see joy, hope, delight. He'd wanted her to throw her arms around his neck and tell him she loved him too.

Instead...

He dropped his head back to the headrest of his chair. Instead she'd stared at him with a kind of stricken horror that had made his heart shrivel.

He understood now how out of character it had been for Caro to fall in love with him so quickly six and a half years ago. How out of character it had been for her to marry him after knowing him for only four months. By nature Caro was a careful person, but she'd loved him back then. She'd trusted him completely, and when he'd left he'd not only broken her heart, he'd broken faith with her, he'd made her doubt her own judgment.

He should have fought for her five years ago!

He'd misinterpreted her reserve as meaning she didn't

love him. Instead of challenging her, though, he'd run away. *Like a coward.*

He'd blown it. He'd get no second chance with her. She'd never let him close again, regardless of the promises he made her.

What promises have you made? What exactly have you offered her?

He frowned at the gathering darkness. With a curse, he leapt to his feet and switched on the lamp before reaching for his laptop. There were no promises he could make that Caro would believe, but he had promised to do all he could to retrieve that damn snuffbox. That was one thing he *could* do for her.

Settling earphones over his head, he tuned in to the listening devices he'd placed in the house in Mayfair earlier in the week. *Give me something!*

Two hours later he pulled the earphones from his head and flung them to the desk.

Eureka!

He backed up the files in three different locations, emailed them to each of his email accounts, burnt them to a CD and loaded them on to a thumb drive as a final precaution. Next he researched the government's National Archive. Forty minutes later he tossed both the CD and the thumb drive into his satchel. Throwing the bag over his shoulder, he set off on foot for Mayfair.

'Mr Jack,' Paul boomed when he opened the door. 'It's very good to see you.'

That wasn't what the treacherous snake in the grass would be saying in ten minutes' time.

'Jack?' Barbara appeared in the doorway of the drawing room. 'Is Caro with you?'

'No.'

He might have misjudged Barbara—just as Caro had

said—but she was still as treacherous as Paul in her own way. Though at least now he understood her.

Barbara moved more fully into the foyer, a frown marring the china doll perfection of her face. 'Is everything all right, darling? Is Caro all right?'

'Caro is fine, as far as I know.' And he meant to keep it that way. 'But everything is far from all right. I need the two of you to listen to something. Do you have a CD player?'

Barbara swept an arm towards the drawing room and directed him across to the far wall, where a stereo system perched on an antique credenza.

'Don't go, Paul,' Jack added, not turning around but sensing the older man's intention to withdraw. 'I want you to hear this too.'

He put the disc into the player, surreptitiously retrieving one of his listening devices as he did so. He'd retrieve them all before he left this evening. He pressed the play button.

'You might want to sit,' he said, gesturing to the sofas.

Barbara and Paul both remained standing.

'This necklace didn't come from Roland, Paul, and we both know it.'

As her voice emerged from the speakers, Barbara sank down into the nearest chair with a gasp, her hand fluttering up to her throat.

'There's only one person who could possibly be responsible for this, and that's Caro.'

A short pause followed, and then Paul's voice emerged from the speakers. *'Yes.'*

Jack could almost see the older man's nod as he agreed with Barbara.

'I don't want to do this any more, Paul. I want Caro to know the truth.'

'We can't! We promised her father! And there's your

*mother to think of. You could never afford her medical
bills on your own.'*

Jack reached over and switched the CD player off. 'I
could let it keep running, but we all know what it says.'

Barbara lifted her head and swallowed. 'I'm glad the
truth will come out now.'

And yet only a couple of hours ago she'd submitted to
Paul's bullying.

'Are you *utterly* faithless?' Paul shot at her.

His words were angry, but everything about him had
slumped, as if he were caving in on himself.

'Faithless?' Jack found himself shouting. 'What about
the faith you should've been keeping with Caro? She loves
the two of you! She considers you her family. And this is
how you treat her?'

Barbara wasn't a woman easily given to tears, but she
looked close to them now. He sensed her regret was genuine. And, considering the bribery Roland had used to sway
her, he could almost forgive her. *Almost.*

He shoved his shoulders back. 'Shall I share the conclusions I've come to?'

Barbara spread her hands in a *please continue* gesture.
Paul said nothing, but his back had bowed and he'd lost
his colour.

'Sit, Paul,' Jack ordered.

The other man's head lifted. 'I'm the butler, Mr Jack.
The butler doesn't—'

'Can it! You lost all rights to butler etiquette the moment
you started this nasty little game.'

Without another word, Paul sat. Jack stared at them both,
trying to swallow back the fury coursing through him.

'Before he died, Caro's father made the two of you promise to sabotage Caro's job at Richardson's in an attempt to
have her fired—so you could force her hand and have her
finally take over the administration of that damn trust.'

Barbara hesitated, and then nodded. 'He thought that by making her the sole beneficiary of his will it would soften her attitude towards both him *and* the trust.'

'And of course the two of *you* were to do everything you could to encourage that softening?'

She winced and nodded.

'I also know that if you succeeded, you were both to be rewarded.'

Barbara's head came up.

'I suspect your mother's hospital bills and her care were to be guaranteed if you succeeded.' He named the medical facility where Barbara's mother resided. 'I know the kind of care she needs, and I know how much that costs.'

She shot to her feet, visibly shaken. 'How do you know about that?'

'I'm a private investigator. I'm trained to follow a lead.'

He'd found out Barbara's mother's name and had tracked her to a private medical clinic in Northumberland. A phone call had confirmed that she had a severe dissociative personality disorder and needed round-the-clock psychological monitoring. She was receiving the very best of care. The fees, however, were astronomical.

Barbara sat again, brushing her hand across her eyes. 'I can't even visit her. It upsets her too much. Making sure she gets the best of care is the one thing I *can* do.'

He couldn't imagine how difficult that must be. 'I'm sorry about your mother, Barbara.'

'Thank you.'

'Roland blackmailed you?'

She glanced up and gave a strained shrug. 'In a way, I suppose. But you see I *did* love him. Ours wasn't a wild, romantic relationship, but… I wanted him to be happy. It didn't really seem too much to ask of Caro, to administer that wretched trust, but…'

'But?'

She lifted her head. 'But, regardless of what the rest of us think or want, Caro has a right to make her own decisions in respect to her life.'

His heart thumped. 'I couldn't agree more.' He just wished she'd made the decision to include *him* in her life. Pushing that thought aside, he turned to Paul. 'What I don't understand is why *you'd* agree to Roland's games. I thought you cared about Caro?'

'I do!'

Nobody spoke for several long moments.

'He just loved Caro's mother more,' Barbara finally said, breaking the silence that had descended.

Jack fell into a seat then too. Paul? In love with Caro's mother?

'I went too far.' Paul rested his head in his hands. 'What are you going to do, Mr Jack?' he asked.

If Caro didn't care about these two so much he'd throw them to the wolves. But she *did* care about them.

It occurred to him then that his idea of family had been utterly unrealistic—a complete fantasy. Family, it appeared, was about accepting others' foibles and eccentricities. It was about taking into account and appreciating their weaknesses as much as their strengths.

He leaned towards the other two. 'Okay, listen carefully. This is what we're going to do…'

Caro was brushing her teeth on Friday morning when Jack's knock sounded on her door.

She knew it was Jack. She refused to contemplate too closely *how* she knew that, though.

She rinsed her mouth and considered not answering.

'Caro? I have the snuffbox.'

His voice penetrated the thick wood of her door. She stared at it, and then flew across to fling it open. 'If you're teasing me, Jack, I'll—'

He held out the snuffbox, and for a moment all she could do was stare at it.

'Oh!'

She could barely believe it. Maybe…maybe disaster could be averted after all.

With fingers that trembled she took it from him, hardly daring to believe this was the very same snuffbox she'd lost. She took Jack's arm and pulled him into the flat, and then ran to get her eyeglass. She examined it in minute detail.

'What are you doing?'

'Making sure it's authentic and not a replica.'

'Well…?' he asked when she set the eyeglass to the table.

She wanted to dance on the spot. 'It's the very same snuffbox I lost last week.'

She wanted to hug him, but remembered what had happened the last time she'd let her elation overcome her reserve. She pressed a hand to her chest to try and calm the pounding of her heart.

'You've saved the day—just as you promised you would. How? How did you do it?'

He shuffled his feet and darted a glance towards the kitchen. 'Is that coffee I smell?'

She suddenly realised he was wearing the same clothes she'd last seen him in, and that he needed a shave. She padded into the kitchen and poured them a mug of coffee each. She set his mug to the table.

'Have a seat.'

With a groan, he unhooked his satchel from his shoulder and dropped it to the floor, before planting himself in a chair and bringing the mug to his lips. 'Thank you.'

She frowned at him. 'Have you had any sleep in the last two days?'

He made an impatient movement with his hand. 'It's no matter. I can sleep on the plane.'

He was returning to Australia *today*? An ache started up inside her.

It's for the best.

Except the misery he was trying to hide beat at her like a living, breathing thing.

She sipped coffee in an attempt to fortify herself. 'How did you find the snuffbox? Who had it?'

'It was all a comedy of errors, believe it or not, and frankly you needn't have hired me in the first place.'

She frowned. 'What are you talking about?'

He eyed her over the rim of his mug. 'You have an army of cleaners coming in to the Mayfair house twice a week, yes?'

'Yes.'

'It appears that when Barbara made her midnight raid on the safe she dropped the snuffbox on the stairs.'

So why hadn't she or Paul found it?

'The next day the maid dusting the staircase found it and placed it in the sideboard in the dining room. She thought it was some kind of fancy spice pot, or something along those lines.'

'And therefore thought it belonged with the dining ware?'

'Of course she forgot to mention to anyone what she'd done.'

She gaped at him. 'So it was never Barbara? Oh, I should burn in brimstone forever for thinking such a shocking thing of her!'

His lips pressed together in a thin tight line.

'It's such a simple explanation! But…how did you find all of this out?'

'I rang the cleaning service you use, spoke to the woman in charge and asked her to check with the staff.'

Amazingly simple—and yet…

'I'd never have thought of that. I did right in hiring you,

Jack.' She swallowed. 'You've saved the day and I can't thank you enough.'

'I'm glad I could help.'

He rose and her heart started to burn.

'It's time I was going.' He barely looked at her. 'Good-bye, Caro.'

She couldn't make her legs work to walk him to the door. It closed behind him and she had to blink hard for several moments and concentrate on her breathing.

Last night's cake box still sat on the table. Seizing it, she strode into the kitchen and tossed it into the bin. Sugar wasn't the answer. Nothing but time would ease the pain scoring through her now.

She limped back to the table and picked up the snuff-box, clasped it to her chest. 'Thank you, Jack,' she whispered to the silent room. 'Thank you.'

She went to turn away—it was time for her to dress for work—when something black and silver under the table caught her attention. She reached down and picked it up. A CD. Had she dropped it? Or had Jack?

It wasn't labelled. With a shrug, she slotted it into her CD player. If it belonged to Jack she'd post it to him in Australia. She glanced at the case again, but it gave no clue.

And then two voices sounded from the speakers and her mug froze halfway to her mouth.

'I don't want to do this any more, Paul. I want Caro to know the truth.'

'We can't! We promised her father!'

CHAPTER TEN

CARO PLANTED HERSELF in a chair and listened to the CD twice more.

'So…' She drummed her fingers against the table. 'The maid never put it in the sideboard after all…' She pressed her fingers to her temples. Paul and Barbara had joined forces to take the snuffbox *together*. She stared up at the ceiling. 'I didn't even think they *liked* each other.'

Actually, the recording didn't change her mind in that regard. Obviously her father had compelled them to sabotage her career. No doubt in the hope that she'd take over that damn trust. What did he have on them? Why would they agree to do such a thing to her? She'd thought they cared about her!

She shot to her feet to pace about the room. Why had Jack lied? Why hadn't he told her the truth? For a moment she wanted to throw things at the walls and shout *No one can be trusted. No one!*

She passed a hand across her eyes. Except that would be histrionic—not to mention an unwarrantable generalisation—and she didn't do histrionics.

With the most unladylike curse she knew, she spun away to storm into her bedroom. She'd just had over a week's leave. The least she could do was get her butt over to Fredrick Soames's house in Knightsbridge and sell him this rotten snuffbox.

* * *

Freddie set the snuffbox to his desk and pursed his lips. 'It's a pretty piece, I grant you.'

'It *is* pretty.' Caro crossed her legs. 'But…?'

'The price is rather steep.'

'That's nonsense, Freddie, and you know it.' She'd known the Honourable Frederick Robert Arthur Soames for her entire life. Her father and his father had both been at Eton together.

He pulled a notepad towards him. 'I'd be prepared to pay…' He jotted down an amount, turned the pad around and pushed it across towards her.

The sum was significantly lower than the price she'd just quoted him.

Freddie loved to play games. And he really loved a bargain.

Caro crossed out the amount and jotted down a significantly higher figure. 'In all conscience I cannot allow my client to accept an amount lower than that. If you choose to pass at that price then we'll take our chances at auction.'

His face dropped comically. 'But…but that's the original asking price.'

She smiled. After all the trouble this snuffbox had caused, she had every intention of getting the best price possible for it.

'Listen, Caro, I know it's your job to do the best for your client, but we've known each other for a long time and—'

'Don't you dare say another word, Freddie Soames. We may have known each other forever, and we may indeed be friends, but I am *not* cutting you a deal on this snuffbox. You should know better than to even ask.'

His shrug was completely without rancour. 'You can't blame a guy for trying. You have a hard-nosed reputation in the industry.' He said it in such an admiring tone that she had to laugh. 'It's so at odds with your personality outside of work that I just…wanted to try my luck,' he finished with a grin.

At odds with her…? That made her grow sober again. Was that why Paul and Barbara had thought they could walk all over her? Was that why…? She gulped. Was that why Jack had left her five years ago?

If she brought the same backbone and strength of purpose to her personal relationships as she did to her work, would it make a difference? If she'd put her foot down and stated, *This is what I expect from all of you—honesty, respect and acceptance. And if you can't promise me that then…then…*

Jack had said he could give her all of those things.

But she hadn't believed him.

Out of nowhere her heart started to thump.

'Caro, are you okay?'

She started, and shot Freddie a smile. 'I'm simply tickety-boo, Freddie.'

It occurred to her that now she had the snuffbox back in her keeping she was curiously reluctant to let it go.

Time to force Freddie's hand. 'Richardson's has given you first option on this beautiful example of a seventeenth-century snuffbox, but you must understand that interest in these items is always high. I'm going to count to three. You have until then either to accept at the asking price—' she touched a finger to the notepad '—or to decline.'

'No need to count, Caro.' He leaned back, fingers clasped behind his head. 'I'm going to chance my luck when it goes to auction.'

She laughed at the light of competition that sparkled from his eyes. As she'd known it would. '*If* it makes it to auction, Freddie. Don't count your chickens.'

She wrapped the snuffbox in a soft cloth, placed it into

a protective box and slipped it into her purse. 'It was lovely to see you.' She shook his hand and left.

She stood on his doorstep for a moment. Freddie Soames lived in Knightsbridge…maybe that was why Lawrence Gardner popped into her mind. She glanced at her watch. The interview with Freddie hadn't taken nearly as long as she'd thought it would. On impulse, she dialled Lawrence's number.

'I wonder if you have a moment or two to spare for me?' she said after their greetings.

'Absolutely, my dear girl. I'm in the Knightsbridge branch today.'

'I'm about two minutes away.'

'So this is the offending item that caused all the trouble.' Lawrence handed the snuffbox back to her. 'I'm very pleased you recovered it.'

'Oh, yes, I am too.' She told him the story Jack had given her.

His gaze slid away. 'All's well that ends well, then.'

She folded her arms. 'You don't believe that story any more than I do. I *know* Paul and Barbara were behind the snuffbox's disappearance…at my father's behest.'

'Ah…'

'Has Jack been to see you since our…uh…unscheduled meeting at the bank on Wednesday?'

He hesitated and then nodded. 'I believe that boy has your best interests at heart, though, Caro.'

She pulled in a breath and nodded. 'I do too.'

'Right, well… Jack came to see me this morning. He wanted a couple of bank cheques drawn up.'

She listened closely to all he had to tell her and her heart started to burn. 'Father blackmailed Barbara and… and threatened to cut off the funds for her mother's care? That's…diabolical!'

Lawrence winced.

'Why didn't she come to me? She had to know that I'd take care of it.'

She suddenly recalled Barbara's words from the night they'd spent in Kent. *'You've always been a funny little thing... It can be very difficult to get a handle on how you truly feel.'* Maybe...maybe Barbara *hadn't* known.

She cursed her own reserve. And Barbara's.

'I can't imagine, though, why *Paul* would agree to do such a thing.' Lawrence sighed. 'He dotes on you.'

'Oh, that's easy.' She rubbed a hand across her chest. 'He was in love with my mother. I believe she's the only woman he's ever loved.'

'Good God!'

She smiled at the appalled expression on Lawrence's face. 'No, no—I don't believe for a single moment that there was anything between them other than mutual respect and friendship.'

'Thank God!' He sagged back in his chair. 'But if you're right it would explain why he'd be so set on you taking over management of the trust.'

'I can't believe I never saw it before now, but all my life he's tried to gently guide me towards it. I thought he was simply trying to be conciliatory—to improve matters between Father and me.'

A sense of betrayal niggled at the edges of her consciousness, but she pushed it away. It would be easy to retreat behind a sense of outrage and betrayal, but what would that achieve? The last time she'd done that it had led to five years of misery.

'So Jack's taken it upon himself to try and put this all to rights?'

Lawrence spread his hands and nodded. 'What are you going to do? Is there anything I can do to help?'

She leaned across his desk to clasp his hand. 'You have

already done so much and I will be eternally grateful.' She pulled in a breath. '*I'm* going to make things right—that's what I'm going to do. Although I could use some help with a couple of practical matters.'

He straightened. 'I'm a practical man. Fire away.'

Three hours later Caro let herself into the house in Mayfair. A voice emerging from the room to her left informed her that Paul, at least, was in. She moved across to the doorway of her father's study and her heart hammered up into her throat, before settling back to bang and crash in her chest.

Jack!

Jack was here. He hadn't left for Australia yet. Somewhere inside her she started to salsa.

The internal twirling faltered when she remembered that flights to Australia didn't usually depart Heathrow until the evening. Her heart nose-dived to her toes. Jack's flight was probably six or seven hours away yet. He still had plenty of time to make it.

Unless she managed to change his mind.

She moistened suddenly dry lips. Her happiness was in her own hands. All she had to do was reach out and take what she wanted.

If she dared.

'Caro, darling!' Barbara shot to her feet, a look of dismay settling over her features. 'Darling, I…' She fell back into her chair, her words trailing off as if she had no idea what to say.

Caro didn't blame her. Squaring her shoulders, she strode up to the desk. 'I'd like to take the floor for a moment, if you don't mind,' she said to Jack and Paul.

She pointed to the two chairs on either side of Barbara, and after a moment's hesitation the two men moved to them.

Paul could barely meet her eye.

Jack stared at her with such undisguised hunger it made her blood rush in her ears, but his gaze snapped away when he realised she'd surveyed him and he shuffled the papers he held in his hands instead. An ache swelled through her.

She slid up to sit on the desk, but had to swallow a couple of times before she could risk speaking. Her voice jammed in her chest again when Jack darted a glance of frank appreciation at her legs.

That sealed it. She knew *exactly* what she was going to do.

But first…

She reached into her purse and pulled out the CD. 'I believe this belongs to you, Jack.'

Barbara closed her eyes. Paul paled.

Jack's eyes darkened as he took it from her outstretched hand.

'It must've fallen from your bag when you visited me earlier. You really should learn to fasten the latches on that thing.'

She could see his mind flicking back to this morning. 'I pulled the snuffbox from it and…'

'And then dropped said bag to the floor when you had your coffee.'

'Without fastening it again.' The pulse in his jaw pounded. He raised the CD slightly. 'Did you listen to it?'

'Oh, yes.'

All three of them winced.

She reached out and plucked the documents Jack held from his other hand. Cheques. One made out to the facility where Barbara's mother resided and the other made out to her mother's trust. Both for huge sums. *Oh, Jack! This isn't your mess to clean up.* Shaking her head, Caro tore the cheques into sixteen fragments apiece.

Barbara pressed the heel of her hand to her mouth to stifle a sob.

'Okay, so here's the deal,' Caro continued calmly, dumping the scraps of paper on the desk behind her. She opened her folder and brought out the first in a series of documents. 'Barbara, this paperwork here, as you'll see, is a contract between the facility where your mother is kept and me. It ensures that your mother's care is guaranteed. I do wish you'd trusted me to take care of this in the first place.'

God, she was magnificent.

Jack stared at Caro and his skin tingled as a rush of warmth shot through him. He hadn't been sure how she'd deal with the truth of all this, but he could see now that he should have trusted her with it. She was all class.

'Oh, I...' Barbara had to wipe her fingers beneath her eyes, to mop up the tears that had started to fall.

'I understand that my...reserve has made you unsure of me. I am sorry for that. I also understand that your loyalty must've felt torn between my father and me as well.'

The other woman lifted her chin. 'The fact of the matter is I did marry your father for his money, darling. I wanted my mother taken care of properly.'

Caro nodded. 'And in return for that my father received a wonderful wife who always went the extra mile for him. I still think he received the better part of that deal. I want you to know that I've had several million pounds transferred into your account—'

'That is absolutely unnecessary! I don't—'

'Humour me, Barbara. I've also had the deeds to the villa in Spain transferred into your name.'

Barbara swallowed. 'You'd like me to move out?' She nodded. 'Of course you do—'

'Absolutely not! I just know how much you love that villa. You and Father honeymooned there.'

'Oh, but, Caro darling, it's all too much.'

'Nonsense.' Caro turned from Barbara to Paul. 'Now, Paul.'

Jack leaned back, folding his arms and enjoying the show.

'It's occurred to me that if my mother's trust means so much to you then *you* are probably the perfect person to manage it. This document here—' she held up a sheaf of papers '—names you as chairman of the trust's board.'

'Miss Caroline, I—'

'Caro!' she ordered.

Paul swallowed. 'Caro, I… I don't know what to say.'

'Say you'll accept the position and that you'll do your best to execute the duties of the post.'

'You have my word,' he croaked, falling back into his seat.

'I've also arranged for a pension for you. Something my father should've taken care of before he died. It will be in addition to the salary you draw from administering the trust.'

The older man's head shot up. 'I won't be drawing a salary from the trust! It will be an honour to administer it.'

Caro didn't look the least surprised by this avowal. Jack would bet she'd factored that in and had made sure that his pension was very liberal.

'Good grief, Caro! I can't accept this,' he said when she handed him the paperwork outlining the details of the pension. 'This is far too generous.'

'You've earned it. You gave my father sterling service for over thirty years. Besides, I can afford it…and it's what I want.'

Caro drew in a deep breath, and such a roar of longing spiked through Jack, his hand clenched about the seat of his chair to keep him there.

'Now, I want you both to know that these things I've set in motion today are set in stone. They cannot be changed.

I cannot revoke or undo what I've just promised you. You are both free to simply walk away from me now, without the fear of any reprisals.'

The room went so still that all Jack could hear was the tick of the grandfather clock out in the entrance hall.

Caro pressed her hands together. 'So now it's time for me to cast aside my wretched reserve and for us to speak plainly with each other. Barbara and Paul—I consider the two of you my family.'

Jack's heart burned that she hadn't included *him* in that number.

'I care about the two of you a great deal. I was hoping my affection was returned.'

'It *is*, darling!'

'I love you like my own daughter!'

'But that didn't stop either of you from trying to sabotage my happiness. If the two of you really care about me then what I demand from you is respect, loyalty and acceptance for who I am. If you can't give me that, then we need to go our separate ways.'

Paul shot to his feet. 'You will have it to my dying day,' he vowed.

'Yes, darling, you have *my* word too.'

Caro's smile was sudden, sweet and utterly enchanting. 'Then we can continue on as we've been doing. I mean to give up my flat and we can all live here in this ridiculous house like the mismatched dysfunctional family that we are.'

Barbara stood in swift elegant motion and pulled Caro from the desk to fold her in a hug. 'Darling, that sounds marvellous.'

Paul waited beside them, impatiently moving from foot to foot, until he had a chance to engulf Caro in a bear hug. 'Splendid! Splendid!'

With a heart that throbbed Jack slipped the strap of

his satchel over his shoulder, stood and turned towards the door.

'Where do you think you're going?' Caro called after him, before he'd had the chance to take two steps.

He pulled in a breath, but didn't turn. 'I have a plane to catch.'

'In what—six hours?'

Acid burned his stomach at the thought of flying away from her. He met her gaze briefly. 'I have to be at the airport in four hours' time and…and there are things I need to do before then.'

Number one on that list was: save face and maintain whatever pride he could.

'I was hoping… Please, Jack, could you spare me ten more minutes?'

He should say no. He should toss a casual *sayonara* over his shoulder and walk away from her with a jaunty stride.

Casual? Jaunty? *Impossible.*

Saying no to Caro? Also impossible.

His shoulders slumped. His satchel slid to the floor.

'Sure. What's ten minutes?'

But they both knew what havoc ten minutes could wreak. Six and a half years ago on a reckless impulse he'd asked her to marry him. On impulse she'd said yes. It had taken less than a minute for them to promise to build a life together.

Five years ago, when he'd thought she meant to abort their baby, it had taken him ten minutes to pack his bags and walk away.

When he'd told her he loved her yesterday, it had taken less than a minute for her to shatter his hopes.

What was ten minutes? It could be the most hellish time of his life, that was what.

Or the most heavenly.

He pushed that thought away. He could harbour no hopes.

He snapped back to himself to find Barbara slipping her arm through Paul's and leading him from the room, murmuring something about tea and cake.

He forced his gaze to Caro's. 'You want to take me to task for keeping the truth about the snuffbox from you?'

She shook her head, her smile spearing into the centre of him. 'It was kind of you to want to protect me from the truth, even if it *was* misguided. It was even kinder of you to offer such large amounts of money to both Barbara and Paul in an attempt to make things right.'

He'd hoped by buying their gratitude it would help offset some of the damage Caro's father had caused.

'If it's not that, what *do* you want to talk to me about?'

Her gaze dropped to her hands and she looked so suddenly uncertain that he took a step towards her. She glanced up and then away again. Finally she reached into her purse and pulled a wrapped object from it. He knew immediately what it was—the snuffbox.

She unwrapped it, placed it on her palm and stared at it for a long moment. 'I bought this earlier today.'

She what? 'You mean to tell me that blasted Soames bloke didn't want it after all?'

'Oh, he wanted it all right.'

Her laugh washed over him and it was all he could do not to close his eyes and memorise it—to help him through tomorrow...and all the days after that.

'But he decided to play games instead—hoping for a lower price—and I found I didn't want to part with it. Regardless of the price offered.'

She held it out to him. 'Jack, I'd like you to have it.'

His jaw dropped. 'That's absolutely not necessary. I told you I didn't require payment, and—'

'It's not payment. I know enough not to challenge you on that. This is a gift. A…a symbol.'

He snapped his mouth shut. He found himself breathing hard, as if he'd just completed the obstacle course at his old police training college. 'A symbol of what?'

She placed the snuffbox in his hand and backed up again, to lean against the edge of the desk. She pushed her bangle up her arm as far as it would go and twisted it.

'I've only just admitted this to myself, but…my heart was lost in the same way that this snuffbox was lost. You found the latter and somehow that helped me to find the former.'

His heart pounded a tattoo against his ribs. He was too afraid to hope. Caro didn't like risks. She avoided them where possible. It would be folly to think she'd risk her heart on him a second time.

'I'm not precisely sure what that means.'

She bit her lip and then looked him full in the face. Her uncertainty almost undid him.

'I never ask for what I want. I'm not sure why that's the case. Habit, I suppose. What I wanted never mattered much to my father, so I guess I thought what I wanted wouldn't matter much to anyone else either.'

'It matters to me,' he said, moving a step closer. 'Caro, are you saying that you want…*me*? That you want to give our marriage a second chance?'

Her eyes suddenly flashed. '*I* want to be the one to state what I want, Jack. I don't want to leave it up to you. I don't want to leave it up to anyone! I don't want to place people in a position where they have to guess at what I want. I want to overcome this hateful reticence of mine and say exactly what I mean—at least around you, Barbara and Paul.'

She'd just put him in the same category as the rest of her family and his heart all but stopped. It took a moment for him to catch his breath.

'What *do* you want, Caro?'

She met his gaze. 'I want *you*, Jack. I want to spend my life with you. I love you.'

He couldn't contain himself a moment longer. He closed the distance between them and hauled her into his arms. 'You know I'm never going to be able to let you go again, don't you?'

Her eyes throbbed into his. 'I like the sound of that. I also very much want you to kiss me.'

He stared at her infinitely kissable mouth and something in his chest shifted.

'You don't need to ask twice.'

He lowered his mouth towards hers and a fraction of a second before their lips met she smiled, as if she suddenly believed that she could have everything she asked for.

Her hope and delight bathed him in a warmth he'd forgotten that he needed. Cradling her face in his hands, he kissed her. Slowly. Thoroughly. Sweetly.

Her hands slid up either side of his neck and she pressed herself to him, kissing him back with the same thoroughness, the same passion and tenderness, and with the same intent to reassure and pour balm on old wounds.

He savoured every moment, something inside him filling up and easing. Then, in a flash and a touch of tongues, the kiss changed to become hungry, hot and demanding. Jack gave himself up to the heady abandon and the flying freedom of it.

He didn't know how long the kiss lasted, but when they finally eased away from each other it seemed as if the very quality of the light in the room had changed—as if a brand new day had dawned.

Caro touched her tongue to her lips, which did nothing to quieten the hunger roaring through him.

'Wow…' she breathed.

A grin stretched through him. 'You should ask for what you want more often.'

Her eyes danced. 'I mean to.' She reached up to touch his face. 'Jack, I promise to be more open and upfront with you. I know that my reserve played a big role in our troubles five years ago.'

He took her hand, kissed her fingertips. 'We can put that all behind us now. It's in the past.'

She shook her head. 'It's only in the past if we've learned from the mistakes we made back then.'

Ah.

She bit her lip. 'Jack, can you promise me honesty from now on?'

He recalled the promise she'd extracted from Barbara and Paul. 'I can promise you honesty, loyalty and acceptance.'

She smiled. 'I never doubted the second and third of those for a moment. But your urge to protect me...'

He pulled in a breath, knowing he couldn't give this promise lightly. Finally he nodded. 'I promise you honesty, Caro. Even if it's hard for me to say and hard for you to hear.'

'Thank you.'

'You promise me the same?'

'I do,' she said, without hesitation.

She bit her lip again, and while her eyes didn't exactly cloud over the light in them dimmed a fraction.

'What?' he demanded, immediately alert.

'I understand your desire for children and a family, Jack, but hundreds and thousands of couples work it out—negotiate it somehow—so I'm sure we can too, and—'

He touched a finger to her lips, halting her rush of words. 'I've been thinking about this a lot, and I think I've found a solution.'

Her eyes narrowed. 'I don't want you making any unnecessary sacrifices.'

'I don't want you doing that either.'

'Okay…'

She drew the word out and it made him smile. 'If you're not totally against the idea of having children—'

'Oh, I'm not. Not now. Being exposed to Suzie's two—being their godmother—has made me realise that I'll never become the kind of remote parent my father was.'

He stared at her. 'I wish you'd told me that was what you were afraid of five years ago.' He didn't want to make the same mistakes ever again where this woman was concerned. He pushed a strand of hair back behind her ear. 'Why didn't you ever tell me?'

One of her shoulders lifted. 'I didn't want you to laugh at me.'

'I would never laugh at you.'

'And I didn't want my fear dismissed as nonsense.'

He nodded slowly. 'The fear isn't nonsense, but the idea that you could be anything less than a loving mother seems crazy to me,' he admitted.

'I'm confident enough in myself now to see the difference.'

He touched the backs of his fingers to her cheek. 'We married too soon, didn't we?'

Five years ago he'd wanted all his dreams to come true then and there.

She caught his hand in hers and kissed it. 'I understand we needed a trial by fire to cement what was really important. I only wish it hadn't take us five years to get through it.'

He wanted to wipe the sadness and the remembered pain from her eyes. 'I promise to never walk away from you the way I did five years ago. I should've stayed and fought for you back then. I will always fight for you, Caro.'

The brilliance of her smile almost blindsided him. 'I think I'm going to have to ask you to kiss me again.'

He laughed. 'How does this sound? When you're ready, we can start a family…and if you want to return to work then that's what you'll do, and I can be the stay-at-home parent.'

Her eyes widened, brightened. 'Really?'

'I'd love it.' He would too. 'My business is doing brilliantly, and I'm proud of it, but it's just something to fill in the time. I can hire a manager to take over operations, or even take on a partner. I might do the odd bit of consultancy work, just to keep my hand in, but building a family with you, Caro, is what I really want to do.'

She smiled back at him with a mistiness that had him throwing his head back and laughing for the sheer joy of it. 'We both have more money than either one of us will ever conceivably need. We can hire all the help we need or want—housekeepers, nannies, gardeners.'

Her eyes shone so bright they made him feel he was at the centre of the universe.

'Would you like to remain in London?' He didn't care *where* they lived.

'Oh! I hadn't thought about it. I love London, but I'm sure I'd love Australia too, and—'

'It's just—' he glanced around '—this house is huge. If we stayed here then maybe, down the track, we could think about fostering kids in need.'

He'd barely finished before she threw her arms around his neck and held him tight. 'That sounds perfect—absolutely perfect! Now, as it appears you won't kiss *me*, I'll just have to kiss you instead.'

His heart expanded until he thought it would grow too big for his chest. Her lips moved to within millimetres of his—

'Darlings, there's tea and cake if you'd like some.'

With a smile that set his blood on fire, Caro eased away to glance at Barbara. 'I'd love cake, but there's some paperwork I need Jack to go over…uh…upstairs.' Taking his hand, she led him out of the room, past a bemused Barbara and up the staircase. 'Make sure you leave us some!' she shot over her shoulder.

He started to laugh when they reached her room. 'You're not fooling anyone with that story, you know.'

'I know—but you can't expect a lifetime of reserve to simply vanish overnight. And the odd polite fiction keeps the wheels turning smoothly.'

He stared at her, barely able to believe he was there with her. 'I love you, Caro. I will cherish this and keep it safe—' he opened his hand to reveal the snuffbox '—in the same way I will always cherish your heart and do all I can to keep it safe.'

Her eyes burned into his. 'I love you, Jack. I will do everything I can think of to make you happy.'

'You promise to always tell me what you want?'

She nodded and then grinned. 'Want to know what I want right now?'

His mouth dried at the look in her eyes. 'What?' he croaked.

'You,' she whispered, moving across to stand in front of him. Reaching up on tiptoe, she pressed a kiss to the corner of his mouth. 'I want *you*.'

'You have me,' he promised, his lips descending towards hers.

'Forever?'

'Forever.'

* * * * *

MEET THE FORTUNES

Fortune (?) of the Month: Wesley "Wes" Robinson. Aka Wes Fortune?

Age: 33—and just a few minutes younger than his twin brother, which still irks him.

Vital statistics: Six feet plus with dark hair you'd love to rumple, laser-blue eyes, and don't forget that sexy brain.

Claim to Fame: Wes is the computer genius behind most of Robinson Tech's success.

Romantic prospects: Mr. Tall, Dark and Gorgeous believes "love" is nothing more than a chemical reaction. He thinks compatibility is a crock.

"I don't believe Vivian's new app can possibly work. Finding your perfect match via smartphone?

"However, I know a moneymaker when I see one. That's why I'm spending so much time conferring with Vivian. It's all about getting the product off the ground. And possibly proving my star developer wrong. It has nothing at all to do with her hazel eyes… or her persistent personality… or the way she gets me to reveal things I'd rather keep buried inside. I've heard enough of my father's Fortune history to know that wishing for a lifetime love is simply a pipe dream. Or is it?"

The Fortunes of Texas:
All Fortune's Children—
Money. Family. Cowboys. Meet the Austin Fortunes!

FORTUNE'S
PERFECT
VALENTINE

BY
STELLA BAGWELL

D1364430

MILLS
BOON®
&
™

First Published in Great Britain 2016
By Mills & Boon, an imprint of HarperCollins*Publishers*
1 London Bridge Street, London, SE1 9GF

© 2016 Harlequin Books S.A.

Special thanks and acknowledgement to Stella Bagwell for her contribution to the Fortunes of Texas: All Fortune's Children continuity.

ISBN: 978-0-263-91959-2

23-0216

After writing more than eighty books for Mills & Boon, **Stella Bagwell** still finds it exciting to create new stories and bring her characters to life. She loves all things Western and has been married to her own real cowboy for forty-four years. Living on the south Texas coast, she also enjoys being outdoors and helping her husband care for the horses, cats and dog that call their small ranch home. The couple has one son, who teaches high school mathematics and is also an athletic director. Stella loves hearing from readers. They can contact her at stellabagwell@gmail.com.

To my husband, Harrell, and son, Jason.
With love to my two Valentines.

Chapter One

"So this little square picture of a key opening a heart is going to change the dating habits of the entire nation. I tap it with my fingertip and magically it will lead me to my true love." With a mocking snort, Wesley Robinson pushed the smartphone aside. "What a crock of crap."

Vivian Blair scowled at the man sitting behind the wide mahogany desk. At this moment, it didn't matter that he was her boss, who also happened to be Vice President of Research and Development at Robinson Tech. Nor did it matter that he happened to be the sexiest man she'd ever laid eyes on. This project was her baby and she had no intentions of letting him make a mockery of her hard work.

"I beg your pardon?" she asked, her voice rising along with her irritation. "This little button you're calling a crock of crap just happens to be a product of your company. A company owned and operated by your family, I might add. Have you forgotten that you approved this idea months ago?"

Ignoring her outburst, he calmly answered, "I've not forgotten anything, Vivian."

Throughout the six years she'd worked for Wes Robinson, he'd rarely called her by her given name, and on each occasion it had never failed to rattle her senses. Her boss was always strictly business. So having her name roll off his tongue was the closest he ever got to acknowledging she was a flesh-and-blood woman.

Vivian shifted on the edge of the wingback chair and did her best to refocus her jolted thoughts on their debate. "Then why are you so intent on degrading the product? I thought you were convinced it was going to make the company a pile of money."

With confident ease, he leaned back in the oxblood leather chair. After slipping a pair of tortoise-framed glasses from his nose, he leveled a somewhat smug gaze on her face. Vivian had the very unprofessional urge to stick her tongue out at him.

"I still believe the app is going to make money. And probably lots of it," he agreed. "But that doesn't mean I believe the theory behind the dating site will hold up. In fact, I'm willing to bet that after a few months the app's popularity will sink, simply because the public is going to realize that My Perfect Match won't fulfill its promise. Still, I'm willing to gamble the initial sales of the app will outweigh its short lifespan."

It was hard enough for Vivian to deal with having his eyes sliding leisurely over her face, but hearing him discount her hard work was even worse.

Leaning forward, she said briskly, "Forgive my bluntness, Mr. Robinson, but you're wrong. Completely wrong. My Perfect Match will work. My scientific research assures me that compatibility is the key to finding a perfect mate. The app will lead the consumer to a list of questions that follows strict criteria of the most important issues and topics in a person's private life. If they're answered truthfully, the computer will be able to match you with the perfect person based on corresponding answers."

His short laugh was weighted with sarcasm. "Sorry, but you just spouted a bunch of hooey. When a man sidles up to a woman at the bar, you think he has a list of questions on his mind?" Not waiting for her to answer, he plowed on, "There's only one question on his mind. And that's whether she'll say yes or no. He doesn't give a damn whether she eats fish twice a week, walks a mile a day or has a cat for a pet."

Vivian's back teeth clamped together as she fought to hold on to her dignity and her temper. "I might remind you that this app isn't an instrument for locating a one-night stand!" She tapped the screen of her phone. "This is a social aid to help lonely people find a perfect partner—one to spend the rest of their lives with happily. Or have you heard of that concept before?"

A wry expression crossed his face, and Vivian allowed her gaze to take a slow survey of his rugged features. At thirty-three years old, he was definitely coming into his prime, she decided. Piercing blue eyes sat beneath an unyielding line of dark brows, while a wide nose led down to a set of thin, chiseled lips. She couldn't remember a time she'd seen his strong, angled jaw without a dark shadow of day-old stubble or his short, coffee-brown hair in a style other than rumpled disarray. Yet she had to admit it was that touch of edginess that often pushed her thoughts in a naughty direction.

Many of Vivian's coworkers at Robinson Tech had trouble telling Wes apart from his identical twin, Ben, who was the newly appointed COO of the company. But Vivian could truthfully say she never got the two men mixed up. Unlike his brother Ben, Wes was rarely ever spotted in a suit and tie. Instead he usually arrived each morning for work in khakis or jeans. Yet it wasn't exactly their fashion choices that set the two men apart. Wes's quiet, reserved manner was totally opposite his brash twin's demeanor.

Clearly bored, he said, "I suppose you're talking about marriage now. I've heard enough on that subject this past month to last me a lifetime."

Since his brother Ben's wedding was taking place in about two weeks, on Valentine's Day, Vivian could only assume he was referring to that marriage. As far as she knew, Wes had never had a long-term girlfriend, much less been engaged. But then, she hardly knew what the man did outside this massive office building. She was only an employee, one of many who worked for the Robinson family.

Moving her gaze to a point just over his shoulder, she studied the skyline of downtown Austin. The capital of Texas had always been her home, yet she doubted that beyond this building, her footsteps had ever crossed Wes's path. Or, for that matter, the path of any other member of his wealthy family. That was just one of the reasons she never allowed herself to look at him as anything more than a boss, rather than a man with enough sex appeal to make a woman swoon.

Giving herself a hard mental shake, she countered his

statement with a question. "What else? If a person finds their perfect mate, the natural progression is marriage."

Vivian's gaze slipped back to his face just in time to see the corners of his mouth turn downward, and she realized this conversation was giving her more peeks into the man's private feelings than she'd ever expected to see. But then she'd never planned for this meeting to turn into a debate about dating or love or sex. Vivian hardly discussed such things with any man, much less her boss. *Awkward* couldn't begin to describe the turmoil she was feeling.

"Marriage is hardly the reason consumers will purchase the app," he said wryly. "But regardless of their motives, the concept won't work. The connection between a man and a woman is all about chemistry. It's the sparks—the fire—that fuse two people together. Not whether their likes and dislikes are the same."

Sparks? Fire? Maybe it would be nice to have a man take her into his arms and set a torch to her senses. But that sort of mindless passion didn't last. She had only to look at her own parents to see what happened between a man and a woman once the heat died and reality set in. Her mother had struggled to raise three children while her father had moved on to a younger woman. Now her mother lived alone, too disenchanted even to try to find a man to love her.

"Maybe attraction does initially pull two people together, but it hardly keeps them together," she argued. "And that's the problem My Perfect Match will fix. That's why it's going to be a huge success. Lasting relationships will eventually prove our product works."

The faint smile on his face was etched with amusement and was far too patronizing for her taste.

"I admire your enthusiasm, Ms. Blair."

He clearly didn't agree with her, and that notion bothered her far more than it should have. Vivian understood that this project had nothing to do with personal viewpoints. It was about producing a product that would ultimately make money for the company. Still, hearing his jaded ideas on the subject of relationships between men and women was maddening to her.

"But you think I'm wrong," she ventured. "If you're so sure this concept is going to be a bust, then why did you agree to it in the first place? In two weeks, on Valentine's Day, the app is scheduled to make its grand debut to the public. Don't you think it's rather late in the day to consider axing it?"

He cocked a brow at her. "What gave you the idea I want to ax it? Just because I don't believe in the concept? Look, Ms. Blair, I'm a businessman first and foremost, and I happen to believe consumers are just gullible enough to fall for this sort of baloney. As far as I'm concerned, whether it works or not is a moot point."

Wes watched as Vivian Blair's spine stiffened and her fingers fluttered to the top button of her crisp white shirt. Clearly he'd flustered the woman, which surprised him somewhat. He'd never seen her any way but cool and professional. During her six years as one of a team of computer developers employed by Robinson Tech, she'd proved herself to be dedicated, innovative and smart. She'd never failed to impress him with her work, but as a woman, she'd never really drawn a second look from him. Until this morning, when she'd snatched off her black-rimmed glasses and glared at him.

Her hazel eyes had thrown heated daggers straight at him, and her fiery reaction had caught him by complete surprise. All at once, he'd forgotten she was an employee. Instead, his mind had taken a momentary detour from work and started a subtle survey of her appearance.

He'd never thought of Vivian Blair as anything more than a coworker, a brainy, no-nonsense developer. She dressed neatly but primly in blouses and skirts that covered her slender frame with enough fabric to make even the strictest father nod with approval. What little jewelry she wore usually amounted to no more than a modest string of pearls or a fine gold chain and cross. Her pumps were low-heeled and pedestrian. And though her brown, honey-streaked hair was shiny and long enough to brush her shoulders, she rarely wore it loose. Instead she favored pulling it back into a bun or some sort of conservative twist.

No. Vivian Blair's appearance wasn't one that caught a man's attention. But seeing all that life sparking in her eyes had shown Wes a different side of her. And now, as her wide, full lips pressed into a tight line, he could only wonder what it might feel like to press his mouth to hers, to make those hard, cherry-colored lips yield softly to his.

Leaning slightly forward, he rested his forearms on the desktop and forced her gaze to meet his.

"Do you have a problem with that?" he asked.

If possible, the line of her lips grew even tighter, while her nostrils flared with disdain.

"Why should I?" she countered stiffly. "Your job is to make money. Mine is to create products. With My Perfect Match, we've both succeeded. Or, at least, we will succeed once the app goes on the market."

She was obviously trying to get her emotions under control, and for a moment Wes considered shooting a remark at her that would stir her temper all over again.

It would be fun to see, he thought. But she wasn't in his office for fun, and he hardly had time for it. Not with his twin brother, the COO of Robinson Tech, expecting Wes to put some new innovative idea on his desk every other day.

"You're on track now, Ms. Blair."

Her expression rigid, she reached for the small notepad and pen she'd placed on the edge of the desk when she'd first sat down for their meeting.

"So is the live remote still on for tomorrow?" she asked.

"I've already spoken with the producer of *Hey, USA* this morning. Our segment is set to be broadcast at nine fifteen central tomorrow. So I expect you to be ready well before that time."

She nodded. "And where do they plan to shoot this remote? The conference room?"

Wes shook his head. "Right here in my office." He jerked his thumb toward the window behind him. "We'll sit in front of the plate glass so the backdrop will be the skyline of the city. I think the producer—she wants an urban feel to the segment. You know, the image of city people hurrying and scurrying—too busy to find a date, so they rely on an app to find them one," he added drily.

"My Perfect Match is more than finding a person a date. It's—"

He held up a hand before she could slip into another sermon about compatibility and long-term relationships. Wes didn't want anything long-term. And he sure as hell wasn't looking to make any woman his wife. He'd seen his mother suffer through too many years of a loveless marriage to want the same for himself.

"Save it for the camera tomorrow," he told her. "The public is who you need to convince, not me."

She clutched the notebook to her chest, and Wes found himself wondering if she'd ever held a man to herself in that manner. He couldn't imagine it. But then, he didn't have a clue about her social life. Could be that once she was away from the Robinson Tech building, she tore off her professional demeanor and turned into a little wildcat. The idea very nearly put a smile on his face.

"Do you have any idea what sort of questions the interviewer will be asking? I'd like to be prepared."

"You've had plenty to say on the subject during our meeting this morning," he told her. "And I'm sure you won't have any problem speaking your mind tomorrow. You'll simply explain the product and how it works. I'll speak for Robinson Tech and what the company stands for. The national exposure will be great."

She dropped the notepad to her lap, but Wes's gaze lingered on the subtle curves of her breasts beneath the white shirt. Damn it, what was wrong with him? He didn't need to be ogling this woman. There were always plenty of women in his little black book who were ready to go out on a date with him. He certainly didn't need to start having romantic notions about Vivian.

"Yes, the publicity is just what the app needs," she said primly. "I only hope everything goes smoothly."

Annoyed at his straying thoughts, he frowned at her. "Why should it not?"

Clearing her throat, she said, "I've never been on television before."

He leveled a pointed look at her. "I'm sure there are plenty of things you've never done before, Ms. Blair. And there's always a first time for everything."

She straightened her shoulders, and once again Wes spotted a flash of anger in her eyes.

"You're very reassuring," she said.

"I'm not your caretaker, Ms. Blair."

"Thank God."

The words were muttered so quietly that at first Wes wasn't sure he heard them. And once he'd concluded he'd heard correctly, he couldn't quite believe she'd had the audacity to say them.

"What did you say?" he demanded.

Louder now, she answered, "I said, are we finished here?"

Any other time he would've upbraided an employee for making such a retort, but seeing Vivian Blair turn into a firecracker right in front of his eyes had knocked him off kilter.

"Yes. Be here in my office no later than eight forty-five in the morning. I don't want any glitches or mishaps happening before the interview."

"I'll certainly be on time."

She quickly rose to her feet and started toward the door. Before Wes could stop himself, he added, "And Ms. Blair, tomorrow for the interview, could you not look so—studious? My Perfect Match is all about romance. It might help if you—well, looked the part a bit more."

Her back went ramrod straight as she fixed him with a stare. "In other words, sex sells," she retorted. "Is that what you're trying to tell me?"

To a woman like Vivian, he supposed he sounded crude. But she should have understood that this was all about business. Still, something about the disdain on her face caused a wave of heat to wash up his neck and over his jaw. He could only hope the overhead lighting was too dim for her to pick up his discomfort.

Clearing his throat, he purposely swiveled his chair

so that he was facing her. He'd be damned if he let this woman make him feel the least bit ashamed.

"Ms. Blair, there's no cause for you to be offended. I'm not trying to exploit you or your gender. I'm trying to sell an idea. Having you look attractive and pretty can only help the matter."

Even from the distance of a few feet, he could see her heave out a long breath. For one split second he was so tempted to see that fire in her eyes again that he almost left his chair and walked over to her. But he forced himself to stay put and behave as her boss, instead of a hot-blooded male.

Tilting her little chin to a challenging angle, she asked brusquely, "And what about your effort in all of this, Mr. Robinson? Do you plan to wax your chest and unbutton your shirt down to your waist?"

It took Wes a moment to digest her questions, but once they sank in, his reaction was to burst out laughing.

"Touché, Vivian. I expect I deserved that."

"I expect you did," she said flatly, then turned and left the room.

As Wes watched the door close behind her, he realized this was the first time in days that he'd laughed about anything. Strange, he thought, that a brainy employee had been the one to put a smile on his face.

Shaking his head with wry disbelief, he turned his chair back to the desk and reached for a stack of reports.

By the time Vivian returned to her work cubicle, she felt certain that steam was shooting from her ears. Before today, she'd never allowed herself to think of Wes Robinson as anything other than her boss. She'd kept herself immune to his dark good looks. A rather easy task, given the fact that he was so far out of her league, she needed a telescope to see him. But their meeting this morning had definitely given her a full view of the man. And what she'd seen she certainly disliked.

"Hey, Viv, ready for lunch?"

Pressing fingertips to the middle of her puckered forehead, she looked over her shoulder to see George Townsend standing at the entrance of her work cubicle. In his early fifties, he was a tall, burly man with red hair and a thick beard to match. Other than a set of elderly parents who lived more than a thousand miles away, he had no family. Instead, he seemed content to let his work be his family. Most everyone in the developmental department considered George a social recluse. Except Vivian.

During the years they'd worked together, she'd grown close to George. Now she considered him as much of a brother as she did a coworker. And she was thankful for their friendship. In her opinion, the man was not only a computer genius but also a kind human being. He didn't care about her appearance. Nor was he interested in the size of her apartment or bank account.

"Is it that time already? I'm not really hungry yet." Actually, the way she felt at the moment, she didn't think she'd be able to stomach any kind of food for the remainder of the day. Thoughts of Wes Robinson's smart-mouthed remarks were still making her blood boil.

"It's nearly twelve," he said with a frown, then added temptingly, "and I brought enough dewberry cobbler for the both of us, too."

Sighing, she put down her pencil and rose to her feet. For George's sake, she'd do her best to have lunch and try to appear normal.

"Okay," she told him. "Let me log out and we'll go."

Once she left her desk, the two of them walked through the work area until they reached a fair-sized break room equipped with a row of cabinets, refrigerator, microwave, hot plate and coffee machine.

Even though it was lunchtime, only a handful of people were sitting at the long utility tables. Since Robinson Tech was located in downtown Austin, most of the employees who worked in Vivian's department went out to lunch. There were several good eating places within walking distance and they all strived to give quick service to the workers on a limited time schedule. But usually Vivian chose to bring her own lunch and remain in the building.

"Looks like most of your friends are out today," George said as the two of them took seats across from each other. "Guess they don't mind walking in the cold."

Vivian didn't mind the cold, either. But she did mind sitting at a table with a group of giggling women with little more on their minds than the latest hairdo, a nail salon or a man.

"The wind was very cold this morning," she agreed. "I was already here at the building before the heater in my car ever got warm."

As she'd readied herself for work this morning, she'd also dressed more warmly in dark gray slacks and dress boots. The gray cardigan she'd pulled over her white shirt had looked perfectly appropriate to her, but now, as she glanced down at herself, she was doubting her fashion choices.

Damn Wes Robinson! What did he know about women and sex and romance, anyway?

Probably a whole lot more than you do, Vivian. It's been weeks since you've been on a date, and that eve-

ning turned out to be as exciting as watching a cater-
pillar slowly climb a blade of green grass.

"Well, Mr. Robinson's office must have been plenty warm," George commented between bites of sandwich. "You looked pretty hot when you got back to your desk."

Vivian shot her friend an annoyed look. "You noticed?"

He smiled. "I just happened to look up. Did anything go wrong with the meeting?"

She let out a heavy breath. "I just don't agree with some of the man's ideas, that's all. And frankly, I'll be glad when the introduction of My Perfect Match is over and done with. I'm a computer developer, George. I don't work in advertising."

"But you are going to do the TV spot in the morning, aren't you?"

The smirk on her face revealed exactly how she felt about being on a national television show that pulled in millions of viewers each morning. "I have no choice. Wes—I mean, Mr. Robinson—wants me to explain how the app works."

"Well, it is your brainchild," George reasoned.

Reaching across the table, she gave his hand a friendly pat. "I could've never created the app without your help, George. You're the wizard here. As far as I'm concerned, you can explain how the thing works far better than I."

He chuckled. "Only the technical parts. All those questions and what they're supposed to do for the person answering them—well, that's more your line."

Vivian had stood in line for nearly ten minutes this morning at Garcia's Deli just to get one of Mr. Garcia's delicious pork sandwiches called the Cuban Cigar, but now each bite she took seemed to stick at the top of her throat.

Shaking her head, she said, "Not really. Those questions were compiled by a set of psychologists who are experts in human relationships. But I do believe in them. And you should, too, George. Otherwise, our little brainchild will be a bust."

And after the way she'd defended the new app to her cynical boss, seeing it fall flat would just about kill her.

He shrugged one thick shoulder. "I'm not worried. We've developed some stinkers before and survived. Not everything we create is going to be a huge success."

No. In this age of fast-moving technology, it was hard to predict what the public would spend its hard-earned money on. Yet Vivian knew first-hand that being lonely was a painful thing. Her many failures at finding true love were the main reason she'd come up with My Perfect Match. At the age of twenty-eight, she would be silly to consider herself an old maid, yet she was growing tired of playing the dating game and falling short of having any sort of meaningful relationship to show for it. Her own frustration led her to believe there were plenty of lonely people out there who'd be willing to give the app a try.

"That's true. But I've really stuck my neck on the chopping block for this project. More than anything, I want it to be a huge success. That's why I can't falter in the interview tomorrow."

George's coarse, ruddy features spread into a reassuring smile. "Don't think about your nerves. Just look into the camera and pretend you're talking to me. You'll be great."

Great? Sitting in front of a television camera with Wes Robinson at her side? She'd count herself lucky to simply hold herself together.

Chapter Two

Back in Wes's office, he was just hanging up the phone with the marketing department when his twin brother, Ben, walked through the door.

"Looks like I need to have a long talk with my secretary." He leaned back in the desk chair and folded his arms across his chest. "Normally, Adelle knows better than to let riffraff come into my office unannounced."

Clearly amused by his brother's sardonic jab, Ben walked over and rested the corner of his hip on Wes's desk. Dressed in a dapper gray suit and burgundy patterned tie, Ben was every inch the business man and more like their father than Wes would ever want to be. Full of brass and swagger, Ben went after anything and everything he wanted with the ferocity of a stalking tiger.

For a while after their father, Gerald, had appointed Ben the new COO of Robinson Tech, Wes had felt worse than slighted. He'd been cut to the core. As vice president of the developmental team, Wes was adept at presiding over operations, generating revenue, analyzing financial reports and motivating staff, along with a jillion other responsibilities that went along with the job. He could've handled the COO position with his eyes closed.

But Gerald had chosen to hand it to his elder twin. And to Wes the reason had been blatantly obvious. Because Ben was their father's favorite. Which wasn't hard to understand, given the fact that Ben had the same aggressive business tactics as their father, while Wes considered hard work and integrity the best way to climb the corporate ladder.

Grinning, Ben said, "I'm glad to see you're getting your wit back."

"I wasn't aware I'd ever lost it," Wes quipped.

Ben thoughtfully picked up a paperweight and held it up to the florescent light. The hunk of gray glass was the shape of a dove, and Wes wondered if Ben was thinking the bird matched his younger twin. No doubt their father would say Wes was the peaceful dove of the two, while Ben was a fierce hawk. The idea stung far more than Wes wanted to admit.

"Hmm. Ever since I got the COO position, you've been about as warm as a polar bear. I thought you'd be over Dad's decision by now."

Wes inwardly bristled while trying to make sure his expression remained bland. No one could rankle him more than his twin, but he hardly wanted Ben to know that. The man was already smug enough.

"I was over it five minutes after Dad's decision was announced," Wes told him.

Ben's expression said he found Wes's statement

laughable. Which came as no surprise. From the years when they were small boys until now, the two of them had been rivals in everything, including their parents' love and admiration. And Wes supposed he'd spent most all of his thirty-three years trying to prove he was equal or better than his slightly older brother.

"If that's the case, then why have you been giving me the cold shoulder?"

"That's all in your mind," Wes told him.

Placing the dove back on the desk, Ben rose to his feet and walked over to the wall of plate glass. Wes watched as his brother stood in a wide stance, his hands linked at his back as he stared out at the city skyline.

"If it's not the COO position that's bothering you, then you're upset with me about my search for our Fortune heritage. I would've thought you'd want to know Keaton Whitfield is our half brother."

Wesley heaved out a weary breath. Crashing Kate Fortune's ninetieth birthday party and creating a scandalous scene had been bad enough. But Ben hadn't stopped there. He'd set out on a wild search to dig up hidden branches of the family tree, and in doing so, he'd already unearthed one of their father's illegitimate children.

"I don't have any complaints about Keaton—not personally. It's you and this dogged search you're making. Just for once I wish you'd stop and consider Mother's feelings in this matter. How do you think all of this makes her feel? Can you imagine the pain and humiliation she must feel to know that her husband cheated on her, not just once, but probably many times?"

"Damn it, Wes, I'm not on a quest to punish our mother. I want Dad's rightful place in the Fortune family to be reestablished. I want the Fortunes, especially Kate, to have to acknowledge the truth publicly."

Wes snorted. "The truth! Regarding our father, we don't know what the hell the truth might be. Dad is hiding things about his past. Rachel already figured out that much when she found some of Dad's old correspondence and the driver's license with his name listed as Jerome Fortune. But as far as I'm concerned, Dad can keep his secrets. I'm perfectly content with the number of siblings I have now. And I sure don't need the Fortune name tacked on to Robinson just to make me feel important."

With a shake of his head, Ben walked back over to Wes's desk, but this time he didn't take a seat. Instead, he stood, his hands jammed in the pockets of his trousers as he gazed down at his brother.

"We see everything about this Fortune thing differently. Wouldn't you like to know the truth about our father?"

Wes answered, "Not if the truth hurts."

Ben grimaced. "Did you ever think that restoring the integrity of our father's heritage might help mend some of the cracks in our family?"

Wes wanted to ask him how uncovering Gerald's true parentage could possibly mend years of their father's deceit, but he didn't bother. Instead, he said, "I'm not the only one against this quest of yours. Most of our siblings side with me on this thing. The Robinson family doesn't need the bad publicity that this expedition of yours might bring to our name and Dad's legacy in the business world." He leveled a challenging look at his twin. "In the end, Ben, what will we really gain?"

"The truth. Justice. Vindication. Take your pick. Although I doubt any of those reasons are enough to satisfy you."

Knowing he was wasting his time and effort on the Fortune family matter, Wes decided to move their conversation elsewhere. "I was about to go to lunch. Was there some reason you stopped by my office this morning? Other than to discuss Dad's hidden past?"

"Actually, I stopped by to ask you about the new app you're promoting for Valentine's Day. I hear you're getting television coverage."

"That's right. Tomorrow, in fact. A colleague and I will be doing a live remote for *Hey, USA* from here in my office."

"A national morning show? Impressive," Ben said, then grinned slyly. "I'm surprised you managed to garner their attention. You must be doing something right, little brother."

Even though physical wrestling matches with his twin had ended in their high school days, there were times Wes still got the playful urge to box his brother's jaw.

"Thanks, but in case you haven't noticed, we do have an excellent marketing department at Robinson Tech," Wes told him. "And given the fact that dating and love and all that sort of nonsense usually garner lots of attention, it wasn't hard for them to snare a segment on *Hey, USA*."

Ben shot his brother a patient smile. "Nonsense? Sorry, brother, but you have a lot to learn. Finding the right girl to love is what life is all about. When you meet finally meet her, you'll understand completely."

Wes couldn't imagine any woman making him want to step into the role of husband and father. Not with the example Gerald had set for his sons.

"There is no right girl," Wes told him. "Not for me.

But that doesn't mean I'm not happy for you. How are the wedding plans coming along?"

"Everything is on track, I think."

"I'm assuming the wedding is going to be a big affair," Wes stated the obvious. He'd already overheard his brother discussing an orchestra and enough bottles of expensive champagne to float a battleship.

"Ella deserves the very best. I've told her she can have anything she wants and I'm going to make sure she gets it." His features grew soft. "When you really love a woman, Wes, you want to give her the world. When the time comes, you'll understand that part of it, too."

Wes could understand his brother wanting to give his fiancée the best of everything. From what he understood, Ella was raised by a single mom in a household with very little money. To make matters worse, her younger brother had cerebral palsy and needed extra care. What did surprise Wes was the amount of love and affection he saw on Ben's face each time he spoke of his fiancée. Wes had never imagined his brother capable of such tender feelings. But somehow Ella had managed to bring out the gentle side of the tiger.

"I'm glad you want to make Ella happy. She does deserve it. But as for me, I'm content to let you be the married twin. I'm staying single."

"Never say never, brother," Ben warned. "When you stand up at the wedding as my best man, the love bug just might bite you."

"I'll be sure and wear plenty of bug spray underneath my tux," Wes replied.

Chuckling, Ben started toward the door. "I'm off to lunch. Good luck on tomorrow's remote. If I'm not in a meeting at that hour, I'll try to drop by and watch you in action."

"I'll do my best not to let the company down."

With his hand on the doorknob, Ben paused long enough to glance over his shoulder. "That's one thing I never worry about."

Wes might have lost the COO position to his twin, but he could never blame Ben for Gerald's decision. No matter the rivalry between the two of them, he and Ben had the special bond of love that most twins shared. As far as Wes was concerned, their bond might get a bit frazzled at times, but it would never be broken.

"Thanks, Ben."

Once his brother disappeared through the door, Wes left his desk and grabbed a heavy jacket from a small closet. Outside his office, he paused at his secretary's desk. At eighty years old, Adelle should have been gray and prune-faced. Instead, her red, perfectly coifed hair was merely threaded with gray and her smooth skin could have been a poster for the Fortune Youth Serum. Wes figured most women Adelle's age had given up working long ago. But Adelle showed very little sign of slowing down, much less heading for a rocking chair. Each day after work, she walked a mile, then stopped at her favorite bar for a gin and tonic.

At the moment, she was peering at him over the top of pink-framed reading glasses.

"I'm going down the street for lunch," he informed her. "Is there anything on my agenda before one thirty?"

She glanced at a spiral-bound notepad lying on the left side of the desk, and Wes inwardly shook his head. The woman worked for one of the most technically advanced computer companies in the world, but she chose to use paper and pencil. Wes overlooked Adelle's archaic work preferences, mainly because he liked her and couldn't imagine his life without her in it. And as a secretary, she was priceless. As far as he was concerned, he didn't care if she used a chisel and stone. All that mattered to him was that she always kept his office running smoothly.

"No. Nothing until two," she declared. "And that meeting is with Mort. I've cut you thirty minutes for him. Is that enough time?"

Mort Conley was a member of the same developmental team that included Vivian Blair. The young guy was a guru at creating computer commands, but he lacked the creative imagination to create an innovate product on his own, like Vivian had with My Perfect Match. Still, Wes respected his enthusiasm and had agreed to look at a new app design related to sports fans.

"Should be plenty," he answered. "And I'll be back before two."

Wes started to move away from the secretary's desk, but she stopped him with another question.

"What did you do to Ms. Blair? She stalked out of your office like she wanted to murder somebody."

It wasn't unusual for Adelle to speak her mind with Wes. After all, she'd been his secretary for many years, and over that time they'd grown close. Still, it surprised him that she'd taken that much notice of Vivian Blair.

"I didn't *do* anything to her. I simply told her to be prepared for the TV segment in the morning."

Clearly unconvinced, the woman smirked at him. "Before today I've never seen as much as a frown on Vivian's face. You must have said something mean—or threatened her in some way. What were you thinking? She's one of the brightest workers on the developmental team! Along with that, she's a sweet little soul who wouldn't swat a bee even if it was stinging her."

Vivian had hardly come off as a sweet little soul this

morning when he'd voiced his personal feelings about her computer-generated idea of dating, Wes thought. To Adelle he said, "I wasn't aware you knew Vivian so well."

His secretary let out an unladylike snort. "You don't have to have supper with a person every night to know her. Women have instincts about other women and plenty of other things. You ought to understand that, Mr. Robinson."

Considering the vast difference in their ages, it seemed ridiculous for Adelle to call him "Mr. Robinson," a fact he'd pointed out to her many times before. But she insisted that calling him Wes wouldn't appear professional, so he'd given up trying to change her.

"Ah, yes. Women and their instincts," he said drily. "They're always right. I'm sure your late husband never argued with you."

"Rudy always respected my opinion, God rest his soul. That's why we celebrated fifty-five years of marriage before he passed on. You need to remember to respect Vivian's opinion—whether you agree with it or not."

Wes stared at her. "Have you been pressing your ear against the door of my office?"

"I hardly need to," she retorted, then turned her attention back to the work on her desk.

As Wes made his way out of the Robinson Tech office building, he mentally shook his head. This morning, he'd heard all he wanted to hear about women and dating and love. Yet as he passed the area where Vivian Blair worked, he found himself wondering if she was still miffed at him. And wondering, too, if she ever went out to lunch with a man, or a romantic dinner in the evening.

While heading down the sidewalk to his favorite bar

and grill, Wes very nearly smiled at that last notion. He couldn't imagine Vivian Blair finding her perfect match in a dimly lit café with violin music playing sweetly in the background and soft candlelight flickering in her hazel eyes. No, she'd be looking for her perfect man in a stuffy computer lab.

The next morning before she left her apartment, Vivian gave her image one last glance in the mirror. Last night she'd agonized for hours over what to wear for the television segment. When Wes had suggested she not look so studious, her first instinct had been to go out and find a dress that showed plenty of cleavage and lots of leg, a pair of fishnet stockings and platform heels. If he wanted a ditzy bimbo to represent Robinson Tech, then she'd give him one. But in the end, she had too much pride to make such a fool of herself. She didn't need to show Wes she could be sexy. She needed to prove that a compatible mate was far more important than flaming-hot chemistry.

Stepping back from the cheval mirror, she adjusted the hem of the close-fitting black turtleneck, then smoothed her hands over the hips of the matching black slacks she'd chosen to wear. The garments weren't frilly or feminine, but their close-fitting cut revealed her slender curves. And her golden hoop earrings were far more daring than the pearl studs she normally wore to work.

Wes Robinson would be unhappy because she didn't look like a sex kitten, Vivian supposed. But she didn't care. She was hardly going to change her style or her viewpoint for him.

Some fifteen minutes later, she parked her car in the underground parking garage of Robinson Tech and rode the elevator up to the floor that housed the developmental team, along with Wes's office.

By the time she neared her work space, George was already there waiting for her to arrive.

Glancing at his watch, he said, "Damn, Vivian, I thought you were going to be late."

"I had a bad night and slept through the alarm," she explained. Actually, *bad night* was an understatement. She'd lain awake for hours, her thoughts vacillating between Wes's infuriating remarks and concerns about the television interview. When she'd applied her makeup, she'd tried her best to hide the circles of fatigue beneath her eyes. "Do I look okay? I mean, for television?"

He let out a low whistle, and Vivian laughed.

"Thanks, George, for your vote of confidence. I definitely need it this morning. My stomach is fluttering like it's full of angry bees."

"I'll go fetch you a cup of coffee with plenty of cream. That should help."

"No! Thank you, George. My nerves are already frazzled enough without a dose of caffeine." To be honest, she was about to jump out of her skin. The notion of being on national television was scary. Especially to someone who'd practically wilted into a faint when she'd been forced to give a salutatorian speech at her high school graduation ceremony. Yet if she was being honest with herself, she had to admit it was the thought of seeing Wes again that was really tying her stomach into knots. Which was ridiculous. She'd worked closely with the man for several years now.

Yes, but she'd never had an argument about love and sex and marriage with him before.

Turning to her desk, Vivian flipped on her computer and locked her handbag in the bottom drawer.

"Hey, Viv, good luck on the TV spot this morning. Are you ready to face the camera?"

Vivian looked around to see Justine, a fellow developer, standing next to George at the entrance of the cubicle. The petite young blonde wearing a short, chic hairdo and a tight pencil skirt was more Wes's style, Vivian couldn't help thinking.

"Thanks, Justine. I'm telling myself I'm ready whether I am or not. Actually, I wish you or George would take my place in this interview. I feel like I'm headed toward a firing squad."

Justine laughed. "George and I aren't camera-friendly. We're tech geeks, right, George?"

The burly man chuckled. "Right. But with you representing us, you can show everybody that it's our team that keeps this company in the black. Without our creations, they wouldn't have anything to sell. If My Perfect Match becomes a hit, we might actually get the recognition around here that we deserve."

"And a bonus to go with it," Justine added on a hopeful note.

"Oh, thanks, you two," Vivian said drily. "I really needed that added pressure right now."

George glanced at his watch. "You'd better head on to the boss's office," he warned. "You don't want to be late."

Already turning to leave, Justine said, "And I'm going to go tune in to *Hey, USA*. Do us proud, Viv."

Moments later, as Vivian headed to Wes's office, the word *proud* continued to waltz through her head. Yes, she had pride in her work as a developer and pride as a woman who had her own ideas of what made relationships work. This morning when the camera started rolling, she had to make sure she was strong, persuasive and full of conviction, even if Wes believed her ideas were a bunch of crap.

When she reached Adelle's desk, the secretary waved her onward. "I should warn you, it's a madhouse in there, Vivian. Don't let the chaos rattle you."

"I'll do my best," Vivian told her, while thinking it wasn't the broadcast crew she was concerned about; it was her irritating boss.

Resisting the urge to smooth her hair, Vivian opened the door to Wes's office and stepped inside. In that instant, she realized Adelle's warning was correct. The place was a jumbled mess of equipment and people. Behind Wes's desk, near the vast window overlooking the city, lights and cameras were being set up to garner the best angle. Cables and electrical wirings were being pulled here and there over the polished parquet, while, across the room, a makeup person was trying to brush powder across Wes's forehead.

"Get that stuff away from me," he ordered the diminutive blonde chasing after him with a long-handled makeup brush. "I don't care if my face shines."

"I'm sorry, Mr. Robinson, but the glare of the light—"

Before the harried woman could finish her plea, Wes quickly walked over to Vivian standing uncertainly in the middle of the room.

"Good morning, Ms. Blair. Are you ready for this?" He waved a hand to the commotion of the crew behind them.

She drew in a bracing breath, while trying to ignore the way his blue eyes were making a slow, deliberate search of her face. What was the man thinking? That she needed help from the makeup woman? The idea stung.

"I think so. I've been going over all the things I

need to say about My Perfect Match. I just hope the interviewer asks the right questions. Do you know what anchorperson will be doing our segment?"

"Ted Reynolds. I rarely watch television, so I'm not that familiar with the guy. Are you?"

Vivian rubbed her sweaty palms down the sides of her hips. "Yes. He's the darling of the network morning shows and the reason *Hey, USA* is such a hit."

"Great. The more star power, the better for us," Wes remarked, then suddenly wrapped his hand over her shoulder. "Are you okay, Vivian? You're looking very pale."

If she resembled a ghost, then the shock of his touch was taking care of the problem. Hot blood was shooting straight from his hand on her shoulder all the way to her face. He'd never touched her before. Not like this. Maybe their fingers had inadvertently brushed from time to time, but he'd never deliberately put his hand on her. Why had he suddenly decided to touch her today of all days?

Don't be stupid, Vivian. The man is simply steadying you because you look like a wilted noodle ready to fall at his feet. That's all it means. Nothing more.

"I'm fine," she muttered. "I just want this to be over with so I can get back to work."

She was trying to decide how to disengage her shoulder from his hand without appearing too obvious, when a member of the production crew spoke up.

"Mr. Robinson, it's nearly time to go on the air. We need you and Ms. Blair to take your seats and let us wire you with earpieces."

The thin young man with a shaved head, red goatee and skintight black jeans motioned to the two of them, prompting Vivian to ask, "Who is he?"

"A guy who wishes he was in Hollywood instead of Austin," Wes said drily, then added in a more serious tone, "actually, his name is Antonio. He's the manager of this affiliate crew."

With his hand moving to the small of her back, Wes ushered her forward. "Come on. Let's go put on our act."

Act? Wes might be planning to put on an act for the camera. But Vivian was going to speak straight from the heart. Whether he liked it or not.

Chapter Three

Five minutes later, Wes and Vivian sat side by side in a pair of dark blue wingback chairs and stared at a monitor positioned in front of them, yet out of view of the camera lens.

A few steps to their left, Antonio stood at the ready, his finger pointed at the monitor. "Get ready," he instructed. "As soon as this commercial ends, Ted will greet you and introduce you to the viewing audience."

Vivian's heart was suddenly pounding so hard she could hardly hear herself think. As much as she wanted to duck behind the chair and hide from the camera, she had to remain at Wes's side and face the viewing audience.

Her hands laced tightly together upon her lap while her mouth felt as if she'd just eaten a handful of chalk. Just as she was trying to convince herself she wasn't going to panic, she felt a hand at the side of her face.

Turning slightly, she realized with a sense of shock

that the hand belonged to Wes and his fingers were gently tucking her hair behind her ear.

"So everyone can see your face better," he explained under his breath.

As if Vivian wasn't already shaken enough, the man had to start touching her like a familiar lover! The idea of being on television must be doing something to him, she thought.

Sucking in a deep breath, she resisted the urge to shake her hair loose so that it would drape against her cheek. "I think—"

Antonio suddenly interrupted her retort. "Here we go," he warned. "Three, two, one—you're on!"

Vivian straightened stiffly in her seat and stared dazedly at the television monitor, while inches away, Wes leaned comfortably back and, with an easy smile, gazed at the camera.

What a ham! During the years she'd been at Robinson Tech, she'd not heard of anyone in the company's developmental team or its vice president being on television. Yet he was behaving as though he did this sort of thing every day.

Just as she was thinking Wes ought to go into the acting profession, Ted Reynolds's image popped onto the screen. Dressed in a flamboyant, brick-red jacket and a blue patterned tie, he had subtly highlighted hair slicked back from his broad face. Through the earpiece she could hear his voice giving the two of them a routine greeting and introduction.

Once they'd responded to his welcoming words, Ted quickly slipped into the role of interviewer. When he asked Wes to give the audience an overview of the company, her boss smoothly went into a brief summary of what Robinson Tech was all about, and the huge strides it had made in recent years at providing the consumer with affordable, up-to-date technology for use in homes and offices.

While Wes was doing a flawless job at praising the company's capabilities and progress, Vivian was trying her hardest to remain focused on the words being exchanged between the two men. But she was rapidly losing the battle. Instead of following their conversation, her mind began drifting to the ridiculous. Like the tangy scent of expensive cologne wafting from Wes's white dress shirt. The way his dark hair lay in mussed waves and the shape of his long fingers resting against his thigh. On his right hand he wore a heavy ring set with onyx, but the left hand was bare. No, she thought wryly. Wes wouldn't be wearing a ring on his left. Not unless a perfect princess came along and swept him up in a cloud of bliss.

Stop it, Vivian! Get your mind back on track! Otherwise, you're going to be lost.

The words of warning going off in her head prompted her to give herself a hard mental shake and stare intensely at the monitor. Maybe if she kept her eyes on Ted Reynolds, she'd forget all about Wes's nearness.

The popular host continued, "In the past few years, Robinson Tech has given us some great products. The tablet for kids—when it first came on the market, my daughter was jumping up and down for it. And by the way, she loves it. Do you believe this new app will be as successful as some of the more popular items your company has produced in the past?"

Vivian looked over at Wes and wondered just how much acting this was going to require from her boss. Successful? She clamped her lips shut to prevent a nervous laugh from bursting out of her. Why didn't he be honest and tell Ted he thought it was a crock of crap? Just as he'd told her less than twenty-four hours ago?

An engaging grin brought the hint of a dimple in his left cheek, and Vivian had to stifle a groan. He'd certainly never shown this charming side of himself when she was around. In fact, she'd never dreamed he possessed an ounce of playfulness. Moment by moment, she was learning there were many facets of Wes that she'd never seen before. Or was this just all a part of his act? she wondered.

"I have a great amount of confidence in our new app. On the surface it might appear that My Perfect Match is designed for young people, but actually it's geared for all ages. After all, love has no age limit. Don't you agree?"

The host chuckled slyly. "I'd better agree, Wes. Otherwise, my wife will have me sleeping in the doghouse tonight."

Oh, please, Vivian wanted to shout. My Perfect Match was nothing to jest about.

She noticed Wes was chuckling along with Ted as though the two of them were sharing a private joke about the opposite sex. The idea stirred her temper as much as Wes's nearness was disturbing her senses.

Ted went on, "So you're telling me that all people interested in finding a mate, no matter their age, can get results using My Perfect Match?"

"I'm absolutely certain of it," Wes answered without hesitation.

The anchor appeared surprised at Wes's unwavering response, while Vivian was downright stunned. She'd expected him to give himself a little wiggle room, just in case the app did fail. Was this more of his pretense? If it was, then what else did he go around pretending?

"Wow, that's quite a statement," Ted responded. "Especially coming from the vice president of the company."

"Vice President of Research and Development," Wes corrected him.

"Uh, okay. Well, can you tell me how this is supposed to work?" A leering grin came over the man's face. "Say I'm a lonely guy looking for a woman to settle down with. How will the app help me?"

"It'll save you a big bar tab," Wes quipped, then softened his response with another charming grin. "Seriously, I think Vivian can better answer that question."

Vivian felt like a million eyes were suddenly focusing on her face. Her heart kicked into an even faster pace, sending a loud whooshing noise to her ears. She darted a glance at Wes, then froze a wide-eyed gaze on the monitor and Ted's smirking face.

"Good morning again, Vivian."

She desperately needed to clear the ball of nerves in her throat, but it was too late, so instead she swallowed. The effort practically strangled her, making her voice sound more like a squeak. "Good morning."

The show host gave her a wide, plastic smile and Vivian promised herself she'd never again tune in to *Hey, USA*.

"I hear you are the brains behind this new technical device to find love," he said. "Would you care to explain to our viewing audience exactly how the app works?"

Shifting slighting on the seat, she resisted the urge to swallow a second time. "Uh—yes, it matches you with the right people. I mean—right person."

"Could you elaborate a little?" Ted urged.

"Oh, well—it's the questions. And how you answer and—that sort of thing."

Oh, Lord, I'm making a mess of this, she thought frantically. She had to pull herself together before she made a complete idiot of herself!

"Okay, say I answer all the questions listed on the program," the interviewer went on. "Then what? A woman out there looking for her perfect man decides if she likes my answers? Isn't that the same premise of all the dating sites being advertised nowadays?"

"No—My Perfect Match is different. A woman won't decide if she likes you—the computer will do the deciding," Vivian attempted to correct him.

The popular television personality chuckled, and Vivian couldn't decide whether she wanted to crawl under her chair or throw her shoe straight through the monitor.

"I'm not sure I follow," he said. "A computer is going to tell me who my perfect mate is? Look, I'm all for new technology, but when it comes to a person's love life, that all sounds pretty cold to me."

She said, "Cold—hot—temperature doesn't come up on the app's questions."

"Then what does come up, Vivian? A criminal background check?" he asked, then burst out laughing at his own crude joke.

How to avoid jerks like you, Vivian wanted to say. Instead, she said through tight lips, "Those types of candidates will automatically be ejected from the system."

"That's good to know," Ted replied. "But I'm still looking for the flawless woman. Tell me exactly how My Perfect Match will find her?"

"I—think—" Her words trailed away in confusion and she darted a helpless glance at Wes.

Thankfully he picked up the rest of her sentence as though they'd planned it that way.

"I think what Vivian is trying to say is that My Perfect Match takes the doubt out of dating. It's all about being compatible, rather than a person's appearance or the chemistry between two people. Isn't that right, Viv?"

Smiling, he looked at her, and for a moment all Vivian could do was gaze into his eyes. She'd never noticed them being so blue before or so full of warmth.

"Oh—yes," she gushed. "Absolutely."

"Well, I must admit this is a new concept. And you definitely sound confident about its abilities," Ted said to Wes. "Would you be willing to trust your love life with My Perfect Match?"

"I certainly would," Wes said without a pause. "I'm more than happy to let the app tell me who I need to be dating."

The morning show host appeared completely amazed by Wes's announcement. "You mean you're telling me that *you* plan to use My Perfect Match?"

"I plan to start tomorrow."

Vivian's head jerked in Wes's direction. Had he lost his mind? To hear him tell it, everything he'd been spouting about the app was pure hogwash. Ted Reynolds and the viewing audience might not know it, but she certainly did. Why had Wes suddenly made such a wild promise? And on national TV!

"Did you hear that, folks? Wes Robinson isn't afraid to put himself on the dating market! He's just vowed to use My Perfect Match to find his perfect lady. I can promise you that *Hey, USA* will certainly be following the outcome of this romantic venture!"

While Vivian was trying to make sense of what had just happened, the interview wrapped up. And even after a crew member removed her earpiece, she continued to sit watching dazedly as the broadcast crew carried its equipment out of Wes's office.

Once the room was finally quiet again, Wes walked over to the wall of plate glass and let out a hefty sigh.

As Vivian watched him stare moodily out at the city, she forced herself to her feet. The past few minutes had twisted her nerves so tight she felt utterly drained, and for a moment she wondered if her legs would hold her upright.

"Well, that turned out to be a hell of a mess," he said.

Vivian winced with regret. Of course he was disgusted. She'd let him down in a big way and made herself look like an imbecile in the process.

"I'm sorry," she told him. "I've never done anything like this before. The second we went on the air, my mind went blank. And Ted Reynolds wasn't helping matters. He was—"

She was searching for the right word when Wes found it for her.

"Being an ass," he finished.

She took a few tentative steps forward until she was standing close enough to see his brows pull into a scowl.

"You noticed?" she asked.

"Hell yes, I noticed."

Realizing she was twisting the frames of her eyeglasses, she eased her grip and thrust her hands behind her. "Well, I'm not going to use him as an excuse for my breakdown. Everything I wanted to say about My Perfect Match came out wrong."

His expression a picture of frustration, he turned and closed the distance between them. "Forget about it, Vivian. It's over and done with. And frankly, what you said or how you said it doesn't matter now. I'm the one who came out of this looking like a fool."

Stunned that he was being so magnanimous about the whole thing, she stared at him. "You? What are you talking about? You didn't miss a beat. You made My Perfect Match sound like something every single person should purchase."

He rolled his eyes. "I realize you were visiting another planet during our interview, but surely you heard me say I'd be using the app for my own personal dating agenda."

She tried to keep the dismay she was feeling off her face. "I heard. But I don't understand your frustration. Ted Reynolds will never know if you use My Perfect Match. I doubt we'll hear from him or the show's producers again."

"If this was just a phony promise made to a jackass television host, I wouldn't care. But I was also speaking to a national audience. Many of whom purchase and use Robinson Tech products. They expect me to be forthright about myself and my company. Not to mention all the curiosity this is going to generate with the public. Everyone is going to be watching like a hawk to see what happens with me and this—dating thing of yours."

Vivian rubbed fingers against her furrowed brow. She should be happy that her boss had managed to get himself in such a predicament. His misery was fitting payback for all that ridicule of My Perfect Match he'd spouted to her yesterday. Yet surprisingly, seeing the harried tension on his face right now didn't give her the slightest feeling of satisfaction.

"I see what you mean," she said thoughtfully. "As a representative of Robinson Tech, you feel obligated to follow through on your promise."

"It's a relief to see your brain is working again, Ms. Blair."

One minute he used her first name and the next he reverted back to "Ms. Blair." His vacillation made her wonder how he thought of her. As Vivian the woman, or Ms. Blair the computer developer? Either way, she wanted to tell him she'd had enough of his insults for one day, but she'd already put her job in enough jeopardy with the interview debacle.

"Well, if that's the way you feel—I mean, if you're actually going through with your vow to use My Perfect Match, then it's only right that I use it, too. After all, I'm the one who has real confidence in the app."

With a faint smirk on his lips, he stepped closer.

"You? Use the app?"

The incredulous tone of his voice made her lift her chin to a challenging angle. "What's the matter? Afraid I'll prove you wrong about My Perfect Match?"

"I hope you do prove me wrong and this blasted thing turns out to be a roaring success," he countered, then slithered a skeptical look down the length of her body. "I just wasn't aware that you were looking for a perfect man."

I'm certainly not looking at him now. Vivian bit down on her tongue to keep the words from leaping out of her mouth.

"In this day and age, the task of finding a perfect man seems like a hopeless quest, but I've not given up the search," she said primly, then shoved her eyeglasses onto her face. "And now that I've created My Perfect Match, I feel much more hopeful of finding him."

The sly grin spreading over his lips was followed by a suggestive gleam in his blue eyes. One that left Vivian feeling so uncomfortable, she wanted to run out of his plush office as fast as her legs would carry her.

"Well, you've just made this whole fiasco more bearable and interesting. I'm willing to bet I find my perfect woman long before you find your perfect man."

Thrilled for the chance to prove him wrong, she stuck out her hand. "It's a deal."

His fingers curled firmly around hers, and Vivian tried to ignore the heat racing up her arm and stinging her cheeks with color.

"Great," he said. "May the best man win?"

The wry taunt in his voice put enough steel in her backbone to make a metal detector blow a fuse.

"You have it all wrong, Mr. Robinson. Let's hope *love* wins. For the both of us."

Wes stared thoughtfully after Vivian as she headed out the door. Adelle passed her on the way into his office.

Since the secretary didn't enter his private work space unless she had good reason, he knew something was up. Given the bad start to his day, he figured it wasn't good news.

While she walked briskly into the room, her high heels clicking with every step, Wes sank into the plush chair behind his desk and wiped a hand over his face.

"Okay, what's happened? It's nine forty-five in the morning and you look like you already need a stiff cocktail."

Stopping in front of his desk, she tapped the eraser of her pencil against the cherry wood. "You've really done it," she quipped. "How do you expect me to get any work done when my phone is jammed with calls?"

"Adelle, you knew this interview was happening this morning. I told you to inform everyone that I'd be late returning calls."

Her eyes rolled toward the ceiling. "Mr. Robinson,

these aren't your usual calls. This is coming from newspapers, television stations, radio and all sorts of media people. Everyone is buzzing with your announcement about My Perfect Match. I've been trying to put them off, but—"

"What do they want? If they're interested in doing advertising for the app, then you should direct their calls to advertising and marketing."

"Thank you for that helpful advice." She shot him a tired look, then asked, "How long do you think I've been working here? A week or two?"

"Probably as long as the world has had white thread," Wes said, not bothering to hide his impatience. He had more important things on his mind than listening to a lecture from his bossy secretary.

"That's right. Longer than you can count. I believe I've gotten the hang of how to direct calls," she informed him. "But I think you ought to know these calls are directed at your personal life. My impression is that the media plans to cover your so-called dates. You and the lucky lady will most likely be followed around like the hottest star of the week hounded by Hollywood paparazzi."

"Oh, damn!"

She thrust her pencil into the hair above her right ear. "*Oh, damn* is right. What were you thinking?"

Ever since the interview had wrapped, Wes had been asking himself that very question. He'd accused Vivian of momentarily losing her senses; well, he'd admittedly committed the same crime.

"Clearly, I wasn't," he muttered, then rubbed his fingers over his closed eyelids. "It's just that Ted Reynolds was doing his best to make a mockery of the app. I wanted to put him in his place."

And surprisingly, Wes had wanted to come to Vivian's defense. In spite of her ridiculous notions about finding everlasting love through a mobile app, he understood she'd worked long, tireless hours to get My Perfect Match to the public. She didn't deserve to have her effort ridiculed in front of a national television audience. And yet, there was a part of him that wanted to open her eyes and show her that love wasn't a cold, clinical pairing between a man and a woman. It was all about overwhelming attraction and desire. At least, that was how he wanted to imagine it. So far in his dating endeavors, he'd never experienced the euphoric state of mind called love.

"Hmm. I suppose if you find a woman who fits you like a glove, you'll make Ted Reynolds look like more of a fool than he already is. Add to that, you'd prove Vivian's theory about compatibility right. Which would be a good thing," Adelle mused aloud. "And now that Ben is about to get married, it's your turn to look for a wife."

Wes grunted. "It's not a written law that twins have to do everything alike, you know."

The cell phone on Wes's desk suddenly rang, preventing Adelle from flinging a disapproving remark at him. He picked up the phone to answer the call, but noticed she was already on her way out of the office.

"Just a minute, Adelle."

Pausing at the door, she glanced back at him. For some odd reason, Wes suddenly wondered how the secretary had looked when she was Vivian's age. Had she been madly in love with her husband? Or had the guy been like Wes's father, Gerald? Unworthy of a good woman's love? What if the dating app led Vivian to such a scoundrel?

"Was there something else?"

Adelle's question had Wes mentally shaking himself. Vivian's personal life was no concern of his. If any of her matches turned out to be cads, then that would be her problem.

"Yes, there was. Concerning my self-test of My Perfect Match, you can inform the media outlets I'll be starting tomorrow. Oh, and you might also relay the message that Vivian will also be using the app—to find her perfect man," he added drily.

Adelle looked at him with dismay. "Vivian? And you approve of that?"

Wes frowned. "Why would I disapprove?"

"Well, why indeed?" she asked with a smirk. "That sweet little thing thrown out there among all those wolves? I shudder to think who she might get tangled up with."

Wes found it hard to imagine Vivian getting tangled up in the bedsheets with any man. She was too prim and calculating to have such a reckless encounter. "Believe me, Adelle, sweet little Vivian, as you call her, knows exactly what she's doing."

With a roll of her eyes, the secretary left the room, and Wes turned his attention to the phone in his hand. Before he could scroll through the call log, the face lit up with another call.

Seeing it was Ben, he drew in a bracing breath and took a seat. No doubt his twin had already heard about Wes's declaration to use the dating app and was rolling on the floor with laughter. Well, Ben could do all the goading he wanted, Wes thought as he swiped to answer the call. When all was said and done, presenting his brother with a hefty sales number from My Perfect Match would shut him up.

* * *

When Vivian got back to Research and Development, George and Justine were waiting at her cubicle. From the guarded looks on their faces, she could tell they'd watched the live remote.

Holding up a hand to ward off their remarks, she said, "You don't have to tell me. I was a complete disaster."

George gave her a sympathetic pat on the shoulder. "It wasn't all that bad."

"Not at all," Justine chimed in. "And you looked great with your hair like that."

Vivian shot her a confused look, then quickly patted the top of her hair. "Like what? Is it all mussed up?"

"No," Justine said with a giggle. "The way it's tucked behind your ear. Gives you a really chic look."

Just the thought of Wes's infuriating remarks had Vivian quickly shaking her hair loose. "My hair was—just a mistake. And my mouth was even worse," she added with a groan of misery. "Every word that passed my lips made me sound like an idiot! I've probably ruined any hope that My Perfect Match will be a big seller."

"I wouldn't think that," George spoke up. "Uh, so what did Mr. Robinson say afterward?"

Before Vivian could answer George's question, Justine pelted her with another.

"Probably angry, huh?"

Exhaling a long breath, Vivian moved past her coworkers and practically flopped into her desk chair. "Not exactly. I mean, Wes—uh, Mr. Robinson—isn't the type to show much emotion. Have you two ever seen him angry?"

George and Justine both shook their heads.

Justine said, "We're not as lucky as you, Viv. We rarely meet with the man."

"I'm fine not to meet with him," George put in. "Makes me nervous to have to talk to the boss."

Justine made a dismissive gesture with her hand. "Technically, he's not our boss, George."

"Don't kid yourself," George said drily. "You mess up with Wes Robinson and you'll be outta here."

"His twin, Ben, is the new COO. And from what I hear, Wes was pretty hacked off that he didn't get the job."

Her nerves already frazzled, Vivian massaged the pain gathering in the middle of her forehead. "Justine, please, give it a rest. Anybody in this building with the name Robinson is our boss. Plain and simple. Now if you two will excuse me, I need to get to work."

"Oh? Orders from *our* boss?" Justine asked slyly.

Dropping her hand, Vivian looked at her coworkers. She might as well let them in on her plan, she decided. They were going to hear about it sooner or later anyway.

"Not exactly. I'm signing up on My Perfect Match. The quicker, the better."

"What?" George stared at her with real concern.

Justine giggled. "You? On My Perfect Match? Are you kidding, Viv?"

"Not in the least. Wes is willing to give it a try. So am I."

The concern on George's face grew deeper as he walked over to Vivian and looked down at her. "Are you doing this just because he is?"

Was she? When Vivian had first come up with the concept of My Perfect Match, she'd certainly not been creating the app for her own personal use. In spite of everything she'd said to Wes, she still wanted to meet her suitors the old-fashioned way. After that, she'd make the decision whether they were completely compatible or not. But when Wes had insisted he was actually going to use the app, she realized she had to step up to the plate and do the same.

"If a person isn't willing to use her own product, George, what kind of impression is that going to give the public? I've got to show Wes and everyone that I believe in this thing."

"Good thing you're not a casket maker," Justine quipped.

George shot the other woman a tired look, then shook his head at Vivian. "Are you sure you know what you're doing, Viv?"

To answer his question, Vivian picked up her smart-phone and scrolled through the pages of applications until she found My Perfect Match.

"I've never been more certain. I'm going to find the man of my dreams. Our likes and dislikes will match precisely. We'll have no choice but to fall in love and live happily ever after."

Justine let out a mocking groan. "Oh, please. That's enough to send me back to work."

George must have had the same thought because he turned to follow Justine out of the small cubicle.

"What? No words of wisdom from you, George?"

Looking over his shoulder, the burly redhead frowned at her. "All I can say is good luck, Vivian. You're going to need it."

Scowling back at him, she asked, "What is that supposed to mean?"

"Just that you've set your goals mighty high."

"Somewhere out there is the man I want to spend the rest of my life with. And My Perfect Match is going to find him for me."

"Hmm. Well, if that's the case, then Wes Robinson is going to find the woman he wants to share the rest of his life with. So this app should make you both very happy."

Happy? Oh, yes, Vivian thought, proving Wes wrong was going to make her ecstatic.

Chapter Four

"Vivian, are you sure you know what you're doing?"

How many times had she heard that in the past two days? The question was becoming a broken record, Vivian thought.

Not bothering to look over at her sister, Michelle, who was standing a few steps away, watching as Vivian applied a coat of mascara to her already dark lashes. Normally she didn't use a great deal of makeup when going on a date, but tonight was special. Or at least she was treating it as such. Tonight was her first date generated by My Perfect Match and she wanted to make a good impression.

"I'm going on a dinner date," she answered, trying her best to sound casual even though her nerves were balled in a knot.

"With someone you've never met before." Michelle shook her head in dismay. "You're far braver than me, sis."

She wasn't brave, Vivian thought. Determined was more like it. "I have to start somewhere. And it's just dinner."

"As far as I'm concerned, you should've never made such a wager with Wes Robinson," she argued. "And just what are you going to get if you prove the app works? A bonus from Robinson Tech? Bragging rights?"

Vivian turned away from the dresser mirror to glance at her sister. Three years older, Michelle was a few inches taller and several pounds lighter than Vivian. Michelle had curly chestnut hair and pale, porcelain skin, and Vivian had always considered her sister to be far prettier than her. And as a high school art teacher, Michelle was far better at communicating with people.

Using the mascara wand to punctuate her words, Vivian said, "Neither of those things. I'm going to get a man. One I can build a family with. One I can depend on to be around for the long haul."

Michelle groaned. "Sis, you ought to consider making a job change. Computers can do a lot of things, but they can't keep a man faithful or responsible."

"Maybe not. But they can weed out the worst of the worst. Besides, I don't exactly see you making any wedding plans." Vivian turned back to the mirror and carefully dabbed on a small amount of lip gloss. Behind her, Michelle walked over to the bed, where Vivian had laid out a brown mid-calf skirt, a white shirt and a camel-beige cardigan to go over it. No doubt her sister was wondering why she'd not chosen something more colorful to wear.

"You're the one who wants a husband," Michelle reasoned. "I enjoy being single and independent—like Mom. When the right man comes along, I'll know it. I don't need a computer to tell me."

Vivian's freshly glossed lips pressed into a thin line. "Thanks for the vote of confidence in my work," she said with a heavy dose of sarcasm. "And open your eyes, sis. Mom doesn't like being single. She's simply too afraid to try marriage again."

"Bah! After the way Dad treated her, she has no interest in being married. If you ask me, she was relieved after she and Dad divorced."

Vivian sighed. "They had nothing in common."

"Only three kids," Michelle said wryly.

Vivian stepped into the skirt and zipped it up, then reached for the shirt. "And we obviously weren't enough to hold them together."

Michelle grimaced. "Well, no. Not when one spouse goes looking for love elsewhere."

Vivian stared at her as she dealt with the buttons on her shirt. "What are you saying?"

Michelle shrugged, then cast a sheepish look at her sister, as though she wished she'd not mentioned anything regarding their father.

"Dad was always on the road," she said. "He had a wandering eye and Mom knew it."

"You don't know that for sure."

"No," Michelle admitted. "But he married very quickly after the divorce was final."

"Some men are needy."

"Exactly my point."

Shaking her head, Vivian said, "I really don't need to hear this sort of thing tonight, Michelle. In fifteen minutes, I'm going to open the door to a man I've never met before, and I don't want to be eyeing him as though he's already under suspicion."

"Oh!" Michelle glanced at her wristwatch. "He's going to be here in fifteen minutes? I'd better go. I don't want to be a distraction. Besides, I have a stack of test papers to grade."

She hurried around to the other side of the bed and smacked a kiss on Vivian's cheek. "Good luck, sissy. Let me know how things go with the search for Mr. Right. And in case you don't know—I'm proud of you."

Twenty minutes later, Vivian stood at the open door of her apartment, her neck bent backward as she peered up at her first date. She'd seen shorter basketball players, she decided, but with his extremely thin frame, he'd be crushed the first time he attempted to make a goal. As for his face, she couldn't tell much about his eyes. They were hidden behind a pair of thick-lensed glasses. The rest of his features were lean to the point of being bony and as solemn as a man who'd just received a death sentence.

The app considered this man an attractive match for her?

Remember, Viv, this isn't about attraction. This is all about likes and dislikes.

"Good evening," she greeted him, hiding her dismay as best she could. "Are you Paul Sullivan?"

He gave her a slight nod. "Yes. Are you Vivian Blair?"

"I am."

"Good. I wasn't sure the GPS in my vehicle was working properly. And the signal on my cell phone loses its mind on this side of town."

And based on her first impression of this man, before this night was over, there was a real possibility that Vivian might lose hers.

Smiling, she said, "Well, you're here, and on time, too. If you'll step inside, I'll get my things and we'll head on to the restaurant."

* * *

By the time Vivian and Paul had finished their salads and started on the main course, Vivian had learned he was an IT technician for a large insurance company. He had four brothers and one sister, all of whom lived in Michigan. Two years ago, his current job had lured him to Austin, but so far the Texas heat had caused him to suffer several heat strokes. A fact that had him dreading the coming spring.

"Perhaps you'll get acclimatized soon," Vivian offered on a hopeful note.

"I doubt it. Everyone tells me you have to be tough to live in Texas."

And Paul Sullivan definitely didn't fit that category, she thought as she pushed her fork into a fillet of grilled tilapia.

"Well, the natives are born that way," she said, her mind drifting to Wes. Was he out on the city tonight, she wondered, squiring around his first date? What sort of woman would the app match him with? Some sort of computer genius? Or maybe a refined woman of the arts who was familiar with his social circles?

Paul's voice broke into her thoughts.

"Yes, that's why I'll probably be heading back home to Michigan soon. I'm afraid another summer here might kill me."

"Oh. That's too bad."

He peered candidly at her. "You mean you wouldn't be willing to move there—with me?"

Vivian nearly choked on a bite of fish. "Uh—no. Texas is my home."

He looked completely dumbfounded. "Oh. But I thought—you see, the app says the two of us are perfectly aligned. That means we'd be happy together no matter where we live."

Oh, Lord, if this was the best the app could offer, she was in big trouble.

"Paul, I think—"

She paused, deciding it would be useless to explain that being technically matched to someone didn't necessarily mean instant commitment. It would only burst his hopeful bubble. And wasn't that what My Perfect Match really stood for? she asked herself. The hope of finding someone to love?

"Yes?" he asked eagerly.

Smiling wanly, she said, "I was just going to say I think I won't have dessert tonight. But feel free to enjoy some if you'd like."

Across town, in a skyline restaurant located in one of the finest hotels in Austin, Wes stared across the table for two at the woman sipping a fruity cocktail. Earlier this evening as he'd showered and changed, he'd been thinking he'd rather be rolled over by a piece of highway equipment than meet Miss Perfect Match.

But later, when the hostess had shown his match to his table, he'd nearly fallen out of his chair. The expectations of his first date had vacillated wildly between a career woman with a scientific mind and a blonde bimbo with an ample show of cleavage. Mercifully, Julia's appearance was neither.

Pretty and friendly, she could even carry on a decent conversation. Perhaps Vivian was on to something with this compatible thing, Wes thought.

Vivian. Earlier today, she'd sent him an email message informing him she was going on her first date tonight. Wes had replied that he'd be doing the same.

Now, as he sipped his drink and the smooth whiskey slid warmly down his throat, he wondered where his developer was tonight and what sort of man the app had picked for her. A muscle-bound athlete with roaming hands, or a suave businessman with a line of phony charm? As far as he was concerned, either image was wrong for her. But then, he didn't think like a computer. Even though his family business was all about the mechanical brains.

"Wes, have I already lost you?"

His date's question brought him out of his thoughts, and he mentally shook himself as he gave her the most charming smile he could muster.

"Sorry, Julia, I was thinking about a project at work."

"Wondering if it will succeed?"

"Something like that."

Smiling provocatively over the rim of her cocktail glass, she said, "I'm certain whatever you're working on will be a winner. The app implies you're a brilliant man."

The app might consider him brilliant, but apparently his father didn't, Wes thought ruefully. At least, not brilliant enough to handle being COO of Robinson Tech. And Vivian—well, she believed his ideas about love were totally ignorant.

But why the hell should he care what Vivian thought about him? She was just a company developer. One of many. And as for his father, he might be one of a kind, but he was the kind Wes didn't want to emulate.

"I'm not sure my work will turn out to be a winner," he said smoothly. "But tonight I feel like one."

Julie laughed, and as Wes drained the last of his drink, a vision of Vivian's disapproving face entered his mind.

She wouldn't go for a line like that, Wes thought. No, that sweet little thing, as Adelle called her, was too smart and stiff to be swayed by a man's glib tongue.

Or was she? The man she was with tonight was supposed to be her kind of guy. He might know the exact words to say to soften her defenses and lure her into his bed.

Bed? No! Not Vivian! For some reason his mind refused to conjure up such a vision.

"Wes? Are you okay?"

He blinked and then, realizing she'd caught him daydreaming for a second time, he felt a wash of embarrassment creep up his neck.

"Sure," he said with feigned innocence. "Why?"

The young woman's gaze zeroed in on the squatty tumbler he was holding. "You're gripping your glass so hard, I'm afraid it's going to shatter in your hand."

Practically dropping the glass to the tabletop, Wes used his forearm to shove it aside, then forced himself to lean attentively toward her.

"Sorry," he apologized again. "I'm just not—myself this evening. But I promise to give you my undivided attention for the remainder of it. Now, tell me all about yourself."

The next morning, Vivian was staring at her computer screen, trying to focus on the work she should've finished yesterday, when a folded newspaper was suddenly thrust in front of her face. The hand holding it was wearing an onyx ring, and the shock that Wes Robinson had bothered to come to her work cubicle had her whirling the chair around to face him.

"What—is something wrong?" she practically sputtered.

A smug expression curved one corner of his mouth, and she instantly wondered if his first date had received a kiss from those same privileged lips.

"Not as far as I'm concerned."

He handed her a folded copy of the *Texan Gazette*. "Page twenty-four in the social section."

Vivian quickly fumbled through the pages. When she reached the right page and spotted a picture of herself and Paul, her mouth fell open.

"That's me!" she said with a shocked gasp. "We were leaving the restaurant. I had no idea anyone was watching us. This is creepy!"

"Creepy or not, it happened. And why the surprise? After our national exposure, you should have known the local media would pick up on our venture."

"I didn't say anything during that interview about personally using the app!" she protested. "You did!"

His expression turned sly. "The media has a way of finding out these things."

Her jaw dropped. "You told them!"

He chuckled, and it dawned on Vivian that he was enjoying this whole charade. The idea was even more surprising than finding a photo of herself in an Austin newspaper.

"Why should I be the only one hounded by the press?" He tapped a finger on another photo at the top of the page. "Apparently you didn't notice this one."

Her gaze followed the direction of his finger, and as she studied the image, she felt herself going hot and then cold.

"Wes Robinson, son of tech mogul Gerald Robinson, was spotted at the Capital Arms Restaurant last evening with a computer-inspired date."

After reading the caption beneath the photo, Vivian glanced up at Wes. "This was your date?"

"That's Julia," he said smugly. "I have to admit, Vivian, so far your app seems to understand exactly what I want in a woman."

Vivian turned her attention back to the photo. Wes's date could easily pose for the cover of a fashion magazine. And the alluring expression she was casting at Wes must have sent him into a dreamy stupor. Vivian had never seen her boss looking so dazed.

Vivian should have been jumping for joy that the app had worked for him, at least. Instead, she felt almost queasy. As if she'd taken a dose of painkillers on an empty stomach. "So you two communicated well?"

"Absolutely. She was smart, funny, interesting—I'm beginning to wonder if I should just stop right now and call her the winner."

The triumphant note in his voice irked her to no end. "Really? One date is all you need to decide she's your perfect mate?"

"I only said I was wondering, not quitting. Besides, if my next dates turn out to be as charming as Julia, why should I stop such a fun quest?"

He'd had fun and she'd gone home with a headache. There was nothing fair about this, Vivian thought miserably.

"Good for you," she retorted. "But frankly, this image of your date has me doubting your honesty."

His eyes narrowed, and Vivian noticed they were abnormally bloodshot this morning, as though he'd downed too much alcohol or had a very late night. Both a product of blonde Julia, she figured.

"What are you talking about? I'm not going to lie about my dates." He pointed to the newspaper image.

"You can see for yourself that she's an attractive woman. I could hardly make that up."

"I'm not doubting that you had a good time on your date last night. I'm just wondering if you answered the questions on My Perfect Match truthfully. What did you put down as your occupation? That you run a modeling agency?"

His short laugh was mocking. "What did you put down as your occupation? That you're a scout for the NBA?"

Disgusted now, she tossed the paper onto her desk. "Very funny. I should expect you to say something like that! You know, Mr. Robinson, not everyone is as flawless as you."

"So you didn't mind breaking a vertebra in your neck to look up at him?"

"For your information, I didn't break a thing," she said coolly.

"So do you plan on seeing him again?"

Not in a thousand years, Vivian silently answered. To Wes she said, "I don't know who I'm going to date next. I'm going to let the app decide that for me."

A clever grin curved the corners of his lips. "Yes, maybe we'd better let the app do its work. That is what this is all about."

"Exactly."

He turned to leave, then pointed to the newspaper. "By the way, you can keep that for a souvenir. I expect it will be one of many. Oh, and don't you think you should start calling me Wes? Now that we're in a dating battle, so to speak, it sounds ridiculous for you to call me Mr. Robinson."

She couldn't have been more shocked. In the past six years she'd worked for the guy, he'd never invited her to be personal with him. But then, they'd never worked on such a personal project together before.

"You are my superior," she reminded him.

"Don't let that stop you."

"All right, Wes."

He gave her a thumbs-up and left the cubicle.

Relieved, Vivian slumped back in her chair and reached for the newspaper. For two cents, she'd push the thing into the paper shredder. The last thing she wanted was a reminder of her disastrous date. And as for Wes's escapade last evening, she wasn't going to waste one more second wondering if he'd spent his night in the arms of the beautiful blonde.

On Friday evening, Wes was standing at the elevator a few doors down from his office when he heard Ben's voice call out to him.

"Hey, Wes! Wait up."

Glancing down the corridor, he spotted his twin stride quickly toward him. The elevator doors chose that exact moment to open, but Wes ignored them and waited for his brother to join him.

"Looking for me?" Wes asked.

"I tried your cell earlier and Adelle wasn't answering her phone. When you didn't pick up your office phone, I was beginning to think you were sick." He eyed the worn leather bomber jacket Wes was wearing this evening. "And you must be if you're quitting work this early in the evening."

Wes punched the down button and the doors opened again. This time Wes stepped inside with Ben following close behind him.

"Sorry about the cell phone. These past few days, I've had to silence the ringer. The constant sound was driving me nuts. But as to my health, I'm actually feeling great. Never better."

With no one else joining them in the elevator, Wes leaned forward to punch the number for the parking garage, and the car moved swiftly downward.

"Hmm. Well, you should be feeling on top of the world," Ben replied. "Marketing informs me the orders are pouring in for the new dating app. It appears all this publicity you've been doing is paying off. Good work, brother."

Wes eased back the cuff of his jacket to glance at his watch. He had less than fifteen minutes to meet his fourth app date at a nearby coffee shop. Normally, Wes didn't cut his schedule so close, but he'd spent the past hour going over cost data for a new processor his department had developed. Since his father had requested the information delivered to him before quitting time, Wes had worked all day going over the numbers, making sure Gerald Robinson could find no gaps in the report. No. Wes wasn't about to let the man find him making a mistake. Not in his work. Or his personal life.

"I wouldn't call it work," Wes told his twin. "It's dating."

Ben let out a low chuckle. "I honestly didn't know you had it in you."

Wes darted him a sharp look. "Had what in me?"

"The ability to land all those good-looking women. How many have you gone out with so far? Three? Four? And from the pics I've seen in the papers, they've all looked pretty darn attractive."

"Hey, you'd better not let Ella hear you saying that," Wes jokingly warned. "She might want to think twice about going through with next Saturday's wedding."

Ben chuckled again. "Ella knows I only have eyes for

her. And speaking of the wedding, that's why I stopped by your office. I wanted to remind you about rehearsal. At the church tomorrow night at seven. So you might want to cross off your dating schedule for tomorrow evening. It might be a little awkward to bring a computer date to a wedding rehearsal."

Leave it to his brother to suggest Wes would do something that crass. True, he wasn't the cool 007 that Ben was, but he knew where and when to show up with a lady on his arm.

Deliberately ignoring Ben's suggestion, Wes asked, "I assume we're having dinner afterward?"

"At the River Plaza."

One of the ritziest hotels in town, Wes thought. When Ben had said he wanted to give Ella everything, he'd obviously meant it.

"Will Dad be there?"

After a long pause, Wes glanced over at Ben. As their gazes locked, Wes knew they were both thinking of their childhood days and how their father had rarely been around for any family event. Instead of looking to their wandering father for male guidance and affection, the twins had always relied on each other. And in many ways that hadn't changed.

Ben exhaled a long breath and wiped a hand over his face. "No. He's leaving tomorrow afternoon for a convention in Chicago. A three-day affair."

Emphasis on *affair*, Wes wanted to say. Typical Gerald Robinson, business and personal pleasure before family. But he kept the snide remark to himself. This was an important time in Ben's life. His brother didn't need to be reminded of their father's shortcomings.

"Sorry, Ben."

He shrugged. "Yeah, well, the old man has promised to be at the wedding. And considering how he feels about this Fortune family search I've undertaken, I'm surprised he's agreed to attend. He's not a bit happy with me, you know."

"Well, not everyone in the Robinson family is happy with this endeavor of yours. But that doesn't mean we've stopped loving you."

The elevator came to a halt, and they stepped onto the dimly lit concrete floor of the parking garage. Wes gestured in the direction of his car. "My car is over there. Was there anything else on your mind? I'm supposed to meet the lady in fifteen minutes and need to get going."

"So you really are headed out on a date," Ben stated the obvious.

"That's right. She's driving up from San Antonio."

"There aren't enough women in Austin for you?"

Wes smirked. "The app is doing the choosing. Not me."

"Ah yes, the app," Ben said with a chuckle. "Well, good luck, brother. Maybe tonight's date will be *the* one."

Wes wasn't looking for *the* one. He'd watched their father make a mockery of marriage far too long to want to jump into matrimony himself.

"I'm sure you'll read about it in tomorrow's paper." Lifting a hand in a gesture of parting, Wes strode off in the direction of his car.

On the following Monday afternoon, Vivian sat staring at the small square logo displayed on her smartphone screen and wondered if she'd created a monster instead of a dreamland of everlasting love. The notion behind the red-and-silver key that represented My Perfect Match was to unlock the secrets of undying love. And once the logo was tapped by an eager finger, it unfurled to show a romantic image of two golden wedding bands bound together on a bed of white velvet.

Everything about the design and the meaning behind it had seemed textbook. That is, until Vivian had started using it. Now she felt as if she'd stepped into a nightmare. One she couldn't escape. Had she been wrong all along about finding a compatible mate? Was Wes right about two people needing a fire between them to make a relationship work? If so, then he was going to win their little wager. Even worse, My Perfect Match would be a total failure.

"We have five minutes left of our break. Are you going to spend it staring at your phone?"

The question came from Justine, who was sitting across the utility table, sipping on a canned soda. Today Vivian's coworker was wearing a tight black sweater and a red skirt that molded to her hips. If the neckline on her sweater had been a half inch lower, the office manager probably would've sent her home for not following proper dress code. But Justine was one to push the envelope and every once in a while, like this very moment, Vivian wished she could be a bit more like risky Justine.

"I'm not staring at my phone," Vivian corrected her. "I'm thinking."

Justine chuckled. "Trying to decide which one of those losers you want to go out with again?"

Vivian glared at her. "That's an awful thing to say. All of my dates have been polite gentlemen."

"A nice way of calling them dull."

Unfortunately, Justine couldn't have been more right. These past few nights, Vivian had been bored out of her mind and wondering how she could endure another evening trying to meet her Mr. Perfect.

After sipping her coffee and realizing it was on the verge of getting cold, she rose to her feet to toss it into the nearest wastebasket.

"Well, I'm not giving up," she told Justine. "Sooner or later, an interesting and good-looking guy will show up. After all, these men are being pulled from the test pool. Once the app goes on sale on Valentine's Day, then the playing field will widen considerably."

"You hope. From what I've seen in the papers, Wes doesn't need a deeper pool of dating candidates to choose from. He looks like he's doing mighty fine."

"He's been lucky," Vivian retorted.

Her phone suddenly chirped, notifying her that she had an incoming text message. Vivian tossed the foam coffee cup, then retrieved the phone from the tabletop.

Come to my office. Now.

What did he want? To gloat, Vivian thought.

Across the table, Justine studied her closely. "What's wrong? You look like you could bite the head off a nail."

If Vivian had an angry look on her face, it was because she was disgusted with the way her heart had suddenly skipped a beat at the thought of seeing Wes again. What was wrong with her, anyway? She'd worked with the man for six years, and in his presence the only thing she'd ever had on her mind was whether he'd approve of her work. But now, that damn app and all their talk about romance and dating and marriage had made her take a second look at him. And instead of seeing her boss, she was seeing a man. A most dangerous thing to be doing. Especially if she expected to hold on to her job and her senses.

"I have to go to Wes's office. Would you stop by

George's desk and tell him as soon as I finish I'll help him work on the equation he needs?"

"Sure, Viv."

Slipping her phone in the pocket of her sweater, she hurried out of the break room.

Although Wes had never been as much of a playboy as Ben, he'd always felt comfortable around women. He couldn't remember a time when he'd felt tongue-tied or nervous about meeting one. Which was a good thing, considering that this past week, he'd been meeting women who were total strangers. But this idea he was going to present to Vivian had turned his mouth to West Texas sand.

What if she refused? He'd look like a total idiot.

The light rap on the door had him looking away from the window to see Vivian entering his office. A dark gray skirt fluttered against her knees, while a white silk blouse was tucked inside the tiny waistband. The clothes could hardly be described as sexy, but as he watched her stride toward him, he decided there was something very charming about the way she looked in them.

"Hello, Vivian." He motioned for her to join him at the wall of glass. "Come look."

When she reached his side, he pointed to a bare-limbed hackberry tree in the small patch of ground behind the building. "A pair of mourning doves is back at the nest. They're getting ready to raise another brood."

"I didn't realize you were a bird watcher," she said.

"I'm not. About a year ago, while I was standing here at the window, I just happened to notice these two. They have a nest in a fork of that big limb on the right side of the tree trunk."

She leaned closer to the window. While she searched

for a glimpse of the nest, Wes found himself looking at the way her warm brown hair was pulled carelessly back from her face and how her lips had a hint of raspberry color on them.

"You couldn't know it's the same doves," she reasoned.

"I might keep my head stuck in a computer most of the time, but I do know a little about the outdoors. Doves usually go back to the nest they've used before. And they're like coyotes or wolves. Once they mate, they're together for life."

"Too bad the human species doesn't possess the same devotion."

The bitter tone in her voice surprised Wes. Had she been hurt in the past by an unfaithful lover? Or was she simply talking about society in general? Either way, now wasn't a good time to pursue those types of questions.

"Well, I think devotion got pushed aside by our higher intelligence," he murmured thoughtfully.

She smelled like a flower after a soft rain. Without consciously knowing it, he'd come to associate the unique scent with her. But then, these past few days, he'd begun to notice all sorts of little things about Vivian that he'd never taken the time to notice before.

He was studying the curtain of hair resting against her back when she suddenly turned from the window and speared him with a questioning look.

"I don't think you called me to your office to discuss the mating habits of mourning doves, did you?"

He cleared his throat. "No. I wanted to talk with you about something else."

Concern marked her brow. "Has something gone

wrong with the app?" she asked quickly. "A glitch in distribution? What—"

He held up a hand before she could go any further. "As far as I know, everything is still a go for the Valentine's Day roll out. Don't worry. Our techs will make sure every available buyer can easily download the app."

She let out a breath of relief, and he wondered if her worry over My Perfect Match was mostly for her own investment in the project, or his.

"Okay. I won't worry," she said. "So you must want to talk about my dates—or yours?"

"No." Even though his dates had been pleasant these past few nights, he wasn't the sort who wanted to be out and about every night of the week. Yet with the media lurking around every corner, he knew if he suddenly stopped appearing around town with a woman on his arm, everyone would suspect he'd found *the* one. The whole thing was getting monotonous. "This is about something else."

"Oh. You have a new project in mind for me or the team to work on?"

"No. Let's sit."

He gestured toward a long, wine-colored couch positioned a few feet away. He followed her over to the couch, then took a seat a few inches down from her. The wary expression on her face made his nerves twist even tighter.

"Wes, if this isn't about the app or work, then what—"

"This is something more personal," he interrupted.

She scooted closer. As Wes took in the look of surprise on her parted lips, he had the crazy inclination to kiss her. What in hell was happening to him?

"Personal?"

He reached for her hand and held it between the two of his. "That's right. I want you to be my date. On Valentine's Day—my wedding date."

Chapter Five

"Date? Wedding?" Her heart pounding, Vivian stared at him in disbelief. "What are you talking about?"

"My brother Ben's wedding is taking place this coming Saturday. On Valentine's Day."

Her heart slowed enough to allow her to catch a decent breath. "Yes, I remember reading the announcement," she said. "I'll go out on a huge limb and guess you'll be in the wedding party."

A wan smile touched his face, and Vivian wondered exactly how he was feeling about his twin getting married. She'd heard the brothers were especially close. Although she'd never understood why. Yes, people talked of twins bonded with a connection that bordered on mystical. But she couldn't imagine such a link between Ben and Wes. Other than looking identical, they were very different. Everyone who worked under the roof of Robinson Tech knew that brash Ben didn't mind plowing over whatever stood in the way of what he wanted, while Wes was the quiet workaholic, content to let his achievements speak for him.

"I'll be standing as Ben's best man."

"Congratulations to your brother. And you," she added.

"Thanks. We had rehearsal over the weekend and let me warn you, it's going to be a massive wedding and reception."

"Warn me?"

"Well, yes. As my date, you—"

She quickly held up her free hand to interrupt him. "Your date? Just a minute, Mr. Ro—I mean, Wes. I don't understand any of this. Why are you asking me of all people to attend the wedding with you? Weddings are family affairs. You should be taking someone special as your date."

Releasing his hold on her hand, he turned his attention toward the windows and the darkening skyline, but she somehow doubted he had the approaching rain on his mind.

"Vivian, don't try to pretend ignorance. You have a good idea of how many hours I spend here in my office. Do you think I have time for a special woman in my life?"

"You don't stay here around the clock," she reasoned. "Besides, how would I know something that personal about you?"

He swiped a hand through his already rumpled hair, and Vivian was beginning to see that he wasn't enjoying any of this. In fact, she got the feeling that he'd thought of her as a last resort date. The notion stung.

"The rumor mill in this place works harder than a

cotton gin in September. If I had a steady, you'd know about it, that's for sure."

Vivian felt herself blushing. The idea that he believed she'd gossiped about his love life was worse than embarrassing. Whatever he might think, she didn't sit around mooning or chatting about him or his wealthy family.

"Maybe not. But you've had a string of steady dates these past few days. Surely the app can provide you with an appropriate date. Why turn to me?"

Turning his gaze back to her, he frowned. "Because it just wouldn't be right to take a strange woman from My Perfect Match to the wedding. She might get the wrong idea about the whole thing. Like I'm getting serious or something. You understand?"

Vivian figured she was gaping at him like some sort of idiot, but she couldn't help it. The more he talked, the worse it sounded.

"I'm afraid I do. You don't want any of your dates getting the impression that you might actually care about them—in a serious way," she added drily.

"That's right. And you being a woman—well, you know how weddings put romantic notions in your head."

"Not mine," she said stiffly.

He shot her a smile of relief. "Thank God you're different and above all that sentimental foolishness. I knew I could count on you to understand the situation."

Oh, yes, she was above it all, she thought sadly. Most men saw her as a practical woman. Not one to bend over his arm and kiss senseless.

Her gaze drifted to his lips. Well, she didn't want Wes Robinson's kiss anyway. To allow herself to dream such dreams about her boss would be like staring in a jewelry store window, pining for a ten-karat diamond. It just wasn't going to happen.

"So you don't think your family will get the idea that there's anything between us?"

He shook his head. "They'd never suspect anything serious going on between us. They know you work for the company."

Trying not to let a hint of sarcasm enter her voice, she said, "And you'd never have serious intentions toward an employee."

A frown pulled his brows together. "I have no intentions of getting serious about any woman. Much less an employee. That would spell nothing but trouble."

Trouble indeed, Vivian thought. She would have liked to grind her heel into the arch of his foot and tell him to go limp off into the sunset. But he was Wes Robinson, her boss. The guy who worked tirelessly. The guy who'd always supported her work and encouraged her imagination to fly into the technical future. If not for him, My Perfect Match would have been tossed into the trash heap with the rest of the department's failed designs and ideas. At the very least, she owed him a favor.

"Okay," she finally agreed. "I'll be your date for the wedding."

"Great. I'll give you all the particulars of when and where later. In the meantime, I should inform you that the women guests are encouraged to wear red. In honor of Valentine's Day. So you might keep that in mind while you're picking out something."

A blank look of despair must have come over her face, because he suddenly seemed to realize she'd never have anything in her closet worthy to wear to a Robinson family wedding.

"Uh, and don't worry about the cost of buying a gown. Just go to Anton's and charge whatever you need to my account."

By now Vivian was so dazed she couldn't decide whether to be insulted or thrilled. Anton's was a high-end department store in Austin. She couldn't afford to breathe the air inside the place.

Pride had her lifting her chin. "Thank you, but I'll find a dress on my own and pay for it myself."

"Nonsense. I'm the one who's put you in this spot. You shouldn't be out the expense of a dress. If it will make you feel any better, just think of it as a work assignment."

And why not? she thought sickly. He certainly was.

"I don't like this," she said frankly. "I don't like the idea of being something I'm not. Of being a decoy."

Vivian was shocked to see a grin spread across his face. Wes wasn't a man who grinned about anything. He smiled on occasion, but never grinned. The playful expression made him all the more appealing.

"I'm sure you can fake it for a few hours," he said.

Fake it? With him? How could she pretend to be his date when being near him made her feel as if she was on a very real one? Oh, this was all so crazy.

Desperate to put an end to the tangled trail of her thoughts, she rose to her feet. "Is that all? I should get back to work—George needs my help."

Rising, he walked her to the door. "No need to keep you any longer. Thank you, Viv. I really appreciate you helping me out."

"I'll do my best not to let you down." With a hollow feeling in the middle of her chest, Vivian left his office and hurried past Adelle's desk before the woman could stop her with small talk.

I have no intentions of getting serious about any woman.

For the remainder of the day, his words haunted her.

She couldn't understand why he'd made a point of telling her such a personal thing. She'd certainly never flirted with the man or made any kind of overture toward him. If he was afraid she might be setting her sights on him, then he was crazy. Nothing about him matched the attributes she wanted in a man. But clearly he'd felt the need to remind her that he was off limits to her or any woman.

The idea was humiliating. By the time her work day ended, she was determined to show him she had no desire to snag him or any business shark. She preferred to swim with her own kind.

On Saturday, shortly after noon, Wes drove slowly through the row of apartment buildings as he searched for Vivian's number. Before today, he'd had no idea where she lived. He'd expected to find her somewhere in the suburbs, in one of the newer apartment complexes that had sprung up in recent years. Now, he was a bit surprised to see she resided in a quaint older area of the city. The huge live oaks shading the yards and the rampant growth of ivy clinging to the brick walls told Wes the buildings had probably been here for longer than Vivian had been alive. But the streets were neat and clean. The sight of kids playing outdoors and the sound of dogs barking from front porches gave the neighborhood a homey feel. Far more than his private estate, which was surrounded by security fencing and locked behind wrought iron gates.

When he finally spotted a driveway marked with the number twenty-two, Wes pulled in and parked his car behind a little blue economy car. As he walked to the tiny porch, he noticed two young boys in the next yard.

They were tossing a football and laughing as though they didn't have a care in the world.

The sight of them had him thinking back to the days when he and Ben had been that age. They'd grown up as privileged children, never wanting for anything. Except the attention of their father.

Attention. Like hell, Wes thought with disgust. Gerald had been too busy hiding his true identity to give his eight legitimate children the devotion they'd needed and deserved. Now Ben seemed to believe it was important to prove Gerald was a long-lost member of the famous Fortune family. But as far as Wes was concerned, none of that mattered. Whether Gerald's name was Robinson or Fortune, he'd been a negligent father and a louse of a husband.

Shaking away the dismal thoughts, Wes punched the doorbell, then glanced over his shoulder to see the boys had stopped their game of toss and were standing side by side, staring at him. Apparently they'd never seen a man in the neighborhood wearing a tuxedo.

The opening door creaked. Wes turned back around to see Vivian standing on the threshold.

"Oh, it's you. I wasn't expecting you for another fifteen minutes."

When she failed to invite him in, he made an open gesture with his hands. "Shall I leave and come back in fifteen minutes?"

With a flustered groan, she pushed the door wide and invited him inside. "I'm sorry, Wes. Please come in. I'm almost ready."

He followed her through a tiny foyer, then made a sharp right turn into a small living room. As she came to a halt in the middle of the floor, Wes was only vaguely aware of his surroundings. His gaze was riveted on Vivian. Something had happened to her. She'd transformed from a professional little developer into a dazzling vision of beauty. One who was practically taking his breath away.

"Viv! You look—" *Gorgeous* was the word he wanted to use, but he didn't want to start the day off by making her feel uncomfortable. "Great," he finished, his gaze sweeping from her upswept hair all the down to the toes of her black high heels.

She turned in a full circle, and as the hem of her dress swayed provocatively against her trim ankles, he had to admit the back of her looked just as luscious as the front. The deep red dress clung to her perfect little curves as though it had been tailor-made to fit. The neckline formed a V low against her back, while the front stopped at a point just above the space between her breasts.

"It took me ages to choose it," she admitted. "And even after I got it home, I had my doubts. What do you think?"

Except for Ben's, Wes figured every male eye in the church was going to be on her. Dear Lord, he'd not been expecting anything like this. How was he going to keep his eyes off all that creamy, smooth skin? How was he going to keep remembering that Vivian was a pretend date and not a real one?

"The dress is nice. Very nice."

"I purchased shoes and a handbag, too. But don't worry. I paid for them myself." She gestured toward a floral couch pushed along the outside wall of the room. "Have a seat while I finish getting ready. It shouldn't take me long."

She hurried out of the room. After he'd taken a seat, he looked around at the simple furnishings and wondered if Vivian entertained much company. She didn't seem like the socializing sort, but outside work, he hardly knew her. If he had, he would have expected to see her change from a plain little daisy into this fully bloomed rose.

Maybe she'd brought one of her app dates here, Wes thought. Maybe they'd sat close together on the very couch he was sitting on. And maybe the man had tasted her lips. Had her cherry-colored mouth been cold and stiff or warm and inviting?

Wes was trying not to think about the answer to that question when Vivian reappeared and announced she was ready. He took the cream-colored cape she was carrying and slipped it around her bare shoulders.

"It's sunny outside, but the wind is cold," he warned as he fastened the garment with a row of rhinestone buttons.

For the next few minutes, as Wes's luxury car carried them toward the church located on the opposite side of town, Vivian stared thoughtfully out the passenger window. When Justine had learned she was going to Ben Robinson's wedding as Wes's date, Vivian had thought the woman was going to fall over in a dead faint. And her sister Michelle's reaction to the news had been loud squeals of excitement followed by words of warning.

"I hope you don't make the mistake of reading any importance into this, Viv. You'd only be asking for heartache to think a man like Wes could see you as a serious date."

Vivian had actually laughed at her sister's ridiculous concern. How could Michelle even think Vivian could foolishly fall for her rich boss? There was no way that could ever happen.

"You're awfully quiet, Viv. Are you dreading this?"

She glanced over at him, then immediately wished she hadn't. She'd never seen him dress in formal clothes before or go without his glasses for more than five minutes at a time. He looked incredibly handsome today with his dark, unruly waves brushed to one side and his jaws shaved clean of black stubble. The tailor-made tuxedo fit his long, lean torso perfectly, and the dark color made his appearance even more dashing.

"A little," she admitted. "I'm not sure how I'm supposed to act."

With his attention focused on navigating the car though busy traffic, he asked, "How do you mean?"

Flustered at his clueless attitude, she let out a long breath. "Wes, it's obvious I can't be myself. I'm not here with you today as your employee, am I?"

A scowl creased his brow. "Look, Viv, if anyone is crass enough to inquire about our situation, then tell them you're my date for the day. Nothing more, nothing less."

Oh, brother, that was going to be easier said than done, Vivian thought. She could only hope she wouldn't have to do much more than say a polite hello to his family members. Like she'd told him, she didn't relish the idea of being a decoy.

"All right," she said drolly. "I'll give you admiring glances, not dreamy ones. And I'll do my best to call you Wes rather than Mr. Robinson. Is there anything else I should know?"

"Not that I can think of. By the time we get to the church, it will be time for me to join the rest of the wedding party. The ushers should seat you somewhere just behind my family. Then, once the ceremony is over, I'll meet you out front and we'll head to the hotel for the reception. That's all there is to it."

Maybe for him, Vivian thought. But she felt as though she was about to step onto a huge stage in front of an audience of VIPs. And to make matters worse, she would have to ad-lib her part of the script.

Vivian flinched in surprise as Wes suddenly reached across the leather seat and wrapped his hand around hers.

"Don't worry. This will all be over soon."

Soon? Their afternoon together was only just beginning, and already Vivian could feel herself tumbling headlong into a situation she couldn't control.

By the time Wes and Vivian entered the church, the members of the wedding party were already gathering to make their way to a vestibule out of sight of the hundreds of guests who were already being seated in the main sanctuary. Wes used the brief moments to quickly introduce Vivian to Ben, younger brother Graham, and two of their sisters, Rachel and Zoe.

Once Vivian left the group to take her seat among the wedding guests, Wes's dark-haired little sister, Zoe, jerked him aside.

"Where did you find her?" she asked, her eyes sparkling with curiosity. "Is she one of your app dates?"

The question irked Wes. He didn't like the idea of anyone linking Vivian to the group of women he'd recently been parading around the city. "No. If you must know, nosy sis, Viv and I work together. She created My Perfect Match."

"Ah, that's why I thought I recognized her," Zoe said. "Photos of her have recently been in the papers. She certainly looks different in person. She's very lovely. Why haven't we seen you with her before now?"

Thankfully, Wes didn't have time to answer that question as the change in music gave the cue that the ceremony was about to begin. Everyone quickly fell into line, then promptly filed into the main sanctuary.

As Wes took his place next to his brother, he noticed the huge church was overflowing with family and guests. Up and down the massive hall and on either side of the altar, candles flickered, while red and white flowers seemed to be everywhere.

The music changed yet again, and to one side of the podium, a prominent singer with the Austin Philharmonic began to sing a song about everlasting love. As Wes tried to concentrate on the lyrics, his thoughts turned to Ben and Ella. His twin had always been focused on Robinson Tech and his career. He'd never expected Ben to make room in his life for a wife. But here he was, about to say his vows in front of hundreds of guests. Wes could only hope the words *love*, *honor* and *cherish* would hold more meaning for Ben than they had their father.

The song ended, and as another began, Wes's thoughts drifted to his parents, who were sitting on the first pew, directly behind Wes and Ben and a row of groomsmen. It often amazed him that his mother and father had been married for nearly thirty-five years. The two appeared as a couple at family and social functions but never spent special private time together. In fact, Wes had never seen any sort of affection displayed between his parents. Bearing eight of Gerald's children was proof that Charlotte had once loved her husband, at least physically. Whether she still held any sort of feelings for the man was difficult for Wes to determine. Sometimes he believed his mother suffered through his father's roaming ways simply because it was easier than getting a divorce and fighting over millions of dollars.

Oh, Lord, Wes wanted no such cold arrangement for himself. If he ever lost his mind long enough to take a wife, he'd want their marriage to be nothing less than warm and loving.

The music finally turned into the wedding march, and every head in the church turned to see the bride make her way down the flower-strewn aisle. Because Ella had no father, her mother, Elaine, walked at her daughter's side. Joining Ella on the opposite side was her little brother, Rory, who walked with the aid of braces and crutches. Yet his struggle with cerebral palsy was completely forgotten as everyone in the audience was focused on the pride and joy glowing on his face.

Moved by the sight, Wes watched Ben's profile. His brother's expression was an overflow of love and humility. In that moment, Wes realized for the first time how deeply Ben felt for Ella and her family.

The bride took her place next to the groom, and the minister immediately requested for all to bow their heads. After the long prayer, the singer stepped up for another song about love. By the time the couple finally got around to exchanging their vows, Wes's mind began to drift to Vivian. Somewhere behind him, she was sitting in that beautiful red dress, watching the ceremony. What was she thinking? That My Perfect Match was going to find the right man to put a ring on her finger?

The questions were rolling through Wes's mind at the same time Ben was pushing the ring onto Ella's finger. And suddenly, a different picture swam before his vision. Instead of seeing his brother or new sister-in-law, Wes was picturing himself pushing a wedding band onto Vivian's finger.

Stunned by the image, Wes snapped himself out of his daze just in time to hear the minister's next words. "You may kiss the bride."

Something about seeing his twin become a married man must have done something to Wes, Vivian thought. Ever since the two of them had left the church and arrived at the reception, he'd been quiet and pensive, as though he was somewhere far away instead of in an elaborate ballroom at the Travis Grand Hotel.

"Hello again, Vivian. Would you care for a bit of company? It seems our twins have chosen to desert us, doesn't it?"

Vivian turned to see the female voice behind her belonged to the new bride, Ella Thomas Robinson. During the elaborate wedding ceremony, Vivian had looked on in awe while thinking the beautiful princess was becoming the wife of her handsome prince. Now that she was up close, Vivian still found it hard to keep from gawking at the woman's gorgeous wedding gown. Done in an intricate rose lace pattern, the dress had a close-fitting bodice with the back making a wide V all the way to her waist. Rows of tiny seed pearls edged the low neckline and the wrists of the long, tight sleeves, while the skirt hugged her hips before falling into a pool of rich fabric at her feet. A band fashioned of pearls and tiny white roses held a single tiered veil to her upswept auburn hair.

Even if Vivian had a whole entourage of beauty consultants, she could never look so lovely, she thought. Or was the beautiful aura surrounding Ella actually a product of love? If so, would she ever experience such a glow? Vivian wondered.

"It appears that way," Vivian agreed. "Wes went after more champagne and got distracted by his mother."

Ella's dreamy smile landed on her husband, who was standing several feet away with his father and several other men Vivian recognized as groomsmen.

"And Gerald has cornered Ben with business, no doubt. I suppose my father-in-law has forgotten what it's like to be just married."

Vivian had met Ella earlier, before she and Ben had cut the giant tiered wedding cake and taken their first dance around the room. She'd been surprised that the COO of Robinson Tech had chosen to marry a woman as young and down-to-earth as Ella. But on the other hand, it was easy to see how he'd fallen in love with the warm-hearted beauty.

"The wedding was the most beautiful ceremony I've ever seen," Vivian told her, then admitted with a rueful smile, "honestly, I was nervous about attending. I'm not used to rubbing shoulders with such important people."

Ella laughed lightly. "Believe me, when I first started dating Ben, I felt the same way. You'll soon find out that they're just people, too. Have you known Wes very long?"

So Ella had the idea that she and Wes were truly a couple, she thought miserably. What would the new bride think if she knew her brother-in-law had brought Vivian to the wedding only because she was a safe date who expected nothing from him?

Vivian tilted a fluted glass to her lips and hoped the bubbly champagne would help ease her knotted nerves.

"About six years," she answered, while instinctively turning her gaze back to Wes and his mother.

"That long!" Ella exclaimed. "Oh, my, he must be a slow worker. I—"

"Hey, can I join in on the fun?"

The British accent caught Vivian's attention, and she looked around to see a tall woman somewhere in her twenties walking up to Ella's side. Slender and elegant, she had straight brown hair, hazel eyes and a faint smile that held a hint of mystery. Vivian was instantly intrigued.

Ella quickly introduced the two women. "Vivian, this is Lucie Fortune Chesterfield. And Lucie, this is Vivian Blair, my brother-in-law's lovely date."

Vivian shook hands with the woman. "Nice to meet you, Lucie. Did you fly in for the wedding? Or do you live in Texas?"

"Lucie is originally from London," Ella inserted, then laughed and gestured for Lucie to explain further.

"But I've been staying in Horseback Hollow with relatives," Lucie went on. "My sister married a cowboy there, and they have a baby daughter. I can hardly resist spending time with my little niece."

"Lucie is the one who helped Ben locate his half brother, Keaton Robinson—or I should say, Keaton Fortune Robinson," Ella added slyly.

Totally confused by this information, Vivian looked from one woman to the other. "I don't understand. Half brother? I didn't realize there was a half brother."

Ella and Lucie exchanged a pointed look.

"Well, the connection was only discovered a few weeks ago," Ella told her. Then, with a curious expression, she asked, "Doesn't Wes talk with you about family matters?"

Vivian felt her cheeks grow warm with embarrassment. "Wes and I have been dealing with lots of work. I guess it slipped his mind."

"Well, then, you don't know that Ben is trying to prove their father, Gerald, is actually a member of the Fortune family?"

Clueless and not bothering to hide the fact, Vivian shook her head. "Fortune? Are you talking about the Fortunes who own the cosmetic company?"

"That's right," Ella answered.

Still perplexed, Vivian glanced at Lucie. "Then if your name is Fortune, you could be related to Wes and Ben."

"We're thinking that could be so."

Stunned by this news, Vivian glanced through the crowd until her gaze landed on Wes. Did she really know the man at all?

Across the room, Wes stood with his mother, Charlotte, as she sipped champagne and commented about the wedding ceremony. Ben was the first one of her children to finally get married, and though Wes had expected her to be happy about the event, she seemed rather pensive.

"What's wrong, Mother? The ceremony went off without a hitch. I don't know much about these sorts of things, but I thought everything looked pretty grand. And everyone appears to be having a good time at the reception. Aren't you happy for Ben and Ella?"

She touched a hand to her short platinum hair and Wes decided, for a woman in her midseventies, his mother looked at least ten years younger. Unlike the majority of female guests who'd worn red in some fashion today, Charlotte had opted to wear a pastel pink dress with a heavy dose of diamonds at her throat. He

supposed she'd foregone wearing red in order to stand
out in the crowd. Or, knowing his mother, she probably
worried the color clashed with her complexion. Either
way, nothing was missing about his mother's appearance, he concluded, except a happy smile.

Charlotte said, "This affair today is hardly what concerns me, Wes. Anyone with money and good taste can
throw a decent party. No, it's Ben whom I'm thinking
of now. I wish a thousand times he'd not jumped into
this marriage so quickly. It's hardly been a month since
he and Ella first got engaged!"

Wes held back a sigh. "Ben never was one to waste
time, Mother. But I wouldn't worry about him. He's
fully aware of what he's doing."

She glanced sharply up at him. "Are you?"

Taken slightly aback by her abrupt question, Wes
frowned, then finally chuckled. "I like to think so. Why
do you ask?"

Her lips pursed with disapproval, and Wes could
only wonder what was going on in her mind. He loved
his mother dearly. She'd always been the glue that held
the Robinson family together. She'd always been the
one who'd made Wes feel special and wanted. But there
were times he didn't understand her way of thinking.

"Are you talking about the articles you've been seeing in the papers about my dates?" he asked. "Mother,
those women have nothing to do with my personal feelings. They're just a part of my job. It's only business.
That's all."

She rolled her eyes until they landed accusingly on
her husband. "I've heard that line a thousand times,"
she said with a heavy dose of sarcasm, then took a long
drink from her champagne glass.

No doubt, Wes thought, his gaze straying over to

his father. Over the years Gerald had probably given his wife endless excuses and lies to cover his deceitful tracks. And now, God help his family, Ben wanted to uncover all of them.

"It's not a line with me," he insisted. "It's the truth."

She turned her gaze back to Wes. "If you say so. I just don't want you making the same mistake of marrying in haste."

Wes frowned. "What are you talking about? I hardly have marriage on my mind."

He followed the incline of his mother's head to see Vivian standing with Ella and another young woman he didn't recognize.

"Mother, Vivian is just a friend. We work together— that's the sum of things between us."

Shaking her head, she said, "I wasn't born yesterday, Wes. I can see the signs—the way you two look at each other. You need to be cautious and take things slowly, son. Please take my advice."

Wes was only half listening to his mother now. His attention was back on Vivian and the way she and her newfound friends were talking intently. Were they discussing him?

"I promise not to do anything rash, Mother. Now if you'll excuse me, I need to get back to my date."

As he walked away, he could feel his mother's eyes boring into his back. Poor woman, Wes thought. She might still look youthful for her age, but her mind was obviously slipping. Why else would she possibly connect Wes and Vivian in a matrimonial way? It was ridiculous.

Why don't you survey the condition of your own mind, Wes? Right in the middle of the wedding cere-

mony, you were picturing yourself slipping a wedding ring on Vivian's finger. That was worse than ridiculous.

Skirting the edge of dancers circling the enormous ballroom floor, Wes made his way over to Vivian. As he neared the three women, the loudness of the live band drowned out their conversation. But it was clear to Wes that whatever they'd been discussing was immediately dropped when he came to stand at Vivian's side.

"Wes, I'm glad you joined us," Ella spoke up. "I don't think you've met Lucie, have you?"

He could feel Vivian watching him closely.

"No. I don't believe I've had the pleasure," he said.

"This is Lucie Fortune Chesterfield. She—"

"Helped Ben locate our half brother." He finished his sister-in-law's sentence, then thrust his hand toward the Londoner. "Nice to meet you, Lucie. I hope your stay in Austin is a pleasant one."

"Thank you. I'm having a great time." Smiling, she studied him keenly. "You look exactly like Ben. It's uncanny."

Wes said, "Yes, but most everyone will tell you that the two of us are not that much alike. Now if you ladies will excuse us, I think it's time I took Vivian for a whirl around the dance floor."

Plucking the champagne glass from Vivian's hand, he placed it on the tray of a passing waiter, then wasted no time in leading her to a vacant space on the dance floor.

As he pulled her into the close circle of his arms, he could feel her body determined to keep a respectable breathing space between them. Wes didn't try to urge her closer. But he damn well wanted to. And the realization rattled him.

"That was rather abrupt, the way you left Ella and her friend, don't you think?"

"This is one of my favorite songs," he lied. "I wanted to dance to it before it ended."

"Considering I've never heard the song, maybe you can tell me the name of it," she suggested.

Sometimes Wes forgot just how clever Vivian could be. "I never was good with names."

"You didn't have any problem remembering Lucie's."

The hand on her shoulder slipped downward until it was lying flat against her bare back. The softness of her skin beneath his palm was all it took to yank his senses in all directions. All these years he'd never stopped to wonder what was beneath her modest clothing. But today he was seeing and feeling for himself, and the sensation was a heady one.

"I have good reason to remember her name. What were you three talking about, anyway?"

"The wedding. Girl things," she hedged.

"And men?"

She frowned. "Not you. If that's what you mean."

Arching a brow at her, he waited for her to continue.

With a tiny groan of reluctance, she relented, "Okay. They were telling me about Keaton Whitfield. Your half brother."

Wes's jaw tightened. "They shouldn't have mentioned any of that. Not today. Not to you."

She looked apologetic. "I'm sorry, Wes. The women started talking and I had no choice but to listen or rudely walk away."

A pent-up breath slipped out of him. "Forget it. Sooner or later, everyone is going to hear about Keaton anyway."

Clearly confused, she said, "You make it sound like he's not exactly a welcome member of the family."

Needing to feel her body next to his, he instinctively drew her closer.

"Welcome," he repeated ruefully. "Is that how siblings should react to their father's illegitimate son? Tell me, because I don't know."

"Illegitimate? Are you sure?"

A curt laugh escaped him. "Well, since he was born about the same time as Ben and me, it's obvious his mother wasn't married to our father. And to make matters worse, there might be other children we've yet to learn about."

"You mean Keaton Whitfield has siblings?"

"I mean children from other women," he said flatly.

"Oh, my."

The two murmured words connected his gaze with hers, and Wes was relieved to find nothing judgmental in the hazel depths, or any sign that she considered his revelation a juicy morsel of gossip to be whispered about the workplace. No, all he could see was concern and empathy.

"Yeah," he said under his breath. "Oh, my."

She gently squeezed his hand, and the unexpected gesture made him realize she understood part of his mixed feelings, at least. It was also waking up something inside him that felt a whole lot like desire.

He was trying to figure out how this sudden attraction for Vivian had started when her feet suddenly came to a stop.

"Uh, Wes, the music has ended," she said softly. "We should probably get off the dance floor before we cause a traffic jam."

With a shake of his head, he said, "Let's wait for the next song."

And the next. And the next one after that, Wes

thought. And even then Wes wasn't sure that would be enough time to satisfy his growing need to hold her in his arms.

Chapter Six

"I'm sorry, Vivian, for sounding so short a few minutes ago," he said moments later as he guided her among
the throng of dancing couples. "It's just that, outside
my family, I've never talked about Keaton Robinson,
or Whitfield, or whatever the hell his name is, to anyone. It feels—well, pretty damn awkward."

A wan smile touched her lips. "There's no need for
you to apologize, Wes. That's your private family business. It has nothing to do with me."

But it did, Wes thought. He didn't want Vivian, of
all people, thinking badly of his family. He wanted her
to be proud of him. Proud that she worked for Robinson Tech.

When he didn't reply, she went on, "Have you met
your half brother?"

He frowned. "No. Ben met him over in London,
where Keaton lives. You see, up until a few months
ago, we had no idea he existed."

"How did you learn about him?" Vivian asked. "Ella said something about Lucie helping Ben find the man. How does she fit into the picture?"

He let out a long sigh. "It's a complicated story, Viv. You see, our younger sister Rachel—the tall, pretty one you met before the ceremony—she suspected something didn't ring true with our father. I don't know what made her suspicious, but anyway, one day when no one was around to notice, she searched through some of Dad's things. Sure enough, she found a driver's license with a much younger picture of Dad on it and the name Jerome Fortune."

"He might have had the license made for a prank or something. It doesn't necessarily mean that was once his identity."

"You're right. But there was more than the license. Rachel discovered several pieces of old correspondence with the same name."

Amazement dawned across her features. "Jerome Fortune? I see the connection to Lucie now. That must have been a stunner for all of you."

"It was stunning all right," he said grimly. "Since then Ben's been possessed with finding out what it all means and why our father would assume an alias."

"Why not just ask your father for the truth? Wouldn't that be the simplest way to find out?"

Wes let out a low, caustic laugh. "Gerald, 'fess up? Are you kidding? His lips are clamped tighter than a pair of vise grips. He refuses to talk about any of it. In fact, he and Ben have been at such odds over the whole issue that I'm surprised Dad even showed up today. He probably decided staying away would create even more gossip."

"How very strange," she murmured thoughtfully,

her gaze straying across the room to Gerald Robinson standing with a group of businessmen. "So Ben's search for your father's background is the reason Keaton's existence was uncovered?"

"Keaton and possibly others," Wes said with a grimace. "To be frank, most of us siblings wish Ben would forget the whole thing. If more offspring are discovered, it will hurt our mother even more."

She nodded ruefully. "That's understandable. So why is Ben so intent on unearthing this information? It's not like you need the Fortune name attached to yours. You Robinsons are already famous in your own right."

Wes sighed. "It's not fame or money with Ben. It's the truth he's after—why our father changed his identity. But as far as I'm concerned, the truth is sometimes better left buried."

As they glided together to the beat of the music, her gaze made a slow survey of his face, and Wes wondered if she was feeling the same sort of hot, sweet awareness that was building in him. He didn't know what was happening, but something about being in her arms was creating an upheaval inside him. She was filling him with desire, and things were coming out of his mouth that normally he would keep carefully locked away.

"Well, at least your parents are still married. Mine have been divorced since I was in junior high school," she said, her voice full of regret. "My sister believes they parted because our father had a roaming eye. But I'm convinced their marriage ended because they had nothing in common. They spent very little time together, and whenever they did, they were both bored out of their minds or squabbling over something silly."

Her revelation had Wes studying the lovely angles and curves of her face. When she'd first come to him with the idea for My Perfect Match, he'd figured the app was merely a product of her fertile imagination. Now he could see the purpose behind the project held a far deeper meaning for her. Because of her parents' divorce, she truly believed passion had nothing to do with a lasting relationship.

"You believe your parents had nothing in common? Believe me, Viv, I've often wondered what drew my parents together in the first place. And I damn well wonder what keeps them together. Their marriage is a disastrous sham. Mother puts up a front and pretends she's happy. But deep down, she has to be hurting over Dad's philandering." He shook his head. "I'm happy for Ben and I wish him and Ella a long and loving marriage. But as for myself, I don't want any part of that."

As soon as his words died away, he expected Vivian to fire a retort back at him. Like how jaded he sounded. Or how he shouldn't allow his father's mistakes to mar his chance for love and happiness. But she didn't say any of that. Instead, she turned a pensive gaze on the couples swirling around them.

The sea of red dresses moving to the music suddenly faded to a blur as Wes's gaze settled on the sweet, tempting curve of her lips. He was aching to taste her mouth. Aching to lose himself in her kiss.

His head leaned toward hers, and a sense of triumph rippled through him as she rested her soft cheek against his.

"I agree. Being married to the wrong person is a tragic situation. It's a mistake I definitely don't want to make."

She pulled her head back just enough to look at him, and Wes very nearly forgot they were in a crowded reception hall with hundreds of couples dancing, laughing and sipping champagne. Her lips were only a scant space away from his, and suddenly he was fighting a war with himself. All he wanted was to capture her lips beneath his and kiss her until they were both breathless and hungry for more.

"You won't make that mistake," he murmured, "if you stay away from marriage."

"That's true. But I still believe marriage can be a beautiful thing when two people are perfectly matched and compatible."

A beautiful thing. Yes, carrying Vivian to a quiet, private place, slipping the red dress off her shoulders and making hot, sweet love to her—that would be beautiful—but crazy and dangerous!

The serious direction of his thoughts was enough to snap Wes out of his dreamy haze, and he quickly stepped back from the tempting warmth of her body. "It's getting warm in here, and I'm getting dry," he said in a husky rush. "Let's go find something to drink."

Not long after they left the dance floor, Wes made their excuses to leave the reception. Seeing the party wasn't anywhere near ending, Vivian was surprised that he was ready to leave his brother's wedding celebration. As he drove to her apartment, she continued to wonder what had come over him. It was as if a switch had been flipped inside him. One minute, they'd been talking and dancing, their bodies snug as they moved to the music. Then, all of a sudden, he'd stopped in the middle of the song and practically jerked her off the dance floor. In the matter of a few seconds, he'd gone from warm and personable to cold and distant.

She'd tried to think of something she might have said or done to cause the change in him, but it was beyond her. Now, as she glanced at his moody profile, she decided it was probably a good thing he'd called an end to their time together. For a while, she'd been enjoying his company far too much. His distant behavior hurt, but it was a good reminder that, for him, today was all pretend. And now the pretense was over.

By the time he parked in the driveway, the sky was growing dark, and a brisk north wind was sweeping across the tiny yard in front of her ground-level apartment. A hollow feeling was creeping over her, but she fought to push it away.

Unfastening her seatbelt, she said, "It's gotten colder outside. There's no need for you to see me in."

He cut her a wry glance. "I don't think I'll die of hypothermia if I walk you to your door."

"All right." Since her cape was already fastened around her shoulders, she grabbed up her handbag and let herself out of the car before he had a chance to skirt the hood and do it for her.

He didn't take her arm on the short walk to the porch. Instead, he kept at least a foot of space between them as he walked by her side. Once they reached the steps, he said in a stiff voice, "Thank you for accompanying me today, Vivian. You've been a good sport about it all."

A good sport. A work buddy. That's all you'll ever be to Wes Robinson.

The mocking voice in Vivian's head was hurtful. Because it was speaking the truth. And that was something she desperately needed to face and accept.

Swallowing the thickness in her throat, she said, "You're welcome, Wes. Thank you for inviting me. The wedding was a fairy tale, and so was the reception. It's been a memorable day for me."

Frown lines appeared in the middle of his forehead

and she suddenly realized he was peering at something over her shoulder. Turning, she spotted a box lying at the foot of the storm door.

"Oh! I wasn't expecting a delivery."

"Maybe you'd better see what it is," Wes suggested. "Someone could be pulling a prank."

She chuckled. "This isn't Halloween, Wes. It's Valentine's Day."

"I'm sure you've broken a heart or two in the past."

"Sure. I'm a femme fatale," she joked.

Vivian collected the box from the concrete floor and quickly pulled off the lid. To her surprise, she found a beautiful bouquet of dark pink roses and a small card with a brief message.

"Looks like you have an admirer," Wes commented.

For one split second before she'd found the card, Vivian had foolishly imagined Wes had sent the flowers as a Valentine's gift. A way to thank her for being his date. She should have known better. Wes didn't send flowers to women who worked for him. He saved that sort of thing for his real dates.

"Roses from one of the My Perfect Match dates," she told him. "How nice of him to remember me on Valentine's Day."

For the first time since the two of them had been dancing together, a genuine smile crossed his face.

"Must be a thoughtful guy. Are you going to see him again?"

She placed the lid back on the boxed flowers and balanced them beneath one arm while she unlocked the entrance to her apartment. Once she had the door open, she turned awkwardly back to him.

"Perhaps. But I'm not about to limit myself. The app went on sale today, so hopefully the pool of bachelors should grow from the small test group. I'm anxious to see what else the computer picks for me."

"I've got to admit, Viv, that so far I'm impressed with the app. I've had some great dates, and it appears that you have, too. Maybe we'll both come out winners in this dating game."

A game. Vivian inwardly sighed. She supposed he would consider the whole matter a contest between them. He wasn't in the market for a serious relationship, and considering the way he felt about his father, she doubted that would ever change.

"I suppose both of us will win if the app is a success," she said simply.

"I couldn't have said it better," he agreed, then leaned over and pressed a chaste kiss to her cold cheek. "Happy Valentine's Day."

Resisting the urge to touch the spot he'd just kissed, she murmured, "Happy Valentine's Day to you, too."

"Thanks. See you Monday. At the office."

He turned to step off the porch, and the sight of his retreating back sent a pang of loss rushing through her. Before she realized what she was about to do, she said, "Uh—Wes, would you like to come in for coffee? The evening is still early."

Pausing, he glanced at his watch as though to calculate whether he could spend any more time with her, and for a second she wished she could take back the invitation. He'd already whisked her away from the reception party at a ridiculously early hour. That should've been a loud and clear signal that he was more than tired of her company.

"It is still early," he agreed. "And after all that champagne and punch, coffee would be nice. Thank you, Viv."

The elation rushing through her was ridiculous, and though she tried to stem it, she couldn't stop a bright smile from spreading across her face.

"Great. Let's get out of the cold."

They entered the apartment, and after she'd secured the door behind him, she gestured casually toward the couch. "Make yourself comfortable. Or if you'd rather, you can join me in the kitchen."

"I'll go with you," he said. "You probably won't believe this, but I can do a few things in the kitchen. Even make coffee."

She chuckled as he followed her through a wide doorway and into an L-shaped kitchen with a small dining area.

"I believe you can drop a little plastic cup into a machine and press a button."

"There's nothing wrong with making coffee that way."

She playfully wrinkled her nose at him. "Go ahead and have a seat. Tonight I'm letting you off coffee detail."

She dropped the box of roses onto the tabletop and wondered why she wasn't feeling more thrilled about receiving the romantic gift. It wasn't often that she received flowers from a man. And yet the app date, who'd been attentive enough to remember her on Valentine's Day, had done nothing to make her heart flutter with eager excitement. When he'd smiled or touched her hand, she'd felt as though she was talking to a brother, cousin or friend. Not a potential lover.

Wes gestured to the box of roses. "You'd better put those in water. You wouldn't want them to wilt."

"I'll take care of them. After all, the flowers might be the only thing I get out of My Perfect Match," she said, then tried to add a lighthearted laugh, but the strained sound resembled a sob more than a chuckle.

He took a seat at the little glass dining table while Vivian removed her cape and draped it over the back of a chair. She would've liked to change out of her dress, but since he was stuck in his formal clothes, she felt it would be impolite to make herself more comfortable. Besides, after tonight, she'd probably never have another chance to wear such a fancy dress. She might as well make the most of it.

He said, "Looks to me like you're off to a good start. And we're just now getting started with our dates. You might find Mr. Wonderful out of this thing."

Strange, but right now she couldn't imagine herself falling in love with any man. Each time she tried to picture herself as a bride or a wife, Wes's face kept getting in the way. Besides not making any sense, it was downright annoying.

"And perhaps you'll find the woman who's ideal for you," she countered.

He made a scoffing noise. "You don't actually believe a person can be perfect, do you?"

"The app is named My Perfect Match, not My Perfect Person," she reasoned.

"I stand corrected."

He drummed his fingers on the tabletop, and Vivian glanced around to see him making a survey of his surroundings. No doubt her modest apartment was unlike anything he was accustomed to. And she'd bet every dollar she owned that he'd never dated a woman of her social standing. Now that he was seeing her in her domain, he was probably wondering what had possessed him to take her to a family wedding. The idea cut into her far more than it should have.

She turned back to the coffeemaker and tried to focus on her task instead of her boss.

Silence engulfed the room before he finally asked, "Do you normally go out on Valentine's Day?"

"On a date?" she asked.

"Any other way doesn't count. It's a day for being with the one you love," he said, then quickly followed that with a derisive little laugh. "At least the one you love on that particular day."

She wanted to ask him if he'd ever been in love, but after the way he'd clammed up at the wedding reception, she decided getting that personal wouldn't be a good idea. Anyway, it was none of her business if Wes had ever loved a woman. And it never would be.

She said, "I've had a few Valentine's Day dates. Some of them were nice and some were stinkers. Funny, but the awful ones are the ones I remember the most. What about you?"

With the coffee brewing, Vivian busied herself finding a vase and filling it with water. Out of the corner of her eye, she saw Wes slipping out of his jacket and loosening his tie. At least he appeared to be relaxing, she thought. The fact help ease some of the tension that had coiled her in knots the moment the two of them had entered the apartment.

"Same with me. You try to forget the bad ones, but those are the ones that stick in your mind. One year Ben talked me into going on a blind double date with him on Valentine's Day. That evening turned out to be disastrous. I thought all four of us were going to be thrown out of the nightclub or arrested."

Laughing at the absurd image, she carried the vase over to the table and placed the bunch of roses into the water. "You being rowdy? That's hard to imagine."

A wan smile curved one corner of his lips. "Anything can happen when you're out with Ben, and I knew better than to go with him in the first place. But he can be awfully persuasive when he wants to be."

She eased into the chair across from him. "I've always thought having a twin must be very different from having just a brother or sister," she said thoughtfully.

"It's a connection you can't explain. Even though we have different mindsets, we're there for each other. That's not to say we don't have our share of disagreements, because we do. But no matter what goes on in our lives, we'll always be like this." He held up crossed fingers.

"I'm surprised to hear you say that," she said. Then, as she watched one of his brows arch in question, she quickly added, "I mean, I've always had the impression that you and Ben were competitive. That must surely put a strain on your relationship."

His eyes narrowed. "Why don't you come out and say you're talking about the COO position?"

Vivian blushed, then shook her head. "I merely meant being competitive in general. But now that you've brought it up, I might as well tell you that I heard through the office grapevine that you were on the outs with your brother. Actually, I heard you were angry with him because he landed the job."

The corners of his mouth turned downward, and a part of Vivian wished she'd not said anything about Ben or the COO position. Now that she'd learned Wes could laugh and smile, she wanted to see that charming side of him, not the harried businessman who often worked himself to the point of exhaustion.

"Who's been talking that nonsense to you? Adelle?"

"Are you kidding? Adelle is your staunch supporter.

She'd never utter anything personal about you to me. No, I inadvertently overheard a conversation going on between some of the other employees."

With a frown still marring his forehead, he said, "Well, it's not true. I wasn't angry with Ben. He didn't appoint himself to the position. Our father made the decision to do that."

"I see."

"I'm not sure you do. Ben is ambitious, but that's hardly a crime. I'm driven, too. Only in a different way. I wanted that position all right, but I can survive without it. I wouldn't want to live without my twin. Understand?"

She smiled. "I do. And you know what I think about it?"

"I'm sure you're going to tell me."

"You're too good at what you do to be working in any other position than the one you're in now."

"Should I take that as a compliment?" he asked.

She laughed softly. "You'd better. It might be the only one you get out of me."

By now the little kitchen was filled with the aroma of freshly brewed coffee. Wes thoughtfully watched Vivian as she left the table and began to gather cups, cream and sugar.

"I have chocolate chip cookies if you'd like some," she offered.

"No, thanks. I'm still full of wedding cake."

"So am I," she told him. "It wasn't enough for me to eat a piece of wedding cake. I had to have a piece of the groom's cake, too."

He didn't know what had made him accept Vivian's invitation for coffee. After the wild feelings he'd been having on the dance floor, the last thing he needed to be doing was spending private time with the woman. But as he'd turned to leave, something about the way she'd looked standing there on the little porch had been his undoing. Now here he was once again wondering how he was going to find the self-discipline to keep his hands off her.

She placed everything on a tray and walked over to the table, where he still sat. "Let's take our coffee to the living room," she suggested. "It's much more comfortable there."

"Fine. I'll get my jacket and you lead the way."

Wes followed her out to the living room, and after tossing the tuxedo jacket over the back of a couch covered in brown suede fabric, he took a seat on an end cushion.

Vivian placed the tray on the coffee table. She joined him on the couch, then reached for the television remote.

"It's nearly time for the local evening news," she said. "Maybe we'll hear something about the app during the business segment."

Grateful for the distraction, Wes picked up one of the cups and settled back against the cushions. "Or the entertainment portion."

She rolled her eyes. "Entertainment? Is that how you view the app? Entertainment?"

"Well, that is what dating is supposed to be, isn't it?"

She opened her mouth to make some sort of retort, then appeared to change her mind. As she poured a measure of cream into her coffee, she said, "I suppose it is entertainment to you."

The screen flickered to life, and Vivian scrolled through the channels until she found a local affiliate. Wes did his best to focus on the television instead of the

woman sitting less than a foot away from him. But that
was difficult to do with her delicate perfume drifting
to his nostrils and the rustle of her red dress signaling
every tiny move she made.

"Did you notice whether any of the media followed
us to the wedding today?" she asked.

He grimaced. "I didn't notice any. But with all the
people around, there was no way of knowing. Anyone
with a cell phone can take photos and videos."

"Hopefully they didn't. The public expects us to be
going out with people from the app."

"That's one of the reasons I invited you to attend
the wedding with me. Everyone knows we're just coworkers."

He'd hardly gotten the words out of his mouth when
a video shot of the wedding appeared on the screen.

"Look, Wes! There we are, heading into the church!"

She snatched up the remote and made the volume
louder just in time to pick up the anchor in midsentence.

"...Robinson Tech. Austin's most eligible bachelor
is off the market. As for his twin brother, Wes, everyone is wondering who the mystery woman is hanging
on to his arm. Since the tech wonder boy made the announcement he'd be using the company's own dating
app to find his lady love, we're all speculating if *this* is
the special one. Who—"

Wes quickly plucked the remote from her hand and
pressed the mute button.

Vivian gasped. "Why did you do that? That was
about you! Us!"

He shot her a droll look. "That social crap is silly.
The media doesn't really know what's going on, but
they damn well like to put stories out there anyway."

Her features tight, she sipped her coffee, then fixed a stare on the TV screen. "Sorry. I misspoke. There is no *us*. Not in the sense they were using it."

Something was bothering her, Wes decided, but he couldn't put his finger on the problem. Could be she'd picked up on all those lustful urges he'd gotten while they were dancing, he thought, and now being alone with him made her feel awkward.

Hell, Wes, if she'd felt that uncomfortable, why did she invite you in? When it comes to women and how they think, you're totally ignorant. You're a tech geek. Don't make the mistake of trying to think like a lover boy. You're not even close to being one of those.

Annoyed at the mocking voice in his head, he handed the remote back to her. "I'm the one who's sorry, Viv," he apologized. "This is your house and your television. I had no right to turn off the sound. I just—don't like my life being made public. But that's probably hard for you to understand."

She said, "You're right. I'm not rich and famous like you are. I don't know what it's like to be in the public eye. Furthermore, I'll never know."

While she scrolled through more channels, Wes sipped his coffee and hoped the hot brew would jerk his senses back to reality. Presently, his brain seemed to be drowning in her presence, and he didn't know how to keep his sanity afloat.

"Be thankful for that, Viv. As kids, we Robinsons couldn't go anywhere in public without a bodyguard lurking nearby. Talk about putting a damper on things. It could get miserable. But Dad couldn't risk any of us being kidnapped and held for ransom. It's only been since we've gotten older that he's eased up and let us go about our lives on our own."

She looked amazed. "I thought something like that only happened in the movies. Or in families with members in high political offices. Gerald must be paranoid."

"My family has always had the kind of wealth that evil people like to go after." He gestured around the neat living room. "I can't live like you do."

She laughed. "You mean, you don't want to live like this."

He shook his head. "Luxury, or the lack of it, is not what I'm talking about. Security is always an issue."

"Oh. I wasn't thinking in those terms." She smiled, then added jokingly, "But I did lock the door behind us."

She placed the remote on the coffee table, and Wes noticed she'd left the sound on mute. The notion that she might consider his company more interesting than the television swelled his ego in a way he never expected.

"I'll bet you've never visited a place like mine before."

Surprised, he frowned at her. "I'm not a snob, Viv. I have friends and acquaintances from all walks of life."

Turning toward him, she tucked her legs beneath her. "Tell me what your home looks like. Do you live there alone?"

"I live on a private estate on the northwest side of the city."

"Where all the mansions are located," she said pointedly.

"Should I apologize for that?"

Another soft laugh escaped her lips, and Wes found himself drinking in the happy sound, the vibrant twinkle in her hazel eyes and the way her teeth gleamed white against her lips.

"No. If living there makes you happy, that's what you should do."

"I don't know about happy. I live there alone. With a housekeeper coming in every other day to tidy up. There are two stories to the house, but I mainly just use the bottom floor. The folks who owned it before me had several kids, so they needed all the upstairs bedrooms."

"Is it an old estate?"

"Originally, an oil magnate had the place built shortly after World War I. I think he and his wife came to the city thinking he could get into politics. But that never happened. In any case, the outside is made of native rock and the inside has open ceilings, parquet floors and varnished moldings."

"It sounds lovely," she murmured.

Had she leaned closer to him or had he scooted toward her? Wes wondered. Either way, her face suddenly seemed much closer to his. So close, in fact, that he could see the gold and green flecks in her eyes, the rim of her black lashes and the faint vertical lines in her lower lip.

How would that lip taste if he ran his tongue over the soft edges? If he gently sank his teeth into the plump curve?

"Maybe I could show it to you sometime," he said, his voice low and thick.

The cup in his hand suddenly felt so heavy, he wondered if it was full of lead instead of coffee. He leaned forward to place it on the table at the very same moment Vivian chose to do the same thing. The two cups collided, and their fingers tangled as they both made desperate grabs to keep them from falling to the floor.

"Oh! Sorry," she exclaimed. She juggled the cup until she finally managed to set it safely back on the tray.

"It's my fault." In a rush to place his cup alongside hers, he very nearly tipped it over before he finally secured in an upright position. "I don't think I spilled any on the floor. But I'm not certain."

"I'm not worried about the floor. What about your trousers?"

He bent forward to inspect the legs of his trousers. When he failed to see any damp spots staining the black fabric, he raised his head and smacked it straight into Vivian's chin.

"Viv! Oh, I'm sorry. Did I hurt you?"

He grabbed her shoulders, more to steady her than anything. At the same time, her hands thrust outward in search of an anchor and ended up landing in the middle of his chest. The sudden contact was like a searing jolt of electricity welding them together. He could hardly breathe, much less find the strength to pull back.

"No. It was just a little bump. No problem—I'm fine."

Her last words were little more than a whisper, but they were enough to beckon Wes to lean his head closer to hers.

"Better let me take a look." Placing a forefinger beneath her chin, he lifted her face. The quick inspection ended with his gaze zeroing in on her moist lips, and the sight brought on a gnawing hunger deep inside him. "I don't see a cut—or anything. I—"

Whatever else he'd been about to say was instantly blotted out as somehow, someway, Vivian's lips found their way to his. Or had he been the one to close the last fraction of space between them? Either way, it didn't matter. The only thing that did matter was that he was kissing her. And she tasted like heaven.

Chapter Seven

Vivian had no idea how she'd ended up in Wes's arms or how her lips had gotten tangled up with his. But now that their mouths were fused together, her brain was on a single mission, and that was to get closer to the man. And to make sure he couldn't slip away, she wrapped her arms around his neck and pressed her upper body to his broad chest.

The masculine scent of his skin mingled with the expensive cologne on his shirt. Together, the erotic mixture filled her head and lured her senses, while the taste of his lips was like nothing she'd expected. Dark and reckless and commanding, his kiss was pushing her to a mindless daze where there was nothing but the two of them. Kissing. Touching. Loving.

Eventually the wild pleasure began to consume her, and a low groan erupted deep in her throat. The sound shattered the silence of the room, and suddenly Wes jerked his head away from hers and stared at her in stunned fascination.

Her face burning, her lips stinging, Vivian sucked oxygen into her lungs and gazed into his drowsy blue eyes. From where she sat, he appeared to be equally shocked by what had just occurred between them.

"Wes, I—"

He didn't wait for her to finish. Instead, the hands he'd already clamped over her shoulders jerked her back to him, and his mouth fastened hungrily over hers.

This time Vivian didn't hesitate to open her lips and invite him to take the kiss to a deeper, sweeter place. He promptly accepted her bidding by thrusting his tongue between the ridges of her teeth. As he explored the walls of her mouth, his hands pushed their way down her back until he reached the flare of her hips.

When his palms cupped her bottom, she uncurled her legs and stretched toward him. She needed to feel the length of his body touching her, warming every feminine cell inside her until she was burning, craving the pleasure he could give her.

He must have been feeling the same hot desperation because the next thing Vivian knew, she was toppling over and he was falling with her. The short tumble was enough to break the contact of their lips, and he used the moment to shift both of them around on the cushions until they were lying face to face, hip to hip. The contact was incredibly intimate, and immediately an aching desire began to build low in her belly.

The search of his mouth on hers was delicious and unrelenting, and the only thought going through Vivian's head was that she couldn't get enough of it. Or him. And when she felt his fingers caressing the cleavage exposed by the low neckline of her dress, she wanted to slither quickly out of the garment. She wanted his hands to touch every inch of her skin. She wanted his tongue to taste every hollow and curve.

Then, just as she was slipping away to a dreamy fog of paradise, Wes jerked away from her and hastily scrambled to his feet.

Recognizing the hem of her dress was hiked up around her hips, Vivian jerked the fabric past her knees. Standing a few steps away, Wes jammed the tail of his shirt back into the waistband of his trousers, then raked a hand through his rumpled hair.

Totally confused, she pushed a question through her tight throat. "Wes, what's wrong?"

Without glancing her way, he snatched the jacket from the back of the couch and jammed his arms into the sleeves. "I'm sorry," he said in a breathless rush. "I shouldn't have—I'm sorry."

Still drunk with desire, Vivian tried to make sense of his behavior, but before she could assemble a second coherent question, he was rushing toward the door.

"Wes—"

"Good night, Viv."

By now, Vivian was overwhelmed, and she watched in stunned silence as he closed the door behind him. Moments later, she heard the soft hum of his car as it backed from the driveway, and the sound put a cold, hard period at the end of the evening.

Talk about a fast getaway, she thought dismally. Wes had just pulled the fastest one she'd ever seen. Why? She could have sworn she'd felt genuine desire in his kiss, an urgency in the way his hands had roamed over her body. But something had caused him to put a swift end to it all.

He raced out of here because he came to his senses

and realized exactly who he was kissing—a lowly employee.

Shoving away the hurtful voice in her head, she went to the door and secured the locks, then collected the tray from the coffee table and carried it to the kitchen.

So much for the ending of a fairy tale day.

Adelle bent over Wes's right shoulder and placed a stack of bound papers in front of him. "Here are the data sheets you wanted."

"Thanks for all your trouble, Adelle."

The secretary skirted the desk and stood in front of him. "That's what you pay me for, Mr. Robinson. But I am wondering what's going on with you. This information is already posted on your computer. What's up? Finally getting tired of staring at a screen all day?"

"Sometimes a man just needs to be able to hold things in his hands." Like a soft, womanly body with a wide, sweet mouth, Wes thought.

He shook his head to rid himself of Vivian's image and quickly wished he hadn't. In spite of the aspirin he'd taken before coming to work this morning, the ache behind his eyes wasn't going away.

"Look who's talking about putting things on paper," he muttered. "You're still living in the Stone Age, Adelle. And if I was a good boss, I'd either make you do things by a normal method, or I'd fire you."

Not the least bit concerned about his threat, she let out a short laugh. "Normal, bah—there is no normal nowadays. Besides, we both know you couldn't do without me. I'm like a long-suffering wife who's never appreciated for the sacrifices she makes for her husband."

Wes groaned. "Please, Adelle, I don't want to hear anything about wives or husbands. Not today."

Her sardonic expression turned curious. "What's the matter? Too much wedding for you over the weekend?"

Leaning back in the leather chair, he pulled off his glasses and rubbed his burning eyelids. "Too much champagne and flowers and sappy romance. It's all a big show for nothing. Do you know how many couples get divorced after only one year or two of marriage? Why bother with a wedding? Why not just jump in the sack for a few months, then when the glow wears off, go your separate ways? Makes more sense to me."

"And you're making me ill," Adelle retorted. "Is that jaded image how you actually think of Ben's marriage?"

Releasing a long breath, he cast a rueful glance at his secretary. "I'm trying not to. I really do want him and Ella to be happy."

"Sounds like it." She slanted a clever glance at him. "Could it be that you're feeling a little jealous that you're not the one on a honeymoon?"

Honeymoon. The word had Wes's thoughts drifting once again to Saturday night and those few mind-blowing minutes he'd held Vivian in his arms. Sure, he could imagine making love to her for two solid weeks. And even that much time might not be enough to satiate this appetite she'd unexpectedly aroused in him. But not on a honeymoon. Not with Vivian. Or any woman.

"Jealous?" He made a scoffing noise. "Adelle, I'm blessed because I'm free. And I have every intention of staying that way."

She had opened her mouth to make a retort, when his cell phone signaled he had an incoming text message. He picked up the phone. "Get out of here. I have work to do," he told her. "And when you get back to your desk, call Vivian and tell her to come to my office. Pronto."

Adelle slowly started toward the door. "I guess it's

not enough that you've ruined my morning with your grumpy mood. Now you want to ruin hers."

There were days Wes wondered why he put up with Adelle's disrespectful mouth. And there were days when he treated her like anything but a secretary. They deserved each other, he thought wryly. Moreover, he couldn't do without her as a secretary and his friend.

He pointed toward the door. "Didn't I tell you to get out of here?"

She stomped off in the direction of his finger. "You sure did. And I hope to heck I don't have to see the inside of this room for the rest of the day."

As soon as Adelle wrenched open the door, then shut it firmly behind her, Wes tossed the phone aside and left his desk. At the wall of plate glass, he stared broodingly out at the city, where dark, wintery skies matched the heavy thoughts swirling around in his head.

After he'd raced out of Vivian's apartment Saturday night, he'd driven straight home and downed a stiff drink of bourbon. But the alcohol hadn't been nearly enough to quench the fire she'd lit in him. Now, after two sleepless nights in a row, he felt like hell.

Kissing a woman shouldn't have been affecting him this way. It certainly never had before. But this whole thing with Vivian was different. Out of the entire team of his developmental department, she was the one he worked with on nearly a daily basis. Of the whole group, she had the brightest, most innovative brain, and he didn't want anything to hinder their productive working relationship. That made her off-limits to any sort of office hanky-panky. And even if she hadn't worked for Robinson Tech, she was hardly the type for a short-term affair, he reasoned. No, when she went to bed with a man, it would mean more than sex to her. It would mean all the things he wasn't prepared to give.

A few minutes later, on her way to Wes's office, Vivian paused at Adelle's desk, where the older woman was digging through a stack of handwritten notes.

"I started to bring you a doughnut from the break room, but I know how carefully you watch your figure," Vivian told the secretary.

Looking up at her, Adelle peered through a pair of black cat-eye glasses. "Honey, I'm the *only* one watching my figure. I haven't had a date in weeks. And the last one I had got so gassed on the dance floor, I thought I was going to have to drive him to the emergency unit."

Vivian studied the secretary's dismal expression. "Maybe you should try My Perfect Match, Adelle. You might find a guy who enjoys dancing and is fit enough to keep up with you."

Adelle let out a short laugh. "Vivian, most men my age are in a nursing home. But your idea about the app might be a good one. At first I was opposed to the dating site. I thought it was a good way to run into a serial killer. But so far, you and Mr. Robinson have dated nice people, and it would give me a chance to meet new guys. And who knows? I might get lucky and find a young one. I'm not too old to be a cougar," she added with a saucy wink.

"I'd certainly give it a try," Vivian said with a chuckle, then glanced at the door leading into Wes's office. "Is Mr. Robinson alone?"

"Yes, go on in. But brace yourself. He's not in the best of moods. The man can't take much merrymaking."

Vivian looked at her. "Merrymaking?"

Adelle thumped her pencil against a notebook lying

on one side of the ink blotter. "Ben's wedding," she explained. "He can't stand being around that much happiness."

"Oh. Well, not to worry, Adelle. I don't figure there's any chance that seeing me will make him happy."

Her chin up, she walked over to the door and, after a light knock, stepped inside the large room. Immediately she spotted Wes standing at the windows with his back to her, his hands jammed in the pockets of his khaki trousers. Even though she hadn't seen his face, the sight of him was all it took to zoom her pulse into overdrive. And as her gaze took in the back of his dark head and the faint ripple of muscles beneath his burgundy shirt, it dawned on her that after Saturday night, nothing would ever be the same between them.

With that realization weighing heavily on her thoughts, she closed the door behind her and walked deeper into the room.

"You wanted to see me?" she asked.

He turned away from the windows and returned to his desk. But instead of taking a seat in the plush leather office chair, he leaned a hip against the edge of the desktop and gestured to one of the wing chairs positioned in front of him.

"Have a seat, Vivian."

This morning, when she'd dressed for work, she'd donned her tightest black skirt and a close-fitting white sweater with a cowl neck that dipped to a provocative spot between her breasts. At the time, she'd thought the sexy clothing would help lift her squashed spirits, but now, as she eased onto the edge of the chair and smoothed a hand over her skirt, she felt like a fool. So far Wes hadn't even made eye contact with her, much less noticed her clothing.

"I appreciate you getting here so quickly. I wanted to talk with you. And it's not something I wanted to discuss over the phone."

Vivian had hoped her heart would've slowed to a normal rhythm by now, but if anything, it had sped up to a dizzying rate.

"I see." She nervously licked her lips. "Is this about the app? I know it's still very early, but have you gotten any sales data in yet?"

He waved dismissively with one hand. "Relax. The app is selling like crazy. If things continue at this pace, we're in for a huge success."

She breathed a sigh of relief. "That's good news. So what—"

"This is about Saturday night," he brusquely interrupted. "I wanted to apologize again. That's not the way I normally behave. I mean, not with an employee."

He might as well have stabbed her, she thought, as anger shoved its way to the tip of her tongue. "Oh, that's right. I wasn't your date. I was an employee pretending to be your date. Excuse me for forgetting that."

"Vivian," he said, his voice rueful, "I'm sorry that you're hurt."

"Hurt! You don't know the first thing about me, Wes Robinson! I'm not hurt. I'm mad as hell!"

His features twisted with frustration, his gaze remaining on her face as he straightened away from the desk. "Vivian, I—"

Certain she'd just burned her bridges, Vivian jumped to her feet to interrupt him.

"Go ahead," she dared, her voice low and tight. "Order me to clean out my desk and get out of the building. I don't care. Telling you what a creep you are is worth losing my job!"

Before she could guess his intentions, he stepped forward and wrapped his hand around her arm. Shivers of heat instantly washed over her, and hating her helpless reaction, she pulled away from him and stepped backward.

Blowing out a heavy breath, he rammed his hands in his pants pockets as though he was afraid he might forget and touch her again.

"I don't want to fire you. I don't want you to quit, either. Your work is very important to me—to Robinson Tech. It's just that—the other night was a result of too much champagne and wedding celebration. Neither one of us was behaving like ourselves. We can't let it happen again."

In other words, he deeply regretted those moments he'd kissed her. He regretted touching and holding her as though she'd meant something to him. The fact shouldn't surprise her. And it certainly shouldn't hurt her. But that night after the wedding, the passion she'd felt in Wes's arms had blotted out her memory. For a few foolish moments, she'd considered herself his equal.

Determined not to let him see he'd squashed her pride, she lifted her chin to a noble angle. "No. You're right. It can't happen again. And as far as I'm concerned, it won't."

His sigh of relief was another kick to her midsection. No doubt he'd spent a big part of the weekend wondering how he was going to worm his way out of this awkward situation between them. While she'd lain awake the past two nights aching to feel his kiss all over again. How stupid could she get?

"I'm glad you feel that way," he said. "Because I think—well, I believe it would be best if we didn't work so closely together for a while. At least until this dating wager between us is over and done with."

When would that time come? she wondered. How long would it be before he found the love of his life and announced it to the world? How many more boring dates would she have to endure before she admitted defeat? Just when she'd thought the weight on her shoulders couldn't get any heavier, it did.

"Fine. I understand completely. If I have anything to say to you, I'll do it through Adelle," she said coolly, then forced herself to meet his gaze. "The same goes for my work. Is there anything else before I go?"

His face reminded her of a piece of stone, and suddenly Vivian was remembering all those critical things he'd said to her concerning his father. Someone needed to remind Wes Robinson that his cavalier attitude toward women was no better than his father's. But she wasn't going to bother with the task. His Ms. Perfect could be the one to set him straight, she thought grimly.

"No," he said. "Except that I regret things between us have become—strained."

Strained? Over. Finished. That was how she saw their relationship now.

"I'm sure you do," she said stiffly. "Now if you'll excuse me, I have work waiting on me."

Her back as straight as an arrow, her head high, Vivian headed toward the door. She was reaching for the knob while thinking it would be a long time, if ever, before she saw the inside of this office again, when the wooden panel suddenly swung forward.

Vivian didn't have time to move as a gray-haired man of considerable age stepped straight into her path, nearly knocking her over in the process.

"Oh, pardon me!" His bony hand grabbed her arm

in an effort to steady her on her feet. "I hope I didn't harm you."

After what she'd just gone through with Wes, nothing could harm her, Vivian thought dismally. To the elderly gentleman, she said, "I assure you there's been no harm done at all."

As Vivian disappeared out the door, Wes remained standing in front of his desk, staring at the tall, slender man walking toward him. How had he gotten past Adelle to enter his office unannounced? Although something about him looked vaguely familiar, Wes was certain he'd never met him before.

"I apologize for interrupting," the man said. "Since your secretary was nowhere to be seen, I took it upon myself to enter your office."

Considering his advanced age, the well-dressed gentleman crossed the room with a surprisingly spry gait. Once he reached Wes, he extended his hand in greeting.

"I'm Sterling Foster," he introduced himself. "Kate Fortune's husband."

Oh, hell, Wes thought as he stifled a weary groan. Meeting anyone associated with the Fortune family was the last thing he needed right now. The awful exchange he'd just had with Vivian was still tearing at him. She'd looked at him as though he was lower than pond scum. And at that very moment, he'd felt even lower. He'd handled the whole situation with the tact of a caveman. Now she would never consider him a man to be respected.

But this new visitor to his office was an entirely different matter. One that Wes wanted no part of. And what was Sterling Foster doing here at Robinson Tech, anyway? To demand that Ben stop his search before more embarrassing family secrets were uncovered?

"Wes Robinson," he replied. With narrowed eyes, he curiously scanned Sterling Foster's wrinkled face. "Is there something I can do for you, Mr. Foster?"

"I didn't make the trip to your office to acquire anything from you, Mr. Robinson. I came to reassure you that Kate hasn't forgotten her promise to meet with your father, Gerald."

When Ben had crashed Kate Fortune's birthday bash, he'd certainly gotten the ball rolling, Wes thought dourly. And now, for Ben's sake, he had to keep it rolling. Otherwise, there'd be hell to pay with his twin.

Deciding to take the diplomatic route, Wes gestured toward one of the wing chairs. "Please have a seat, Mr. Sterling," he invited politely. "Would you care for a cup of coffee?"

"Nice of you to offer, young man, but I won't take up that much of your time." He eased into the nearest chair and waited until Wes had taken the seat across from him before he continued. "I actually came here this morning to speak to Ben, but I was told he's gone on his honeymoon."

"That's right. He was married this past Saturday and won't be returning to Texas for the next two weeks or more."

"I see. Well, as you might have heard, my wife has been very ill. She's out of the hospital now and doing better, but her doctors are insisting she remain here in Texas. The winters in Minneapolis are extremely cold, and they believe she'll recover better here in the milder climate."

"The weather here in Austin can be fickle. We've even been known to have ice storms. But let's hope, for the sake of your wife's health, that we'll have an early spring."

"Thank you. I am praying she'll be back on her feet soon. And as soon as that happens, I'm sure she'll be contacting Gerald about a meeting between the two of them."

Wes could hardly keep from letting out a loud snort. He could have told this man that Gerald Robinson had no desire to meet with Kate Fortune or anyone connected to the Fortune family. In fact, Gerald knew nothing about a meeting. What Ben was planning was an ambush between the cosmetics mogul and their father. But Wes wasn't about to reveal such a thing to this man and ruin his brother's plans. This was all Ben's baby, and Wes didn't want to get involved. Not if he could help it.

"Well, I'll be honest, Mr. Foster. This whole thing between my brother and your wife really has nothing to do with me." He paused and took a breath, but refrained from passing a hand over his aching forehead. Not for anything did Wes want Sterling Foster to think his visit was causing him any undue stress. "Tell me, have you tried seeing Gerald this morning?"

A wry smile crossed Sterling Foster's face. "No. I don't expect just anyone can meet with your father. And in any case, when it comes to my wife's personal affairs, I wouldn't presume to speak for her. She'll do her own talking."

Wes breathed an inward sigh of relief. He wasn't sure how his father would react if any member of the Fortune family showed up here at the office, wanting to ask him awkward, personal questions. Most likely he'd have security escort them off the premises. Yet in spite of Sterling letting himself into Wes's office, he got the impression this elderly gentleman appeared to have more tact than to take that approach.

"I'm sorry I couldn't be of more help, Mr. Foster. But like I said, this interest my twin has in the Fortune family is his, not mine. Unfortunately, I'm afraid Kate will have to wait until Ben gets back to set up a meeting with Gerald." *And that might actually happen when hell freezes over*, Wes thought.

Sterling weighed his suggestion for a moment before he inclined his head in agreement. "As far as I can see, that's not a problem. Right now Kate's still weak, and I'm trying my best to keep her home and out of the cold and away from flu germs. The extra time will allow her the chance to get stronger."

The tender affection in Sterling's eyes when he spoke of his wife surprised Wes. Probably because he'd never seen his own father display any sort of love toward his mother.

Deciding the man couldn't be all bad, Wes gave him a genuine smile. "I'm glad the wait won't cause problems for you. And I'll make a point to let Ben know about our meeting today. I can assure you that as soon as my brother returns to Austin, he'll be contacting you."

Sterling rose to his feet and extended his hand to Wes, who quickly stood and obliged the man with a handshake.

"Thank you, Mr. Robinson. You've been very helpful."

Wes walked him to the door. "Good day, sir. And best wishes to your wife's health."

"That's very kind of you. Goodbye."

Wes shut the door behind Kate Fortune's husband, then walked over to his desk and flopped into the leather executive chair. Dear God, what a morning, he thought as he blew out a long, weary breath. And it wasn't half over yet.

Moments later, as he searched through a drawer in his desk for more aspirin, Adelle walked into the room. From the look on her face, he could tell she was fuming about something.

"I'm glad you're here," he told her. "Would you get me a cup of coffee? I need to take something for my headache."

"I'll just bet," she quipped on her way across the room to a coffee pot and tray of pastries on a small, round table.

"Okay, Adelle, I don't have the time or energy to read your mind. What's wrong now? Not that I should be asking. I should be chewing on your you-know-what for letting Sterling Foster slip his way into my office! Where in the hell were you, anyway?"

Tilting her nose toward the ceiling, Adelle carried the coffee to his desk and plunked it down in front of him. "This might come as a shock to you, but I do have to go to the ladies' room now and then. How was I supposed to know anyone would show up and be bold enough to barge their way in here?"

He shot her a tired look, but instead of that riling her more, Adelle suddenly looked curious. "Who was that man, anyway? I didn't recognize him. But he was rather attractive—for his age, that is."

"Adelle, your last dying thought will be about sex. I'd make a wager on that," he muttered. He tossed the painkillers into his mouth and gulped down a mouthful of coffee. "For your information, he was Sterling Foster. Kate Fortune's husband."

The secretary's mouth sagged open. "Are you kidding me?"

"I'm hardly in the kidding mood! And don't ask me why he was here. It's none of your business or even mine, for that matter." Then, feeling a bit ashamed of himself, he added in a gentler tone, "He wanted to speak with Ben. That's all."

She squared her thin shoulders. "I have no intentions of questioning you about the man. What concerns me is why Vivian came storming out of here a few minutes ago. She flew by my desk without a word, looking like she had homicide on her mind. Most likely yours."

The pained expression on Wes's face was partially hidden behind his coffee mug. "Look, each time Vivian leaves my office, you're in here giving me the third degree. I'm not a suspect here. I'm the boss—in case you've forgotten that fact. If Vivian isn't happy with me, that's her own problem. Not yours. And furthermore, Vivian and I won't be working together in my office anytime soon. If I have any messages for her, I'll send them through you. And vice versa. Got that?"

Her face a picture of very real concern now, Adelle looked over his shoulder to the windows beyond, as though looking at the city skyline would reveal as much or more than his face.

"Yes, I got it. There's a rift between you two. Why—"

Not wanting to hear more, he firmly interrupted, "That all I'm saying on the matter, Adelle."

"Oh, Wes, please, don't mess up something good," she said gently. Then, with a dismal shake of her head, she walked out of the office.

Once he was alone, Wes slammed the coffee mug onto the desktop, then dropped his aching head into his hands. He didn't know what sort of spell Vivian's kiss had put on him, but he had to shake it off, and quick.

Chapter Eight

The only bright spot Vivian could find in the following week was the apparent success of My Perfect Match. Social media was buzzing about the app and its capabilities, while sales data confirmed there was a wild demand for the product. The dating program she'd created was going to make a huge amount of money for Robinson Tech. It was a proud achievement for Vivian, and yet she couldn't help thinking that it had, in an inadvertent way, contributed to the wall that now stood between her and Wes.

In spite of that sad fact, she'd already started work on several spinoffs. My Perfect Employee, My Perfect Roommate and for all those animal lovers, My Perfect Pet. Through Adelle, Wes had given her the go-ahead for each project, and since that time, Vivian had buried her head in her work and tried hard to forget Valentine's night, when he'd kissed her senseless, then raced out of her apartment.

"Working late again tonight?"

Vivian glanced over her shoulder to see Justine buttoned up in a plum-colored coat. A designer handbag was slung over one shoulder, and a mustard-colored scarf was wrapped around her throat.

"Mmm. I'm researching information about the most popular pets across the United States and what makes people love them."

The blonde wrinkled her nose in distaste. "Sometimes I worry about you, Viv. Researching animals has nothing to do with building a computer application."

Vivian bit back a sigh and reminded herself that Justine's job was mainly one of creating commands for a computer to process. Anything more seemed to be beyond the young woman's imagination.

"Not exactly," Vivian replied. "But I can't build an application without a general sense of the subject, now can I?"

Contemplating, Justine tilted her head first one way and then the other. "I guess not. But I sure hope you're getting overtime for all this extra work you're doing. Every evening this past week, I've left you sitting here at your desk, and George tells me you've been putting in long hours."

"My Perfect Match is selling like crazy. Now is the time for other apps to follow on its coattails. So I don't have a minute to waste."

"Well, I wanted to see if you'd like to walk down the street with me to Jack and Jane's. I realize it's cold outside, but a piña colada might make us feel like we're on a warm beach. At least it's a try."

Frowning, Vivian turned her chair toward Justine. "Jack and Jane's? That's a great bar and grill, but a bit too pricey for my taste."

"True, but a girl needs to splurge once in a while,"

she said sheepishly. Then, stepping into Vivian's cubicle, she continued in a hushed voice, "Okay, I confess. I've heard the new guy stops by there in the evenings for a drink. I thought we might get a chance for a closer look at him."

The crease between Vivian's brows deepened. "New guy?"

Her voice dipping even lower, Justine said, "Come on, Vivian, I know you can be a nerd at times, but even you aren't blind or dumb. Think! The new guy. Joaquin Mendoza. He's Rachel Robinson's brother-in-law. Surely you've seen him around the building!"

Oh, yes, Vivian had heard through office gossip that Robinson Tech had hired a new business consultant from Miami. Two days ago, she'd spotted the man getting on an elevator. No doubt on his way up to a meeting with the higher echelon of the company.

"Yes, I've seen him," Vivian said curtly.

Justine was incredulous. "That's all you have to say? Every woman in the building has been swooning over the man. He's gorgeous!"

"I suppose he is nice-looking. But I have other things on my mind." Like trying to get Wes's face out of her mind. Like trying to forget how his kiss had momentarily turned her into a wanton hussy.

Justine was obviously crestfallen at Vivian's lack of enthusiasm. "Oh, I'd almost forgotten. You have your app dates to keep you occupied. So how's that going?"

"Actually, I've skipped these past few days. Work has kept me late every evening."

Justine's grin was sly. "It doesn't appear as though Mr. Robinson has let up on his dating quest. You can't pick up a paper without seeing him with some beauty on his arm. No wonder he wants you to make all the new apps. This one has been great for him."

Her features stiff, Vivian turned back to her desk. "I've seen Wes—I mean, Mr. Robinson, leaving the building these past few nights—heading out to his dates. I hope he finds the perfect one soon."

At least that way, she could forget about him once and for all. The thought barely had enough time to whiz through her head before another one followed.

"I've changed my mind, Justine. It might be fun to go to Jack and Jane's. Give me a moment to shut my computer down after I save my work, and grab my coat and we'll be off."

"Great! Now you're thinking," Justine said happily.

Minutes later, the two women were standing at the elevator, waiting for a ride to the ground floor. In spite of the corridor being fairly empty and Justine chattering a mile a minute, Vivian sensed that someone had walked up behind them.

As she cast a glance over her shoulder, everything inside her suddenly stopped, including her breathing. Wes was standing less than five steps away, and from the looks of him, he wasn't headed home with a briefcase jammed under his arm. No, he was dressed impeccably in a dark gray suit and coral-colored tie. The bright shade was definitely a bold move for him, and Vivian could only think this must be an important date for him.

"Good evening, ladies," he greeted them, his cool blue gaze assessing both women. "Headed home for the evening?"

"Yes," Vivian blurted.

At the same time, Justine piped up, "No, we're on our way to have cocktails. Would you like to join us, Mr. Robinson?"

With strangulation on her mind, Vivian cut her friend a sharp look of warning, but it seemed to go over Justine's head as the other woman cast Wes an inviting smile.

His handsome face a stoic mask, Wes straightened the knot of his tie. "No, thanks. I'm meeting someone."

Even though his announcement came as no surprise, it still managed to cut her deep.

You're a little fool, Vivian. Just because the man gave you a few kisses, you got the idea he cared. That's laughable. Women like you are an afterthought for Wes Robinson.

Her jaw tight, her fingers curled into her palms, Vivian stared at him. "Going on one of your app dates?" she couldn't resist asking.

The smirk on his face made Vivian wish she could slap it off.

"That's right. I'm beginning to think this lady might be the one. My Perfect Match appears to be delivering exactly what you promised it would."

Was that sarcasm or sincerity she heard in his voice? Vivian couldn't decide which. Either way, it shouldn't matter to her. But it did matter. Far, far too much.

"I couldn't be happier," she said stiffly, while wondering if the elevator had gotten stuck on a higher floor. She'd never had to wait this long for the doors to open.

Oblivious to the tension between Vivian and Wes, Justine spoke up jokingly, "Hey, maybe I better try the thing. I'm getting tired of my lame dates."

Wes narrowed his eyes on Vivian. "What about you? Found Mr. Perfect yet?"

For a few seconds that night in her apartment, she'd been certain she'd found him. But that misjudgment had shown her how easily a woman could be confused in the heat of passion. After dealing with Wes's hot and cold attitude, she could see how her mother had made the mistake of jumping into a marriage that was doomed from the start.

"I'm going on a second round tomorrow night," she said in the brightest voice she could muster. "With David—my Valentine date."

The word *Valentine* must have caught his attention, because his eyes narrowed and the corners of his mouth tightened. "Valentine?"

"Yes, you ought to remember—the rose man."

"Yes, I do remember. Vaguely."

Unable to stand another second in the man's company, Vivian grabbed Justine's arm. "Come on. Let's take the stairs. It'll be quicker."

As Vivian hurried her friend toward the stairwell, Justine nearly stumbled.

"Viv! You're acting like the fire alarm just went off. What has come over you?"

"I've been in a foggy haze, Justine. But everything has just become crystal clear. That's what." And the next time she got within ten feet of Wes Robinson, she promised herself, she was going to feel nothing. Nothing at all.

The next evening, Vivian was so busy with George on the technical routes for the new Perfect apps, she almost forgot the time.

"Oh, no!" she exclaimed as she noticed the clock in the corner of the monitor. "I have less than an hour to change clothes and be across town!"

Jumping to her feet, she started tossing her cell phone and a few more personal items into her purse. George looked up from his scribbled notes.

"Another date with Wes Robinson?"

Vivian paused. "Wes? Why in the world would you think I'd be going out with our boss?"

The big man shrugged. "I saw pictures in the paper of you two together at Ben's wedding. I assumed—"

"You assumed wrong," she cut in quickly. "That was simply business. Nothing more. I'm meeting one of my app dates."

"Oh. My mistake. I just always thought you and the boss were friendly."

"*Tolerant* is a better word. And right now we're not even that." She gestured toward the notes spread in front of him. "Why don't you put the work away and head home? We'll start again in the morning."

"Yeah. I think I will. Liz hasn't been feeling well. She wants to roam at night—looking for a boyfriend, I suppose, and the cold weather has given her a cold. Anyway, it will be time for her medicine soon."

Liz, George's black-and-white cat, was the closest thing he had to a family. Vivian had often watched the man leave from work and wondered if he ever got lonely. Vivian had once asked him why he'd never attempted to take a wife and have children. He'd told her he enjoyed his own company.

"I'll see you in the morning, George. And take good care of Liz—she can't help that she wants a man once in a while."

Vivian left the cubicle with her purse and the dress and heels she'd brought to work with her. As she headed to the nearest restroom to ready herself for her date, she wondered if George might have a good idea. Being alone was better than being miserable with the wrong person. Better yet, maybe she should forget about finding the right man and simply enjoy being single and independent, like her sister Michelle.

But that wouldn't get her the children she wanted or a home filled with all the special things that having a family could give her, she mentally argued as she pulled a cream-colored sweater dress over her head, then shoved the clingy material down her hips.

She wasn't the least bit convinced that David, or Mr. Valentine, as she thought of him, was going to be that man, but she had to start somewhere. And if a date with him was enough to push Wes from her mind, then she'd consider the whole night a huge success.

With her dress and high heels on, Vivian quickly refreshed her makeup, then turned her attention to her long brown, honey-streaked hair. The rainy day had brought out the frizz, but she didn't have time to do more than flick a brush through it. But her hair was hardly a worry. David didn't place much interest in physical appearances. He was the intellectual sort who enjoyed discussing fine arts and foreign travels. And tonight she was determined not to be bored. Instead, she was going to be an attentive listener.

After one last glance in the mirror, she left the restroom and was halfway to the elevator when she suddenly remembered she'd forgotten her coat. And since the temperature was far too low to try to brave it without the garment, she had no choice but to head back to her work cubicle, where she'd left the coat hanging on the back of a chair.

For the past week, Wes had hardly lifted his head from his work, and in spite of what he'd told Vivian last night as they stood waiting on the elevator, he'd dated a new woman every night. He certainly wasn't on the brink of finding his lifelong mate.

But then, Wes wasn't looking for love. He was simply following through with his vow to the public to use My Perfect Match. After his date last night, though, he'd decided he needed a break from wining and dining and trying to remain on his most charming behavior. Frankly, he was tired of women and tired of work.

So why are you walking straight to Vivian's work area? he asked himself. *Why aren't you leaving for home, where you can grab a tumbler of Scotch and turn on an NBA game?*

The questions going off in his head caused Wes to pause in the middle of the corridor and ponder his motives. Several days had passed since he'd worked with Vivian. He'd missed seeing her and talking with her, even about something as simple as the weather. And now that she'd started creating more of the Perfect apps, he had every right to stop by her desk and see how her work was progressing.

The idea pushed him forward, and that was when he spotted her rounding a corner. A cream-colored dress clung to her body, outlining each and every curve she possessed, while her brown hair swirled about her face like a dark cloud tipped with gold dust. And a crazy thrill of pleasure rushed through him as he watched her graceful strut carry her straight toward him.

That day at Ben's wedding, he'd believed it would be impossible for her to look any lovelier. But tonight, as he drew closer to her, he realized he'd been wrong. There was something different about her, or maybe it was something he was just now noticing. Either way, there was a sensuality about her that stole his breath away.

"Hello, Viv. Fancy running into you this evening."

"Go figure. I'm at least twenty feet from my work area. Who would ever guess I'd be hanging around this part of the building?"

"Hmm. I just happen to be the vice president of the developmental department. It's just a wild chance that I'd be on this floor."

"Okay," she conceded, then arched a brow at him. "So what's up? Adelle gone home to leave you with the dirty work of talking to me?"

His nostrils flared as his gaze roamed the familiar lines and angles of her face. "Since when did your mouth get so full of sarcasm?"

"I refuse to answer that question on the grounds it might incriminate me."

She infuriated him. So why was he having to fight to keep from grabbing her right there in the corridor and kissing her senseless? He was losing his mind. That was the only excuse for the crazy feelings that seemed to hit him out of nowhere.

"You're all dressed up this evening," he observed. "You look enchanting."

Her gaze darted away from his, and then she swallowed. Wes wondered what she was thinking. About the date she was about to meet? The notion slashed him with jealousy so strong it staggered him.

"I'm going out," she said. "With David."

His stomach clenched. "Good for you. Maybe he'll send you more roses. But right now we need to talk— in my office."

He didn't know why that last had come out of his mouth. But now that it had, he felt a weird measure of relief.

"Talk? Now? I don't have time!"

"I'm sure Mr. Valentine will wait," he said smoothly.

Then, wrapping his hand around her upper arm, he urged her down the corridor to his office.

Except for a tiny night-light glowing on Adelle's desk, the secretary's work space was quiet and dark. Wes didn't bother switching on another light. Instead, he led her straight through to his office and shut the door behind him.

A small ceiling lamp, which was always on, sent a pool of dim light over the couch. Between its glow and that of the city lights filtering through the plate glass behind his desk, it was enough to see his way.

After he'd switched on a banker's lamp situated on one corner of his desk, he turned back to Vivian. She was standing a few steps away, her back rigid, her mouth pressed into a flat line. Even in an irritated state, she excited him. Which didn't make sense at all. He'd worked closely with the woman for years and never stopped to look at her. Never felt her presence touching him, enticing him. What had happened to make everything suddenly change? he wondered wildly.

"Okay, here we are," she said in a strained voice. "What do we need to discuss? Have you decided you want me to shelve the plans for the other Perfect apps?"

"No. Quite the contrary. I'd like for you to build them as quickly as you can."

She stepped toward him, her lips parted with faint surprise. As Wes's gaze zeroed in on them, the twisted knot in his gut unfurled, then burst into a simmering fire.

"Then what? I need to go—"

Yes, she needed to go to her new man, he thought, feeling sick. And he needed to think up some legitimate reason for bringing her to his office before she guessed he was simply playing a stalling game.

Snatching at the first thing that entered his mind, he said, "I'm concerned about these new applications you're creating. If any one of them is larger than My Perfect Match, a cell phone processor can't handle the load. The phones will stall or lock up."

"I learned all about overloads in high school. George and I will keep the size of the sites as marginal as possible. Certainly within the size of Perfect Match."

Strange how the weather was very cold outside, yet the office felt like a hot, humid July night. The air around them felt so heavy, Wes was finding it hard to breathe. And each time he did manage to draw in a deep breath, it carried her scent to his nostrils.

"If the sites can only be used on phones with high megahertz, I don't have to tell you that sales will be very limited."

With a frown that was almost comical, she took another step toward him, then spluttered with disbelief. "I just told you that George and I will handle it. And if that's all you needed to caution me about, you could have sent a short email."

By now, Wes didn't care if she'd guessed this trip to his office had been spawned from jealousy. He wanted her, and he didn't care whether she knew that, either.

"Yeah, I should have sent an email. But then I wouldn't have been able to do this."

Before Wes could stop himself, he snagged a hold of her wrist and tugged her forward.

She stumbled straight into his chest, and Wes didn't waste the opportunity to wrap her in the tight circle of his arms. Immediately her head flopped backward, placing the shocked O of her lips in the perfect position to be captured by his.

The taste of her mouth was even better than he remembered, and his mind went blank as he moved his lips over hers and slid his hands slowly down her back until they reached the flare of her hips.

With his hands cupping her bottom, he pulled her hips tight against his aching arousal and held her firm while he continued a hungry feast of her lips.

In the back of his mind, he recognized her body was surrendering as the soft fullness of her breasts pressed flat against his chest, her head tilted to allow him better access to her lips. By the time her arms slipped around his neck and her fingers pushed into his hair, sanity had ceased to exist. He was on fire with the need to make love to her.

Desperate to be closer to the object of his desire, he lifted her off her feet, then with a half turn sat her on the edge of his desk. A groan of compliance sounded deep in her throat, and then her legs were wrapping around his waist, causing the hem of her dress to slip decadently up around her hips.

Even as his lips sought the soft skin of her throat and his hands cupped the mounds of her breasts, a slice of sanity was still trying to penetrate his overloaded brain. Vivian wasn't the type of woman to have spur-of-the-moment sex with him, or any man. And certainly not on an office desk. But his mind refused to listen to that common-sense reasoning. The only thing it could follow was the urging of her hands on his hips, the hot thrust of her tongue between his teeth.

Seconds ticked by and he continued to kiss her until he was certain he was going to explode behind the barrier of his trousers. And with a frantic groan, he finally managed to break the contact between their mouths.

"Viv! You can't—"

"I can. You can," she said between frantic gulps of air. "Now, Wes. Now!"

It didn't matter that somewhere across town an app date was waiting for him. Or that Mr. Valentine was sitting somewhere, twiddling his thumbs, waiting for Vivian to arrive. To hell with them, Wes thought. At this very moment, the only thing that mattered to him was having Vivian in his arms. Having Vivian give him every sweet inch of her luscious little body.

"Protection?" He could barely get the one word question past his gasp for oxygen.

"The pill."

With a grunt of overwhelming relief, his hands dove beneath the hem of her dress and quickly yanked her panties down her legs and over her feet. The process knocked her high heels loose and the shoes fell one by one, plopping loudly on the wooden parquet.

"Wes, oh, Wes, hurry. Don't stop now!"

Her frantic plea was like throwing diesel on an out-of-control fire. Gripped by a desire so intense he thought his body was going to combust, he freed his manhood from the fly of his trousers and quickly thrust into her.

And as her body rose to meet his, the pleasure was so enormous his legs very nearly buckled beneath him.

"Viv. Viv."

She heard him whisper her name, and after that Vivian knew nothing except the incredible sensations bombarding her from every direction. Her hips instinctively lifted to match the rhythm of his hard, driving thrusts, while his hands seemed to be everywhere. On her breasts, in her hair, over her thighs and around her ankles. She wanted him to keep touching her; she wanted him to keep plunging into her, asking her for more and more.

She didn't know how they'd gotten to this point, or why. And she no longer cared. Wes was making wild, sweet love to her, and that was the beginning and end of everything she wanted.

Far beyond the walls of the office, she heard the faint jaunty whistle of a janitor, then the roar of a vacuum. Back inside, somewhere on the desk near her head, a clock ticked, while above them warm air rushed through the vents in the ceiling. Yet none of those sounds could compete with Wes's sharp, raspy intakes of breath or the groans in her throat that went on and on.

Everything began to spin, and then suddenly she felt his body straining over hers, felt the beat of his heart hammering against hers. She locked her hands at the middle of his back, while her legs tightened in a vise-like grip around his waist. Wherever he was taking her, she had to follow. She had to hang on and weather the wild, relentless storm whirling around inside her.

Then, just as she was certain the ecstasy of it all was going to tear her apart, his body grew rigid. As his face hovered over hers, she could see his features gripped with an intensity that transfixed her. And then as his hot seed began to pour into her, she felt a part of her lifting away. Floating, spinning, whirling until there were no walls around her or cherry wood beneath her. There was nothing but Wes holding her tight as the two of them shot through a sky of brilliant stars.

When Vivian finally returned to earth, Wes had already climbed off her, and she turned her head slightly to see he was standing a few steps away from the desk, straightening his clothing.

With her breaths still coming in rapid gulps, Vivian

scrambled to a sitting position, then slid off the desk and jerked down her dress.

Now that the contact between their bodies had ended, she felt dazed and more than a little embarrassed. Never in her life had she behaved with such reckless passion. How had it happened? How had she let it happen?

Biting back a helpless groan, she swiped the tumbled hair out of her eyes and bent to scoop up her panties and high heels.

She was hurrying toward the door when Wes's hand snaked a hold on her wrist.

"Viv, wait! Where are you going?"

She forced herself to meet his gaze and was surprised at the earnest look on his face. She'd halfway expected to find indifferent amusement twinkling in his blue eyes.

"To the restroom," she blurted.

With a flick of his wrist, he pulled her close and covered her mouth with a kiss deep enough to start another fire in the pit of her belly.

"Use my private one. And hurry. We're getting out of here."

Her head swimming, she frowned. "I don't understand."

His hands briefly cupped her jaw, then slid into her tangled hair. With his lips nuzzling her ear, he murmured, "No. I don't think you understand how much I want to make love to you again. But you will. As soon as I get you home."

Home? His home? Too shaken to think about it all now, Vivian pulled away from him. "Give me five minutes," she said hoarsely.

Later, in Wes's car, Vivian stared out the windshield at the endless taillights moving in a slow, steady stream along the thoroughfare. But her mind wasn't on the busy flow of traffic; it was consumed with Wes and what had just happened in his office. Now, every cell in her body was wildly aware of the man sitting behind the steering wheel. Only minutes ago, he'd made reckless love to her. And now he was whisking her off to his home. What did it mean? That he was so hot for her that one time just wasn't enough? That idea was hard to swallow. Wes wouldn't have to beg or even look very far for a sex partner. So what did that make her? At this very moment, she didn't want to think about the answer to that question. Making love to Wes, under any circumstances, was too heady to resist.

"This might be a ridiculous time to bring this up, but we both had dates tonight—with other people," she said. "I was supposed to be there more than thirty minutes ago. And considering how the media is covering My Perfect Match—especially your part in it—this might look embarrassing."

"What do you mean, embarrassing? No one knows we're together. Not really together. As for our dates, we'll be at my place soon. I'll call mine and you'll call yours and we'll both give them some legitimate excuse for not showing up."

He made it all sound so easy and reasonable. Maybe that was because he'd learned how to be a cheater from an expert, his father Gerald.

"Yes, that should work." She turned her head toward the passenger window in hopes he'd miss her sigh.

He didn't.

"Okay, what's wrong?" he asked. "Do you really care that much about Mr. Valentine?"

Vexed by his cavalier attitude, she frowned at him. "No. It's just that sneaking around isn't my style."

"Would you rather disappoint me and keep your app date? Would you rather tell the whole world that our app dates are off and the two of us are on?"

They were *on* all right, Vivian thought wildly. But for how long? One night or two? She'd sworn never to let herself fall into a meaningless affair with a man. But this was Wes, and for a few minutes back there in his office, he'd shown her what real passion was all about. And now that she'd found such thrilling pleasure, she didn't want to give it up.

Reaching across the plush leather seat, she placed her hand on his forearm. "No. I'd rather be here with you."

He glanced away from the traffic long enough to flash her a promising grin. "And I'd rather be with you. It's that simple."

Simple. She wasn't naive. Everything about the two of them being together was worse than complicated. But for now, Vivian wasn't going to allow herself to worry about the future. At this very moment, with Wes looking at her as if she was the most special woman in the world, she felt like a princess in a fairy tale. And even fairy tales lasted for a little while.

Chapter Nine

Wes's home was located in the elite section of the city, where estates stretched for acres and acres, and the houses were elaborate, multistoried structures set in perfectly landscaped lawns.

Black iron gates stretched across the driveway to Wes's property. On either side, the low-hanging limbs of two massive oak trees gave Vivian the feeling she was entering a Gothic novel where a cold stone mansion was waiting to trap her.

The narrow asphalt drive wound through sloping grounds until the car was climbing a sharp incline edged by more live oaks. When the house eventually came into view, one look at the massive, two-story structure was enough to convince Vivian she was way out of her league.

By the time he'd parked inside the five-car garage, she was huddled back in the seat, chewing thoughtfully on her bottom lip.

"Viv, we're here. You can't get out of the car unless you unbuckle your seat belt."

His voice jerked her out of her deep thoughts. Without glancing his way, she began to fumble with the straps locking her into the plush seat.

"Sorry. I was—" Filled with sudden doubt, she glanced over at him. "Wes, I'm not sure I should be here."

Groaning with frustration, he reached for her and pulled her across the car seat until she was wrapped in the tight circle of his arms.

"Why shouldn't you be?"

Her nose pressed against the warmth of his neck, she murmured, "This place is—you are—"

Even though she was unable to voice her doubts to him coherently, he seemed to understand them anyway.

"Viv, I'm not royalty living in a palace. I'm just a man who happens to have money. That's all. None of that has anything to do with you and me."

Perhaps it didn't to him, but Vivian knew what it was like to stand on the floor and try to reach a hand to the top shelf of the cabinet. Without something to climb on, it never worked. And the way Vivian saw it, she didn't have anything to help her make the climb from her lowly position to his.

But then, she'd been aware of the differences between them long before she'd agreed to come here to his home. It was far too late to get cold feet now.

"You're right, Wes. None of it matters."

He planted a thorough kiss on her lips, then helped her out of the car.

They entered the house through a side door, and Vivian found herself standing in a large kitchen equipped with modern stainless steel appliances, but decorated in a distinctly homey fashion from an earlier era.

"Let's get our calls out of the way before we head upstairs," Wes suggested.

Vivian pulled her phone from her purse. "Fine with me. I'm nearly an hour late as it is."

While she explained to her waiting date that an emergency had come up and she needed to cancel their evening together, Wes stood at the opposite end of the kitchen, doing the same with his date.

Once they both ended the brief calls, Wes walked back over to Vivian. "That was unpleasant," he confessed. "I think the lady guessed I wasn't being totally forthright about needing to break the date."

Feeling equally guilty, Vivian shook her head. "My date was hardly convinced I had an emergency to deal with. But what could I say? That I'd run off with another man?"

Chuckling now, Wes curled his arm around the back of her waist. "You have run off. We've run off together."

He urged her out of the kitchen and down a narrow hallway. When they stepped into a large family-type room, Vivian got the impression of high ceilings, rich drapes at the windows and floral wingback chairs in front of a long fireplace. The furnishings looked as if they'd been taken right off a 1940s movie set.

Amazed by it all, Vivian asked, "Did you have the place purposely decorated with this era in mind?"

He smiled. "What? Were you planning to see my home filled with chrome and glass and sterile furniture?"

His hand was wrapped tightly around hers as they moved out of the room and toward a tall curved staircase. The warmth of his fingers was so comforting and inviting that he could have led her straight into a wall of flames and she wouldn't have resisted.

"Well, you are a computer geek," she reasoned. "You're all about cyberspace and the future."

"That's at work. I'm different at home."

"Hmm. I'm beginning to see that."

"Actually, I can't take the credit for the furnishings," he said. "This is the way the place looked when I first bought it. When my mother first laid eyes on the furnishings, she gasped with disbelief. Then, when I told her I had no intention of changing them, she was horrified. But I was adamant about keeping everything the same."

"I would've never pegged you to be the homey sort."

As they started to climb the stairs, he said, "The story goes that the couple who originally built the house, the pair I told you about before, had two children. A son and a daughter. They lost the son in World War II, and they were determined to keep the house as it was when he left for Europe. Years later, when they passed the property on to their daughter, she carried on with their tradition. And I—well, it's a comfortable escape."

And he clearly had a bit of a sentimental streak in him. The fact surprised Vivian a lot and tugged on her heartstrings even more.

They both remained quiet while climbing the last of the staircase. Once they reached the stairwell, Vivian saw no point in asking where they were going. It was obvious he was taking her straight to his bedroom.

After traveling several more feet down another narrow hallway, he opened a wide door. She followed him over the threshold, into a room illuminated only by a tiny night lamp near the head of the bed.

Vivian barely had a glimpse of a four-poster covered

in a dark green-and-gold-patterned spread, a tall armoire and matching chest, before his hands caught her waist to pull her backward and into his arms.

Bending his head, he whispered against her ear, "Finally. I have you alone—exactly where I want you."

Goose bumps raced over her skin as his teeth nibbled at her earlobe. "We were just together. On your desk. Or have you forgotten?"

His low, sexy chuckle fanned the side of her face. "I won't be forgetting that anytime soon."

He began to bunch the lower part of her dress in his hands, and her breath caught in her throat as the fabric slowly inched upward until it was gathered around her waist. Then one hand slipped between her thighs, and his finger stroked the aching flesh covered by the silky fabric of her panties.

"Wes. Oh, I didn't know I could want you this much! Not —so soon! We were just together in your office."

Her voice was so thick with desire it sounded strange to her own ears, but Wes didn't seem to notice. He was too busy stroking her, teasing her to the point of torturous pleasure.

"You're going to feel a whole lot more, my sweet Viv. I'm going to make sure of that. This time is going to be slow and special. So—very—special."

With each syllable, he moved her backward, until her legs were pressed against the side of the bed. Once there, he wasted no time in pulling her dress over her head. Then, slowly and purposely, he removed her undergarments.

As he placed the bundle of clothing into a chair near the foot of the bed, it dawned on Vivian that she'd never been so completely naked in front of any man before.

A month ago, the idea that she'd be standing without a stitch of clothing in the middle of Wes's bedroom would have been nothing more than a far-fetched fantasy. A laughable one, at that. And yet tonight, she was amazed at how right and natural it felt for his gaze to devour the sight of her.

Standing in front of her, he weighed her breasts in his palms, then skimmed his hands downward over the curve of her hips. "I didn't expect you to be this gorgeous, Viv. All those years—I never dreamed your skin would be so soft—your lips would taste so good. So good."

As though saying the words intensified his thirst, he bent his head and captured her mouth with his.

Vivian emitted a helpless groan as every bone in her body melted. Each muscle quivered weakly as she succumbed to the wild magic his kiss was wielding over her.

Longing to experience his bare skin, she tugged the tails of his shirt from the waistband of his trousers and thrust her hands beneath the finely woven cotton. The fiery heat of his flesh seared her fingers as she traced the tips over his flat stomach and up and down the faint bumps of his ribs.

The more her hands roamed over his torso, the more she could feel him leaning into her, deepening the kiss until the need for air was causing her head to spin at an even dizzier rate.

Finally, his lips gave hers a reprieve, and as she gulped in long breaths, her fingers went to work on the buttons of his shirt.

"I think it's time I make this fair play and get you out of your clothing, too," she whispered.

* * *

Wes stood motionless as Vivian slowly undressed him. Starting with his shirt and tie, she traveled on to his belt, trousers and finally his shoes. Once she'd tossed the black wingtips over to join her discarded high heels, she straightened and reached for the band on his navy-blue boxers. By then his insides were already simmering and his arousal achingly apparent.

With her hand outside the thin fabric, she touched him there, moving her fingertips against his hard shaft in a caress that sent agonizing pleasure rifling through his loins.

"Viv!" he choked out her name. "This is—more than I can take!"

Brushing her hands aside, he quickly removed the last piece of clothing. Then, with his hands at her waist, he lifted her onto the high four-poster and followed after her.

As soon he stretched out next to her, she rolled toward him and curled her arm around his waist. He immediately shifted onto his side so that they were lying face to face and his free hand could access the curve of her hip.

"This isn't right," she murmured as she planted a series of kisses across his chest.

Wes dug his fingers into her hair and, with his nose nuzzling her forehead, combed them through the long strands. She smelled like sunshine, flowers and woman. His woman.

"What isn't right? Being in my bed? We can go to a guest room if that would make you feel more comfortable."

The soft chuckle she emitted caused her warm breath

to skitter across his skin, and Wes decided it was as seductive as the touch of her fingers.

"Whether we're in this bed or one down the hall—it doesn't matter. What isn't right is the way you're making me want you. I feel like a jezebel."

"Mmm. You feel like an angel to me."

"You better take a look at my back," she whispered. "You won't find any wings there."

"Maybe not, honey, but you can still fly me up to heaven."

Tilting her head back, she looked at him, and Wes was suddenly struck by the tenderness he spotted in the hazel depths of her eyes. He'd not expected that from her. But then, he'd not expected all this fire and passion, either. Wes realized he was just beginning to peel back the multiple layers of Vivian Blair, and so far everything he'd uncovered was a new delight.

"You're delirious," she mouthed against his lips.

"Yeah. And it's about time you cured me."

He kissed her until she was moaning deep in her throat and her hands were digging into his shoulders. Then, rolling onto his back, he pulled her on top of him.

With no hesitation, she positioned her knees on either side of his waist and slowly lowered herself over his hard arousal. Inch by inch, her soft flesh consumed him, and the pleasure surrounding him was so great it was practically unbearable.

Unable to wait, he grabbed her bottom and jerked her downward. She growled with desire and then, tossing her hair back from her face, she bent and placed her mouth on his. Instantly, Wes thrust his tongue past her lips at the same time he arched his hips and drove himself deep inside her.

Vivian began to move furiously against him, and in

a matter of seconds, Wes ceased to think. All he could do was hang on to her and wait for the fiery desire to consume him.

He had no idea if minutes or hours had passed when he felt her velvety bands tighten around him and heard her choked cries of relief. He wanted the ecstasy to continue. To go on and on. But her climax was all it took to nudge him over the edge. And before he could stop it, he was falling into a dreamy abyss.

He was still trying to gather his senses when she lifted her face from his shoulder and glanced around, as though she'd just realized where she was. Wes wasn't surprised by her reaction. He was just now recognizing the walls of his own bedroom.

"Oh. Sorry," she said. "I must be squashing you."

He anchored an arm across her back to prevent her from climbing off him. "You don't need to go anywhere," he said huskily. "I like you right here. Like this."

A gentle smile curved her lips. Then, with a sigh that was almost too poignant for him to bear, she lowered her head and pressed a kiss to his damp cheek.

Wes tucked her head in the crook of his shoulder, then stroked a hand over her hair. He'd never felt so satiated, so complete, in his life. And the realization was completely terrifying.

He'd not only broken his rule never to bring a woman home with him, but also put her in his own bed. And even worse, he wanted to keep her there.

"You know, I don't think we've eaten," she said after a moment.

"I hadn't noticed." His hand traced gentle circles upon her back. "But if you're hungry, I'll have something delivered."

That was enough to have her scooting off him and

sitting cross-legged in the middle of the bed. "Are you kidding? Surely you have something in the refrigerator to snack on!"

"Probably. I just wanted to treat you with a nice dinner."

A frown pulled her brows together. "For services rendered, I suppose."

She started to slip off the bed, but before that happened, Wes managed to catch her and tug her back to his side.

"Why would you say such an awful thing?" he asked.

Her gaze drifted to a shadowy spot on the far side of the room and, as Wes took in her solemn profile, he felt an odd pain shoot through the middle of his chest.

What the hell is wrong with you, Wes? Having sex with a woman shouldn't be making you all soppy and soft-hearted. You've never really cared what your bed partners thought about Wes Robinson, the man. It shouldn't matter to you now.

No. But damn it, it did matter to him, Wes thought grimly.

"Sorry. I shouldn't have said that." She looked at him, her expression rueful. "But you and me—there's a huge chasm between us and—"

"I'm not going to allow you to continue with that sort of nonsense. I told you earlier that my wealth, home or lifestyle has nothing to do with us. And you're not just insulting me with such a comment. You're also demeaning yourself."

She rested her head on the pillow next to his, their faces only inches apart.

"This is all new for me, Wes. I've never been like this with a man like you."

"And I've never been like this with any woman. Especially one like you. But I think we'll figure it all out.

In fact, I'm more than eager to see how we fit together. And if tonight is any indication, I'll go out on a limb and predict the fit will be perfect."

She groaned. "Please, Wes, don't say that word. Right now I don't want to think about My Perfect Match. It seems rather superfluous now."

He tossed a corner of the bedclothes over their naked bodies, then pulled her close against him. "Yes. But it's our work. And we don't want the whole thing to implode. That's why we have to be cautious about being seen together in public."

After a stretch of silence, she said, "You're right. So I suppose I should take a taxi home tonight. That way, if the media are lurking around, expecting you to meet an app date, they won't see you taking me home."

He buried his face in the side of her silky hair. "You can take a taxi to work in the morning. Tonight you're staying here with me."

She reared her head back enough to look at him. "All night?"

"All night."

"But Wes—"

He prevented the rest of her protest by pressing his lips to hers. "No arguments. Or I won't let you raid my refrigerator," he teased.

Her lips smiled against his. "And what if I tell you I like breakfast in bed?"

"Then we'll have breakfast right here. Together."

Shortly before lunch the next day, Vivian was busy at her desk when a delivery boy showed up at the entrance of her cubicle with two dozen red roses arranged in a crystal vase.

Even though she'd spent an incredible night with Wes,

and even though he'd come through with his promise of giving her breakfast in bed, she'd not expected flowers from him. And before she'd opened the small card stuck within the greenery, she'd expected to find the sender to be an app date, one whom she'd gone out with after the dating site had become available for public purchase.

But she'd guessed wrong, and now each time she glanced away from her work to the gorgeous bouquet, her heart did a little flip.

"Wow! Wow! When did you get those?"

Vivian turned away from her computer to see Justine hurrying over to the roses. No doubt her friend would be stunned if she knew Wes had actually sent the bouquet.

"A few minutes ago. Beautiful, aren't they?"

"I'll say. These aren't your cheap run-of-the-mill grocery store roses. So who's the romantic guy? One of your app dates?"

Avoiding Justine's gaze, Vivian looked down at some scribbled notes lying in front of her. "Uh—I guess you could call him that."

Being her usual nosy self, Justine plucked up the small card and read aloud, "To my perfect Valentine, W." She looked slyly over to Vivian. "W? Come on, what's his name?"

She snatched at the first thing that came to her mind. "Wayne. He—er, works in computers. Like us."

Losing interest now, Justine shoved the card back among the rose stems. "Oh. How boring. I thought you might have gotten hooked up with a doctor or lawyer or some professional like that."

"Justine, the app is all about putting two compatible people together." Oh, God, she felt like a complete fraud. But she'd promised Wes to keep their relationship under wraps. And considering the truth would likely hurt both of them, she didn't have much choice but to follow his wishes.

"So you think this guy is The One? He's completely compatible with you?"

She nearly barked with laughter. Other than working in the field of computer technology, she and Wes had nothing in common. Unless you counted red-hot sex, she thought. And all she had to do was look at her parents' failed marriage to see that sex, no matter how glorious, was hardly the glue to hold two people together. So what did she think she was doing? Leaping headfirst into heartbreak?

You're being a woman, Vivian. A woman who wants to be held and kissed and loved.

Mentally blocking out the voice in her head, she said, "I don't know, Justine. I'm going to need some time to figure out exactly where he fits into my life."

Justine thoughtfully touched a finger to one of the rosebuds. "Hmm, well, one thing is obvious. The man has class and money."

Vivian glanced sharply at her. "What makes you say that?"

Justine gestured to the bouquet. "Not just any man could afford these."

"Believe me, Justine, I actually wish he couldn't."

Frowning with disbelief, Justine asked, "What does that mean?"

"Nothing," Vivian answered before changing the subject completely. "Is it time for lunch?"

"I'm on my way. Want to come along?"

"No, thanks. I'm going to eat with George in the break room."

Justine turned to leave, then paused to glance back

at Vivian. "Are you okay? You don't seem like your-self today."

Because she wasn't herself, Vivian thought. And after the night she'd just spent with Wes, she wasn't sure she'd ever be the same again.

Was she falling in love with the man? No! She might be infatuated. But she'd never allow herself to love a man who had nothing in common with her except sweaty bedsheets.

"I'm fine, Justine. Just a little tired. I stayed out later than usual last night."

Glancing at the roses, Justine smiled cleverly. "I see what you mean."

With a cheerful wave, her coworker departed, and Vivian let out a long sigh of relief. If this was what liv-ing with deception was like, she wasn't sure how long she could keep up the pretense.

After holding several meetings throughout the morn-ing, Wes finally had the chance to get to work at his desk, only to be interrupted by the in-house phone.

As soon as he lifted the receiver to his ear, Adelle said, "Ben is on line three. He says it's important he talk with you."

"Thank you, Adelle. I'll take it." He punched the but-ton on the phone. "Hey, Ben, doesn't a man have more to do on his honeymoon than call his brother? Don't tell me you're already getting bored with Ella and those Caribbean beaches."

Ben's low chuckle told Wes what he thought of that assumption. "This place is dreamy, and so is Ella. I'm not sure I ever want to come home. But for now, Ella's at the hair salon. I'm using the time to catch up on some calls. You're first on the list."

Wes pulled off his glasses and tossed them onto the desktop. "I guess I should feel flattered. If I was on my honeymoon, I don't think I'd be calling you. Or anyone, for that matter."

There was a pause before Ben said in a surprised tone, "Why, Wes, you sound like you know what it's like to be madly in love."

Lust. Love. Was there really that much difference? he wondered. His father could definitely give him the lowdown on lust, but the man clearly flunked out in the love department. And his mother? If what she felt for her husband had caused her to endure thirty-five years of hell and humiliation, then Wes wanted no part of it.

"I have a good imagination," Wes told him.

"Yeah. That's why you're so innovative. You can see things I never could."

Receiving the compliment from his twin was nice, but Wes knew it didn't come without a price. "You must be buttering me up for something. Let me have it."

Ben chuckled again. "Actually, I'm calling to ask a favor. Since Ella and I won't be home for several more days, I want you to a hold a family meeting for me."

Closing his eyes, Wes pinched the bridge of his nose. Facing his siblings with more Fortune news was not anything he relished.

"Is that really necessary?"

"Very. I think I might have located Jacqueline Fortune—our grandmother."

Grandmother! "Hell, Ben, you've not yet determined Dad is actually a Fortune!"

"Wes, do I have to show you a roadmap? Surely you can see that all the signs point in that direction. And finding Jacqueline will definitely help solve the mystery."

"And how many more of our father's offspring are you going to discover along the way?"

"There's no way I can predict. But if they're out there, we need to know about them, don't you think? And they should know about us. As far as I'm concerned, blood kin should be aware of each other."

No matter what the cost or who it hurts, Wes thought grimly. Biting back a heavy sigh, he said, "And just where do you think this Jacqueline might be located?"

"I'd rather not go into that just yet. Not until I make a few more contacts, but I expect to do that soon. Tell everyone I'll be calling in the next few days with an update."

"All right. I'll call the meeting, but I don't expect any of our siblings to appreciate showing up for this news. You can't give me more?"

"Not yet. Soon."

Wes swiped an impatient hand over his face. "Well, I should tell you that I had a visitor a few days ago. Sterling Foster came to my office."

"Kate's husband? What was he doing contacting you?"

"He actually came to see you. But since you were gone, I suppose he figured I was the closest he could get to you. He said to tell you that Kate hasn't forgotten about the meeting with Gerald—she thinks she's going to have a meeting with Dad. Ben, there's no way in hell you can make that happen."

"I'll think of some way to work it," Ben assured him. "All I have to do is get them in the same room together. It'll be like setting a keg of dynamite near an open flame and just waiting for it to combust."

"Great. Just great," Wes said cynically. "And what's left after the explosion?"

"The truth."

Wes sighed. "Somehow I expected you to say that."

"I can always count on you to read my thoughts," Ben said with amusement. Then, in a more serious tone, he asked, "Is that all Foster had to say?"

"Very nearly. He talked about his wife being gravely ill for a while. Apparently, she's not been out of the hospital long. She's planning on remaining here in Texas, at least until winter is over, and from what Foster said, she's still too weak to make engagements. So I wouldn't expect to set up a meeting anytime soon."

There was a thoughtful pause before Ben replied, "That might work to my advantage. It will give me more time to gather evidence related to our father's real identity."

To Wes's relief, the private line between Wes and Adelle began to blink. "Uh, Ben, Adelle is calling. It has to be important for her to interrupt."

"Sure. I'll be in touch," Ben told him.

"Enjoy the rest of your honeymoon."

"Don't worry, I intend to," he replied, then laughingly added, "And this is one time I don't wish you were here, little brother."

Ben ended the call, and Wes punched Adelle's line. "What's up?" he asked the moment she answered.

"Sorry to interrupt you and Ben, but your father wants to see you in his office in fifteen minutes."

Damn! The last thing Wes wanted was to face his father today. Especially after the information he'd just exchanged with Ben. How could he look the man in the eye without speculating and wondering who he really was and why he refused to be forthright with his own children?

Just pretend, Wes. The same way your mother has

pretended for the past thirty-five years that Gerald Robinson loved her.

Shaking away that dismal thought, Wes asked, "Do you know why he wants to see me?"

"I think it's something to do with My Perfect Match. I'll print up its latest sales data so you can take it with you."

"Thanks, Adelle. And once you finish with that chore, would you tell Vivian I'd like to see her in my office in about an hour?"

"Vivian? You mean you two are back on speaking terms?"

Speaking terms was a long way away from his relationship with Vivian, but Wes wasn't ready to tell Adelle, or anyone, about his growing feelings for his coworker. Mainly because he didn't know how to even describe his feelings for the woman or where they might be headed.

"We—uh, have settled our problem," Wes told her.

Instead of replying, she abruptly hung up the phone. After staring comically at the receiver, he was tossing it back on the hook when the door opened and Adelle stepped inside.

Without a word, she marched over to his desk and, before he could guess her intentions, leaned forward and planted a kiss in the middle of his forehead.

"Adelle, since when did you start having cocktails at lunch?"

She wagged a finger at him. "It isn't necessary for me to be half-intoxicated to kiss you. That's a thank-you."

"For what? Keeping you out of an old folks' home?"

She chuckled knowingly. "No. That kiss is for not being like your father."

"I don't get it. What does Dad have to do with me and Vivian?"

She cast him a clever smile before heading out of the room. "For a while there I was afraid you were growing as heartless as he is. Thank God I was wrong. Congratulations."

Chapter Ten

When Vivian arrived in Wes's office later that afternoon, he immediately locked the door and pulled her straight into his arms. After kissing her thoroughly, he pressed his cheek against her silky hair.

"I've been waiting all day for this!"

His eagerness lifted her heart, and she laughed softly as she pressed her palms against his chest and looked up at him. "Wes, we had breakfast together this morning. It's only been a few hours since we parted."

"It feels like days to me."

Rising on the tips of her toes, she planted kisses along his jawline. "Thank you for the roses. They're gorgeous."

He rubbed his nose against her cheek. "Mmm. I'm glad you liked them."

"Justine read the card and wanted to know who W was. I made up the name Wayne and told her the roses were from an app date. Afterward, I felt a little ashamed."

His warm hands roamed her back, and Vivian was amazed at the familiar flare of desire shooting through her. Even after their long sessions of lovemaking last night, her body was already craving more. The reaction was shocking and frightening at the same time. It was one thing to want a man, but she was on her way to losing all control.

"I understand you don't like deceiving your friends. But for right now, I don't see any other way of handling the situation."

Situation. Yes, Vivian supposed that was what she was to Wes. But even that knowledge wasn't enough to douse the fire his touch built in her.

"So did you call me to your office for work or just to see me?" she asked.

"I want to do more than see you. I want to carry you over to the couch and make love to you. But unfortunately, I have more meetings this afternoon—the next one in less than ten minutes—so I won't. We'll save that for tonight."

A thrill rushed through her. "Tonight? We're meeting tonight?"

"I'll come to your place."

"What about the media following you? We're supposed to be going on app dates," she reminded him.

"To hell with app dates. I'll be careful and shake any media who might be tailing me."

Another sobering thought struck her, and she pulled away from him and walked across the room to where the warm, wintery sun slanted across the polished wooden floor.

"That interview with *Hey, USA* is going to be coming up in a few days," she said. "How are we going to handle that? I'm not sure I can sit there beside you and pretend you're just my boss."

He walked over to her and drew her back against him. "It'll be easy. I'll talk about all the great dates I've been on, and you'll chat about the wonderful men you've met. We're going to make it sound like a success, whether it is or not."

Two weeks ago, all that mattered to Vivian was that she proved the theory of My Perfect Match would work. That compatibility was the only thing a man and woman needed to bind them together. Now, she was going against everything the site stood for. Something crazy had happened to her. And yet she'd never felt so exhilarated or happy in her life.

"I wanted it to be a success," she said in a small voice. "I still do."

"And it will be, Viv. It is already. In fact, I just got back from a meeting with Dad. I was expecting him to harp on the products with sluggish sales this past quarter. Instead, he was praising my initiative on My Perfect Match. He's ecstatic over the sales, and he's expecting our exposure on *Hey, USA* to boost them even higher. I assured him we wouldn't let him down."

Surprised, she twisted around to face him. "Mr. Robinson has taken notice of My Perfect Match? I can't believe it. I mean, Robinson Tech offers all sorts of items to the consumer. The app is just a little minnow swimming among some huge fish."

"In spite of Dad's questionable personal past, everyone will admit he's a hell of a good businessman. He takes notice of everything. And he's eager for the rest of your Perfect apps to be developed."

"Oh! That means I need to be working late nights until they're finished."

"Not on your life! Your nights are going to be spent with me, not here at Robinson Tech."

The possessive note in his voice sent a rush of excitement through her. Yet at the same time, she wondered how their clandestine affair was going to play out. With her on the losing end?

Don't think about that now, Vivian. For once in your life, grab the pleasure Wes is offering you and let tomorrow worry about itself.

Heeding the words of advice going off in her head, Vivian wrapped her arms around his waist and snuggled the front of her body next to his.

"Hmm. Spending my nights with you does sound more gratifying. I think I'll follow my boss's orders," she murmured as she tilted her face up for his kiss.

"Yeah. This boss," he said just before his lips came down on hers.

The next week passed like a whirlwind for Vivian. Since she'd never had an affair with a man before, she wasn't sure if the romance had her head in a fog or if keeping the relationship a secret was the reason it seemed as though her life was spinning out of control. In either case, she was slowly starting to wonder if she'd made the worst decision of her life. Or the smartest one.

Most any woman in Austin would have jumped at the chance to have a red-hot affair with Wes. Thanks to Robinson Tech, his family was known nationwide. He had more money than most regular folks would know what to do with, plus he was about as good-looking and sexy as a man could get. And yet she couldn't help but wonder if he was the right man for her. If she took away the mind-blowing sex, what did they really have in common? He could dine at the finest restaurants or have a personal chef if he wanted. Vivian had to make do with cooking something economical for herself or bring home a meal from a fast-food diner. He lived in a two-story mansion, while she called home a one-bedroom apartment. He could travel to far parts of the world just for the fun of it, while she had to save up just to travel down to San Antonio to watch a Spurs game. No, other than the fact that they both talked computer language, the main points of their lives were hardly compatible.

Tonight, as she moved around the small kitchen table, preparing the place settings for a meal she was planning to share with Wes, nagging doubts continued to travel through her head. Last evening she'd pushed her hair into a winter cap and donned a pair of dark glasses before taking a taxi to Wes's place. And each time he'd come to her apartment, he'd driven an old, beat-up pickup truck and worn a disguise to throw any media off his trail.

The ringing of her cell phone caused Vivian to pause, and, thinking it might be Wes, she walked over to the countertop to glance at the caller ID. Instead of Wes, the number belonged to her sister, Michelle.

With one hand still clutching several pieces of silverware, Vivian scooped up the phone and managed to swipe it before jamming it to her ear.

"Hey, sis, are you busy?"

Vivian returned to the table to finish her task. "Hi, Michelle. I'm busy, but I have a few minutes for you."

"Oh. With it being Saturday night, I expected you were probably getting ready to go out on one of your app dates."

Vivian inwardly groaned. A few days ago, the idea of keeping her relationship with Wes under wraps was a bit thrilling. Each time they'd made plans to meet, she'd felt a little like Mata Hari. But this evening she was wondering if Wes would ever invite her out to a real dinner date; would he ever feel comfortable showing the public that she was his woman?

"Actually, I'm having someone over for dinner tonight. In fact, he'll be here in a few minutes."

"Really? I'm surprised you'd invite a stranger to your apartment."

Vivian frowned as she moved around the table, placing the last pieces of silverware on folded napkins. "What makes you think he's a stranger?"

Michelle made an impatient noise. "Well, if he's an app date, it's clear you've not known him long."

Finishing with the silverware, Vivian leaned a hip against the edge of the table. "It could be a case of love at first sight, you know."

Michelle replied with mocking laughter. "Oh, please, Vivian. You? You're the most careful, cautious and reserved person I know. You'd be the last woman on earth to come down with a quick case of lovesickness."

A flash of annoyance shot through Vivian, but then a cool breath of reality quickly followed. Michelle was right. Up until she'd developed My Perfect Match and this thing with Wes had boiled out of control, she'd approached every date as though it was an amber caution light.

"Don't worry, sissy. This guy doesn't have murder on his mind." Unless breaking a heart could be considered the same as committing homicide, she thought grimly.

"I'll sleep better tonight just knowing that much," Michelle said drily, then went on, "I was actually calling to remind you that Tuesday is Mom's birthday. I'm going to cook dinner for her, so I thought you'd want to come over. Maybe bring her a little gift. I got her a CD collection of disco music. So you might find her a book or something. You know how she likes to read."

"Disco music! For Mom?"

"That's right. She grew up during that era. I thought it might give her the urge to get out and go dancing."

Even though her sister couldn't see her, Vivian shook her head. "I thought you didn't want Mom to consider marrying again."

"Who said anything about marriage? Sometimes she seems lonely. I just want her to get out and have some fun. Not get hooked up with some dirtbag who'd ruin her life all over again. And since you brought up the *M*-word, how are you doing on finding the right man to spend the rest of your life with?"

Was Wes the right man? Or had she fallen in love with the wrong man?

She purposely evaded Michelle's question. "I can't predict that just yet," she said, then couldn't stop herself from adding, "I do have one I'm seeing exclusively for right now."

"Hmm. Well, why don't you bring this favorite man to Mom's birthday dinner? We'd love to meet him. And it would give him a chance to meet your family."

"I'll give it a thought, sis."

Michelle's suggestion stayed with Vivian all through the evening until finally, after she and Wes had finished their meal and a long round of lovemaking, she brought up the subject of her mother's birthday.

"I suppose you'll be going," he murmured.

The two of them were cuddled in the middle of her bed, and now his hand was gently stroking up and down the length of her bare arm.

"Of course. You wouldn't miss your mother's birthday celebration, would you?"

He paused for a moment before he said, "That depends on the guest list. Besides, my parents are always hosting some sort of party. But I always acknowledge Mother with a card and gift."

"That's a cop-out."

"Thanks. I love being told I'm a negligent son."

She shifted in his arms so that she was facing him. "I just meant that your mother would probably choose your company over a gift."

"Yeah. You're probably right. Most of us kids are busy with our own lives now, and Dad—well, he's never showered her with attention. Not the kind a husband should show his wife."

At least Wes recognized his father's faults, Vivian thought. The encouraging sign had her touching her fingertips to his cheek. "I was wondering, Wes, if you might like to go with me Tuesday night. I'd really like to introduce you to my sister and mother."

He went quiet for so long that she knew his response wasn't going to be the one she wanted to hear.

"It's nice of you to ask, Viv, but I'm not sure it would be the right thing to do. Your family might not understand."

"I could just bring you as my boss. Since we're working closely together on the Perfect apps, it wouldn't look like anything more than a coworker relationship."

He groaned. "Viv, do you honestly think we could pull that off? Your mother and sister would have to be blind not to notice the electricity popping between us."

She sighed. "I suppose you're right. But what would be so wrong about them knowing the two of us are romantically involved? Neither one would say a word to anyone if we asked them to keep it private."

His gaze dropped from hers, and Vivian tried to ignore the little pain that was slowly winding its way between her breasts.

He said, "I'm sure they wouldn't. But I—just don't think we're ready for that sort of thing just yet, Viv. You understand, don't you?"

"Sure. No problem, Wes. Let's forget it, shall we?" She smiled in an attempt to cover up the deep disappointment she was feeling. "The night is still young. We don't want to waste it all on talk, now do we?"

Gathering her close, he pressed his lips against hers. "Now you're speaking my language."

By the time Wednesday rolled around, Wes was beginning to realize that something was going on with Vivian, and whatever it was, he didn't like it. For the past three nights, she'd come up with excuses not to see him, and though he wanted to question her head-on, he didn't. After all, he didn't have a claim on her. He couldn't expect her to make her life his. Also, a part of him feared that, if he did confront her, she might just come out and end everything between them. Wes wasn't ready for that. Not by a long shot.

Maybe if he knew what he'd done or said to put her off, he might have a chance of fixing things. As it was, the only thing he could figure was that she'd decided he wasn't compatible with her.

Compatible, hell! The sex between them was perfect! What more could she want?

Think about it, Wes. The woman wants love. Marriage. Children. All the important words you've not so much as breathed to her. What do you expect from her? To be happy spending her time with you in the bedroom? Since Ben's wedding, you've not even taken her

on a date. You've hidden her as if she was something
shameful in your life.

Not liking the mocking voice going off in his head,
Wes reached for the phone on his desk. "Adelle, would
you kindly see if all my siblings are gathered in the
conference room?"

"Hold on and I'll check." In less than a minute, she
came back on the line. "Everyone is present. They're
waiting on you."

"Thanks, Adelle. If you need me for anything in the
next half hour, I'll be with my family."

"It's about time you showed up," Graham, the rancher
of the family, spoke up as Wes entered the room. "We
were all about to decide you'd ducked out of the building."

Except for his sisters Sophie and Olivia, who were
busy helping themselves to coffee and pastries, and Ben,
who was still on his honeymoon, his siblings were already sitting at the long conference table. Seated next to
his brother Graham was Zoe, the youngest of the family.
Next to her was Rachel, then younger brother Kieran.

Wes started to take a seat at the end of the table,
but when he noticed all eyes were on him, he decided
to stand. "Sorry. I didn't mean to keep you waiting. I
wanted to make sure everyone was here before I started.
And thanks, Rachel, for making the trip all the way
over from Horseback Hollow. I realize you're a busy
woman."

"No problem, Wes," his pretty sister replied. "Since I
feel responsible for starting all this mess, I'm certainly
not going to quit on it now."

"It seems you're the only one of us who's heard from

Ben since he and Ella left on their honeymoon," Graham said to Wes. "Is everything okay with him?"

"Lying on a sunny beach with his new bride," Kieran spoke up with a sly grin. "I'm sure everything is more than okay with our brother."

"Ben and Ella are having a great time," Wes replied. "No problem there."

"So what is our dear brother up to now?" Zoe asked. "If he says he's found another half sibling, I refuse to believe it."

"This whole thing has gone to Ben's head," Olivia commented as she and Sophie took their places at the conference table. "He's beginning to think he's Mike Hammer. Next thing we know, he'll be wearing a wrinkled trench coat and smoking unfiltered cigarettes."

The group chuckled at Olivia's observation, except for Zoe, who frowned in confusion. "Who's Mike Hammer?" she asked. "I don't understand."

Graham shot his baby sister a patient look. "A fictional PI in books and movies," he explained. "And I have to agree with Olivia. Ben is just about as brash as the famous detective."

"You got the brash part right," Kieran grumbled good-naturedly.

Deciding the comments about Ben's endeavor weren't going to improve, Wes went on with the announcement.

"I think it's safe to say Ben doesn't give a flip what we say about him or his quest to trace Dad's past tracks."

"That's right. He doesn't care about any of us. Especially Dad," Zoe spoke up. "Ben or any of you don't care how this must be affecting him."

All eyes instantly turned on Zoe, and the attention turned her cheeks a bright pink.

"Well, Dad does have feelings," she said defensively. "I see them. Even if all of you can't."

"That's because you're the only one of us kids who Dad gives a damn about," Graham said.

Everyone in the room except Zoe seconded that notion.

"Dad has feelings, all right," Wes said. "And they're all self-directed. But we're not gathered here today to argue that point. Ben has asked me to give you an update on the progress he's making. Apparently, he believes he's very close to finding the whereabouts of Jacqueline Fortune."

"And who is she supposed to be?" Zoe asked candidly.

"From what Ben believes, she would be our grandmother," Wes explained.

The group of siblings exchanged shocked glances before everyone began to talk at once. Long ago, Gerald told his children he had no parents. All during their childhood and up until now, the Robinson brood believed they had no paternal grandparents. Everyone at the table, including Wes, agreed that if Gerald had willfully deprived them of knowing their grandparents, it was a despicable thing for him to do.

Rachel finally managed to get a pertinent question heard above the din of voices. "Does Ben know exactly where this woman is living?"

All siblings looked to Wes for an answer, and he had to shake his head in response. "I asked. But Ben wouldn't go into the particulars. He wants to search out a few more contacts before he tells us anything definite. But I can assure you that he sounded very confident about finding her."

"Are we to assume this woman is alive?" Graham asked.

Wes removed his glasses and rubbed his weary eyes. Vivian was distancing herself and breaking his heart, but he also had to be the bearer of his brother's unnerving news.

"I suppose so, Graham. At least, that's the way I took it. He didn't say he'd located her grave. He said he believed he'd discovered the woman's whereabouts."

The brothers and sisters began discussing the prospect of having a real grandmother. For now, it was hard for them to wrap their minds around such an idea.

With the conversation still buzzing, Wes used the moment to step over to the coffee machine.

He was standing with his back to the group, taking a long sip of the fresh brew, when Zoe and Graham walked up behind him.

"What's wrong, Wes? You seem tired," Zoe commented.

Wes glanced over to see his youngest sister was helping herself to a cup of coffee. Bubbly and petite, Zoe was always full of life, and normally Wes enjoyed her company. But today he wasn't ready to answer questions about his personal life.

"I've had a lot of work to deal with this week," he told her.

The explanation was true enough, but who would believe it? Everyone knew he thrived on work. Yet he could hardly confess to his siblings that for once in his life, he was having trouble concentrating on his job. Doubts and questions about Vivian were consuming his thoughts.

Graham chuckled knowingly. "I think Wes has been spending way too much time with all those ladies he's been dating. That's why he looks like he's been shoved through a wringer."

Wes grimaced at the thought. The mere idea of taking out another app date made him want to curse a blue streak. He didn't want a woman the computer matched him with. The only woman he wanted was Vivian.

"My Perfect Match has had me preoccupied," he admitted. "Not the ladies. Vivian and I have to fly to Los Angeles at the end of the week to appear on *Hey, USA* again to promote the damn thing."

Any other time he'd be excited about the trip. Spending a night with Vivian in a plush hotel would be special. But the way things were going, he wasn't sure if she'd be receptive to being in his arms for ten minutes, much less a whole night. One thing was certain, though, Wes decided. He couldn't let her continue to avoid him. Not without finding out why.

Studying her brother over the rim of her coffee cup, Zoe said slyly, "I think Wes is following in his twin's footsteps."

"How's that?" Wes asked, thinking she meant he was joining Ben with the Fortune hunt.

She cast him a clever smile. "I think you've fallen in love."

Before Wes could voice a loud protest, Graham laughed.

"Zoe, we're not all hopeless romantics like you. Wes loves his computer. Not a woman."

Later that same afternoon, Vivian was at her desk, trying to immerse herself in work on the new Perfect apps, but her thoughts kept straying to Wes. And the huge bouquet of white daisies sitting a few inches away from her left elbow wasn't helping the situation.

This morning when the flowers had arrived, she'd stared in confusion at the attached card. "She loves me? She loves me not? W."

Where did Wes come off using the word *love* with her? During all of their times together, he'd never so much as breathed the word to her or even hinted that he felt anything close to it. In fact, the only time he'd discussed the emotion was the day they'd argued about My Perfect Match and whether it would ultimately fulfill its promise. And even then he'd dismissed the word as though it was something that only happened in fairy tales.

For the past three nights, she'd come up with an excuse not to meet him at his place or her apartment. While here at work, she'd done her best to avoid running into him in the building. Today, she'd been expecting him to call her to his office and demand some sort of explanation from her. And the idea had her nerves frayed to the breaking point. She wasn't sure how she could explain her behavior. Mainly because she couldn't exactly explain it to herself.

Wes had become everything to her. That much was clear. It was also plain to see that she was caught in a one-sided love affair. One that was heading nowhere fast. The fact was ripping her apart. And yet, in spite of all that, there was a tiny part of Vivian that wanted to believe Wes might eventually love her. She understood it was stupid wishful thinking on her part. But her heart refused to let go of the notion.

"Hello, Viv."

The sound of Wes's voice interrupted the turmoil in her head, and she slowly turned to see him walking into her cubicle.

Wearing dark-rimmed glasses and a white shirt

tucked neatly into a pair of black khakis, he looked all business. But what sort of business? she wondered. Did he have the progress of the Perfect apps on his mind, or planning a night of sex with her?

"Hello," she replied, her throat thick. "What are you doing here?"

The question sounded worse than inane. He was her boss, and this was the Robinson Tech building. There could have been all sorts of legitimate reasons for his visit to her cubicle. But his sudden appearance had rattled her senses.

He walked over and stood to the left side of her desk chair. With his hand resting near the vase of daisies, he said, "I wanted to talk with you."

Her heart was hammering for him. And for everything wrong about their relationship. "Why didn't you let me know? I would've gone to your office."

"I just came from the conference room, so I didn't have far to walk."

Dropping her gaze from his, she tugged at the hem of her chocolate-colored skirt, but the fabric refused to cover her knees. "Oh. Big meeting?"

"A family thing. It didn't last long." He gestured toward the flowers. "I hope you liked the daisies."

"Thank you. They're lovely."

She looked up to see his narrow gaze was cutting a path across her face. "But you viewed them as a cop-out. Like giving a gift to my mother instead of giving her my time. Right?"

She frowned. "I didn't say that. But I'll admit I didn't understand the card."

His expression turned stoic, and Vivian realized this was more like the old Wes she'd known before My Perfect Match rolled onto the scene. This was the blunt, no-nonsense businessman, driven by his job rather than personal relationships. This wasn't the Wes who'd held her in his arms and given her more passion than she'd ever dreamed possible.

"The card shouldn't have confused you. You either want to spend time with me or you don't. And with all these flimsy excuses you've been giving me for the past three days, I can't help but think that you don't," he said flatly.

So the card hadn't been asking whether she loved him, Vivian thought dourly. She should've known a question like that had never entered his mind. "I've been busy. And in case it slipped your mind, one of those evenings was my mother's birthday celebration—the one you refused to go to," she added caustically.

"Your mother's little party couldn't have lasted that long. We could've met afterward. And what about the other two nights? Maybe you had app dates? Is Mr. Valentine still after you, even though you stood him up for me?"

He was making her, and everything connected to her, sound deliberately awful.

It is awful, Vivian. You knew better than to jump into bed with Wes, yet you made the leap anyway. Why are you suddenly expecting him to give you some sort of promise, a sign that you're special to him?

Sick with the hopeless feelings stirring inside her, she swung her chair so that she was facing him head-on. "I've not been out with anyone! Why? Have you?"

One of his dark brows arched in question. "No. I wanted to take you out, remember? But you turned me down."

She didn't have to be standing in front of a mirror to know fire was flashing in her eyes. "Take me out? Out? Really, Wes? Out where?"

As her voice rose, his gaze darted furtively around them as though to make sure no one had overheard her outburst. The idea rubbed the raw wounds in her heart even more.

A sheepish expression suddenly stole over his face. "Okay, you know what I mean. I wanted us to get together." Bending his head closer to hers, he added, "And you know we can't do that in public."

Truth be told, they would never get together in public, she thought sadly. Not unless it was a pretend sort of thing like their date of convenience for Ben's wedding.

Feeling more defeated than she ever had in her life, she looked blindly down at her lap. "Well, none of that matters, Wes, because I—I've been doing a lot of thinking these past few days, and I've decided that we need to slow down. This thing between us flared up so quickly that neither of us has had a chance to consider what it might do to us or the sales of My Perfect Match."

His eyes narrowed, and when he spoke his voice was low and strained. "Oh, so the app sales are more important to you than us?"

They weren't, but pride had her saying otherwise. "Of course. This is my work. It means everything to me."

His nostrils flared, and she wondered what he could possibly be thinking. Were his thoughts already moving on to some other woman sharing his bed? The idea was so unbearable, her mind slammed a door, shutting out the mere thought.

"I see. Then you've not forgotten that we'll be traveling to Los Angeles in a couple of days for the *Hey, USA* show?"

"No. I've not forgotten. Adelle informed me that she's already booked our flight and made hotel reservations for us."

"Separate rooms, I'm sure," he quipped.

Her chin lifted. "Adelle is a free-spirited woman. Especially for her age. But she wouldn't expect us to be sleeping in the same room. And neither would I. If anyone happened to notice—well, you know, we can't have that, now can we?"

"Okay, Viv. I get your point. You're getting annoyed with all this sneaking around. But you've not stopped to think what you're asking of me. It's too much."

She gave him a wan smile. "You don't have a clue what I'm asking of you. And that's the whole problem, Wes."

His lips a grim line, he shot another quick glance over the walls of the work cubicle. To make sure no one overhead his next phony line, Vivian decided.

She was drumming her fingers on the desktop, waiting to hear what sort of excuse he was going to come up with, when his head suddenly bent downward. The moment his lips landed on hers, she sat frozen in place, too stunned to react.

Like the swift touch of a hot iron, his mouth seared hers, and for a split second all Vivian wanted to do was hang on to him, to pull his head closer and kiss him until both of them forgot where they were.

But before that could happen, common sense stepped in, and then it was all over as he abruptly pulled away from her. "You don't know what I'm asking of you,

Viv. So think about that kiss and perhaps you'll figure it out."

He walked out of the cubicle, and Vivian turned back to her computer screen. But instead of seeing her work, all she could see was a wall of hot tears.

Chapter Eleven

The rest of Wednesday passed in a miserable blur for Wes, and Thursday wasn't much better. Even though he'd just spent the past hour with Vivian in his office, he might as well have been working with a complete stranger. She was as cool and distant as a snowy mountaintop and just as unreachable. The invisible wall she'd erected between them was always present, barring him from carrying her to the couch and making love to her right there in his office.

Now, with their work for today concluded, Wes watched with a sick heart as she gathered her things to leave. He desperately wanted to take her in his arms and remind her how good things had been before she'd had this stubborn change of mind. He wanted to promise how wonderful it would all be again, if she'd only let him make love to her.

"I hope you've not forgotten our trip to Los Angeles tomorrow," he said.

She pulled the dark-framed eyeglasses from her face and dropped them into a pocket on her blazer. "I'll be ready."

When she didn't elaborate, he said, "We'll need to be at the airport by eight in the morning, at least. I'll send a taxi around for you. That way you won't have to leave your car in the airport parking lot. Better yet, I'll come pick you up myself."

She looked at him, her expression unyielding. "No, thank you. We'll only be gone for one night. I'll drive my own car."

Out of the blue, Adelle's voice whispered through his thoughts. *Could it be that you're feeling a little jealous? That you're not the one on a honeymoon?*

At the time, he'd scoffed at his secretary's suggestion. Him, married? And on a honeymoon? The idea was ridiculous. So why was he wishing their night in LA wasn't going to end with just one? Why was he picturing her at his side long into the future?

His intimate thoughts put a husky note in his voice when he replied, "If that's the way you want it. I'll meet you at the airport."

She squared her shoulders and lifted her chin. "Yes. We should probably go through security together."

They should go through everything together, Wes thought. Like each day of their lives. How or when he'd decided that, he didn't know. But the reality of his feelings was settling in on him, scaring him with their depth.

Rising to his feet, he skirted the desk and dared to wrap a hand over her shoulder. "Vivian," he said gently, "I hope tomorrow we can—"

When he couldn't find the right words to explain his feelings, she was quick to prompt him.

"Yes? You hope we can do what?"

Spend the rest of our lives together.

The thought stuck in his throat and refused to budge. Was he losing his mind or his heart? Had he actually fallen in love and was just now realizing it? The questions were tumbling wildly through his head when she apparently grew tired of waiting on his reply and turned away.

Wes forced himself to speak. "I was—just going to say I hope we have a safe trip."

On her way to the door, she glanced over her shoulder and frowned at him. "Why would you say that? Are you expecting trouble?"

He was already experiencing big trouble, and it was standing right in front of him. "Uh—no. But one never knows about flying."

Shaking her head, she said, "Appearing on *Hey, USA* is much riskier than stepping on an airliner. But this time I'm going to be ready for any question Ted Reynolds throws at me. What about you?"

A strange sense of resolve suddenly settled inside him. During the interview, he had to be honest with himself and everyone else. But he had no idea if Vivian would even be interested in the truth.

"I know exactly what I'm going to say. So don't act surprised when you hear it."

The next morning, as soon as the big jetliner lifted off the ground, Vivian pulled out a book and began to read, giving Wes a loud and clear message that their trip was nothing more than the business of promoting My Perfect Match.

After he'd stared absently out at the passing clouds for more than ten minutes, he had to break the silence or he was going to end up ramming his fist into the seat in front of him. And since he doubted the male passenger would appreciate the jolt, he said to Vivian, "I can't remember the two of us ever taking a business trip together. This is a first."

She pulled off her glasses and propped the open pages of the book against her abdomen before she looked over at him. Wes felt his heart do a little flip as his gaze scanned her lovely face, downward over the pretty blue dress cinched in at her waist, and on to the pearls dangling from her ears. Had she always looked like this and he'd been too blind with work to notice? Or had she changed on the outside these past few weeks, the way he'd changed on the inside?

She said, "We never had a reason to take a business trip together."

When she'd first approached Wes with the idea to create My Perfect Match, which now seemed like eons ago, he'd never dreamed the dating app would affect his life so much. He didn't know how that little square with a red heart and silver key, the one he'd mocked and ridiculed, had managed to open his eyes to many things. Especially how he viewed love and marriage and women. During these past weeks since the app had evolved, Vivian had quickly and surely become an important part of his life. Yet with each day, each hour, he could feel her pulling away, and he didn't know what to do to stop her.

Why don't you try being forthright with her, Wes? Why don't you simply take her in your arms and tell her how important she's become to you?

For the past week, the pestering voice in Wes's head had been haunting him with those questions. Yet each time he felt the urge to follow the simple suggestion, he backed down.

Vivian wasn't stupid. Nor was she gullible. He'd already told her he was against love and promises of forever. Was she honestly going to believe he'd had a change of heart? No. She would view his words only as a way to get her into his bed. As far as he could see, he had to find some other way to show her the sincerity of his intentions. But how? And would she ever give him a second chance to do that?

"Have you ever been to LA?" he asked.

"No. I can count on one hand the times I've been out of Texas."

"That's good. I mean, this will be a good opportunity for you to see the sights. There are plenty of interesting places in the area to visit. And we'll have this afternoon free to do whatever we'd like."

Her brows lifted. "Are you offering to show me around?"

"Of course. Why wouldn't I want to show you around?"

She shrugged and glanced away from him. "I assumed you would have a bunch of meetings scheduled. What with Robinson Tech always interested in buying out other companies, I thought you'd want to make the most of this visit to LA."

"Buyouts are Dad and Ben's forte, not mine. While we're in LA, I have no plans to step foot in any tech company's offices. And the only meeting I have scheduled is the one we're doing with *Hey, USA*."

Vivian groaned. "Just the thought of getting back in front of the camera and answering Ted Reynolds's ridiculous questions gives me the shakes."

He reached over and took her hand. To his relief, she didn't pull away. "Don't think about it, Viv. Now that you have that first interview behind you, your nerves will be steadier."

"I hope you're right. I'm going to try my best not to

get brain paralysis this time. No matter how Ted Reynolds comes across, I want to do a good job stating my case for My Perfect Match."

His fingertips made lazy circles on the back of her hand, and suddenly he was remembering back to that moment at Ben's wedding when he'd imagined himself slipping a wedding ring onto Vivian's finger. Was that what she wanted from him? A long-term commitment?

You're not ready for an engagement or marriage. You're not even sure if you know what love really means. Ben has already taken a wife. But you can't compare yourself to your twin. Ben landing the COO position was proof of that. Besides, Vivian wants a man who's completely compatible with her way of life. And you're far from it.

In spite of the inner voice of warning, Wes didn't release his hold on Vivian's hand. Instead, he held on to her until the plane landed at LAX.

Later that night, as she sat across the dinner table from Wes, it was easy to see he was making an all-out blitz to convince her to spend the night in his bed. French cuisine, a bottle of expensive wine, candlelight and soft music in the background were definitely romantic. And earlier in the day, as they'd toured around the city, he couldn't have been more attentive and thoughtful.

She had to admit, at least to herself, that she'd enjoyed every minute the two of them had spent together. Even so, she understood she couldn't let her guard down and cave in to more of what he had to offer. Long before this day had arrived, she'd been telling herself that this business trip was going to remain just what it implied. Business. As much as she ached to be back in Wes's arms and to feel his lips sending her to heights of incredible passion, she was resolved to stick to her guns.

Having an affair with a handsome, wealthy businessman was exciting and pleasurable. But having and needing were two different things. And she needed a man in her life who wanted more from her than just being his sex partner.

"There's dancing in the next room," Wes said as the two of them finished coffee and dessert. "Would you like to take a few whirls around the dance floor?"

And have his arms wrapped tightly around her, crushing her body close to his? No. That much temptation would be too much for Vivian to bear.

She looked across the table to the soft candlelight flickering over his rugged features and had to fight hard to hang on to her resolve. "No, thanks. The flight was tiring, and we've had a long day. I'd rather just go to my room and call it a night."

Something like disappointment flickered across his face, but it came and went so fast, Vivian couldn't be sure. Especially when his response came out carefully measured.

"Fine. If you're ready, I'll settle the bill."

Throughout the taxi ride back to the hotel, they exchanged only a few words between them, but Vivian could feel the tension building around them like steam in a hot shower. And with only a handful of inches separating them on the seat, it would be very easy for Vivian to reach over and touch him. But she was smart enough to know that one touch was all it would take to start their affair rolling again.

Maybe she should be satisfied with that, Vivian thought as the taxi braked and swerved its way through the heavy city traffic. Judging from the years of romantic drought she'd gone through, finding a man who could fly her over the moon was not something to toss away lightly. She might never find another guy who could make her feel the things she'd experienced with Wes. But heaven help her, she wanted more than meeting a man in secretive shadows. She wanted one who'd be proud to be seen with her. She wanted a husband and children, a family to share the rest of her life with. She was determined not to be like her mother, alone and afraid to try love again.

Even though it was a relief when the taxi finally pulled to a stop in front of the hotel, Vivian still didn't have a chance to escape Wes's company. With their rooms on the same floor and separated by only three doors, they were forced to ride the elevator together.

When the doors of the lift swished open and they stepped into the corridor, Vivian desperately wanted to sprint away from him and lock herself inside her room. But more than making her look childish, it would prove to Wes that she was having to fight to keep her distance. And she didn't want to give him that much satisfaction. He'd already taken her heart; there was no need to let him have her pride, too.

Without speaking, they walked side by side down the wide hallway, their footsteps silent on the ornately designed carpet. Every guest on this particular floor was either still out to dinner or already gone to bed, Vivian decided. No one else seemed to be around, and by the time they reached her door, it felt as if the two of them were the only ones in the whole hotel.

"It's still early," Wes said as he watched her fish an entry card from her handbag. "You could invite me in for coffee or—something."

She tried to give him a sly smile, but the longing tugging at her heartstrings prevented her lips from forming the expression.

"I could," she said. "But I won't."

He stepped closer, and Vivian's breath caught in her throat. She wanted him desperately, and no doubt he knew it.

"Viv, we can't go on like this. I don't know—" He paused, shook his head and started over. "That's not exactly true. I do know one thing. That night you asked me to go to your mother's birthday get-together with you, I didn't understand just how much it meant to you. Then later on, I realized how I'd made you angry. And I'm sorry about that."

Closing her eyes to block out the image of his troubled face, she said, "Forget about it, Wes. I did really want you to go, but later...well, the whole thing made me see that we just don't belong together. No matter how wonderful the sex is."

Her eyes were still closed as she suddenly felt his hand cupping the side of her face, and then his lips were brushing against her forehead, sending shivers of delight over her skin.

"Wes," she whispered. "Don't—"

He didn't allow her to finish. Instead his lips swooped over hers, and for the next few moments the only thing she could do was kiss him with all the hungry desperation she was feeling.

Eventually, the sound of the elevator doors was quickly followed by voices. Wes instantly lifted his head and took a step back. While he glanced around at the intruders, Vivian used the moment as an opportunity to escape. She jammed the card into the door and jerked it open.

"Good night, Wes. I'll meet you down in the lobby in the morning."

He whirled back to the door just as she was shutting it, but not before she'd glimpsed the shocked look on his face.

"Viv! Open up!" he urged in a hushed voice. "We're not finished."

She tried to swallow away the aching lump in her throat. "I said good-night, Wes. And I meant it."

Expecting him to start banging on the door, she was surprised when long moments of silence stretched into more minutes. She finally decided he'd given up and gone to his own room.

The reality shouldn't have left her feeling lonely and miserable, but it did. She was cutting away all the sweet, romantic ties she had with Wes. It was the right thing to do. At least, she spent the rest of the night trying to convince herself it was right.

Wes was hardly in the mood to sit in front of a television camera and answer questions about My Perfect Match, he thought as the taxi driver steered him and Vivian toward the network broadcasting station. After tossing and turning for most of the night and fighting with himself to keep from walking down the hall and banging on Vivian's door, he felt like hell.

Never in his life had wanting a woman ever consumed or tortured him the way this thing with Vivian was. Why couldn't he simply forget her and move on? There were plenty of women who were more than willing to go out with him. And a high percentage of those women would eagerly jump into bed with him at the first invitation. Unfortunately, most of them would try every angle they could think of to get their claws into him and the Robinson wealth.

But not Vivian. No. She didn't care about his money

or his name. Dear God, his name. He wasn't even sure about that anymore, he thought grimly. Maybe he actually was a Fortune, but even if he was, he was smart enough to know that belonging to the famous family wasn't the key to winning Vivian's heart.

Is that what you want, Wes? Her heart? I thought all you wanted was her hot little body. Someone to snuggle up with for a while, then say goodbye to once you tire of her.

Tormented by his mouthy conscience, he glanced over to see she was staring thoughtfully out the car window. If she was nervous, it didn't show. In fact, she looked cool and collected. As if she'd made up her mind as to what she was going to say and was confident she'd say it right.

And that sexy coral dress draped over her curves would certainly make the male television audience sit up and take notice, he thought. Since when had she started dressing like that? After he'd gone and fallen hopelessly in love with her?

The answer to that last question shook him so deeply he didn't say another word until they were inside the television studio, being ushered to the green room.

"Are you all right, Wes? You look pale or sick, or both," Vivian told him as they sat waiting on an orange couch.

"I'm fine. Just feeling a little jet lag," he lied. "I've been going over in my mind what I plan to say."

"That's hard to do when we don't know the questions Ted Reynolds will be asking."

He heaved out a long breath. "I have a pretty good idea what the questions will be. I'll have to talk about all the beautiful dates the app has generated for me.

And you'll have to talk about the great guys you've been seeing. Think you can manage?"

Her hazel eyes were dull as she looked at him. "It'll be a snap. You see, you've taught me how easy it is to pretend."

"Viv, I—"

Before he could say more, a young woman stuck her head through the doorway and beckoned to them. "Okay, you two. It's time to take your places on the set. Follow me, please."

Wes quickly rose from the couch and reached a hand down to help Vivian to her feet. Once she was standing beside him, she said, "You were about to say something. Was it important?"

Probably the most important thing he'd ever said in his life, Wes thought ruefully, but he'd missed the chance. And now it would have to wait until Ted Reynolds attempted to skewer them in front of a national audience.

"We'll talk later," he murmured, while urging her out of the room.

Being in an actual television studio was far different than the remote telecast they'd done in Wes's office, Vivian quickly concluded. There were cameras and bright lights pointed at them from every angle, not to mention the set itself, which up until now she'd viewed only on a television screen. The bamboo furniture, accented with bright pillows and shaded with tropical plants, gave the seating area a real Hollywood flair, while behind them, a plate glass wall revealed a view of a street lined with tall palms and filled with bustling traffic.

Before the cameras started to roll, the director seated

Vivian and Wes close together on the couch. Ted Reynolds was apparently using the break between segments to stretch his legs. He was walking around the set with a coffee cup in one hand and a pompous expression on his face.

What a phony, Vivian thought as he barely nodded a greeting in their direction.

Maybe you'd better take a good look around you, Vivian. There's more than one phony on the set of this morning show. You and Wes have been doing a pretty good job of faking an image and attempting to prove to a gullible audience that My Perfect Match delivers what it promises. Now you're going one step further and pretending you've not fallen madly in love with your boss. Who's the biggest phony here?

"Three, two, one, you're on!"

The set director's shout of warning pulled Vivian out of her dismal fog, and as their host introduced them, she forced a smile on her face. She'd gone this far; she could surely fake her way through the next few minutes.

After a brief introductory chat with both of them, Ted said, "I have to admit I'm a bit shocked at how this dating app has become a huge craze across the nation. Robinson Tech must be feeling very happy right now. I certainly hope *Hey, USA* helped to push the sales."

"No doubt about that," Wes agreed. "Everyone watches your show, Ted. You've helped millions learn about My Perfect Match."

Wes's compliment put a smug expression on Ted's face. "Well, it's been great fun following this project. So tell us about your dates. The audience is anxiously waiting to hear the juicy details."

Wes and Vivian exchanged glances.

"Who would you like to go first?" Wes asked.

Smiling slyly, Ted gestured to Vivian. "Ladies first, of course."

Without naming names, Vivian related general details about the men she'd met through the app and the dates they'd been on around the city of Austin. And with a few chuckles added in, she even admitted that a few of them had turned out to be a bit boring.

She definitely wasn't having any problems spitting her words out this time, Wes decided.

"So have you two found *the* special one?" Ted asked.

"Yes," Wes quickly responded.

At the same time, Vivian blurted out, "No."

Wes glanced over to see Vivian was staring at him in wonder. Their gazes connected and remained that way until Ted's laughter finally caught their attention.

"I see you're at odds here." He gestured to Vivian a second time. "I'll start with you again, Ms. Blair. I believe your answer was no. However, I thought I detected a doubt in your voice. Could it be you've found Mr. Perfect and just don't want to admit it?" Ted asked cleverly.

Wes could feel her gaze returning to his face, but he couldn't bring himself to look at her again. Hearing her talk about the men in her life wasn't exactly pleasant. Actually, he'd never felt so empty in his life.

"Well, I answered no because—I'm not yet certain whether he's the perfect man for me. I'm still trying to make up my mind," she said cautiously. "But I'll say there is one who's at the top of my list."

"Would you like to give us the name of this lucky guy, Ms. Blair?"

"I'd rather keep that to myself, but I do have a nickname for him—Mr. Valentine."

Wes whipped his head in her direction. Was this more of her pretense, or was the man who'd sent her roses on Valentine's Day actually beginning to steal her heart away? The impish expression on her face told him nothing except that she was adept at fooling people, especially him.

Sickened by the idea, Wes missed the last exchange between Vivian and Ted. It wasn't until the morning show host turned a question on him that he managed to mentally shake himself back to the present.

"Wes, your dates have been well documented in the papers. So the viewing audience is already aware that you've wasted no time in squiring around a bevy of beauties." Ted's grin was close to being lecherous. "I'll say one thing. If I wasn't already married, I'd be tempted to try the app myself."

The sick feeling in the pit of Wes's stomach refused to go away. "I just happened to get lucky."

"Sure," Ted drawled. "I'd like to know how you answered the computer-generated questions, but we'll leave that for next time. Since our time together is running out, I need to get straight to the point. You said you've found your special lady. Can you elaborate on her identity?"

"Not yet. Right now, the lady's name is private."

"Oh, come on, Wes," Ted goaded. "You've traveled all the way from Texas to give us this interview. Surely you don't want to waste this opportunity to reveal your new lady love."

"There are circumstances that prevent me from doing that today."

"Okay. Maybe you can answer this question. Do you see your relationship with this woman lasting far into the future? Or is she just perfect for you at this time in your life?"

Wes swallowed as emotions threatened to close his

throat. "I can assure you that through My Perfect Match, I've found the woman who will always fit me perfectly."

The conviction in Wes's voice must have taken Ted aback a bit, because his smug tone turned thoughtful. "Well, now, I think you're really serious about this. So why not come out and tell us her name?"

"Sorry. Her name is off-limits. She means too much to me to reveal her name before we have—everything settled between us."

"Oh, so it sounds like an engagement is soon coming," Ted said happily. "Another reason for *Hey, USA* to follow the trials of My Perfect Match. And we'll certainly be doing that."

Ted went on quickly to wrap up the segment, which happened to be the last one for the show. Once the cameras had quit rolling, Wes helped Vivian from the couch, hoping the two of them could exit the set before Ted could catch them. Now that he'd practically revealed his feelings to millions of viewers, he had all sorts of things he needed to say to Vivian, and he couldn't do it fast enough.

"Excuse me, Wes. Before you go, could I have a word with you?"

Glancing around to see their host walking toward them, Wes groaned under his breath. "There's no need for you to stay," he told Vivian. "I'll meet you out in the lobby."

"Fine," she said and briskly strode away from him.

Surprisingly, Ted chatted with Wes much longer than he expected, and by the time he finally excused himself, Wes was close to screaming with frustration. He practically ran off the studio set and through the empty green room. But once he reached the entrance to the outer lobby of the building, he came to an abrupt halt and stared.

Across the wide room, Vivian was standing with a young man he recognized as a recruiter from a competing tech firm. What in hell was he doing here? Had he followed them to snoop? Maybe he'd hoped to catch Vivian alone and pry sales data from her? Or had he wanted to talk directly to her about another matter?

The sick feeling he'd been dealing with all morning intensified as he forced himself to stride across the room. Unlike Ben, he hated confrontations, but Vivian was more than his employee; she was his woman, and this man needed to know it.

"I'll have to agree it sounds like a great offer, Mr. Clemente. I've never thought of leaving Texas before, but California does have its sunshine," Vivian was saying as Wes walked up.

The young black-haired man gave her a charming smile. "Please call me Gino. And we have much more to offer than sunshine. This is a mecca for innovative technology. And with your rich imagination, you could zoom to the top. Our company does plenty of business with the film industry. Are you interested in the movies, Ms. Blair?"

Vivian glanced awkwardly over to Wes, and it was clear she wasn't comfortable with him overhearing her conversation.

"Are you, Ms. Blair?" Wes prodded.

With a nervous lick of her lips, she looked back to Gino Clemente. "I'd have to think about that before I could give you an answer."

"Surely," he said smoothly. "I do hope you'll give it careful consideration. I promise it would give your career a huge leap."

"Thank you for thinking of me, Gino. I have your number."

"I'll be looking forward to hearing from you."

He shook Vivian's hand, then walked off without bothering to acknowledge himself to Wes. Which was okay with him. As far as he was concerned, he never wanted to see the guy within two thousand miles of Vivian again.

"So you want to tell me what that was all about?"

Vivian shrugged, then glanced away as she tucked a loose strand of hair behind her ear. "I'm sure you heard enough to figure it out. Mr. Clemente was here on the behalf of World Vision Mobile. My Perfect Match has caught their attention, and they're offering me a position with them." Her gaze returned to his. "It would mean a much larger salary and a higher position than the one I hold now."

The challenging glint in her hazel eyes sent a shock wave through him. Why had it come to this point to make him realize what a gem he'd always had in Vivian? Had he taken for granted that she would always be around to work with him? Moreover, that she'd be willing to be a hidden mistress?

His throat tight, he asked, "And what did you tell him?"

"You heard."

"I only caught part of the conversation."

"I don't want to discuss this now. Not here."

She turned toward the exit, but Wes instantly wrapped his hand around her upper arm.

"Well, I do. Now. And right here."

Wes glanced around for a quiet spot in the room and noticed an atrium connected to one side of the lobby. He led her over to the plant filled room and seated her on a wicker couch. Once he was sitting beside her, he drew her hands gently between his.

"Viv, are you unhappy at Robinson Tech?"

The dainty flare of her nostrils told him he'd not asked the right question, so he tried again.

"A few minutes ago you told Ted Reynolds that Mr. Valentine was at the top of your list. Are you really thinking he might be your special man?"

She frowned at him. "No. That was only for the camera. Remember? You said we needed to look convincing."

He let out a heavy breath. "Well, you fooled the hell out of me."

Her eyes narrowed as she continued to study his face. "And what about you? You said you had found *your* special woman. Was that just for the sake of My Perfect Match?"

Suddenly his heart was brimming over with love for this woman, and he finally understood what Ben had been trying to tell him about finding the right one.

"I have really found her," he said gently. "I just didn't want to use her name to promote a Robinson Tech product. I love her too much for that."

Her head bent forward, and a curtain of hair went with it, making it impossible for Wes to see her face.

"Then it probably would be for the best if I accept Gino's offer," she mumbled.

Wes stared numbly at the top of her head. Had he made such a mess of things that she no longer cared what he was feeling?

"Is that all you have to say?" he asked, his voice full of dismay. "That it's best you leave?"

She lifted her head, and Wes could see a cloud of

confusion in her eyes. "Do you think I want to stick around and watch you with some other woman?"

The meaning of her words smacked him like a fist to the face. "Viv! You think—" Pausing, he shook his head in disbelief. "When I said I'd found my woman, who did you think I was talking about?"

She stared at him in blank confusion, and then her lips began to tremble. "Are you saying—do you want me to believe you were talking about me?"

"You'd better believe it, Viv. Because I can't live without you. And I don't intend to try."

Her mouth fell open. "But I thought you considered this whole thing with us as a temporary thing. Especially when you wanted to keep everything secret."

He groaned ruefully. "At first that was the only way I figured we could work things. The whole world was watching, expecting us to find a special love through My Perfect Match. I didn't want to squash the chances for the app to be a success. Especially when you kept telling me how important it was to you."

She squeezed his hands tightly as a rueful groan slipped past her lips. "It was important. It still is. But not nearly as important as you are to me. Oh, Wes, I thought you were ashamed of me! I'm so—we come from such different worlds. And I—"

Releasing his hold on her hands, he wrapped his fingers around her shoulders. "Look, Viv, I understand that we're not compatible in your eyes. And I know how important that is to you. I even agree that passion in the bedroom eventually burns itself out. But my feelings for you go much deeper than that. I love you. Maybe it's too soon for you to believe that. But I'm willing to spend a lifetime proving it to you."

Tears spilled from her eyes and onto her cheeks. "I

never fully understood what passion was all about until you, Wes. You made me feel things I'd never dreamed possible. We have that special spark together. But even if the fire dies, I'll still love you, Wes. Always."

Happiness such as he'd never known soared through him, and at that moment he felt as though he could jump the moon. "And what about all that compatibility you've been worried about? You think we can find enough in common to keep us together for the next fifty years?"

Her face leaning toward his, she chuckled softly. "Let's shoot for sixty."

Closing the last bit of distance between their lips, he gave her a kiss filled with love and promises for the future. A future they would share together.

"What do you say we start those sixty years by going to the hotel and proving to each other just how compatible we really are?"

Laughing, she jumped to her feet, pulling him along with her. "I say we're wasting time."

Much later that night, after an evening of dining and dancing at a seaside resort, Wes and Vivian walked down to the beach. Standing on the wet sand, with the moon bathing them in silvery light, they watched the waves of the Pacific roll onto shore.

The salty wind carried the scent of tropical flowers growing nearby, while farther in the background, the faint sound of music drifted from a cabana. With Wes's arm curled around her waist and her cheek resting against his chest, Vivian was certain she was in heaven, or very close to it.

"When you phoned Adelle and told her we'd be staying in California for another night, did you tell her why?" she asked, her voice drowsy with contentment.

"Not exactly," he answered. "I told her we still had business to take care of before we returned to Austin. But don't start worrying that I'm still keeping secrets about our relationship. I wanted to surprise her and everyone else back home."

"Surprise them? How?"

With his hands on her shoulders, he turned her so that they were facing each other. "I was going to wait until we got back to the hotel to do this. But I've decided now, right here on the beach, is better."

"To do what?" she asked impishly. "Kiss me and tell me how beautiful I look in my new dress?"

Because she'd only expected to spend one night in Los Angeles, Vivian had packed just enough things to fill her carry-on bag. After Wes had made the decision for them to stay over, he'd taken her on a shopping spree, buying her a whole suitcase full of dresses and other clothing to wear when spring arrived in Texas.

His eyes glittering with love, he smiled at her. "I've already done that."

"A second time won't hurt."

"In a minute," he promised. "Right now, there's something else I want to do." He slipped a hand into the front pocket of his trousers and pulled out a small jewelry box. "I confess, while you were trying on dresses, I did a little shopping on my own."

She stared at the little white box while trying to guess what might be inside. "Earrings! You've already spent too much on me today, Wes." Slipping her arms around his waist, she snuggled the front of her body close to his. "I don't need gifts from you to make me happy, darling. You're all I need."

"But this is a special gift. One that goes along with those sixty years we're going to have together." He flipped open the box and held it up for her to see. "Will you marry me, Viv?"

She gasped at the sight of a rather large diamond winking in the moonlight. "Wes! That's—it's—an engagement ring!"

The shock on her face had him chuckling softly. "That is what a man usually gives a woman when he asks her to become his wife."

"Yes. But you told me you—" She broke off as confusion and joy collided inside her, scrambling her senses. "You told me you never wanted to get married. That seeing your parents' troubled marriage had put you off the idea completely."

The wind was whipping her hair about her face, and he reached up to gently snare the wayward strands with his fingers. "That's true, Viv. For years now, I've told myself I wanted no part of having a family of my own. My parents had eight children together, but their marriage is cold and loveless. I've never understood what went wrong between them, or if it was ever right. I only knew that I didn't want that for myself. Ben told me I'd think differently if I ever found the right woman. I didn't believe him. Until I fell in love with you. Having you in my life has changed me, Viv. You've taught me there's more to what goes on between a man and a woman than red-hot sex."

Her heart overflowing with emotions, she cradled the side of his face in the palm of her hand. "And you've taught me that a man and a woman need more than simply being compatible to keep them together. Without a spark of fire, things could get pretty boring."

"They'll never get boring with us. I promise. And you do look very pretty in that dress." He kissed her thoroughly. Then, with his lips hovering close to hers, he said, "I'm waiting for your answer. Are you going to wear my ring or not?"

"Yes! Yes, I'll marry you! But what about My Perfect Match? What about your family and friends and all the employees at Robinson Tech?"

He pulled the ring from the box and slipped it onto her finger. "When we walk back into the Robinson Tech building Monday morning, I want everyone to see we're engaged. And as for My Perfect Match, well, it did manage to bring us together. So we're proof the app delivers what it promises. A perfect match to love, honor and cherish. There's only one thing left for you to consider, Viv."

"What's that? If you're worried I'll be wanting a wedding as big as Ben's, then don't be. Any kind of ceremony will do for me."

"We're going to have a grand wedding," he promised. "But for now, you don't actually know if your name will change to Robinson or Fortune. Is that going to make a difference?"

"I'm not marrying a name, Wes. I'm marrying the man I love."

Rising on tiptoes, she closed the gap between their lips. As the kiss swirled them into an erotic cocoon, she didn't worry what the future might hold. Her future was right there in her arms.

* * * * *

MILLS & BOON®

Cherish™

EXPERIENCE THE ULTIMATE RUSH OF FALLING IN LOVE

A sneak peek at next month's titles...

In stores from 11th February 2016:

The Greek's Ready-Made Wife – Jennifer Faye *and*
Fortune's Secret Husband – Karen Rose Smith
Crown Prince's Chosen Bride – Kandy Shepherd
and **"I Do"...Take Two!** – Merline Lovelace

In stores from 25th February 2016:

Billionaire, Boss...Bridegroom? – Kate Hardy *and*
A Baby and a Betrothal – Michelle Major
Tempted by Her Tycoon Boss – Jennie Adams *and*
From Dare to Due Date – Christy Jeffries

Available at WHSmith, Tesco, Asda, Eason, Amazon and Apple

Just can't wait?
Buy our books online a month before they hit the shops!
visit www.millsandboon.co.uk

These books are also available in eBook format!

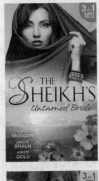

MILLS & BOON®

Why shop at millsandboon.co.uk?

Each year, thousands of romance readers find their perfect read at millsandboon.co.uk. That's because we're passionate about bringing you the very best romantic fiction. Here are some of the advantages of shopping at www.millsandboon.co.uk:

Get new books first—you'll be able to buy your favourite books one month before they hit the shops

Get exclusive discounts—you'll also be able to buy our specially created monthly collections, with up to 50% off the RRP

Find your favourite authors—latest news, interviews and new releases for all your favourite authors and series on our website, plus ideas for what to try next

Join in—once you've bought your favourite books, don't forget to register with us to rate, review and join in the discussions

Visit **www.millsandboon.co.uk**
for all this and more today!